# NEVER TOO LATE

## SUSANNAH HUTCHINSON

*Never Too Late*
**UK Edition**

# DEDICATION

I'm dedicating this book in memory of my late mum, who is always in my heart.

Also, to the many women who had the courage to speak about their experiences to me for my research.

# TABLE OF CONTENTS

# TABLE OF CONTENTS

# TABLE OF CONTENTS

# ACKNOWLEDGMENTS

Thank you to the Norfolk Constabulary for assigning me a police officer to help with the research for this book and future novels so I could get the police procedures right.

Writing is a solitary process. A world of imagination and storytelling made easier by trusted and loyal support from the right people. It's been a long two years for me as I laboured to bring *Never Too Late* to life. Three inspirational people gave me the confidence and self-belief to write this novel, rooted for me, grounded me, and always told me the truth, to which I will always be grateful.

First, I would like to thank my extraordinary fiancé, for his love and patience, and for his superb instincts and candour as front line editor.

My late dad used to say to me, 'You can count on one hand the amount of true friends you have in a lifetime.' I found this to be true. By chance, I met author, Robert J. Watson, who took me under his wing and taught me how to fly. Thank you, Robert, for your support and belief, and for those times I needed a shove. Consider yourself on my hand.

To another extraordinary person, Caroline Smith, a dear friend. There are no words to describe this amazing woman. If it wasn't for her, this book might not have been written. Thank you for everything, and I mean everything, much love.

Without people on the sidelines, you never know if your book is flowing correctly or the pace is right. I would like to give a big Thank You to those who read for me and gave an unbiased opinion. You know who you are.

I would also like to give LDB Press, and its imprints, a special thank you for giving me the chance to fulfil my dream. Also, to Nancy for doing a great job of editing and who understands the writer's needs. I look forward to working with you again in the future.

I would like to end with one of my favourite quotes.

*Life should not be measured by how many breaths you take,*
*But the moments that take your breath away.*

# CHAPTER 1

**T**INA squeezed herself between several parked cars and stepped onto the pavement, jogging the last hundred yards to her home. Hot and out of breath, she blotted her forehead with the edge of her sleeve. The thought of what waited for her behind the front door made her heart race. Her hands trembled as she reached into her pocket for her keys. They slid through her fingers and hit the ground with a loud chink.

*Damn it!* she thought, and bent down to pick them up.

She rolled her shoulders to ease the tension and slid the key into the lock, promptly letting herself in. Her mouth grew dry as she set one foot on the doormat. There he was, sitting at the bottom of the stairs, a position he assumed when things didn't go his way.

"You're late. Where have you been?" Clive asked, his hands locked together, elbows balanced on his knees.

Tina's face paled as she stared at him. "I'm only a little late. You know I've been to see Sam."

She kicked off her trainers and then remembered to place them neatly with the other shoes in the rack.

Clive's eyes narrowed as he stared back at her. "You should have left earlier."

"I got carried away chatting."

She hung her coat on the hook and leant forward to peck her husband on the lips then stroked his right cheek, hoping that it would ease the hostility between them.

He brushed her hands away and said, "We *said* eleven o'clock.

1

You will not see her again. Do you hear me?"

"It's only a few minutes. Why do we have to go through this every time I see her?" she asked. "You know she's my oldest friend."

Clive's lips thinned to a tight line. Her body tensed as the words left her mouth. He stood and approached her, clutching her shoulders and pinning her against the wall.

"You won't see her again," he repeated. "Is that clear?"

Tina's cheeks tingled as Clive's breath puffed across her face as he spoke. She cowered before him, dreading what was to come.

"I—I'm sorry! I didn't mean to answer back. Please, let me go!"

Clive increased the pressure upon her shoulders, his eyes boring deep into hers. "I'm not making myself clear, am I?"

The scent of sour milk and garlic invaded her nostrils as his breath blew across her cheek. Tina's spine pressed against the wall as she tried to back away from him to no avail. Clive wrapped his hand around her throat, pushing her jawbone upwards. His grip tightened, restricting her airflow. She slumped against the wall, feeling a little woozy. Spittle oozed from the corners of her mouth, dripping onto his shirtsleeve. Incoherent nonsense came from her lips when she tried to speak.

A searing pain invaded her abdomen, causing her to double over. Through watery eyes, she watched as Clive shook his hand and flexed his fingers. The smug look on his face betrayed his enjoyment. A stream of urine slowly trickled down her thighs. Tina clamped her legs together, hoping to shield the wetness that was now seeping into her trousers from her husband's view.

Her eyesight swam and she soon rolled to the floor. Curled up in the corner, Tina wrapped her arms around her middle. Her nostrils flared as she struggled to breathe, hoping that it would cure the dizziness she now felt.

Clive stared down at her and said, "You will not talk back to me again, bitch. Stop snivelling! I hardly touched you."

Cowering against the wall, Tina tried to suppress her tears. She knew if she cried, it would fuel his anger.

"S—Sorry. I didn't mean . . . to . . . answer back." She paused and looked at him from the corner of her eye. "You've really hurt me this time!"

Using the telephone table for balance, she stood on unsteady feet. Clive shook his head in disapproval.

"You've pissed yourself. Sort it out. It stinks." He offered her a hand. "Come on. I'll make you a tea."

Tina allowed him to lead her through to the kitchen. He helped her into a chair near the table, and set about in preparing a cup of tea. Her knuckles whitened to the point of hurting as she clenched her fists across her lap. He flipped the switch on the kettle. Neither of them spoke until he placed the cup in front of her.

"Thanks," she said, her voice barely a whisper.

Her throat felt dry as her gaze landed on the cup. She reached for it, the heat of the porcelain mug warming her palms.

"I'm going to bed." He smirked. "I want you up by midnight."

She nodded, afraid of looking up at him. "Yes, darling. I'll drink this and have a shower."

He bestowed another of his smiles upon her before he departed the kitchen. Tina's calm façade dropped as he made his way upstairs. A quick glance at her watch told her it was eleven forty-five. Fifteen minutes was all she had to finish her drink and get to bed. There was no time to decide on a suitable plan tonight. Though, the sooner he was gone, the better.

Tina stood and poured the mint tea down the sink. They'd been together for a little over two years and he still insisted she drink this crap. She washed and dried her cup, placing it in the cupboard with the others, ensuring that all the handles faced the same way. Re-folding the teacloth, she placed it dead centre on the rail. Rituals she loathed, but had become accustomed to after she married Clive.

Upstairs, she entered the bathroom to undress. The linoleum felt cold through her socked feet. She shoved the soiled garments into the bottom of the laundry basket. A slight smirk spread across her lips. This was something she couldn't get wrong.

Tina grimaced at her reflection in the mirror. A tired-looking face and dark circles reflected back. After brushing her teeth, she looked down and assessed her damaged body. She ran both hands over the bruise on her flat stomach. The area was still orange and green from a previous blow. Her attention turned to her purple mottled thighs and her chin quivered.

Once showered, she patted herself dry and applied moisturiser to her hands. She toyed with the loose marital band around her finger, the only piece of jewellery she had left. Sighing softly, she remembered her special day. Clive had gotten rid of the rest some time ago, saying it made her look cheap. He'd thrown the items into a bin along with her cosmetics.

His cruel words flashed into her mind. *"Make-up is for slappers and you will not wear any."*

Clive hadn't always been this way. He'd been loving and attentive once. Soon, however, she would be free, and be able to leave the pain and heartache behind.

Tina unclipped her hair and used her fingers to untangle the shoulder-length locks. By the time she was done, it was five minutes to midnight. Creeping barefoot into the bedroom, she saw the short blue nighty laid out across the bed. With reluctance, she tugged it over her head. She winced as the thin strap caught the edge of the scabbed wound on her shoulder.

The crisp duvet would have looked inviting if not for her husband's presence. She slid beneath the covers and lay on her back, eyes open. Clive's hot breath on the side of her neck made Tina stiffen as his rough hand sidled up her leg. She pushed it away and looked at his silhouette within the dark room.

"I'm not up to it tonight, darling. I don't feel so good."

"You were okay earlier. Not too ill to go out," his gruff voice whispered in her ear.

She balked as his hand mauled her breasts as if he owned them. His tongue glided over her stomach. Its slimy wetness repulsed her. She would need another shower. The pads of his fingers walked across the top of her inner thigh, making their way to her bush before his thumb slid between her unaroused lips. Clamping her legs together hadn't kept him away. He'd found a way inside, nonetheless.

"Please, not tonight. I'm a bit sore from where you hit me earlier."

"You're my fucking wife and I will do what I want. Stop fucking around and turn over."

Tina lay rigid on the bed with her arms locked to her sides. Clive's hold on her tightened, causing a wave of bile to rise to the back of her throat. She closed her eyes for a moment, hating the fact that he made her feel afraid and insignificant.

*It will be over soon.*

"I said, turn over."

Her body and limbs felt heavy and refused to move. "I can't."

His shaven face was inches from hers when he shouted, "Don't make me use force!"

The scent of decay emanated from Clive's teeth and gums. She breathed through her mouth to stop the chance of an involuntary gag. Tina didn't want another beating, and knew she had no other choice but to surrender.

She flipped herself over, her breasts flattened against the mattress. The pressure of his weight as he mounted her restricted her movements. She felt smothered and gasped for breath. His erection felt hot against her lower back. A whimper came from her lips as she clenched her bottom.

"You're going to enjoy this," he said.

He gripped her buttocks so hard that her eyes watered.

*I doubt it,* she thought. *Just get it over with!*

"Open, bitch."

Tina relaxed her taut limbs and lifted her bottom in submission. He thrust into her, uncaring of the fact that he was hurting her. Tears ran down her cheeks. She shrieked as the sensation burned and ripped at her insides. The more vocal she was, the faster he pumped into her. Her knuckles whitened as she gripped the sheets, unable to reach for the pillow that would muffle her whimpers.

His body shuddered as his release came. She turned her head and saw the look of pleasure spreading across his face. Clive soon withdrew and lay on his back. Although she felt relieved that he never lasted long, the disgust she felt for letting him violate her body plagued her mind.

*Why can't I stand up for myself?*

"I told you, you would enjoy it. I heard those whimpers. You should play hard to get more often."

A partial laugh escaped him. He sounded pleased with himself, like a caveman that had fulfilled his manhood. Tina refused to reply. Instead, she focused on the wall across from where she lay and waited for morning to come.

\*\*\*

A beam of light shone directly into Tina's sensitive eyes and caused her to stir. Clive had opened the blinds, and the fragrance of his shower gel lingered throughout the bedroom. He sprayed on his deodorant, its cloying scent invading her nostrils, making her cough. A faint snap sounded as the wardrobe door closed. Several minutes later, the bed dipped under his weight.

She buried her head under the quilt, refusing to acknowledge him. The bed shifted as he stood. The stairs creaked, moments later, as he descended. Happy, she sighed and stretched out like a starfish, enjoying the fact that she now had the space to herself.

The sound of clanking pots and pans echoed through the house. She groaned as the radio began to play in the background. Clive's voice soon followed as he started to sing.

"Shut up! You're killing that song!" she mumbled, using the pillow to block out his discordant tone.

Clive yelled at her from the kitchen. "Breakfast! Are you coming down yet? It's getting cold."

Tina groaned and flung back the covers. Her sore and clumsy

limbs slowed her down. She shielded her eyes from the sudden glare, reaching for the gown hanging on the back of the chair and toeing her slippers.

"Coming," she said, and made her way downstairs, dawdling into the kitchen.

Clive's eyes narrowed, his lips pursed with displeasure. "You're not dressed. You should try and make yourself more respectable in the morning."

He placed a cup full of mint tea next to her plate. Her heart raced as she avoided his intense scrutiny. She wanted to voice her true thoughts, but kept them to herself instead. Tina apologised and took a seat.

"I'm going," he said. "I'll be late for work."

Clive kissed her forehead and grabbed the car keys, heading for the front door. Tina glanced down at the plate. A smiley face of boiled eggs and soldiers stared up at her from their holders. She saw a toasted finger for a nose, three fingers for the mouth, and drawn on the shells were two felt-tip eyes. It was a fun thing to do, a genuine gesture. She'd have found it humorous had it come from a playful husband, but not from Clive.

Tina pushed the cup away without taking a sip. The smell alone churned her stomach. Propped against an eggcup was the dreaded note, written in bold red pen. He'd left the job list for the day.

Crumpling the paper into a tight ball, she threw it across the room. Tension and frustration coursed through her veins. Tina stood and swiped her arm across the table. The sound of the smashing crockery satisfied her momentarily.

Tea spewed across the tiles, and splashes of the murky liquid trickled down the fridge. It dripped onto the floor, joining the fragmented china covered in gloppy yolks. She stepped over the remains and reached into the depths of the top cupboard to retrieve her hidden chocolate powder. Clive had forbidden her from drinking it, but the luxury was one of the few remaining pleasures she had left.

"You're not that bloody clever," she said under her breath.

# SUSANNAH HUTCHINSON

Frothing the chocolate, she added a sprinkle of cinnamon for devilment. She then took it with her as she opened the patio doors and sat outside. The sunny spring morning was just what she needed to think about her life and make sense of her crumbling marriage.

# CHAPTER 2

**T**INA sipped her drink and licked the residue from her top lip. She sat on the patio chair with her legs tucked beneath her and closed her eyes. Could she really contemplate murdering her husband? Maybe it was too extreme. In her heart, however, she knew it would be justified. Clive hurt her every day. She couldn't live like this anymore.

Her heart clamoured for freedom. She wanted to live her life as peaceful as possible without having to worry about looking over her shoulder. With Clive around, she couldn't do that. As the morning sun warmed her face, she let her mind drift back to when it all started.

\*\*\*

**I**T was a warm day in May. Pungent smells from popping sausages, sizzling steaks, and fresh green salad mingled with the perfume of Wisteria, which clung to the side of the house. Clusters of purple flowers drooped off their thin stems, announcing that spring had arrived. Clematis covered the trellis and formed an arch across her best friend's garden.

Tina wore a short ruffled dress and a squirt of her favourite fruity perfume. Her size twelve figure was toned and curvaceous. A dusting of blusher on her cheeks was all she needed to make her skin glow.

Most of the other guests were couples, engaged or married.

9

Some were there with children. All were gathered to celebrate Sam's birthday. A shirtless handsome man wearing only shorts and flip-flops sat in a shaded spot under a tree, sipping his Bud straight from the bottle. His dark hair was short and groomed. As she walked by with a glass of wine in hand, he spoke.

"Care to join me?" he asked with a cheeky smile. "You smell lovely."

He stood, like a perfect gentleman, and waited until she sat next to him.

"I get the impression we may have been set up. We are the only singletons here."

Tina blushed and smiled. "I think so. Hi. I'm Tina."

She offered him her hand. He took it and kissed the back of it. Tingles shot up her forearm.

"I'm Clive." He kissed her hand once more. "Blythe." Another peck. "Pleased to meet you."

Her smile broadened. "Can I have my hand back now?"

***

**I**T had been a perfect beginning to a great relationship. The reaction she received from her family at the announcement of their wedding was no surprise. Her brother, James, thought it was too soon, but stood by her decision to keep the peace, nonetheless. She also recalled being disgusted by her mother's outburst in front of friends and family.

"Thank God, someone wants to marry my failure of a daughter!" her mother had cried.

Some looked puzzled upon hearing her mother's outburst, their jaws dropping open with surprise. They'd probably gossiped behind her back later on.

***

**T**HREE months later, on August 25, 2011, she and Clive were married in a registry office. Tina didn't mind. She was never one for a fussy ceremony. The meaning of matrimony meant more to her than the act itself.

Their honeymoon, which should have been the best time of their lives, was on the beautiful Greek island of Kos, a cliché of turquoise seas and golden sands. Lemons hung from sagging branches, their tangy scents wafting through the air whenever a gentle wind swept by. When the heat subsided and the evening breeze came, you could dine on the beach and watch as the sun went down over the horizon.

At two in the morning, people were dancing to the music from nearby bars, the loud sound reverberating through the streets. The pavements heaved with holidaymakers taking advantage of the warmth and cheap booze.

The top floor of the Toto Bar was open air. Visible in the night sky, the large Mediterranean moon shone through the occasional cloud and the stars dotted the sky.

"I've never seen the moon that big," Tina said.

"It's amazing, isn't it? We'll sit here," Clive replied, pulling out a chair for his new bride.

"Thanks. We're right on the edge of the dance floor." After downing her drink, she asked, "Do you fancy a dance, Babe? It's Beyonce's "Crazy in Love," my favourite."

Tina smiled and pushed herself to her feet. She reached out to clasp his hands, pulling him out of his chair, like a schoolgirl at a disco.

Clive resisted. "No, you go ahead. I'll sit this one out. Stay close where I can see you."

Her hands slipped from his and she made her way into the crowd. Tina swung her hips from side to side, accentuating her curves, imitating the dance moves. Her arms coordinated with her thrusting hips as she did the booty shake to the opening beats of the song.

Everyone on the floor was in the mood and joined in. A Greek waiter watched her dance, and looked her up and down. Sensuality oozed as her head moved to the rhythm, left then right. When the song faded and another took its place, she made her way back to her husband and flopped into the seat.

"I'm out of breath! It's been ages since I've danced like that. I need a drink. Do you want one?"

She stood, wrapping her arms around his neck and kissing him on his small plump lips. The scent of his Hugo Boss cologne wafted up her nose. It tasted bitter on her tongue.

"Just sit down," Clive said, reaching up to slide her arms from around his neck. "You're embarrassing yourself and me. Calm down!"

A blank expression spread across his face as he stared into her brown eyes. He pulled her arms down and away from him.

"I'm having fun. Sorry, Mr. Grumpy!" she said in a cheerful childlike voice.

The effects of the Retsina she'd drunk earlier were starting to take effect. Tina felt a little merry because of it. The Vodka and Cokes amplified the feeling surging through her system.

"What were you doing out there?" He pointed to the dance floor. "Are you drunk?"

"Having fun. You should have joined me."

"You've had too much already. I'll get the drinks."

"Bloody cheek! Can't a girl enjoy herself?" was on the tip of her tongue. Tina held the words back, not wanting to spoil the mood between them.

"Okay. Just a Coke, please."

"I won't be a minute."

Tina's eyes followed Clive as he moved through the dancing bodies to the bar. She watched until the back of his head disappeared into the crowd. Gathering her composure after such an exuberant dance, she settled back against her chair. The waiter approached their table and collected the empty glasses.

"You pretty lady, yes," he said in fragmented English.

"Thank you."

"You holiday with husband?"

"Husband, yes. It's our honeymoon," she shouted over the noise, and flashed her ring at the waiter.

He put down the glasses, took her hand and kissed it, stroking the back of it with his thumb. "Many congratulations. You come back here before go home. Drink on house."

Before she could say thank you, Clive stormed across the dance floor. He slammed the drinks onto the table, their contents sloshed with the momentum. The waiter turned. Clive's punch caught him on the mouth. He stumbled backwards, crashing into several chairs and falling into the people at the next table before ending up on the floor.

"Come on, bitch," Clive said. "We're leaving."

He grabbed her arm and yanked her to her feet. She shook her head at the crowd. Clive mouthed an apology, trying to excuse his behaviour and eyeing the waiter's bloodied lip. Tina tried to shrug off his grip, but it was no use. His grasp was too tight. She rebelled against him and planted her feet. Her high heels screeched and gave way, moving her further toward him. On the way out, she gave the waiter an apologetic nod.

"How dare you call me a bitch? What is the matter with you? Get off me!"

"Let's get back to the hotel. I don't want to have to drag you, now move!" He tugged her arm, guiding her to where he wanted to go.

"Let go, please!"

She broke free of his hold and folded her arms across her chest. The streets were quiet as they walked back to the hotel. A slight breeze cooled the heat from their bodies, and the noise from Toto's faded in the distance. The silence was broken by the chirp of crickets and cicadas.

Tina refused to say a word, not until they'd reached their room. She was tipsy, but not that drunk. It was not her style to make a scene.

No one was at the reception desk upon arriving at the hotel. They took the lift to the fifth floor in silence and walked to their room. Tina swiped the key card into the slot, aware of Clive's presence behind her. She strode into the room and tossed her shoes into the corner closest to the wardrobe. Sitting down on the corner of the bed, she clasped her hands around her knees.

"Care to explain what just happened at the bar? Don't ever treat me like that again!"

A muscle twitched along Clive's jaw as he stared at her. "The waiter, the fucking sleaze, was trying to get into your knickers and you led him on." He pointed at her face. "You were showing me up, behaving like some cheap slapper."

"How dare you! You . . . You showed yourself up. The waiter was only being friendly. He was asking about the honeymoon."

"You what? You bloody idiot! That waiter . . ." Realisation dawned on him. "I thought you were giving him the eye."

"Don't be silly. What have you got to be jealous about? I married you! This is our honeymoon, Clive. What were you thinking?"

A flush of colour flooded his cheeks. "I'm sorry. I don't know what came over me. Please forgive me. I guess I had too much wine with dinner and then the Jack Daniels. I . . ."

His voice faded. He knelt in front of her and nestled himself in between her smooth legs. Clive hugged her waist and then buried his head in her lap.

"Don't do it again," she said, stroking his hair.

Tina could forgive this little outburst. Dominant males liked to protect their prize, their actions fuelled by drink and too much testosterone. These things happened quite a bit. She'd seen it before in clubs and pubs.

She'd begun to worry when he'd directed his temper at her. It felt as if Clive had waited for the marriage to begin and their holiday to end before he showed his true colours.

**C**LIVE no longer asked for forgiveness like he'd done in the hotel room back then. He no longer cared about anything. Her life had changed in an instant, and she now lived in a nightmare.

The phone rang in the hallway, startling Tina back to the present. She'd forgotten about the scheduled call. She moved back into the house, stepping over the crockery's shattered remains, and hurried to answer.

"That was nearly five rings," Clive said. "Where were you?"

Tina's pulse raced as she tried to compose herself. "Hello, darling. I was upstairs cleaning." She cradled the receiver in the crook of her neck, knotting the belt of her dressing gown.

"You should have answered the one in the bedroom."

"Sorry, force of habit. Everything alright?" She made her voice sound full of genuine concern.

"How are you getting on with that list? You're at work tomorrow, so I want it done before then."

Her body prickled with annoyance. "Yes, darling."

"We're going out for dinner tonight with Maggie and Ray. I will shower and change at work, and pick you up at six-thirty. Wear that dress I bought you. Don't let me down."

The line went dead.

"Goodbye. See you soon," she said to the dialling tone.

Tina glanced at the clock in the hall. She had seven hours to clean up. Two hours of daydreaming this morning, and she still hadn't come up with a suitable plan. A feeling of nausea rose to the back of her throat. She ran to the kitchen and retched over the sink. Chocolate bile drizzled down the plughole. Dry heaves soon followed, indicating there was nothing left.

*It's stress,* she thought.

By late afternoon, Tina found herself immersed in her shower. She let the steamy water flow over her body, the pounding jets easing aches and massaging her cramped muscles. Taking extra care with her right shoulder upon drying herself, she padded to the bedroom. She had an hour before Clive came to pick her up.

The purple pinstripe dress with three quarter sleeves and a ruffled neck looked hideous. She'd worn it once, not wanting to seem ungrateful when Clive had first bought it. The thought of wearing it again made the hairs on the back of her neck rise. She didn't want a confrontation tonight. Her body was too weak to take another beating. She removed the garment from the wardrobe, and laid it on the bed along with the plain, unsexy underwear. Tina then set about in styling her hair.

The hair dryer blasted the side of her cheeks, making them redden. She teased the heat down each strand, hoping a curl would form at the bottom, but gave up and left it straight instead. She slipped the dress over her head and popped her feet into her shoes. A quick glance at the cheval mirror confirmed her image.

*I look like a frump.*

Smoothing her palms over her hips, she sprayed on his favourite perfume. She was finally ready. Tina made her way into the living area, waiting for Clive to arrive.

A sofa filled one side of the small room. Secured to the bare magnolia wall, a large flat screen television sat in full view. A Blu-Ray player rested on the shelf below. Three *What Car?* magazines lay neatly on a nest of tables tucked into the corner. She'd wanted to hang her paintings by a talented local artist, but Clive had refused the notion, leaving most of the walls bare. The paintings remained in the loft, covered up, along with all the family and wedding photos. His excuse for this being that he didn't want the clutter.

The early evening sun shone through the bay window where she sat. It brightened the living room, illuminating every available space. The painter's light, as it is known, did nothing to ease her worries. Tina squinted through the sudden glare, dreading the sight of the navy-coloured Audi. Clive had never let her anywhere near the steering wheel. He insisted on always picking her up and dropping her off, giving him more control on her freedom.

The home reminded Tina of her childhood. Her father kept the decor simple and impersonal. The less clutter, the better. Yet she wished she could have something of her own to remind her that it was her home, too.

Since her husband was nowhere in sight, Tina sprawled herself across the couch. She closed her eyes, allowing her thoughts to drift.

When the first slap had come, Tina had been shocked. As the slaps turned to punches, her shock turned to fear. She made excuses for him, just as her mother had with her father. What had made this loving man change into this monster?

"What have I done? Is it my fault?" she said aloud, breaking the silence of the room.

The walls didn't answer. Her chin dimpled and started to quiver. Tears welled up from deep within as the memories engulfed her.

Her reflections turned to her dead father. Not a day went by when he wasn't under her skin. The guilt she'd tried so hard to bury always resurfaced. Her mother had been just as bad, blaming her for his death. Using the guilt trips to her advantage, her mother claimed that she was 'too demanding and put too much pressure on his weak heart.'

Of course, her mother adored Clive. They had long friendly chats on the phone. "He's the best thing that ever happened to you," she would say. Tina could hear her whiny voice inside her head. She always did wear blinkers.

"Bitch," Tina replied with annoyance.

Her mother was another unwanted accessory in her life she needed to ditch. Nothing she did was ever good enough for her. In her mother's mind, Tina was a waste of space, unworthy of her affections.

She closed her mind off to the memories, refusing to devote her time to wasted emotions. Whatever plan she came up with, Clive would track her down, even if she were able to escape this sordid life. He might even kill her in a rage.

After the shoulder incident, she couldn't take the chance. Her best course of action, she decided, would be to confront him about getting professional help, a conversation she dreaded having with Clive. Waiting until the weekend before approaching him would give her some time to do some research. If that failed, she could see no other way out but to turn to her last resort. She had to do it, didn't she?

Tina opened her teary eyes and darted into the downstairs toilet. She splashed cold water on her face to cool her cheeks. Disguising the telltale signs, she refused to let Clive see that she'd been upset.

A vehicle pulled up outside. The horn blasted three times. She recognised its distinctive pitch. He'd arrived.

*How many times do you have to pip?* She rubbed her palms over her face, and traced her eye bags with her thumbs. *Give it a rest!*

Tina paused at the front door. She took a deep breath and held it for few seconds, before releasing a slow, controlled breath through her teeth. Opening the door, she hoped the evening meal would be uneventful.

The cool air brushed against her face, dark clouds forming in the distance. Gravel crunched beneath her feet as she walked to the car.

"Hi. Ready?"

She glanced at him and nodded. A smug look crossed his face. His Ray-Ban's were balanced on his nose, and his jaw clenched as he chewed gum.

*You look like a cow chewing fodder,* she thought, and climbed into the passenger seat.

"You look great. Hungry?"

Tina nodded once more. The music rattled the seats, jarring her nerves. The song, "Bonkers," blared through the open window of the vehicle. She was sure the whole street could hear it. The tyres screeched, trying to find some traction as they sped off.

*What a prat!* she thought, wishing she could have stayed home.

# CHAPTER 3

**T**HE Coach House was a recently renovated trendy restaurant four miles outside of town. It had built up a reputation for fine English cuisine.

Tina paused on the pavement before they entered and winced. Clive's arm was wrapped around her shoulder, pressing against the healing wound. With his other hand, he turned her head toward him. She hated it when he used two of his fingers to pull her chin around to face him.

Silence enveloped them. The glare on his face said it all. Tina tried to slide out of the awkward embrace as she looked down the road. Anything was better than facing him. His grip tightened, bringing tears to her eyes.

"Now, now. Don't be like that."

He pulled her close. Spit speckled her face. She resisted the urge to wipe it off.

"Can I loosen my grip now? Are you going to behave like a good girl?"

She grimaced. "Yep."

Clive's eyes bored into hers. "Let's go in."

As they approached the restaurant, a staff member held the door open for them. Tina nodded at him in acknowledgment.

"Thank you," Clive said, and followed Tina inside.

"You're welcome. Enjoy your meal."

In the foyer, Tina felt him grasp her forearm. He pulled her back, refusing to allow her to go any further. She'd forgotten that

Clive liked to lead the way and show off to anyone who gave a shit.

The heat from the kitchen seeped into the air. Three ceiling fans worked hard to keep an ambient temperature. The food smelled wonderful as a waitress passed by, holding two plates of Beef Wellington.

The maître d' salon led them to a brown rustic table. The matching chairs were upholstered with soft green cushions and backs. Carnations arranged in small vases were placed in the centre of each one. Wine and water glasses completed the simple place settings.

"Your waiters will be with you shortly. I hope you enjoy your evening," the maître d' said.

"Thank you. I'm sure we will," Clive replied.

Tina sat at the table set for four with her back to the room. She faced the window, Clive sitting opposite her. Silence surrounded them once more. A few minutes later, an attractive girl wearing a green skirt and a white blouse appeared at Tina's side. She snorted with amusement and rolled her eyes.

*Even the staff matches the décor!*

"Would you like a drink while you wait, sir?" the tall waitress asked, holding a pen and pad in anticipation. Her long hair was neatly tied in a fashionable messy bun, her oblong spectacles perched on her long nose.

Clive smiled and said, "Yes, please. I'll have a large Jack Daniels and Coke, one cube of ice, and a jug of water for the lady. We will have a look at the menus as well, please."

"We have mineral water. Sparkling or still?"

"No, just tap water will be fine."

"Ice and lemon?"

"No, as it comes."

"Thank you." With a glance at Tina, she wrote Clive's instructions on her pad and walked away.

"I was going to have a drink tonight," Tina said through gritted teeth. She straightened her place mat and fiddled with the shiny cutlery.

"You're having water."

A few minutes later, the waitress returned with their drinks. After placing them on the table, she took two menus out from under her arm, and passed one to Tina while offering the other to Clive.

"It's okay. We only need the one," he replied, snatching the menu from Tina's hands and passing it back.

"Would you like to wait for your guests before ordering?"

"No, we'll order first. It will save time when they arrive. That's all, for the moment. Thank you."

"I'll give you a few minutes to decide." With that, she moved to an adjacent table.

"Shouldn't we wait for Maggie and Ray, and order together?"

"We'll order now." Clive looked through the choices offered on the menu.

"I thought I might try the beef. It looked and smelt lovely." Tina's stomach grumbled as she remembered the sight that greeted them earlier. With her eyes fixed on Clive, she waited for a response, though nothing came from him. "What about you? What do you fancy?"

The waitress returned several minutes later. "Are you ready to order, sir?"

"Yes." Clive looked up, cocking his head to the side to read the name badge pinned to her blouse. "May I call you . . . Helen?"

"Of course, sir. What can I get you?"

"I'll have the salmon with Mediterranean vegetables and the sautéed potatoes, no starter. Again, no starter for the lady, but she will have the halibut. Can it be steamed and not pan-fried, and served with a salad with no sauce? Could you also make that a small portion? We will wait for our guests to arrive before we eat and order wine." He slapped the menu shut and passed it back to her. "Thank you."

Helen glanced at Tina once more, a look of curiosity on her face. She then ripped the page from her pad. Tina watched the waitress until she reached the saloon doors leading to the kitchen and then looked back at Clive.

"I was going to have the beef. I don't even like fish that much."

"You're getting fat, Tina. I don't want to be married to a dumpling." He laughed in her face.

*Cheeky bastard!*

Tina gripped the sides of her dress under the table, creasing the fabric between her fingers. "There's nothing on me, even this dress is too big. How can you say th—"

She bit down on the side of her mouth, watching Clive swill the liquid around in his glass. He knocked it back, crunching on the ice cube like a boiled sweet. The urge to pour the jug over his head rose to the surface. She took a breath and counted to ten. The pain of digging her nails into her thighs took her mind away from the festering anxiety.

Clive glanced at his watch. "They'll be here any minute."

*Great. Can't wait!*

Tina knew Maggie and Ray had arrived by the scent of Maggie's overbearing perfume. It travelled through the dining room like a dense fog, lingering and never clearing. She preferred Maggie when she was sober. Her tongue loosened with the more wine she drank, unable to control what came out.

"Ah, they're here."

Clive nudged his chair back and stretched out his hand, waiting for his best friend to take it. Tina closed her eyes for a moment, taking a deep breath and forcing the air out through her teeth.

"Be nice. Be nice," she said under her breath.

Ray took Clive's hand and shook it hard.

Clive moved onto Maggie and said, "How are you? You look amazing." He kissed both of her cheeks, his hands staying a little too long on her curvy hips. "You smell lovely."

"I'm great, thanks. You look fit yourself," she replied.

Maggie sat down, her dress riding up her thighs. Inadequacy built up inside of Tina. It wasn't jealousy. That faded long ago. She'd hoped they would have an affair. At least she would have a good excuse to leave, but deep down, Tina knew it would never happen.

Maggie's attention turned to Tina. "And how are you?"

"Fine, thanks."

Tina prepared herself for a night of the same mindless drivel. Maggie was an attractive woman, a voluptuous size twelve. She refused to wear a size fourteen, which would be a better fit. Her large firm breasts pushed themselves out of her low-cut red dress that barely covered her backside. Auburn curls danced upon her quivering chest. She rubbed her hands together, ready to eat whatever she wanted.

"It's good to see you, Buddy," Ray said, pulling his chair closer to the table. "How are you, Tina? All right?"

He leaned in and pecked her cheek. Tina stiffened as Ray's stubble scratched her face, invading her space.

"Fine, thanks."

Ray was the most irritating man Tina had ever known. Not to mention a letch and a creep. She held him responsible for her wounded shoulder. He was shorter than Clive, and had a potbelly that hung over his black trousers, his shirt buttons under strain and his hair a shade lighter. Tina guessed that Maggie was attracted to his money and being civil to him was all she could muster.

"We've ordered already. I hope you don't mind," Clive said, clicking his fingers to attract Helen.

They browsed through the bill of fare, unsure of what to order.

"Are you having a starter?" Ray asked as he glanced at Clive.

"I wasn't, but I think I'll change my mind and have the garlic king prawns."

Ray nodded. "What about you, Tina? Are you having a starter?"

"She's on a diet. Aren't you, dear?" Clive interrupted and shrugged. "I don't know . . . *women*."

Tina ignored his jibe and sat in silence as they placed their food orders and selected the wine. The men chose a dry white. Maggie insisted she wanted a red to accompany her Beef Wellington.

*She just wants the bottle to herself,* Tina thought. She sighed softly and eyed the ceiling above her.

Throughout the first course, Tina noticed Clive leering at Maggie, who, as always, lapped up the attention. Ray defended what was his and kept a tight hold of her hand, in case his best friend muscled in. The flirting continued. She wondered why Ray didn't do more or say something.

Tina listened to their conversations with slight disinterest. The men talked about cars and football. Maggie butted in on occasion, fishing for compliments. Then the inevitable work chat began and their egos clashed.

A droning sound rumbled in her ears. No longer able to decipher their words, her mind shut off. She stared at the flowers in the middle of the table, hoping to find the answers to the misery that surrounded her somewhere amongst the petals.

The plate placed in front of her brought Tina out of her daze. She nodded and thanked the waitress. Once all the food was served, they ate. The restaurant, to their credit, did try to make Tina's halibut look appetising, but there was no disguising the blandness of the dish. She choked it down, though she had to admit the food on the other plates looked delicious.

"Is that all you're having? You should really try to eat more, Tina," Maggie said as she scooped the beef into her mouth. "This is really tasty."

Tina glared at her and smiled politely.

"Mine too," Ray replied through a mouthful of salmon.

"That's what I keep telling her. She needs fattening up."

Clive placed a quieting hand on top of hers across the table. She snatched it away and listened to Maggie's insistent nagging instead.

"It's not a good look being scrawny. What do they call it?" She clicked her fingers and tried to remember. "Heroin chic, that's it! It's never looked good. Girls walking around like sticks. It's stupid. Men like curves." A cheeky look spread across her face. "I can sort you out at my salon, if you like. Give you a makeover." Maggie took another sip of wine, followed by more beef.

"I'm alright. Thanks."

Tina pushed the rest of her meal out of the way. A slight tremor coursed through her body. She was unsure of how much longer she could keep up the pretence.

"I don't mean to be rude, my love, but are you wearing that dress as a joke? It's hardly en vogue."

Tina bristled with annoyance. Everyone laughed, making her feel uncomfortable.

"Clive bought it for me. Don't you like it?"

Clive sat up straight in his chair, his eyes focused on Tina. "No, I didn't. That's your mother's. I wouldn't buy you shit like that. You should dress more like Maggie."

He kicked Tina's shin under the table. Pain shot up her ankle. She held back the tears as the bullies feasted upon her.

"Tell me, Maggie. Are those breasts real?" Tina asked, saying the first thing that came to mind.

Maggie grinned. "Well, a little enhancement does a girl good. You should try it."

Tina's attempt at baiting Maggie had failed. Unwilling to remain amongst them any longer, she pushed herself to her feet.

"Excuse me. I'm just nipping to the ladies," she said.

She then made her way to the powder room. Once out of sight, she stormed into a cubicle and slammed the door closed. With her arms placed above her head, she leant against the wall, the wood cool against her forehead. Frustrated, she kicked the bottom repeatedly.

"Bastard!" she cried.

Tears flowed down her cheeks. The sound of the main door opening made her hackles rise as she waited for Maggie to call her name. Relief surged through her body several seconds later.

*It's not her! Phew.*

She took several slow and deep breaths until the toilet flushed. The sound of the tap running and the noise from the drier muffled any sobs that may have escaped from her lips. The door soon closed, and she found herself alone again.

Composing herself, she slid out of the cubicle and headed for the nearest sink. She splashed water on her face for the second time that evening. Her reflection in the mirror showed she'd been crying.

*Damn! It'll have to do.*

With no other option but to return to the table, she exited the bathroom and made her way back to the group. Coffee cups replaced their plates, and Helen poured smooth, rich coffee from a cafetière.

"How long does it take to go to the ladies?" Clive asked, eyeing her flushed face. "I ordered you a coffee."

"I don't want one, thanks."

Tina placed her hand over the top of the cup as Helen went to pour. The brandies arrived for the men, as well as a Drambuie for Maggie. Without attempting to savour the warming amber liquid, Clive downed his in one gulp as if it were a contest.

Tina stared at him with disapproval. "You're driving, Clive. Should you be drinking that much? You've had wine as well."

The words rolled off her tongue without her giving them any thought. His eyes locked on hers. She knew the look on his face well and it wasn't forgiving.

"It's okay. I've eaten well." He stroked her hand as it rested on the table. "Women! They worry far too much."

"We'd better go. We have some unfinished business to attend to," Ray said, staring at Maggie with hungry eyes.

Maggie smiled at him as if she'd read his thoughts. "Your place or mine, Baby? We'd better go. I wouldn't want to disappoint." She pouted her lips at him, egging him on.

"Could we have the bill, please?" Ray asked as he saw Helen pass by. He opened his wallet, selected the relevant plastic card, and slid it across the table.

"Are you getting this? Thanks, Ray. My shout next time," Clive said.

Tina looked on in disgust. Every time they came out to dinner, it was Ray who paid the bill. Clive always said he would get the next one, but he never did.

They left a good tip, thanking Helen on their way out. In the car park, they stopped by Ray's BMW to say their goodbyes. Tina watched Clive take great delight in hugging Maggie, who was a little unsteady in her heels, trying to remain decent as she got into the car.

"See you soon, Buddy," Ray said.

"Yes. Don't forget. It's on me next time."

"Bye, Tina," Maggie replied. "Give me a ring." She gestured with her fingers. "We can get your wardrobe and make-up sorted."

*Another snipe. That's not going to happen!*

She nodded at her. With two blasts of the horn, they drove away. Clive and Tina walked to their car in silence. Only when they were both inside, and Clive had pulled out of the car park, did Tina know she was in trouble.

# CHAPTER 4

**T**HE quiet hum from the air conditioner kept the interior refreshingly cool. The scent of polish and leather added to the clean smell of the new Audi. The headlights flashed across the uneven tarmac, the road ahead clear.

Tina had learned when it was best to remain quiet. From the corner of her eye, she saw the thunderous look building on Clive's face. The car was powerful and needed handling with respect, not steering with one finger hooked over the bottom of the wheel. His doing so made her nervous.

He broke the silence between them and glared at her. "Bitch, how dare you question me in front of my friends?" He pointed a finger directly at her face.

"Please, calm down! Let's not end the night like this."

Tina swatted his hand away, concerned that he wasn't paying attention to the road ahead. She felt too drained for another row. He placed his hand back on the gear stick.

"Don't tell me to calm down! You're a fucking mess, an embarrassment."

Clive snarled through clenched teeth. His eyes widened.

"Slow down a little. Please!" Tina gripped the soft foam that filled the plush seat.

"You had to mention the drunk driving, didn't you? You couldn't resist humiliating me in there."

The car drifted. The tyres vibrated as they skimmed over the reflective cat's eyes in the middle of the road.

"What about me? You treat me like dirt."

She glanced at the speedometer and then at Clive. Fear invaded every inch of her body as the needle crept upwards.

"What? Am I going too fast now?"

"Please! Look at the road."

Her heart hammered within her chest as the engine growled and the speed quickened. For a brief moment, he looked ahead and then back at Tina.

"Don't you like speed, you stupid bitch?"

"Stop talking to me like that! I'm your wife."

He snorted with derision. "Try acting like it, then."

"You're on the wrong side of the road. Move over!" She stretched her legs into the spacious foot well, instinctively braking on imaginary pedals.

Clive ignored her and said, "Look at Maggie. She's not a frump like you."

"No, she's a fake Barbie throwback. Slow down, please, and move back to the other lane."

"You want to go back to the other lane? Fine."

He turned the wheel a fraction. Their bodies swayed to the side with the force of the momentum. Tina reached for the door handle and held it tight. He moved back into the wrong lane and stayed there.

"Don't slag off Maggie. You're only jealous."

"Move over! There's something coming. Please!"

She leaned back in the seat and glimpsed at the speed dial. It rose to eighty-five. Two headlights danced over a dip in the road. An oncoming vehicle approached, heading straight for them.

Clive smirked, hatred shining in his eyes. "Let's have some fun."

Dread overwhelmed her as the car picked up speed.

"Please, look at the road ahead."

"What do you think? Will we get over in time?"

Clive laughed, tapping his hand on his thigh. The lorry's main beams flashed.

"Who the fuck does he think he's flashing?"

"You're going to kill us both, you maniac!" She shrunk in her seat, eyes scrunched tight, waiting for the aftermath of his little game.

"Open your eyes," Clive demanded. "I said, open your fucking eyes!"

Tina shook her head, refusing to do as he'd asked. "No, I won't."

A burning sensation travelled up her scalp. He'd grabbed a clump of her hair and yanked her head back. She tried to resist, but it was no use in being defiant. Opening her eyes, they widened in panic.

"I wouldn't want you to miss the finale. Now, scream if you want to go faster."

"Oh, God! Please help me. Stop! Please, I don't want to die!"

She braced herself for impact. Her kitten heels dug into the mat and she sunk lower into the seat. Her hands ached from gripping the foam tight. Her life flashed in streaky blurs across her eyes. With a head-on collision, their bodies would resemble burnt toast.

*At least I will be free,* were her final thoughts before the presumed impact.

Swerving at the last minute, the back of the car fishtailed as he fought for control. The continuous honk of complaint from the lorry rang in their ears as it passed. Her knuckles white and face pale, she was unable to move, tears rolling down her cheeks. The car started to slow down.

"That was exciting. What are you crying for? You're fucking weak. Get a grip," he said, stroking her inner thigh.

His hand moved beneath her dress, the tips of his fingers grazing the edge of her knickers. She clamped her knees together, shoving his clammy hand aside.

"You're mental. You loved that. Give you a buzz, did it? I hate you!"

She stared out the passenger window, watching the muted hues of the Norfolk countryside flicker past. Tina tried to make sense of what happened, yet her mind refused to do so. She couldn't believe that Clive had the audacity to do such thing in order to elicit a reaction from her.

Ten minutes passed before Clive cleared his throat and spoke once more. "Darling."

His soft voice was the essence of a man she once knew.

"Hey, sweetheart. Look at me, please."

She turned and looked at his softened face. "What?"

"Don't 'what' me."

He smiled, his lips turned up at the corners. Clive curled his left hand around the wheel, exaggerating the movement. Tina's reflexes responded with a flinch.

"Darling," he said once more in a soft voice.

"What?" she asked.

"Sweetheart, look."

She looked in his direction once more. The back of his hand whacked her face, coming at her hard and fast. The bridge of her nose felt like it would explode. The pain seared along her cheeks and rattled the bones of her face. Stunned, she screamed through watered eyes and her body trembled. He laughed. The vehicle's tyres skidded across the loose gravel as it came to a stop.

*Bastard!*

Clive opened the driver's side and stepped out of the car. He hurried around to her side, anger lurking in the depths of his eyes. Tina panicked, dreading what was coming.

"No! Please, not here," she cried, trying to find the button that would lock the interior doors, but he was too quick and had already opened hers.

"Please, don't. Get off me!"

She pulled at the handle to keep him out, but he was too strong and won the battle. Clive reached out to try and yank her out of the car.

"No, stop! Please, don't do it!" she pleaded.

Defending herself, she thrashed in his arms, slapping his face and shoulders. Clive ignored her blows, unwilling to relinquish his hold on her.

"Shut up!" he said in a brusque voice.

Tina bit into his forearm. The pressure of her clenched jaw triggered renewed pain across her nose. She cried out, her mind in a daze, trying to wriggle free. He yanked her hair once more and attempted to pull her from the Audi's depths.

She resisted, holding onto the car's metal frame. "Get off me!"

"Get out of my fucking car!"

Tina lost her grip and tumbled out of the vehicle, losing a shoe. "Please don't do this. Don't leave me out here!"

"You hated me a minute ago. Fucking stay here where you belong!" He held the collar of her dress and shook her hard. "You should have thought about that before you started with the backchat."

The blow to her chest winded her. It sent a stabbing discomfort through her breasts, the pain so unbearable, she lost her balance.

"Please don't leave me! We can talk this through," she said, falling to the ground. The thought of being alone sent waves of insecurity through her broken body.

"Bloody women always want to talk. Stay here until you can learn how to behave."

Clive turned his back on her and slid back into the car. The last thing she heard was his music blaring as he drove away.

Long spiky grass pricked the backs of her legs. She hiccupped. Tears coursed down her cheeks and her chest heaved. Tina leaned back against a wooden fence post and took inventory of the damage. Physically, she was okay, apart from a sore head and a few niggles, here and there.

She skimmed her hands over the tops of the long grass, and smelt the wild fragrant flowers that filled the surrounding area where she sat. The smell of lush vegetation and salad crops calmed her. Tina tried to stand, but soon gave up, too exhausted to move.

A brief smile crossed her face as a vixen crossed the road, cubs in tow. She looked skyward. Several wisps of clouds mooched over a bright half-moon. Silver dots, millions of them, blinked back at her.

*What have I done to deserve this? Damn you for doing this to me!*

Tiny screeches sounded from the Pipistrelles flying overhead. The sight always held her fascination. Her fingers rubbed her throbbing nose, the skin tender to the touch. Dropping her head into her hands, she began to sob.

# CHAPTER 5

**TINA** held onto the fence post and pushed herself to her feet. She couldn't be bothered to remove the remaining shoe, not caring that it made her walk to the pavement harder.

The main road was clear as she looked about. To her right sat a bench. Limping as if one leg was longer than the other, she shuffled toward it. Her spine protested. With her hands pressed against each hip, she arched her back, thankful for a rest.

Moss had formed around the edges of the bench's wooden frame. Well-worn indentations from previous use had left the seat smooth. She placed her hands underneath her thighs to prevent the cold slats from penetrating her dress as she sat down.

Looking ahead, she gazed at the regimental order of the houses on the opposite side of the road. All of their brickwork was identical. Faint glimmers of light came from each one. Some of the curtains were drawn, their cars perched on gravel driveways.

The night air was mild and had a calming effect on her nerves. She didn't care about the predicament Clive had left her in. Sitting out here gave her a sense of freedom, a place with no falsities or aggravation. A sudden thought occurred and destroyed her moment of bliss.

*I have work in the morning. How will I get home without money or a phone?*

She could turn to the dwellings nearby for help, but with that came a barrage of questions and risks she didn't want to take. Nor did she want to involve someone else in the matter. The need to answer him back in the restaurant added to her confidence and fuelled Clive's rage. He'd scared her tonight more than on any other occasion. The stupid prat was going to sacrifice both of their lives just to prove a point.

Mucus clung to her sleeve as she wiped her nose across its edge. Her heart no longer pounded against her ribcage as the hysteria began to fade. The torn hem of her dress made the corners of her mouth lift into a genuine smile. Despite the fact that he'd unsettled her, Tina was still alive, though a little worse for wear.

She'd loved Clive. He'd been a man who tweaked her nose in the morning after a succulent kiss, left messages of love around her old flat, and told her how beautiful she was while rubbing her feet after a hard day at the office. Her mind sometimes refused to fathom the fact that he'd changed into someone else entirely.

Her reluctance to give up on her marriage and leave was incomprehensible. That would be another failure in her life, but she could take no more abuse. Escaping this emotional prison would be the hardest thing she'd ever do. Channelling her frustration, she kicked the dirt with her shod foot, creating a divot with the heel.

A distant thrum of a car made her look up. The hairs on her neck stood at attention and her muscles stiffened.

"Please drive past. Please drive past," she chanted. The hum grew louder. "Don't be him!" The vehicle whizzed past, leaving a rumble in its wake. "Thank you!"

Emptiness engulfed her once more. Several hiccups escaped her. With it, came a fresh wave of tears. She fiddled with the hole in her dress, twirling it around her fingers before she ripped it and made it bigger. Tina was determined in never wearing the dress ever again.

Several cars passed by. It was getting late, though she was unsure of the actual time. She decided to walk the four miles to her home. Not knowing what mood Clive would be in made her feel anxious, but she would worry about the consequences later.

Standing on unsteady legs, she stumbled and sat back down for a minute or so. Nausea surfaced and the contents of her stomach rose to the back of her throat. Pressing her hands against her knees, she threw up between her feet. She wiped her lips with bottom of her frock once her stomach stopped rebelling and waited for the sick feeling to pass. She stood once more, removing her shoe as she strolled down the path that ran alongside the road.

"Ouch! Ooh ya."

She cussed, hopping from one foot to the other as the grit and stones dug into her flesh. Music echoed in the distance, getting louder as a car approached. She knew it was Clive from the sound of the music blaring from its speakers.

*At this time of night? Drive past. I want to walk.*

She held her shoe strap with a little finger and swung her arms outwards, reflecting the tentative movement of the sharp steps. Taking several deep breaths, she continued on and prepared herself for whatever his mood might be.

Tina stopped and looked to the right, staring at the car rolling alongside her until it came to a halt. Music poured through the open door as Clive got out of the vehicle. He stood in front of her, his arms stretched out, ready for a cuddle as if nothing had happened.

"Hey."

"Hello." She gave him a cursory glance and aimed her eyes at the ground.

"Would you like to come home now and join me for a hot drink? You look cold."

"That would be nice." Tina took his offered hand and followed him to the passenger side.

"Dust yourself off. I don't want bits in the car," he said, holding the door open.

Tina brushed herself off and climbed in. He'd moved to the other side and slipped into the driver's seat, revving the engine and driving off.

"I have a headache. Would you mind if I turned the music down?"

She picked the debris from her feet. Tina buzzed the window open about an inch, careful to not drop the bits onto his foot mat, and flicked them outside.

Clive lowered the volume. "It shouldn't have come to this." He squeezed her knee with affection. "You're cold. Let me put the heating on."

"I feel okay. I don't feel cold, but that would be nice, thanks. I would like to talk, work things out between us."

*Keep him sweet. Play his game.*

"Sure, I'm cool with that," he said, his eyes fixed on the road ahead as he turned down and switched the CD to the radio. Johnny Cash played in the background.

"Thank you," she replied, not knowing what was worse, his good mood or bad. Both were equally damaging.

***

"**CAN** you walk to work tomorrow?" Clive asked as he brought their hot drinks through to the living room.

Tina reached for hers and thanked him. "Sure, I start at ten. It's Sam's night. Is it okay to see her? I can cancel if it's a problem."

"You only saw her two days ago."

"She is going away for a bit, so I won't see her for awhile."

"It's about time you cut ties with that snob." He shifted in his seat. "Mrs. Goody Two-Shoes needs bringing down a peg or two. When will you be back?"

"Is eleven okay?"

"Make it ten." Clive slid across the edge of the sofa.

"That's not a problem. I can fit it in around you," she said, blowing at her tea before taking a sip.

"Let's get that nose seen to," he said.

Clive stood and hurried out of the room, returning a few seconds later with the first aid kit. He dabbed her nose with witch hazel, soothing the contours of her face. She backed away from his touch, tamping down the sudden flinch.

"Pass me the vanity mirror, could you?" she asked. "It's in the plastic box."

He rummaged about until he found it and handed it to her. "Here."

She tilted her head left and right, and looked at the damage. "It's fine. You hardly touched me."

The line slipped from her tongue. He'd hit her with more force than he'd intended. The skin around her nostrils was starting to swell. She'd have a bruise soon enough.

"I know I hardly touched you. It could have been worst. I could have busted your fucking nose."

"Can I get some foundation from the chemist before work tomorrow? I wouldn't want anybody making comments."

He leaned forward, circling her face with his finger. "Good idea. You'll need to trowel it on to hide that ugly mug." He sniggered, and after a few minutes, he spoke again. "I won't see you in the morning, since I'm starting early."

He gathered the bits and put them back in the kit. Tina flexed her fingers around the cup and hid her rising anger with the sound of a loud slurp, hardly tasting the mint in the tea. Why did he think he was being funny? Ignoring the jibe, she took another sip. The moisture rejuvenated her dry lips and settled her nerves. He tipped his head back and let the final dregs of coffee fall onto his tongue.

"Wash these cups and put the first aid kit away. I'm going to bed."

"Bastard!" she said softly once he'd gone upstairs.

Tina finished her drink and did as Clive had asked of her. She would play the obedient wife, for the time being. Doing so would give her enough time to sort out her future.

*Two can play this game,* she thought, and turned in.

# CHAPTER 6

**A**WOKEN by the sound of the car moving out of the driveway, Tina stretched and flipped back the quilt. She slid out of bed, heading for the bathroom to take a shower. The twinge in her nose when she yawned was a reminder of what Clive had done.

Despite the events from the night before and the lack of a full night's rest, she felt rejuvenated. She decided wearing a pair of black trousers and a cardigan over a vest top would suffice for her day at work. After choosing a pair of flat shoes to go with the ensemble, she glanced in the mirror. A look of disappointment spread across her face.

*My face is a mess.*

Tina shook her head and walked out of the bedroom. She headed for the kitchen, eager to tackle the coming day. Her gaze fell upon the counter. Clive had left her a note propped against the bread bin.

*Don't be late.*

She ignored it and set about in making herself something to eat. Tina sat down and dug in, enjoying her breakfast. Eating the last corner of toast and downing the tea, she then headed out the door.

The sunlight stung her eyes, making them water. Tears ran down her face and trickled into the corners of her mouth. She licked her salty lips and palmed the moisture away. Two old dears passed and gestured a good morning in her direction. She was almost certain they saw the bruises on her face.

*What will people think?*

Tina dipped her head and focused her eyes on the pavement. Her aching nose felt huge. She cursed under her breath for forgetting her sunglasses. They wouldn't have hidden her nose, but at least she could hide behind them. It would have given her a false sense of security, but at least it would have worked.

The heady fragrance from the blooms in the neighbour's gardens wafted long after she passed and birds chirped in trees. She enjoyed starting work at ten o'clock. It meant she missed the rush-hour traffic and the kids were already at school. Crossing the road, she walked into Basle the Chemist. The cool air blasted from above the automatic door and blew wisps of hair into her face.

The end of the isle sign directed her to the make-up section. She tucked the loose strands behind her ears before browsing the tubes and selecting a colour that matched her skin tone. The woman at the counter gave her a knowing smile as she handed over the goods. Tina passed the money and left in a hurry.

She made her way to the nearest public bench in a shaded spot to apply the make-up. Putting a pea-sized amount on the back of her hand, she targeted the worst areas, and then replaced the cap, wiping away the excess with a face wipe. With a quick glance in a mirror stitched inside the flap of her bag, she sighed.

*That will have to do.*

She stood, tossed the wipe into the nearest bin, and strolled into work. Kobalt Advertising was a thirty-minute walk from her home. She'd been working there for almost twenty-two months, two days a week. The half day on a Saturday gave her most of the weekend off.

Tina liked her job, but preferred her previous one. Thanks to the bullies and the troubles at home as a child, she left school with no qualifications. She'd trained at night school, juggling two jobs to become a legal secretary, and was proud of her achievement. However, that changed after she moved in with Clive. He insisted she go part-time in a place he knew of close by, so he could keep an eye on her.

Tina climbed the concrete steps and held onto the rail for balance. She pressed the intercom and stared at the freshly polished brass plaque screwed to the wall. The system buzzed. Yanking the door, she stepped through.

The aroma of ground coffee drifted down the carpeted corridor on her way to her desk. Firing up her computer, she put her bag on the floor next to her workstation. There were eight desks in the office, all equipped with the same thing. She looked at the pile of paperwork. It would keep her busy for most of the day.

"Morning, Tina," Martin, another office clerk, said when he saw her. "How are you? Did you have a nice few days off?" He fiddled with the coffee percolator.

"Fine, thanks. You?" she asked, keeping her head down, avoiding any visual contact.

"Great. I've been run ragged with the little one. Want a drink?"

"Err, no thanks. I've just had one."

She hoped her quick reply would be sufficient to deter him from coming anywhere near her. It was too late, however. He was soon standing behind her, talking over her shoulder with baby photos in hand.

"Thought you might like to look at little Drew. He's walking now." He placed the photographs on her desk.

Tina's hair flopped over her face as her head dipped a little lower. "He is getting to be a big boy now."

The worst part about working in an office was having to put up with people's life stories and photos when she had enough to contend with herself. Annoyed that there were several pictures to look at, she thumbed through them and gave him her usual reply to this sort of situation.

"They are lovely, so sweet."

She passed the pictures back to Martin, accidentally dropping one on the floor. Martin bent down to pick it up. As he stood, he caught sight of her face. Tina turned her head away.

"What have you done? Have you been mugged? Someone's had fisticuffs? It wasn't your hubby, was it?"

"Of course not! Why would you think that?"

Her stomach burned with the indigestion brought on by stress. *Does he suspect something?*

She put her hand to her lips, tilting it back and forth as she tipped her head back to gesture a drunken motion. "I had too much wine."

His eyebrows furrowed with concern. "But you don't drink."

"Two glasses of wine," she said. "I was out of it." She swayed in her seat, her arms flailing about. "I walked into the kitchen door."

Disappointed, she kicked herself under the table. She'd hoped the foundation would have done a better job.

"I bet Clive will get some stick. People will think he did it. He's such a nice bloke, your hubby."

"He is. Aren't I lucky? Who else is in today?"

She changed the subject, hoping it would ease the sudden tension that now surrounded her. The grin on her face was starting to feel heavy.

"Two others. Some are coming in late. The boss left those on your desk. He wants the figures for the new clients as soon as possible."

"Thanks. I better make a start then."

With that, he got the hint and shuffled back to his desk. Switching on the desk fan, she let the cool breeze lift her hair and dry her damp neck. She picked up the first lot of paperwork and started her workload.

Lunchtime came and everyone ate at their desk. Mouse, the office geek, opened her egg sandwich, the foul smell wafting through the room as the fans circulated around the office. Tina pinched her nose, bringing sudden tears to her eyes. She couldn't put up with the putrid scent that now surrounded her.

*Bloody woman! Why can't she choose a less smelly sandwich?*

# NEVER TOO LATE

Martin popped his bag of prawn-flavoured crisps. No longer able to take the mingled smells, Tina rushed to the ladies room. She stood over the sink and waited fifteen minutes. Once the odours from lunch had dispersed, she went back to her desk. Tina removed her mobile from her bag, and hid it under the table from prying eyes. She typed a message and hit send.

*Hi, Sam. Cover me tonight. If Clive rings, tell him I'm busy or something. x*

The mobile phone vibrated instantly, and she read the reply.

*Yes, are you okay? Seeing Daddy tonight. xx*

She could never understand why Sam, a grown woman, would call her father, Daddy. Tina shook her head and sent the next message.

*Planning a surprise. Need the time away from him to do that. You know how close we are. x*

Another reply soon came in.

*Too close. I will get my messages forwarded in case he rings. When will I see you again? Are we up for next week? I could ring. xx*

Tina smirked and sent the final message.

*May not see you for awhile. Lots on. Do not ring. Will explain soon. Enjoy the time at your dad's. Love you. xx*

Sam's reply quickly followed.

*OK. You know where I am. Love you, too. S x*

Tina deleted both the in and out box, in case Clive took a crafty look. She then popped the phone back into her bag. A deep sigh escaped her. She'd never mastered the self-preservation skill to handle her resentment. The relationship with Sam and her father always left her feeling hollow and alone. She'd met Sam's father on numerous occasions. He was a charming man and devoted to his daughter. She shrugged the feeling away. Things were trying enough, making her avoid situations she couldn't control.

Mouse approached her desk. "May I borrow your calculator? The batteries have gone in mine."

Tina stiffened and lowered her head. "Sure, but I want it back, though. Things disappear in this office."

"Of course," Mouse said, her eyes narrowing as she gazed at Tina's face. "Oh, what have you done to—?"

Tina sighed and repeated her story for the umpteenth time. She was fed up with the questions about her nose and face. Her desk phone flashed, giving her a nice reprieve. She smiled at Mouse and picked up the phone, speaking into the mouthpiece.

"Good morning, Kobalt Advertising."

***

**I**T was now seven o'clock. Tina noticed Mr. Manning enter the office to do his final checks before heading home. He glanced in her direction and shook his head.

"Are you still here? Home time was ages ago."

"I just have a few more things to do. Is it okay to stay a bit longer?"

Her portly boss looked down through his specs at her. "I admire your dedication, but I can't pay you overtime."

Tina nodded with understanding. "That's okay. I want to get these reports finished, that's all."

"You will have to use the back entrance when you leave. The cleaners will lock up after you. Oh, and sorry to hear about your nose. Good night, Tina," he said, and hurried off to complete the task at hand.

"Good night, Mr. Manning."

*Bloody gossips!*

Once the office was empty, Tina typed in the keywords, untraceable murder, into the Google Chrome browser and hit search. She'd already printed off the relevant information to help Clive, and hidden it in the secret pocket of her bag, ready to present it to him over dinner tomorrow.

The screen flickered, showing her several options. She scanned the list, amazed by the amount of information at her disposal. Weapons, how to commit the perfect murder, trace evidence, DNA—the list was endless.

*Not quite what I had in mind.*

She changed her search options and waited for the screen to respond. Several clicks later, she found something a little more feasible.

"That could work," she muttered, while memorising the details. "Drowning!"

*Why didn't I think of that before?*

The idea was perfect. She could use her father-in-law's boat to get the job done. Of course, he would take some persuading, being the cantankerous git that he was. Her mind raced with ideas.

Changing the search to accidental drowning gave her an idea of what to expect. Her mouth grew dry from the anticipation. She read the information again and committed it to memory.

"Perfect."

Content with the fact that she finally had the guts to start her plan, she sat back in her chair and fantasized about what was to come. Clive had two choices, seek help or die. Her hand shot to her mouth. She pinched her lips between her fingers, fearing she'd scream aloud because of the excitement surging through her veins. For the first time in a long time, she felt alive and ready to fight.

The main office door swung open, startling her. The cleaner had started her rounds, it seemed. She wore a tabard and pink rubber gloves. The squeak from the wheels on her trolley set Tina's teeth on edge. As the lady passed, it was full of household items and black bags. Tina minimised the screen in case she decided to be nosey.

"Evening."

"Evening," Tina said, and glanced over her shoulder to look at the woman as she began to clean the other end of the office.

Satisfied, she carried on and opened the tab. Without warning, she felt a presence standing behind her several minutes later. Tina looked over her shoulder to find that the cleaning lady had snuck up behind her. She clicked close on the browser, but the computer was too slow. Clicking repeatedly seemed to freeze the screen. Her heart raced and the room felt hot.

"What you looking at?" the woman asked, and leaned in. "Drowning?"

Tina's breath hitched as she tried to reply. She wracked her brain for a fast excuse, but nothing came to mind.

"Who you gonna drown?" The woman quirked a brow in her direction. "Your husband? I would, too, if he did that to my nose."

Tina gulped. *Don't reply to the jibe. Be nice and calm!*

She seemed to find her voice once more and said, "Research. I'm doing a paper for a college course."

"Oh, right. That sounds hard. Think I shall stick to my cleaning. Can I empty your bin and hoover here now?"

Tina sighed inwardly. She reached up to reopen the browser and erased the history.

"I'm finished here. Give me five minutes to shut down and it's all yours," she said.

She packed up her things and pushed herself to her feet. Nodding at the woman, she headed for the door. Ten minutes later, she made her way home.

\*\*\*

**A**s she entered her house and strode down the hall, Tina recognised the sound of Ray's voice and her heart sank. She popped her head around the living room door. Clive lounged nearby, his feet propped on the table, a beer in one hand and the remote control in the other. She knew he was showing off. He hated putting his feet up on the table. Ray sat next to him.

"Hi, Tina. How are you doing?" Ray asked.

The corners of Clive's mouth tightened as he looked at her. "You're early. I thought you were seeing your mate. I rang, but you were in the garden."

His fingers curled around the remote. Jabbing at the button, he found the sports channel and put the control on the table. She nodded and gave Ray a false smile. Tina met Clive's inquiring eyes and gestured toward the kitchen.

"Can I have a word?"

A muscle twitched along Clive's jaw. He stood and followed her into the kitchen with his beer in hand.

"Why are you here early? We said ten." He looked at his watch. "It's only eight o'clock."

"That's okay, though. It's just two hours early."

Tina sensed Clive's displeasure. She hated making him angry, but there was nothing else she could do about it. She'd come home early, and that was that.

*Can't win with you, can I?*

"No, it's not. I'm having a sports night. Why are you early?" he repeated.

Tina pretended to feel a little annoyed. "Sam was getting on my nerves. We had a little fall out, and I won't be seeing her again."

Clive smirked with amusement. "Oh, good! About time you ditched her." He reached out to hug her to him. "Are you going to bed? I want to watch the program. Men only, I'm afraid."

He stared at her, waiting for a reaction. Tina nodded with understanding.

"No problem. You won't hear a peep out of me. I just wanted to ask if we could have a romantic meal tomorrow night. I would like to try and cook your favourite."

A look of incredulity spread across Clive's face. He laughed and shook his head.

"You . . . cook? You're shit at cooking, Tina. Burnt offerings more like."

She counted to ten and then replied, "I could try. I just thought that after last night we could . . . you know . . . try."

With reluctance, she rubbed her hand across his forearms, hoping to garner the reaction she wanted from him. Clive's eyes narrowed as he assessed her.

"Alright. I see you got some slap for your face. Camouflage didn't work, did it?"

He flicked a finger against the tip of her nose. Tina's eyes watered. Standing her ground, she refused to cower before him. She dabbed at her wet eyes with the corner of her cardigan instead.

"Don't pick me up tomorrow," she said.

His eyes narrowed with suspicion. "Why not?"

"I need to go to the butcher and the supermarket for some bits for dinner. I can walk back and then get started on the housework. Will that be okay?"

Clive nodded. "Yep. Take your phone with you."

"I will," she said. "Good night. I'm going up."

She kissed him on the cheek and hurried out of the kitchen. Tina paused at the top of the stairs, listening in on the men's conversation. Ray agreed with everything Clive discussed, never forming his own opinions, overawed by her pig of a husband. Their raucous behaviour continued. She shook her head and made her way to bed.

"More fool you," she mumbled along the way.

# CHAPTER 7

**L**ADEN with several shopping bags, Tina plonked them down on the counter. Her hands carried the indentations the bags had made across her fingers. Rubbing the life back into them, she put away the groceries. She opened a bottle of wine and left it on the table to chamber. Pouring herself a small glass, she smelt the Chianti's dry floral notes before taking a sip.

Tina then donned an apron and started the preparations for their romantic meal. Clive had requested steaks before he left that morning, and insisted on a pudding of rhubarb pie and cream. Although more than capable of baking her own, buying one seemed like an easier option. This way he wouldn't grumble about a sour filling or feathery pasty.

Above the cooker, the clock read four forty-five. Clive would be home soon. The juicy rib eye's under the grill smelt of deliciousness, their scent wafting downstairs. She stirred the peppercorn sauce, the heat from the oven scorching her face as she turned the chunky chips. Washing her hands, she dried them on the bottom of her piny. Hearing the car pull into the driveway, Tina took a generous mouthful of wine and removed her apron. Counting his footsteps down the hall, she soon greeted him.

"Hi! Good day at work?"

"Busy. Your face is all red, and what's that burning greasy smell?"

"That's dinner cooking, I'm hot and flustered, that's all."

Tina took his coat and hung it up, though not even a thank you or a kiss came.

"You're not cooking already, are you? I need a shower."

Her shoulder nudged the wall as Clive barged past and strode into the kitchen.

"They're on a low heat. We always eat first."

Tina watched him move about from her perch in the doorway. He snatched the oven mitt from the hook, and removed the steaks from the grill, slamming the pan on the side.

"They'll be fucking cremated. You know I like my meat medium-rare."

Tina tensed, knowing what would come next.

"Why is this crap on the table?" He pointed to the flowers sitting in the middle of the table, reaching for the thin stemmed vase and hurling it into the sink. "I fucking hate flowers."

Rose petals fell into the suds at the bottom of the plughole. The blue glass broke in two, the pieces scratching the stainless steel sink.

"They were only on a low heat. S—Sor . . . ry!"

Tina hurried into the kitchen. A look of annoyance clouded her beautiful features. He'd messed up her routine and broke her favourite vase.

"Can I get you a glass of wine?" she asked.

Without waiting for his reply, she reached for the bottle and began to pour him a glass, passing it to him. He took a hefty swig, holding the liquid in his mouth for several seconds, before spitting it into the sink.

"That tastes like shit. Are you trying to poison me?"

Tina's head recoiled as if he'd slapped her. "It's your favourite! The one you always have." She held the bottle up for him to study the label. "See?"

Clive snorted with derision. "Well, it tastes like vinegar. I'll be down in twenty minutes. Then you can dish up this pile of crap you've made me for dinner," he said, and stormed off.

She heard him bound up stairs, chuntering along the way. She couldn't understand the harshness of his actions. After the conversation they'd had the night before, it was supposed to be an attempt at a fresh start. She needed him calm and amicable so that she could approach the taboo subject. This wasn't how she'd pictured the evening going.

*Just relax. You can do this.*

Clearing the petals and glass from the sink with her fingertips, she pushed the bin's pedal with her foot and tossed the fragments inside. A blob of blood appeared on her thumb. She hadn't noticed that she'd nicked it. Tina ran it under the tap and sucked at the tip, satisfied that the bleeding had stopped. She then carried on with the evening meal.

Clive soon appeared. He took a seat at the table. His aftershave was so strong that it tickled the back of her throat and left a bitter taste on her tongue.

She turned to face him and said, "Do you feel refreshed now?"

He drummed his fingers across the table's surface, his mouth pursed with impatience. The stern look on his face unsettled her as he waited for his dinner.

*What? Am I your serving wench?*

Tina set about in preparing their plates. "Wine?" she asked as she put the food down on their placemats.

"Water for me," Clive said. "You can pour that shit down the sink."

Unable to help herself, she replied, "I like it. It's a nice drop of wine."

"You would. You have no taste." Clive looked down at his plate. "I wanted the sauce separate. It's smothered now."

Tina glanced in the same direction. "It's a little bit of sauce on the side. There's more in the pan if you want it."

She twisted the cap on the bottle of mineral water and filled his glass.

"Can I get you anything else before I join you?" She hovered near the cooker and waited for his reply.

"Sit the fuck down, and have your dinner."

Obediently, she sat down, placing the cotton napkin over her lap, and started to eat. Her eyes lifted from her plate at the sound of Clive stabbing at his meat. He'd spread a small amount of sauce on the cut piece, twiddling his fork in the air, examining it before it entered his mouth. She rolled her eyes at him with disbelief.

*Eat your bloody meal, you pretentious prick!*

"It's overcooked!" he said. "Old fucking boots! Why do you bother, you stupid mare?"

He spat out the mangled piece of beef. It fell onto his plate, and saliva drooled from the corner of his mouth. Tina lowered her head and put her cutlery down before she reached for her glass.

"Sorry! I just wanted it to be—"

He pushed his plate aside and gulped down some water. "You can take that now. I'm finished," he said, cutting off her reply.

Tina stood and cleared away the dishes. "Shall I serve the pudding now?"

"Did you make it?" he asked.

"No, I bought it."

He nodded at her. She fetched the pie and set it down on the table.

"Cream?"

"Yes, I'll have some, but I want my pie cold and the cream on the side. Can you manage that?"

Tina ignored his jibe and slid the knife from the block. It felt heavy in her hand. A sudden thought rushed through her mind. She could slit his throat and end it all now. Yet she wasn't sure if she could do it. Instead, she took her anger out on the pie and hacked it into quarters.

"Where's your piece?" he asked as she passed him the slice of pudding.

"I'm not hungry." She paused and prepared herself for the next question. "Can we talk, please?" Her heart started to race.

"Oh, yes, the chat," he quipped, his voice full of heavy sarcasm. Clive put down his fork and pushed the plate aside. "I don't want this. The cream isn't whipped. And what did you cut it with? A butter knife?"

Clive folded his arms across his chest. The look on his face added to her apprehension.

*If only things had gone the way I'd planned them*, she thought.

"I have something I want to show you," she said.

Tina collected her bag from where she'd left it on the worktop. She unzipped the secret pocket and found nothing, frantically searching the other compartments. The documents she'd stored earlier were nowhere to be found.

*I'm sure I put the information in here.*

"Looking for these?" Clive asked.

He pulled the A4 sheets he'd taken from her bag out of his pocket. Unfolding them, he slid the papers across the table one by one.

"Anger management, relate counselling, and let's not forget this one, domestic abuse advice! You've been busy."

Tina's face paled. "How did you get those? They were in my . . . You went through my bag!"

"You can't keep anything from me, Tina. I own you."

Her mouth quivered as fear coursed through her veins. "How did you—?"

"Know? I didn't, but you can't hide anything from me. You should know that."

"Those . . ." She pointed at the papers. ". . . are what I wanted to talk to you about."

"Are you saying I have a fucking problem, bitch?"

"N—No."

The corners of his mouth deepened. "Sit down. NOW!"

Tina sat down on the nearest chair. She curled her hands into fists beneath the table. Her heart pounded inside her chest. Nothing was turning out the way she thought it would.

"Please, I was only trying to help. I thou—"

Clive's harsh tone cut off the rest of her reply. "You just don't think, and that's your own fault. You're the one that makes me like this with your snivelling and disobedience."

Tina's mouth dropped open with surprise. "How can you say that?"

He leaned forward, his eyes focused on her face. "I say it because it's true. Can't you do anything right?"

"I've done everything you've asked me to do!"

Clive slammed his hands down on the table. "You never do it right!"

"But . . ." she began. "I—I can't talk to you when you're like this. I need to use the bathroom."

Tina pushed her chair back and prepared to stand. Clive jumped to his feet and skirted the edge of the table. He towered over her several seconds later.

"Where do think you're going?"

His hand descended upon her injured shoulder. It began to hurt as he pressed against it, pushing her back down onto the chair. She didn't resist, trying to keep her wayward emotions at bay. He let go of her. She reached up and rubbed her collarbone.

"You thought you could hide this from me until tonight?" Clive moved toward the worktop and leaned against it. He pointed his finger at her, shaking it at the same time. "With this . . . *I will cook your favourite meal* bullshit, you thought you could dissuade me, didn't you?"

Tina refused to let him bait her. "You had no right to root through my belongings!"

Clive laughed. "I have every right. I'm your husband. All you have to do is toe the line. Instead, it all goes to shit."

"We could make this work if you sought help."

"I'm not the one that needs help. You are. You're damaged goods, always have been."

Clive moved forward and flattened his hands across the table. He leaned in, inches from her face. His stinking breath blew across her cheeks. The foul scent invaded her nose. A wave of revulsion rose to the surface. She needed to get out of the kitchen and make it to the bathroom. She could lock herself in once there, but there was no means of escape for her.

Anger took hold of her. Tina did the one thing she swore she'd never do. Unable to hold herself back, she spoke back to him, moving in closer as her eyes focused on his.

"Why . . . marry . . . me . . . then?" Tina wailed, blinking rapidly to keep her tears from falling.

"Because you're easy to control. Nothing but damaged goods. Always grateful for anybody's attention," he said through grinding teeth.

The fount broke and tears flowed down her cheeks. "Stop snarling at me! I've done nothing but support you." She hiccupped. "It—It's not true."

Clive laughed once more. "Yes, it is. I've spoken to your witch of a mother, who gladly filled me in on a few things."

Tina's mouth dropped open with surprise. "She had no right to tell you anything!"

"No? Why not?"

"Because it's nothing to do with you."

"It has everything to do with me! Causing your dad's death must have got to her, I bet. Or was it because you're a failure?"

"Stop it! Please!" she shouted, and rose to her feet. "Please, just stop." She gripped the edge of the table, her legs trembling with the effort.

Clive leaned forward once more, staring deep into her eyes. "Would you like me to carry on? I've plenty more where that came from. And you say I need help!"

Tina's heart raced. Clive enjoyed showering her with abuse. It made him feel strong and quite manly. This was his way of controlling her, to make her do and say exactly what he wanted her to.

"Okay, I was wrong," she said, her voice barely a whisper.

Clive cupped his hand around his ear. "What's that? I didn't hear you."

"Sorry!"

Tina moved forward, squeezing past Clive to try to get to the sink. From there, she would be able to make a dash for the door and run.

Clive grinned, a malevolent light invading the depths of his eyes. "Too right you are. And now you have to be punished like the slut you are."

Pinned against the sink, Tina felt Clive grind his pelvis into her backside. His hands gripped her hips tight. She felt his penis grow hard as it pressed against the small of her back.

"No! Leave me alone!"

"Why? Everyone else has had a piece of you."

She reached for the nearest object she could put her hands on. Tina pushed him back with all her might as she turned and hurled a pan at him. Lukewarm sauce splattered his white t-shirt. To her dismay, she'd missed his face. While Clive checked out his soiled clothes, she made a run for the other side of the kitchen, hoping for a clear exit to the door.

Clive turned around and headed straight for her, blocking her escape. "Bitch!"

"Get away from me!"

Tina changed directions and ran to the other side of the kitchen. The hateful look on Clive's face frightened her. Her husband would not be deterred.

"Come here, bitch!"

She edged along the sink's counter, moving closer to the door. His bulk filled the door's frame. He lunged, cornering her against the table and the wall. Tina swallowed past the lump forming at the back of her throat. She was trapped.

Diverting his attention by grabbing the papers off the table, she threw them at his face. Her sudden action caught him off guard, giving her enough time to reach the bottom of the stairs. Tina caught a glimpse of Clive as he moved in her direction. She took the stairs two at a time. Adrenaline kicked in, giving her a burst of energy.

Tina's foot slipped and she stumbled across the top three steps. Regaining her footing, she managed to get to the landing before she felt his hand grab her ankle. Clive pulled her back down. She kicked him away, hoping to dislodge his grip.

"Get off me!" she screamed.

"Where the fuck are you going?"

She lashed out at him, her body thrashing about. His hold on her ankles tightened and he yanked harder.

"Leave me alone!"

Tina felt one last tug on her feet. Her elbows scraped the carpet as she tumbled down the stairs. The last thing she remembered was a boot slamming into her ribs.

# CHAPTER 8

**CLIVE** nudged Tina's inert form with his foot. "Get the fuck up." He tried to rouse her once more. "I said, get up!"

He knelt and checked the side of her neck with his index finger. Blood dripped from her lower lip. She'd landed on her back with her legs splayed, one arm by her side and the other flopped across her chest.

"Oh, shit." He cupped his chin and paced the hall as panic set in. "Think, think. What shall I do? Oh, shit. Shit!"

Several minutes passed before he covered his wife with his jacket and decided to change his shirt. He then walked into the kitchen. The dirty dishes were scattered across the table. He balanced the crockery on top of each other and dumped them on the draining board. Clive then picked up the papers and put them in his pocket to dispose of later. The mess bugged him, but he wasn't washing up. In his mind, it was women's work.

Opening the top cupboard, he reached for the first aid kit, annoyed by the fact that Tina had put it back the wrong way round. He found what he was looking for, and shoved the small green bottle into his pocket. With a quick flick of his hand, he put the kit away, making sure it was exactly an inch away from the other stuff in the cupboard. He then slammed the door closed.

Clive took a moment to compose himself before he made the call to summon the paramedics. It took fifteen minutes for the ambulance to arrive. During that time, he focused on a scuff mark on the wall and answered the controller's questions on the other end of the phone while he sat at the bottom of the stairs.

"Yes, she is," he said. "No, I've not moved her."

He tapped his foot with impatience and scratched at his scalp. The woman was getting on his nerves, and he was anxious to get rid of her. It took every ounce of his self-control not to tell her to piss off. Several shapes soon appeared before the half-moon glass of the front door. Relief flooded every inch of Clive's body, though it didn't lessen the slight trepidation he still felt within him.

"Ah, they're here."

He ended the call and slid the phone into the back pocket of his jeans. Clive took several minutes to compose himself before answering the door. He retrieved the bottle he'd stashed in his pocket and tipped his head back, letting the drops fill each eye. Fluttering his lashes for the desired effect, he darted to the door before they knocked again.

"Please, help. My wife's had an accident." He glanced at Tina and back at them.

"Don't worry. What's your name?" one of the paramedics asked as they entered.

"Clive." He nodded and pinched the bridge of his nose to conjure more tears from his eyes. "She just fell and . . . I didn't know what to do. I . . ."

"It'll be okay. I'm Lucy, and this is Steve."

She turned and gestured. Steve smiled and said hello. He dropped the bulky bag he was holding to the floor.

"How long has she been unconscious?" Lucy asked, positioning herself in front of Clive to block his view, wanting his undivided attention.

"I'm not sure. An hour, maybe less." He put his thumb to his mouth and bit the nail.

"Could you tell me what happened?"

"I've just told the lady on the phone."

"I know, sir, but if you could repeat it, that would be very helpful. Why don't you take a seat?"

Lucy led him into the living room and took out her patient assessment form.

"We were having dinner." Clive paused and swallowed. "She dashed up stairs. The next thing I hear is a rumble."

"Does she always run up the stairs that quick?"

Lucy withdrew a tissue from her deep jacket pocket and passed it to him.

"Yes, she does." He took the tissue and wiped his nose before blotting his eyes. "Will she be alright?"

"Steve is just checking her over. Sit down, Clive. We don't want you passing out as well, do we?"

She stroked his shoulder, encouraging him into the chair. Clive allowed her to lead him to it and slowly sat down.

"She must have slipped. Those stupid sandals didn't help. We had a wonderful dinner. Help her, please!"

Lucy glanced at the form and said, "I just need to ask you some questions."

Clive wiped his thumb on his shirt and flicked the piece of skin out of his mouth with the tip of his tongue. He began to tremble, hoping Lucy hadn't noticed.

"Would you know if she has any allergies? Is she taking any medications? Any outstanding illnesses?

"No, none." He inched toward the edge of his seat.

"What's her full name and date of birth?"

"Tina Blythe. 4/4/1987."

"Have you been together long?" Lucy asked, and filled the relevant boxes on the sheet.

"What does that matter? How is that going to help?" he snapped.

"I'm just making conversation. It's a stressful time, but I need you to stay calm for me." Lucy looked him in the eye. "I'm going to assist Steve now."

"I need a glass of water," Clive said as she walked away from him.

He stood and averted his gaze as he passed by his wife to enter the kitchen. Splashing water in his eyes did nothing to redden them. He peered around the door's edge. Both of the paramedics were working on Tina. Clive stepped back and out of sight, adding more eye drops.

Clive panicked. *What if I'm found out? How can I? It was an accident. She would have fallen anyway.*

He began to feel a little paranoid. Clive squeezed a good portion of the drops into his eyes before he pocketed the bottle. All of a sudden, Lucy appeared in the doorway. His heart pounded and his hands shook as he stared at her.

"Everything okay?" she asked.

"Fine. Just looking for the Paracetamol."

"You'll need to pack a few things. She may have to stay overnight. It's best to be prepared."

Her sleeve got caught on the door handle as she turned to join Steve. She adjusted it and moved into the hall.

"Thank you," he said, though he wasn't sure she'd heard him.

The muttering coming from the hall unnerved him. Had Lucy seen the drops? He punched his thigh and kicked at the floor with his heel. Taking a deep breath, he stretched his back and rotated his shoulder blades before flexing his fingers, ready to front it out.

"How is she doing?" Clive asked as he leaned against the doorframe.

"Her blood pressure is low and she's in shock. We have put a neck brace on her and set up a drip," Lucy replied as she squatted beside Tina.

"Will . . . she be . . . ?"

"We will get her in as soon as we can."

"What about the blood coming from her mouth?"

Steve returned with the spinal board. He nodded at Lucy, ready for the next step.

"She may have bit her tongue when she fell. It's too soon to say.

61

She's doing fine. We'll take good care of her."

"Thank you."

Clive stepped back to give them room. Though he appeared to be calm, he was anything but that. He hadn't meant to cause Tina's accident. He'd only meant to scare her.

"Before we move her, I'm going to give her a mild sedative and 3 milligrams of Morphine to help relax her muscles and take away any pain."

Clive nodded in approval. Steve eased her limbs and straightened her out.

"After three," Steve said.

They rolled her onto her side and slid the board underneath her body. A clear bag lay at Tina's side. Standing at each end, they carried her to the wheeled trolley outside the front door. Clive supported her head, hating the fact that she'd caused such an unfortunate accident.

***

**T**INA slowly awoke, feeling the movement and pricks on her skin. The warmth crept up her arm and hit her brain. A blanket of happiness soon surrounded her. The pain was a distant memory.

Muffled voices echoed in her head. She opened her heavy eyelids. The bright light made a tear run down each temple. She reached up to tug at the tight elastic wrapped around her ears, pulling at the plastic cup that covered her face.

"Hold on, Steve," Lucy said as she caught sight of Tina's movements. "Stop a moment, please. You need to leave that on, Sweetie."

Lucy pressed Tina's arm back to her side. Tina mumbled as she tilted her head to the right. The slight shift was restricted by some kind of stiff plastic.

"Don't move your head. Keep still if you can."

She felt something stroke her palm before she floated into

62

oblivion.

\*\*\*

**C**LIVE followed as they wheeled her to the back of the ambulance. Steve pressed the button and the ramp lowered. It hit the ground with a soft thump. With the patient now secured, the ramp ascended. Lucy climbed into the driver's seat and hit the ignition. The engine idled as Steve spoke to Clive.

"You can come with us, but it's probably best if you follow on later. We won't know anything until the full assessment can be made. She could be a couple of hours."

Clive nodded with understanding. "I'll come later. I need to get her things together."

"We are taking her to the Queen Elizabeth Hospital's A/E department. Everything will be fine."

"Thank you."

Clive sniffed. Steve climbed aboard the ambulance. Five minutes later, the blue lights flashed as it turned onto the main road. Shaking his head, Clive strode toward his house.

"What's happened? Can I help?" Mrs. Conerly peered over the garden fence. "Where have they taken her? Can I get you anything?"

Clive nonchalantly walked past without answering her and slammed the front door.

"Fucking nosey old cow!"

He cussed under his breath and took the stairs two at a time. Clive threw some of Tina's things and toiletries into a canvas bag he'd pulled from the wardrobe. Once done, he trudged out of the bedroom and hurried downstairs, tossing the bag near the door.

He would leave in an hour or so, he decided. For now, he grabbed a beer from the fridge and carried it through to the living room. Clive snapped the ring pull and took a hefty glug. Turning on the television, he sat down to watch his favourite sports channel.

*If that bitch says anything, she's fucking dead!*

# CHAPTER 9

A grey cuff inflated around the top of Tina's arm. As it squeezed, she opened her eyes.

"Evening. Sorry to wake you. How are you feeling?" a young nurse asked.

Tina grimaced. "I have a headache."

"That will be the sedatives. I will get you some pain relief. Drink plenty of water. It flushes the drugs from your system quicker."

"No . . . pain relief. What am I doing here?" Tina croaked.

The nurse fiddled with the cuff. "You had an accident. Open your mouth for me."

A woman lying in a bed nearby cried out. "Sue . . . Help . . . Sue."

Tina glanced at a frail old woman. "Is she okay?"

"She has dementia, poor lady. Open wide."

The thermometer felt heavy under her dry tongue. Tina raised her arm, feeling confused, wanting to remove the foreign object from her mouth.

"That's normal," the nurse said, ejecting the disposable end into the paper bag taped to Tina's table for rubbish. The blood pressure cuff deflated. She removed it and placed it on the trolley beside the monitor. "Your saturation levels are good, too." She filled in the chart before sliding it into a metal slot at the bottom of the bed.

"Is my husband here?"

"I will check for you. The doctor will be along in a minute. Can I get you a cup of tea and a sandwich?"

"I'm not hungry, but a cuppa would be nice." Tina's chin dimpled and her bottom lip quivered.

The nurse nodded. "Let me get your tea. Do you take milk and sugar?"

"Just milk, thank you."

"You're welcome. If you want to sit up a bit, I've left the remote to your bed over there." She pointed to it and poured iced water into her glass, moving the table closer so that Tina could reach it.

Tina pressed the blue arrow on the control pad, and her bed lifted with a gentle hum. Her bony fingers reached for the water. After downing the whole glass, she refilled it, resting her head back onto the plump pillows and straightening the thin blue blanket covering her.

The nurse appeared, carrying the beverage. "Here we are, my dear, a nice cup of tea."

"Thanks. Is my husband here?"

Tina accepted the cup, wincing as she leant forward to take a sip. The brew was tepid and weak, but welcome, nonetheless.

"He's in the waiting area, but the doctor wants to see you first. He won't be long."

A buzzer sounded as Tina prepared herself to ask another question. The nurse held up a hand momentarily and shook her head.

"Coming, Mrs. Wright. Enjoy your tea," she said, and strode to the next patient.

Another nurse approached. She was quite cheerful and carried a clear bag in her hand.

"Hello. I'm going to change your drip." She snapped on a pair of latex gloves and fiddled with the clear tubes. "What happened to you?"

Tina's eyes lifted to the sound of the pleated blue curtains being drawn, relieved to be rescued by a tall man wearing blue scrubs. He squirted gel on his hands and rubbed them together. The strong smell of ethanol filled the confined space.

"Hi. My name is Doctor Harper. I'm one of the team here. What would you like me to call you?" He looked at his chart and pulled a chair to her bedside. "Mrs. Tina Blythe."

"Tina's fine."

She nervously bit down on her bottom lip and sat up. The doctor was young, handsome, and couldn't have been much older than herself. The nursed finished with the saline and binned the gloves. She left, swishing the curtain behind her.

"How are you feeling?"

"A bit confused. I can't seem to take a deep breath without my chest hurting."

"I'm not surprised. You have hairline fractures on two ribs. Nothing we can do, aside from letting them heal. Because of the fracture's location, we decided not to strap them."

Tina nodded and rubbed her lips together. A bright sheen of moisture shone in her eyes as she did her best to hold herself together.

Dr. Harper continued. "We kept you sedated until we finished the tests. We're just waiting for—"

A sudden commotion in the corridor startled them. Tina's eyes widened and her body tensed. Dr. Harper became aware of her reaction and stood.

"Excuse me for a moment."

The ward sister popped her head between the flaps. "I'm sorry, Doctor. He demanded to see his wife."

Dr. Harper shot Tina a glance. She nodded an approval.

"Let him in."

Clive strode into the cubicle with an angry expression on his face. "I've been waiting. No one told me anything. I'm her next of kin. It's not good enough!"

The doctor sighed and shook his head. "I'm Doctor Harper. I'm looking after your wife." He stretched out his hand, and Clive shook it. "The patient has only just come round. I was about to finish her assessment and apologise for the wait."

"I've been very worried. Other patients have had visitors." Clive played with keys in his pocket.

"It depends on their circumstances. As I said, she has only just come round from the sedation." He looked at his watch.

Beads of sweat formed on Clive's brow. "May I have some time alone with her?"

"Yes, but she needs rest. I'll give you a few minutes. Then I need to finish her assessment." Dr. Harper walked away, looking over his shoulder as he left. "I will be back soon, Tina."

She gave the doctor a thin smile and closed her eyes, waiting for Clive to speak. Tina felt Clive's tender touch upon her face. He pressed a kiss to her forehead.

"How are you feeling?" He took a seat, stroking her arm at the same time.

"Sore." Tina forced her eyelids open and looked at his unshaven face.

Clive snorted and rolled his eyes at her. "Well, it's your own fault."

"I'm a bit groggy from the medications."

Remembering what the nurse had said, she reached for her water. Clive pushed the table away. He smirked at her, pleased that he'd kept her from drinking.

"What have you said?"

"Nothing. Didn't you hear what the doctor said?"

Clive walked his fingers down her arm and rubbed at the cannula in her right hand with his thumb. "You're in your element in here. All these drugs . . . No wonder you're spaced!"

"That's not fair! You put me in here." Her voice rose above a whisper, and tears started to form in her eyes.

"Keep your fucking voice down!"

She tensed and looked down at her hand. The sight of his thumb circling the cannula upset her. Tina was afraid he'd take drastic measures to make sure she'd keep mum about what happened.

*He can't hurt me in here.*

Clive leaned forward to whisper in her ear as he pressed down on the needle. She tried to pull away from him, but his grip was too tight.

"I will fucking kill you if you say a word to anyone. You will get home tonight."

"Please, stop! I won't say anything."

Her delicate veins felt like they would pop because of the pressure. The point of the needle dug into the soft tissue and a burning sensation travelled up her forearm.

"I won't say anything!"

"Are you sure?" he asked, adding more pressure.

Tears leaked out of the corners of her eyes. "Promise. Just let go!"

The twitch of the curtain made them both jump.

Clive cleared his throat and said in a loud voice, "I love you. Get better soon. Take as long as you need." He reached out to stroke her head.

An auxiliary soon appeared. "Would you like your water refreshed?" the woman asked. She put a fresh jug on the table before either of them could reply. "Oh, you can't reach it. Let me push this a little closer for you."

"Thank you," Clive said, and smiled.

"You're lucky to have such sweet attentive man, honey." She smiled at Tina and then moved to the next cubicle.

Clive lowered his voice and looked at Tina. "How many blacks work at this bloody hospital, and why is that old bag shouting so much? Fucking depressing!" Clive folded his arms across his chest.

Tina wanted to shush him, but thought better of it. "The nurses have been nice. Could you pass me a drink now, please?"

The old woman moaned as she lay in her bed. "Sue . . . Help . . . Sue."

"Get it yourself when I've gone. There she goes again. What's up with that wrinkly old bag?"

"Did you bring me some things? I can't go home in this blue gown."

Clive's eyes narrowed as he reached for the bag and set it down at the bottom of her bed. "I'm going. It's too warm in here. Get them to ring when you're ready to be picked up. I've a surprise for you tomorrow."

He glanced over his shoulder before leaving and put a finger to his lips. Unconditional love and a warm embrace from her mother was what Tina craved. Instead, she was alone in a strange place. The staff was wonderful, but they were no substitute for genuine empathy.

Tina wiped her face with the corner of her gown. The surgical tape that kept the needle in place was loose. She rubbed the corners back down and gently flexed her fingers to ease the stinging.

Dr. Harper re-appeared and closed the gap in the curtains behind him. He sat down beside her, eyeing her wet cheeks. She wiped away the fresh wave of tears again.

"I can't seem to rest in here. I'm a bit disorientated. When can I go home?"

"I need to go through some things with you first," he said, glancing at the papers in his hand. "What do you remember?"

Tina inched herself up to ease the slight pressure upon her ribs. "Nothing."

"What about before your tumble?" He perused his notes.

"I ran up the stairs too fast and slipped. There's not much after that."

He nodded and jotted down a few notes. "You have cuts and bruises, some of which are a cause for concern, as they're not consistent with your accident."

Tina stiffened. She'd known they'd ask about her previous injuries, but she'd unrealistically hoped they wouldn't.

"Why blue?" she asked, hoping to move the subject away from her cuts and bruises.

The doctor frowned. "Pardon?"

"It's monotonous. Everything is blue." Tina pointed to the cup. "Even the cup and saucer is blue."

He grinned and chortled. "So it is. We have to get them as a job lot. It was either that or bright pink, but it's not very clinical, though."

After the banter settled, Tina asked, "How do you know?"

Dr. Harper nodded, pleased with the fact that she'd veered back to his previous question. "We needed to cut off your clothes to get you into a gown and run scans. You were on a spinal board when you came in."

"I remember something around my neck."

"We restricted your movement. We had no idea what damage was done to you."

A soft sigh escaped her. "Can I go home?"

"We shall see. You've been very lucky. It could have been much worse." He checked his notes again. "Apart from your fractured ribs, no other bones were broken. The brain scan was clear. There's no swelling or pressure in there. You do have mild concussion, however. We also ran some bloods."

*I don't feel that lucky.*

"I tripped a few weeks back," she blurted. "I bruise easy and they take ages to fade." Tina wiggled her toes.

"What about your nose?"

"I had too much to drink and walked into a door."

"I've heard that excuse many times," he said. "Please, let me help you."

"Help me with what? A few bruises that will fade on their own?" She scratched her knee and looked away.

"You know what I'm talking about. Let me keep you here overnight. You can get some rest and a little respite from everything." Dr. Harper wrote something on the chart as he spoke.

Tina blinked rapidly to keep her tears from falling. "I want to go home," she whispered.

"Because Clive said so?"

"You're assuming things." Her chin quivered as she tried to hold herself together.

Dr. Harper pointed to her injured shoulder. "You did a good job on your shoulder. It's healed well, considering it would have needed stitches. I'm afraid it will leave a nasty scar, however."

Another sigh escaped her. "I used Steri-Strips, and I kept it clean, too. Look, as much as I would like to tell you about it, I can't. It'll only make things worse."

The doctor's lips thinned to a tight line. "It looks like a stab wound."

"It's not." Dread threaded through Tina's veins as she realised the doctor was looking for a way to implicate Clive because of the injuries she'd sustained.

"Stay in for a few days," he said, refusing to be deterred from what he thought would be in her best interest. "We can get you to a refuge. We have a great support team here."

Tina shook her head, unable to meet his intense scrutiny. "Please, just let me go home, and keep your nose out of my business."

His pager beeped. He snapped it from his belt and looked at the number.

"I'll be back. I have an emergency. I'll chase up your bloods soon enough."

The doctor stood and nodded at her. He threw back the curtain and left in a hurry.

"Clear. Shock him!"

Tina heard the resuscitation team shuffling about outside the curtain. She stared at the patterned ceiling tiles and hoped the person survived. Someone soon called the time of death. Heartache rippled through Tina's body as she clutched at the bed sheets. It reminded her of her father.

It wasn't long before the hooks on the runners squeaked across the plastic pole. Dr. Harper appeared once more.

"We have your results back."

"Shame, isn't it? That poor person!"

"Sorry you heard that. Sometimes, we just don't have time to move the patient."

She nodded with understanding. "You must be strong to deal with death every day."

"You get used to it. You're my main priority now." He took a seat. "Have you given any thought to what I said earlier?"

How could she accept his offer? It seemed like a good idea and would finally end her misery, but she knew it wouldn't work. No matter where she went, Clive would find her. No amount of court orders or injunctions would stop him. She would build her strength and be a dutiful wife instead, succumbing to his ways while she worked on her permanent solution.

"I think I'll just go home. I know what you're thinking, but it's easier for me this way."

A look of dismay crept across the doctor's face. "I am not thinking that at all. I see a vulnerable woman who needs help. I do need to ask you a couple questions, though. Have you ever had an eating disorder?"

Tina's eyes widened with horror. "No, never."

"You're underweight, and your tests show borderline malnutrition. You also have a B12 deficiency, but with a proper diet that can be rectified." He flipped the page on his chart.

"I don't eat much at the moment, but that's because I'm a bit stressed."

"I also did another routine test for a woman in your position. Have you been trying for a baby?"

"No, I have not."

He raised an eyebrow in her direction. "The test shows you're pregnant."

# CHAPTER 10

**T**INA stared at the water jug on the table. Tiny bubbles floated to the top. An echo came from the bedside, mumbled and distant. All she could feel were the vibrations rattling in her ears from a distant buzzer. Everything else seemed so surreal.

"Are you okay?" Dr. Harper asked, waving the palm of his hand in front of her face.

Something flashed in front of her eyes. The voice sounding in her ears was calm and pleasant, so unlike her husband. The doctor grabbed the glass of water and pressed it against her hand.

"You're awfully pale. Here. Sip this."

Tina's hands shook as she lifted the glass to her mouth. It knocked against her teeth.

"No . . . I . . . I can't be!"

He leaned forward to pat her free hand. "I understand. It must be quite a shock. Did you . . . ?"

"H—How can I be pregnant? The last time we had sex was several days ago. It can't happen that quickly. It just can't!"

Then it dawned on her. She'd had unprotected sex several times against her will.

"You don't take any form of contraception?"

"That's none of your business. I need to get rid of it. Please, help me." She burst into tears.

*Why is all this happening to me? Damn you, Clive, for controlling everything!*

"It's quite a shock," he repeated once more. "You need time to

73

think about it."

Tina swiped a hand across her wet cheek. "What about the morning after pill?"

Sadness invaded the depths of the doctor's eyes. He stood and left the room, returning several seconds later with a box of tissues. She snatched a couple and blotted her eyes.

"It's too late for that," he said. "You're just over five weeks gone. I can refer you to a clinic, but you must think it through first. The wrong decision will haunt you for life. I will be back again in a minute."

Tina nodded as he left. She blew her nose and threw the sticky tissue into the paper bag. Now was a good a time as any to think things through, but her mind refused to make sense of her current predicament.

*I'm a bad person. How can I think about getting rid of it so quickly?*

Termination is a selfish decision, but she could not subject the child to Clive's wrath. Nor would she be able to cope if it had his looks. How would she get to a clinic without Clive noticing? She sighed and tipped her head back, staring at the ceiling.

The doctor returned. "I've brought you these." He handed her the leaflets. "These are some services you may find helpful."

She set them down by her side. "You can't tell my husband. I don't want your involvement, either. I will see my GP." Tina gasped for breath, tears filling her eyes.

"It's alright. We can keep it confidential. What's best for you is what matters."

"Thank you." She sniffed and grabbed another tissue.

"You're going home tonight, then. How is your pain on a scale of 1-10? Your notes state that you were Tramadol dependant." He flipped through the chart's pages.

"I'll manage without, and that was years ago." Tina picked at a bit of cotton on her gown.

"We can give you something else."

She shook her head. "I don't want anything, thank you. I . . . I get fed up with being labelled and nobody understands."

"I do understand. You don't have to explain anything to me."

"When I was eighteen, I had a riding accident. A dog ran out and spooked my horse. I fell and fractured my spine. They put me on narcotics to kill the pain until the hospital came up with a treatment plan." She swallowed and looked up at the doctor, his gaze firmly settled on hers.

"Six months, I was on them. I got better, but after I stopped taking them I would get an indescribable ache all over my body. Even my teeth hurt. The twitching of my limbs would keep me awake at night, so I went to my GP, who said it was withdrawal and placed me on a weaning program. My parents called me a druggy. Now, I touch nothing. It wasn't my fault!"

"Don't feel ashamed." He smiled. "We, doctors, are more aware of how easy these things can happen, and we're more vigilant when we prescribe something to a patient."

She nodded her appreciation and took a sip of water.

"You need plenty of rest. Do you sleep well?"

"Yes. I mean, sometimes I . . ."

"I'm going to give you Zopiclone. It's a sleeping pill with a mild sedative. Take it at night half an hour before you go to bed. Only take it when you need it, as it can become habit forming."

It wasn't a dig at her previous predicament, she realised. His response was just a standard thing they said to all the patients.

"Okay, when can I leave?"

Dr. Harper continued speaking as if she hadn't spoken. "They shouldn't be taken whilst pregnant, but you're in the very early stages of pregnancy, so I don't think it would do much harm. I'd rather you get some proper rest, however. I'll get your discharge paperwork sorted and then you're free to go."

Overwhelmed, she sat up straight, wincing at the sudden pressure she put on her ribs. "Can you ring my husband?"

"I will instruct the receptionist to do so. Look after yourself." He held out his hand, and Tina shook it. "The nurses will take it from here."

He turned and left. Tina chastised herself for giving a piece of her soul away. She couldn't deny that it had eased the burden on her shoulders. He was a professional and would keep things confidential.

Discharge was tedious. She tapped her foot on the bottom of the bed, hoping the nurse would bring her the medication before Clive arrived. Riffling through the leaflets the doctor had left behind, Tina tried to memorise some of the details before she tore them into pieces and tossed them in the paper bin. Her concentration was broken as a nurse walked into the cubicle.

"Hi," she said. "My name is Eve. I'm your discharge nurse. You can go home now. I have your meds and your husband is on his way."

"What about this?" Tina raised her needled arm.

"Someone will be along in a minute to take the cannula out." Eve put on her spectacles and read the instructions listed on the paperwork. "The doctor prescribed you six Zopiclone tablets. You need plenty of fluids when you get home and lots of rest."

She put the small box of medication on the table and carried on. Tina reached out to grab them, sliding the medication onto her lap and thanking the nurse.

Eve separated the paperwork. "This is yours." She held up the pink sheet. "The bottom copy is ours, and the third one is for your GP."

Tina snatched it out of her hands. Eve looked at her as if she were nothing more than a six-year-old.

"Sorry," she said, and read the information. Folding the papers in four, she tucked them under the covers.

"Someone will be along soon to help you. Any questions?" Eve removed her glasses and looked at Tina.

"No. Thanks."

A slight commotion took place nearby. "Sounds like your husband's here," Eve said, and left.

Tina scrambled to open the packet. Six tablets fell onto her palm. The foil crinkled as she slid them under the mattress, and shoved the box and the papers under her pillow. She heard several voices exchanging pleasantries. Sliding her arms to her side, she tensed as Clive appeared and approached the bed. A look of displeasure spread across his face.

"You're not dressed yet! You can't go home in that gown." He leant over and stole a kiss. "How you doing?"

"Fine. I couldn't reach the bag." She glanced at the bottom of the bed.

"You're not crippled. You could have reached that or got one of the nurses to earn their money and pass it to you."

Tina lowered her head, her eyes pinned to the blanket covering her legs. "Could you pass it to me now so I can change?"

"Why do I have to do everything?"

Clive moved forward and dumped the holdall closer to her. A rotund nurse entered the room with a grey tray in hand.

"Hello. Home time for you, my dear," she said. "Let's take your drip and needle out."

"Why couldn't you do that earlier?" Clive asked. "Now we have to wait God knows how long." He tapped his foot and stood with his hands in his pockets.

"I'm sorry, but we are busy and short-staffed."

"You bloody nurses are always whinging."

"Your wife is not the only emergency we have today. There are other patients. Are you in a hurry?"

"Yes, we are, and I want to get home."

"Well, you're not the concern here. The patient is." She slid the needle out and applied pressure to the cotton pad she'd set on top of Tina's hand. After dabbing it a few times, the nurse put a plaster on it.

"That's left a bruise."

*It'll match the others,* Tina thought.

Gathering the swabs and tubes, the nurse turned and said, "There, that didn't take long."

Tina admired the gutsy nurse for putting Clive in his place. She reached into the bag and took out the clothes he'd packed for her. Clive snorted and shook his head.

"Fat bitch! She eats too many pies."

*Leave the poor staff alone, you ignorant and nasty prat. You're so out of my life soon!*

She thought about the pills she'd hidden and an idea came to her. For the first time since her fall, Tina felt the floor beneath her feet as she eased herself into a sitting position. Her weak legs shook as she tried to bear the weight. Flexing her calves seemed to help. She sat down on the edge of the bed and began to change.

Tina eyed the pyjamas he'd brought her. "You could have brought my new ones. These are faded and tatty."

"Why do you keep them, then?" he asked. "You should throw them away."

Tina held them up. "Look! They have holes in the knee."

Clive slapped the garment out of her hands. "Stop moaning and put them on. Since when have you been bothered about your appearance?"

She glared at him and reached for them once more. "I keep them because they're comfortable. A dear friend bought me these years ago." With careful precision, Tina put the bottoms on underneath the gown. "Why don't you get yourself a coffee while I change?"

Clive's face brightened. "Good idea. I saw a machine at the end of the ward. Back in a minute."

He pulled out some pocket change and left. Tina waited until he disappeared and lifted the pillow. She searched for the papers, but couldn't find them.

*Damn it!*

Lifting the pillow, she found nothing. They hadn't dropped to the floor either. She inspected the inside of the pillowcase and sighed with relief.

*There they are.*

Tina retrieved the silver strip, and slid the items down the front of her knickers. She smoothed them down, making sure they were flat against her skin. Bending her arms back, she tried to untie the four knots that held the gown in place.

"How long does it take for you to bloody change?" Clive asked as he walked in holding a plastic cup.

Tina turned around. "Could you untie me, please?"

Clive snapped each one, not bothering to fiddle with the knots. "No one can use that again."

She caught the gown as it dropped from her shoulders and held it against her. "You put holes in it. Look!"

He snatched the garment out of her hands, and threw it across the cubicle. "So what? Just get fucking dressed!" he said, and sipped his coffee.

She pulled the top down over her hips and gathered her things, sliding her feet into a pair of sandals. "What are you laughing at?"

Coffee squirted from his mouth, dribbling down his chin and making a small puddle on the floor. "That stupid logo on your shirt."

"It's a joke from a friend."

"Well, it's shit. Carry on Regardless, whatever next. And those sandals . . ." He wiped his chin with the palm of his hand.

"You didn't bring any slippers or proper clothes. I can't go barefoot, can I?"

Clive ignored her and said, "What do you look like? What a mess!"

Tina handed him the bag. He stared down at her and then turned away.

"You can carry that."

Tina's mouth grew dry. She realised that he was going to be difficult. It didn't matter that he'd caused her accident. He refused to lift a finger to help her.

"The porter is here to take you to the main entrance," a rotund nurse said as she drew the curtains aside.

A lanky man shuffled the wheelchair toward them. "It has a

mind of its own."

The nursed nodded at her. "Take care."

"Would you like me to help you?" the man asked as the nurse left.

Tina moved forward, intent on sliding into the chair.

"We don't need that contraption. She can walk," Clive snapped.

The porter glanced in his direction. Tina pressed her feet against the footrests and did not attempt to move.

"It's best for the patient," the porter said, placing her belongings upon her lap.

He clipped off the brake with his foot and pushed her out of the ward toward the hospital's entrance. Tina mouthed a thank you to Dr. Harper when she saw him. He had a phone pressed to his ear as he stood at the nurse's station. Their gazes clashed, and he nodded at her.

The long corridor to the lift was busy. Medical staff carried hot drinks as they walked along. Several patients lay on waiting beds near the entrance to the theatre doors. Tina caught a glimpse inside. Rows of different apparatuses lined the internal corridor.

Clive walked on ahead. "I'll take the stairs and meet you out front," he said.

Tina's eyes fell on Clive as the porter pushed her chair into the lift and down to the main entrance. Their car was nowhere insight.

"Where's the car?" Tina asked as she stood up.

"Goodnight, and have a safe journey," the porter said, wheeling the empty chair about as he left.

Clive stared down his nose at her. "Over there in a disabled bay. Come on."

"We don't have a badge," she said, struggling with her bag.

"Who gives a fuck at this time of night?" He strode in the direction of the car, uncaring of the fact that she had a hard time in keeping up with him. "Get in!"

Tina sunk into the front seat, holding the bag across her knees. It pushed against her pelvis making the package hidden beneath her pyjama bottoms scratch her skin.

"Did you say anything?" Clive asked, starting the car.

"No. I made something up." Tina clicked her seatbelt into its holder.

"All you had to do was behave. None of this would have happened."

He set the car in reverse and edged the car out of the parking space. The vehicle temporarily stopped moving. Clive cupped Tina's face and kissed her forehead before screeching out of the car park.

"I have learned my lesson," she said. "I just want to go home now."

"I'm sorry, too. That's why I have a surprise for you."

Tina stiffened. She'd forgotten about that. She smiled, nonetheless, unsure of what to expect.

\*\*\*

**T**HE excuse Tina made for sleeping on the couch was that she could not manage the stairs. Clive fetched the quilt from the spare bedroom and threw it down before turning in.

To her surprise, she'd slept well. He'd left before she woke. It was the first Sunday he'd worked for months. Double time and extra money were his motivation, however.

Tina moved around the kitchen and soon found what she was looking for in Clive's personal drawer. Standing over the sink, she slipped the hospital paperwork from its warm hiding place, and lit the corner with a match. Flames flickered before the paper turned to black dust. She then washed away the evidence.

The smell of the singed paper and the stale food made her feel queasy. The dishes still sat in the sink, and the contents of the saucepan she'd pelted him with had dried hard on the floor.

*He could have cleaned up.*

She scanned the room for a suitable place to hide the sleeping pills. Tina had no intention of taking them. They'd come in handy for what she in mind for Clive, though. Spiking his drink before she drowned him seemed plausible. It would make him woozy and amicable. If they did blood tests after his death, she'd say he was stressed and that he'd taken her medication.

*Excellent,* she thought.

She found the perfect hiding place between the skirting board and the fridge. He'd never look there. Bending, and then rising a little too fast, put pressure on her ribs.

"Ouch."

She rubbed the sore area, taking slow and careful breaths. After a glass of water, she climbed onto the sofa and snuggled against it. She now had the time to think about her plans.

*How do I convince him he needs a holiday?*

# CHAPTER 11

**TINA** kicked the duvet from her legs and eased herself into a sitting position. The sofa was surprisingly comfortable. The morning sun shone through the bay window and illuminated a thin layer of dust coating the furniture. Her ribs hurt as she yawned, but the pain was bearable.

Clive entered the room with one arm behind his back. The sight gave her goosebumps.

*What's he hiding?*

"Here, these are for you," he said, thrusting a bunch of blooms into her arms.

The cellophane covering the flowers crinkled in her hands. As she gave them a courteous sniff, three dead buds fell to the floor.

"Thanks."

This was the surprise, a bedraggled bunch bought from a garage forecourt with the price tag still on. Still, it was better than a punch in the mouth. It was the thought that counted.

"I thought you hated flowers in the house."

"Make the most of 'em. It won't happen again."

"I'll put them in water," she said. Her body ached, and as she tried to stand, her legs weakened.

"I brought these down for you, too." He handed her a dressing gown and a pair of slippers. "You must try and dress. You can't sit around here all day in your night things."

"Thanks."

She stretched out her hands in the hopes that Clive would help her to her feet. He stood there instead, watching her struggle. Tina sighed and stood up, trying to ignore the sudden flare of pain.

The pile of dishes greeted her upon entering the kitchen. Clive hadn't bothered to wash them. The only thing missing were the self-help papers.

*Crafty, he's gotten rid of them.*

Pain rippled through her chest as she bent down to hunt for a vase under the sink. The pressure made her nose pound and her temples pulsate. She held onto the worktop, trying to steady herself.

"Let me get it." He filled the vase with water and set it aside on the counter. "I'm going to work soon and won't be back until late."

Numerous petals fell from the bunch as Tina arranged them in some kind of order. She set the vase on the windowsill next to the cactus.

"I need to sit down for a moment," she said.

Clive helped her to sit. He looked about the kitchen.

"It's a mess in here. I want this cleaned up by the time I get back," he said with his back to the sink. "There's washing to do as well."

"The doctor said I needed to rest."

"I don't care what he said. I want this done by the time I get home."

"I'll see how I feel."

Clive turned around to face her. A rap on the front door made Tina jump. They weren't expecting anyone this morning. The last time Jehovah's Witnesses came to the door Clive had humiliated them. She hoped that would not be the case today.

He motioned for her to stay seated. "I'll get it."

Feeling light-headed, she stood up and made her way back to the sofa to lie down. Moments later, Clive appeared with a smile on his face.

"I have a surprise for you," he said. "Look who's come to see you."

He stepped aside to allow the guest through. Dressed in an old duffle coat as if it were middle of winter, her mother stood in the doorway. Grey curls poked out from her hat and an ancient handbag hung over her arm. The corners of her mother's mouth titled downward.

"Up to your old tricks again, I see," she said.

Tina's mouth dropped open with surprise. "Mother!"

Her mother moved into the lounge. She flopped down into the nearest chair. Clive nodded at her mother and smiled.

"I'm going to work now. Enjoy your day." A big grin spread across his face. "I can take you to the train station later, Joan, if you want me to. I may be back late."

"My train leaves at four. I'll manage and take my time." Joan looked down at her knobbly knuckles and rubbed her bent fingers. "It's this damn arthritis. I get no help from my family."

She glared at her daughter. Tina eyed the two of them, and her stomach sank.

"Why are you here, Mother?"

"To keep you company and make sure you don't have any more silly accidents," Joan replied, and smiled at Clive.

"I will leave you to it. Bye."

Tina sat up once he'd departed and stared at her mother. "You have to leave. I don't want you here."

"According to Clive, you do. Attention seeking again, he said." Joan rubbed her knees. "It's cold in here."

"No, it's not. It's mild. And what do you mean by that?"

"Nothing. You do look a fright. Are you going to offer me a drink? I've travelled a long way to see you."

"Get it yourself, and you only live an hour away," Tina snapped. "I'm okay. Thanks for asking."

"There's nowt wrong with you. Try living with this." She held up her crooked talons again.

"Mother, please. I need to . . . ." Tears welled in her eyes.

"Don't you start those tears with me! Your father would turn in his grave."

"I wondered how long it would be before his name cropped up." She rubbed her hand across her face.

"You killed him." Joan huffed and folded her arms.

"Not this again! He had a heart attack."

"All the stress you caused him brought that upon him."

"What stress? He brought it on himself."

"Your goings-on and the accusations . . . How could you do that to him?"

"It wasn't my fault with those boys. I was seven when . . . they ganged up on me. I thought they left me infertile. You couldn't even support your own little girl!" Tina cried.

"It was that man in London that finished him off. The shame you brought on this family . . ." Joan tilted her head and looked away.

"I was fifteen."

"You should have known better. A little slag, you were."

"He groomed me. How do you think I felt? I needed you."

"Your father always said you were old enough to know better."

"He was jealous because I was his special girl. Don't you see, or are you blind as always? He'd beat me when I refused, and when I was naughty, he'd smash my toys into smithereens."

"You deserved it. We never had any trouble with James. He had to discipline you somehow. You were out of control." Joan stood. "I'm going to make myself a cup of tea."

This should have been the proudest moment in a person's life; a new life born, the next generation. A perfect home and husband all slotted into nice, neat holes. The congratulations from family members, proud grandparents getting out their knitting needles— they were things she'd never know.

Tina sighed and bowed her head. She wanted to tell her mum and watch her face as they shared the excitement. Instead, no one would know. Was it fair to have it aborted? After all, it wasn't the baby's fault. From the recesses of Tina's body, an ache filled every bone. She'd never felt so alone.

"It's a mess in there," Joan said as she brought the mug back with her and rested it on her lap.

"Could you help me wash up?"

"With my hands?" She held up her bent fingers. "I don't think so."

*Mother and her bloody hands!*

"You could make yourself a drink."

"Well, you didn't offer."

"Did you make me one?" Tina sat on the edge of the chair, ready to stand.

"No, I didn't. Besides, your legs are younger and stronger than mine." Joan licked the dribbles from her mug, a habit that annoyed Tina.

"Why are you here?"

"To keep you out of mischief."

"It doesn't have to be like this, Mum. Can't we try and get on?" Tina reached for her mother's hand. "Please, I need you."

"I can always tell when you want something when you call me mum."

Joan ignored the offered hand. Tina knelt at her mother's side and waited for a kind and comforting gesture. A stroke on the head or a handhold, anything to make her feel wanted.

"Look at you. Selfish! That's your trouble. You always have been." Joan turned in the seat, giving her a cold shoulder.

"I need to . . ."

"Self-pity won't work. Pull yourself together. Your father would turn in his grave. God rest his soul."

*He does a lot of turning,* she thought.

Moving back to the sofa, venom built inside of Tina and she let it rip. "You really are a blinkered old cow. You live your life in denial, instead of concentrating on what matters now." Not wanting to give her mother the satisfaction, she held back her tears.

"Don't you use that tone with me! I'm your mother."

"Then act like it!" Tina cried, surprised by the words as they left her lips. "Leave, Mum. Now! I want you gone."

"My train leaves at four."

"Catch an earlier one, then."

"Clive will have something to say about this!"

Fuelled by adrenaline, Tina stood and yanked the mug out of her mother's hands. The dregs splashed the floor.

"Get up." Tina hooked her arm under her mother's elbow and urged her out of the chair.

"He must be a saint to put up with your antics."

Joan shrugged out of her grip and stood in front of her daughter.

"Just go, now. Shoo! Go on. Get out!"

Joan sniffled and shook her head. "James never treats me like this. You never ask about him. When I'm dead, you'll get nothing. Nothing! Do you hear?"

"I don't want your money, Mother."

Tina ushered her out of the house and watched her walk away and out of her life. Deep inside, she hoped it was forever.

After slamming the door closed, she reached the bottom landing before her legs gave way. Tina dropped onto the first step, stretching her legs out in front of her. Her hands lay by her side as she stared at the blank wall.

She felt empty and numb inside. Tina had become accustomed to such feelings most of her life. The constant bickering over the years with her mother was the most draining, however.

*Come on. You can do this,* she thought. *Stick to your plan and all this will be history. You don't need anyone, Tina. You can do this alone. Come on now. Get on your feet!*

Repeating the mantra, she stood and took a deep breath to steady herself.

*No one will ever get me down again.*

Tina moved up the stairs, making her way to the bathroom. She showered and used the water to soak the dressing from the back of her hand. It came away easily, but it left a bruise behind.

She changed into casual clothes. Working her way through the endless chores was a slow process and took most of the day, but the house was now ready for his arrival. Making herself a hot chocolate, she grabbed a banana from the fruit bowl, ready to put her feet up in the lounge when the phone rang.

"Hello."

"So you got rid of the witch, then." Clive laughed. "Joan called me from the station."

"Yes, I did. She was under my feet."

"Snatched her tea from her hand and forced her out, huh? Can't you ever play nice with your old mum?"

Tina rolled her eyes. "You knew she would be like that. Why invite her?"

"I thought it would be fun. Shake some life into you."

Tina bit her lip. "It worked. I've done the housework. It's all ready for you."

"I won't be home till later. Having a meal with Ray."

"Oh, okay. I'll see you when you get back, then."

"Don't wait up. I spoke to my parents this afternoon. We're going to see them next weekend."

Tina straightened, ignoring the sudden pull upon her ribs. The news was unexpected. She kept her voice even as she spoke to Clive.

"I shall rest now for the rest of the day."

"Did you hear what I just said?" Clive asked, sounding annoyed.

Tina swallowed, feeling a little nervous. "Yes, I did," she said. "It'll be nice to see them."

Several echoes, voices, and drills sounded in the background.

"Got to go," Clive replied, and hung up.

A weekend with his parents took the excitement out of having the evening to herself. However, she could use the weekend to her advantage. It would solve a dilemma, she realised. Clive still needed convincing to take a holiday. With his dad's backing, she'd be able to turn him to her way of thinking. Her plan should work.

*This could be interesting,* she thought.

She relaxed in the lounge with her drink and fruit in hand, a slight smile darting across her lips.

**L**ATER that Monday evening, Tina worked on her next problem, her unborn child. She decided to surf the internet for information. A laptop and desktop were the only devices the household used and she trusted neither. Even if she cleared the browser's history, Clive would still be able to retrieve the information. Using her smartphone also carried risks, but she had no choice. Being home alone gave her the perfect opportunity to browse without having any nosey work colleagues to look over her shoulder.

She remembered the time she'd bought a gift for Clive online. The next day, he'd questioned the link and the monetary value. From that day forward, he monitored her usage.

Curled up on the sofa with another hot drink, she tapped the screen and waited for the options to form a list. The name for the abortion clinic in Norfolk showed up on the screen. There were several procedures available, one of which was day surgery, though it still required follow-ups and aftercare. If Clive decided to use her for his satisfaction, that would not be feasible.

Tina twiddled her lower lip with her thumb and forefinger, a mannerism she'd picked up from her father. In a couple of months, she would start to show. A shiver ran down her spine. It needed doing. Sooner, rather than later.

Making a mental note of everything, she cleared the screen. Clive would have to die first before he got the chance to check her phone. Tina eased back into the chair and closed her eyes. She would deal with the recuperations later.

She could do this with careful planning and caution. Going to see the in-laws was another hurdle she needed to tackle. The weekend would be trying enough. Joyce and Len Blythe were cantankerous and set in their ways. She would play along until she got what she wanted. Exhausted, she cleared her mind. She'd done enough thinking for today.

\*\*\*

**T**HE slice of rhubarb pie looked pathetic on the large plate sitting in the fridge. Tina knew she would have to eat it. Carrying it through to the lounge, she settled on the sofa and turned on the TV to the comedy channel.

Crumbs fell down her front as she laughed. She'd seen the film many times before and it always made her smile. Flicking bits from her top onto the floor, she set her plate to the side. She'd vacuum later before he returned.

Her shoulders bounced up and down as she laughed hard. Meryl Streep's bottom cheeks lifted one by one, and looked like a teenager's pert bum. Her breasts no longer hung south. A magic potion of eternal youth had done its job, until the end when cans of spray paint covered her decaying flesh. Still giggling, she wiped her eyes as a slice of Goldie Hawn's shoulder fell off and Bruce Willis' character stuck it back on.

A commercial break broke the flow of *Death Becomes Her.* She struggled to the loo, ready for the next instalment. A little bit of heaven for a vulnerable woman who was about to commit a crime.

*** 

**O**AK Avenue is a quiet street in King's Lynn. Tina liked the area, but upon Clive's death, the property would eventually be up for sale. How could she continue to live in a place full of negativity?

Tyres crunched as the car pulled into the drive. She peered out the window and grimaced. Picking up the plate and any crumbs that had fallen on the floor, she hurried into the kitchen. Tina washed the plate and made it back to the sofa just in time for his entrance.

Clive popped his head around the door. "Hi." He scanned the lounge. "Alright."

"You're home early. I thought you were going out with Ray."

"I need a shower first," he said.

Tina followed as Clive checked every downstairs room. He must have been satisfied that the house was to his specifications because he leaned forward to kiss her forehead.

"You've done well for someone who should be resting."

"I wanted to make sure everything was right for you." She smiled and moved back to the lounge area.

"What's this crap?" He picked up the remote as she sat down and the TV went black.

"I was watching a film."

"Not anymore. When I come down, I want a beer."

For half an hour, she waited, using the sound of the creaky floorboards as an indication that he was on his way down. Clive appeared, dressed in a shirt and tie.

"I'm ready for my beer now."

The scent of his cologne invaded her nostrils. *How much Hugo Boss does he need? It feels like he bathed in it.*

She passed him the bottle and said, "You look smart. Where you going to eat?"

"Curry House, then a game of pool."

"Have a nice evening. I'll be in bed when you get back"

"I would have asked you to come with me, but you're a mess." Clive took another swig of his beer and wiped his lips with the back of his hand.

"Will I see you in the morning?"

"Maybe." He finished the last drop and set the bottle aside. "I'm going."

She waved him off as she stood at the front door. "Bye."

Tina swung the door closed once the car disappeared into the distance. Shuffling back into the living room, she turned the telly back on. The film was on the part where Goldie Hawn had a hole in her stomach. She tittered and settled down to watch what was left of the movie.

# CHAPTER 12

**A** week later, Tina had their overnight bags packed and ready to head out on Saturday morning. Boston, Lincolnshire was an hour's drive away. Clive had rung his parents the night before and agreed that eleven o'clock would be a good time to arrive.

Pulling over to the kerb outside the dreary bungalow, he said, "Bang on time," and turned off the engine.

Feeling apprehensive, Tina rubbed her sweaty palms across her jeans before getting out of the vehicle. The garage door was open. She observed Len fiddling with something inside. He must have heard them pull up because he made his way over to greet his son. They met halfway across the small gravel drive. Tina trailed behind, pulling her top down over her hips.

"Nice to see you, boy." Len playfully slapped his son on the top of his arm.

"You too, Dad."

Len nodded at Tina as she walked up the path. "Alright?"

"How is your knee?" she asked. "I noticed you're still limping."

He flexed his calf and tapped his implant with his knuckles. "Bionic man me, tough as nails."

She smiled. "Operation went well, then."

"No, it was shit. They know nothing, these doctors. Not complaining. I just get on with it."

Clive gave her a nudge and shot a look of annoyance in her direction. "The garden looks neat, Dad."

"Hard work, that's all it takes."

Len pointed at the various plants and structures that had changed since their last visit. Taking an interest, she scanned the garden. It needed height and multilayers of planting. Tina disliked the set-up, as it had no personality to it.

"You could put some trellising up the back wall," Tina said.

Len glared at her. "It's fine as it is."

Clive looked away, shaking his head. The side door opened, the sound breaking the silence.

"Watch out. Here comes trouble. They've arrived," Len shouted.

Joyce waddled down the path. Her pink two-piece clung to her body. Ever since Tina had known her, she'd been a large woman. Joyce blamed it on her thyroid. Tina knew it could be that, but a bad diet and lack of exercise was the more probable cause.

"Come on, Nelly," Len said in a loud voice.

"Coming, Duck," she replied.

"That's not a nice thing to call her," Tina pointed out. The look the men gave her made her wish she'd kept her mouth shut.

Len glanced at his son. "Your wife is a silly cow."

"Mum collects elephants, you daft bint."

Clive moved closer to his dad. They turned their backs on Tina and waited for Nelly to arrive. Annoyed with herself for not remembering a simple fact, she chewed on her lip and stared at the ground.

*How dare they speak to me like that?*

Tina watched Joyce's approach. Her calves were thick set, and fat oozed over the top of her slippers. Her toenails were so long, they poked out of the front. She stood for a moment to get her breath back.

"My precious boy." She held out her arms and Clive walked into her warm embrace.

"Nice to see you, Mum. You're squeezing the life out of me!"

"I've missed you." She stroked her hands across his cheeks. "Smooth as a baby's bum."

"You okay standing, Mum? We should get you inside," he said, reaching for her hand.

"I'm okay, Ducky. I'm so pleased to see you." She rubbed her nose against his.

*He used to treat me like that, so loving and sweet.*

Envious of the bond between them, Tina looked away. Her stomach churned. She wasn't sure if it was because of the morning sickness or insecurity.

"My daughter-in-law." Joyce kissed her cheeks and gave Tina a half-hearted hug.

"How are you?"

Tina patted her back and held her breath. The scent of stale sweat emanating from Joyce's armpits stung her nose.

"What have you done to your face, Ducky?" Joyce asked, her arms now pressed to her sides.

"I wanted to ask that, too. Knowing her, she walked into a door," Len said.

Both men sniggered.

"She did, Dad."

Len shook his head at Tina. "What a daft mare, you are."

Tina's chin dimpled. "I guess I am."

"Now, now, can't you see you're upsetting the poor girl?" Joyce cupped her face. "Did you, Duck?" Her eyes bored into hers and Joyce's double chin shook when she spoke.

"Yes, I did." She stepped back, not wanting this woman touching her face.

"You're a clumsy clot."

Len tapped his watch. "Nelly, coffee time."

"It's ready. I'm waiting for you." She turned and trudged down the path, heading back inside.

"Hang on, Mum. Wait!" Clive hurried to his mother's side and took her arm.

Joyce patted his hand. "I'm okay, Duck."

Clive turned and looked straight at Tina. "Get the bags out of the boot while I help Mum."

Tina stood, rooted in place. She stared at their faces before she moved to unload the car.

"Mind the door." Len laughed. "Leave Nelly be, son. She can manage." He pulled the keys for his Bellingo from his pocket. "Put your car in the garage. We'll be using mine this weekend."

"It's easier to use mine, Dad."

"We are using mine. Just do it."

"What is the point of that?" Tina muttered, moving toward their car.

Pain shot across her breastbone as she lugged the two bags up the driveway. Tina stopped halfway to take a breath. She then waited patiently by the front door. While the men played swapsie with their toys, she stared at two gnomes with rosy faces that sat on either side of the doorstep.

Tina rolled her eyes and sighed. The one thing she'd learned from Clive was to never enter the Blythe property without an invitation. It would have been easier to follow Joyce inside, but no, she had to wait on the doorstep like a lemon until Len had finished faffing with the cars.

"You can go in now. We'll be right behind," Len said. "You know where your room is."

Tina faked a smile and walked down the hallway to the room at the end of the hall. She plonked the bags down on the bed and unzipped the first one. Hearing her husband walk into the bedroom, she looked up.

"Leave that. Dad wants a drink."

"It will only take a minute."

"I said, leave it. It's already ten minutes past their coffee time."

"What difference does it make? Can't we have one when we're ready?" she snapped.

He glared at her. "Stop with the backchat shit and do as you're told."

Tina hung her head, her heart hammering inside her chest. "Sorry. I will come now."

Two glass mugs sat on a tray on the table in their living room. Joyce sat in her usual place opposite a portable television. Len sat next to her in his armchair.

"It will be cold now." Len sipped his instant coffee and rested the mug on his chest.

Tina winced as Joyce gulped her drink down. The slurping sound made her feel a little nauseous. Clive took a seat and reached for a mug.

"It's quiet in here, Dad. Put the radio on."

"Maybe later, son."

"I will make a fresh cup," Tina offered. "I fancy a tea anyway."

"No, you won't. We have coffee at this time of day, and we have one cup. We do not have waste in this house," Len said. "It's that or nothing." He gestured at Tina, ordering her to sit.

Tina took her seat. She swallowed past the lump in her throat, trying to hold herself together.

"Look at you, Nelly. You dribbled again."

Joyce mopped her chin with the hankie she kept tucked under her sleeve. She then dabbed at her chest and licked the moisture from the bottom of her jumper. Tina looked away in disgust.

"How can you miss your mouth, Mother?" Clive laughed.

"Don't mock her. She has thyroid issues. It can't be helped." Len reached for Joyce's chubby hand.

"I know, Dad. I was only teasing."

Tina sipped her warm, weak coffee and eyed the ceiling. She counted down the hours until it was time for them to leave.

Excusing herself, Tina finished unpacking. Although there wasn't much, she took her time. Any time away from them made her feel human. With no TV or radio in their room, it meant more endless drivel to put up with. It was like living in another century.

Len had never warmed to technology and refused to have it in the house along with mobile phones. When the digital switchover came, it was a battle to get him to see sense. Clive came over that day to make sure things were done properly. Now, all Len does is rave about the extra channels.

Clive popped his head around the door's edge. "Are you nearly done?"

"I'm coming."

Tina slid the stiff drawer shut. She heard his dad grumble from the other end of the hall.

"Tell her dinner's ready in half an hour. How long does it take to put a few clothes away?"

*Already? And it's lunch, you prick.*

Unpalatable odours drifted through the bungalow. Tina folded her arms across her chest and made her way to the living room.

"We're in here," Clive shouted.

She doubled back and walked through to the steamy kitchen.

*Open a flaming window!*

The magnolia walls reminded her of their marital home.

*That's where Clive gets it from!*

A whistle sounded and Len removed the kettle from the electric ring. It's been years since she'd seen a cooker like that and even longer for the kettle.

*Do people still use those?*

The house itself was tidy, although cluttered, with mismatched furniture, knick-knacks, and odd-sized tables. Overall, it seemed homely, though Tina felt out of place in it.

"Something smells interesting," she said, sounding polite.

"It's the boy's favourite."

Len filled the sink with the boiled water and re-filled the kettle. He placed it on the back ring. Joyce leant on the surface next to the cooker, watching her veggies boil. Clive sat at the table and read the paper.

Tina looked in the pans on the stove. "What are we having?"

Joyce's mouth drooled as she spoke, nearly losing her false teeth. She manoeuvred her tongue and pushed the plate back in.

"Double-cooked Lincolnshire Snorker, Duck."

"Lovely."

Tina had wondered if that's what she'd make. Joyce made this dish every time they came over, convinced it was Clive's favourite. Sausages, pre-cooked and left on the side to cool overnight, were reheated in the oven the next day. The last time they'd eaten them she nearly broke a tooth.

"Shall I get rid of this for you? The birds would love that." Tina stared at a pan full of brown jelly, a spoon stuck in the middle.

"That's my gravy. It renders down," Joyce said, wiping her brow with the teacloth.

"Sorry. How do you get it that thick?" Tina asked.

The mixture had started to bubble and melt around the edges as Joyce gave it a stir. "I just add all the fat and juice from the meat we cook." She lifted the spoon and let the gloop fall back to the pan. "Then I add an Oxo and flour, now and again."

"Looks like there's a lot there for the four of us."

"It will do a few meals that. Excuse me." She brushed Tina out of the way. Her fat bottom looked like a beanbag as she bent to attend to the oven. "Ten minutes, and it will all be ready."

They sat around the cramped table. Globules of half-rendered gravy fell from the spoon as Joyce served it.

"No, thank you. I have enough here." Tina looked at the cremated sausages and the sloppy vegetables sitting next to them.

"You like gravy. Mum has gone to a lot of effort." Clive smiled at his mother. "Put some on, Mum. She will eat it."

Len ate his sausages with his fingers. "Tasty, Nelly. Very good."

As they tucked into the feast, Tina felt sick. Joyce slurped and gulped loudly as usual, and Len licked the gravy from his fingers. Clive used the cutlery to cut his sausages, praising his mother with every mouthful.

Tina increased the pressure on her knife, hoping to cut one in half. It pinged off her plate and fell onto the carpeted kitchen floor. Len picked up the piece and shoved it into his greedy mouth. Disgusted, Tina put her utensils down.

"Sorry, I need to be excused." She rose and hurried to the

bathroom.

***

"**WHAT'S** up with her?" Len asked, scraping his knife around the edge of his plate before licking it.

"Is she pregnant?" Joyce inquired.

"No, she's just attention grabbing, that's all. Ignore her." Clive helped himself to Tina's untouched meal.

"Well, she should be. I want a grandson."

"It's not for the want of trying." Clive thrust his pelvis forward as he sat in the chair.

"We will have none of that crudeness here." Joyce smiled as she said it.

"Did you take the suggestion I made?" Len asked.

"Yes. I made her stop taking contraceptives and I watch her closely."

"Does she want a baby? It's awfully strange if she doesn't. A woman of that age in her prime . . ." Sniffling, Joyce pulled the hankie from her sleeve once more. "I was denied the gift of another child."

Len rubbed her broad shoulder. "Have you asked her?"

"Of course, I have. She says eventually, but trust me, I'm working on it." Clive half rose from the table. "I'm going in the other room. I hate it when she gets upset."

"Sit your arse back down and support your mum."

Clive leaned over and gave Joyce a hug and a kiss. Len nodded his approval and then allowed his son to leave.

# CHAPTER 13

**TINA** overheard the group's mumbling echoes through the bathroom wall. She rested her arms on the toilet seat and heaved into the bowl. After flushing, she sat on the bath's rim. Her stomach was still in knots, but the pressure on her ribs had begun to ease.

The bathroom reflected the rest of the house. The cistern sat high above the loo, and had a long silver chain with a rubber handle attached to it. A showerhead, about the size of a hubcap, was corroded and green, old-fashioned pipes holding it in place. On the windowsill, a plastic doll covered in a knitted dress sat on top of a spare toilet roll.

Once she felt a little composed, Tina twisted both taps to fill the basin. As expected, the hot water ran cold. She splashed the water across her face and then gargled to clear the sour taste from her mouth. The towel smelt musty as she patted her face dry.

Tina paused at the door. She took a breath and replayed the conversation she'd overheard in her mind. She hated the fact that she was surrounded by so much negativity. This wasn't the life she'd always envisioned for herself.

*You can do this. Stay calm. Use the situation to your advantage.*

After the count of three, she made her way to the kitchen. Len was washing up, and Joyce stood nearby drying the dishes.

"Sorry about that. I came over feeling a little funny."

"You must stop this childish behaviour. You're a grown woman, Duck," Joyce said, her back turned to Tina.

Taken aback, Tina gasped. "Can I help you with anything?"

"Stop creeping. Your dinner is in the bin. We don't have a lot of money and you wasted it." Len turned and shot her a stern look.

"My appetite, it's . . . not so good lately." Tina bit her lip and swallowed. "Please accept my apologies. I can be silly at times. I—"

The look on Len's face eased. "It's okay. Don't do it again."

"We are having a cup of tea. Do you want one?" Joyce asked.

"I would love one, thanks. I wondered if I could have a shower later. It may make me feel a bit better."

"No, Duck. It's Saturday. We don't put the water on until Monday. We are pensioners, you know." Joyce put the mugs on the tray.

"Boil the kettle and wash in the sink. That's what we do, isn't it, Nelly?" Stroking her shoulder, Len squeezed past her to reach the teabags.

"Yes, Ducky. Go in there and join the boy. We'll be through in a minute."

Tina did as she'd asked and joined Clive. He read the paper with his feet propped on the pouf. He glared at her and shook his head. She sat in her designated seat and crossed her legs. Sitting anywhere else would get her ticked off by the mighty Len.

The clock on the mantle read three. Bored and resting her head back, she stared at the walls. A wide shelf, about a foot from the ceiling, circled around the room. China, plastic, and metal elephants filled them, their trunks pointing upwards, a sign of good luck. To the left, a sacred chair covered in cuddly toys sat in the corner, a shrine to Joyce's miscarriage.

It melted her heart. She might not like the in-laws, but no one deserved to lose a baby. She pressed a palm to her abdomen. A pang of guilt twisted her gut.

Joyce's shuffling through to the lounge broke her train of thought. She turned her head toward the door.

"Let me take those from you, Len."

"No, sit. Tea up." Len balanced the tray well, considering his limp, and placed it on the table before he sat down.

Joyce carried the biscuits and put them down next to the drinks. The chair creaked and the air from the cushions puffed in complaint.

"Tea up," Joyce said, her eyes focused on Clive.

"Oi, Mum's talking to you. Put the paper down and stop being so rude."

"Sorry, Dad," he said, putting it in the magazine rack.

Tina reached for her tea and took a sip. It was strong and quite welcome.

"Custard creams, my favourite."

Len leant forward and slapped the back of her hand. The biscuit she'd grabbed fell back onto the plate.

"People who don't eat lunch are not allowed treats."

Tina froze and then smiled. She thought he was teasing, but the look in his eyes said otherwise.

"You tell her, Dad." He laughed and rested his mug on his lap.

Joyce scoffed down three creams, the remnants of the last one scattered across her front. Clive and Len nodded at one another.

"Do you feel better now? Not pregnant, are you?" Len asked.

Shocked by his direct question, Tina swallowed and remained neutral. "Why would you think that?"

Joyce's gut rumbled, the sound filling the whole room. "I'm sorry it must be the biccies."

"You think, Mum?" Clive teased.

Pleased by the diverted conversation, Tina smiled. Back on point, Len repeated the question. This time, she was ready and the answer slipped easily from her tongue.

"No, I'm not. I've only just come out of hospit—"

"She has fainting spells, Dad," Clive said. "It makes her feel funny."

"Dizzy duck, dizzy duck!" Joyce replied in a jesting tone. "Maybe it's time to think about it."

"You may be right. Are we going out this afternoon for a drive?" Tina asked.

"No, not this time. My knee is sore."

"We could take my car, Dad."

"No, I don't think so. Anyway, your mum wants to play Scrabble."

Clive nodded. "I'll get the board."

Len cleared a space on the table. "It's in the spare room."

For two hours, they played the word game until Clive got huffy because he was losing. The dictionary exchanged hands several times to check Len's spelling, while Joyce nodded off.

"Look at the time! I better start preparing our tea," Len said.

"Can I put the telly on, Dad?" Clive asked.

"Keep it low. I don't want to wake your mum, and put the game away first."

"Can I help you, Len?" Tina offered.

"If you must. Bring those cups through. Make yourself useful." Len stretched and stroked Joyce's head like a pet dog as he passed by.

"Cheese or tomato sandwiches, children?"

"Cheese and tomato, please," Tina replied.

"As they come for me, Dad."

"It's one or the other. We don't have both together. We're not made of money."

Len had plenty of money stashed away, according to Clive. He was just a miser and could live more comfortably than this if he wanted to.

"Any way you want to do them." Tina stood, the cups knocking together as she moved.

"Careful with that. You're a clumsy clot."

Len followed her as she moved into the kitchen. Standing in the middle of the room, Tina waited for him to take the tray. He filled the kettle and placed it on the stove.

"Put that over there. You can wash up when the kettle is boiled."

She slid it on the side. While Len had his nose in the fridge, she crept to the door and pushed it closed.

"Pass me the chopping board," he said, and turned. Putting two overripe tomatoes on the table along with a block of cheese and a tub of Stork, he then attended to the kettle's whistle and poured the water. "You can wash these cups now."

Tina added cold water. Len leaned across and turned off the tap.

"What is the point of me boiling the kettle if you're going to run cold water into it?"

"It's too hot, Len. I can't put my hand in that."

"I manage." He grabbed the loaf from the bread bin.

Tina rubbed her lips together. *You would.*

"Where do you keep the liquid so I can wash the dishes?"

"We don't use it for cups, only greasy pots and pans."

She should have known. *The stupid old git!* Holding the cups by their handles, she rinsed and dried them. Finished, she sat at the table and watched Len as he added the filling to the over greased bread.

"Len . . . Could I talk to you for a moment?" Her chin rested on her fist.

"Oh, yeah. Is that why you wanted to help? Crafty," he said, putting the top slice on the first sandwich.

"No, no, not at all. I need your help with something."

"Fire away. I'm all ears."

"I want a baby."

"I am too old, dear. I can't help you with that."

Tina reddened and forced a smile. "We've been very busy lately, and it's been quite stressful."

"For him, maybe. You do nothing all day."

She ignored his jibe and kept calm. "I was thinking we could have a little weekend away, just the two of us." Tina watched his reaction. "It would be nice to have a romantic break. What do you think?"

"What are you telling me for? Just do it. Oh, I get it! It's money you want?"

"Of course not. I just thought it would be a nice setting to, you know, make a baby." She paused for a moment. "On the water, surrounded by fresh air."

"Oh, the boat?"

"Just think, your first grandchild conceived on your boat." Tina smirked.

"Good idea. I'll go and tell him."

Tina grabbed his arm. "No, wait. I don't want him to know it was my idea." She gulped. "He would only say he was too busy for a holiday if it came from me."

"Yes, he would. The boy's like that."

"He gets it from you. You should be very proud of his hard work." Tina's stomach knotted as she forced out the words. "He looks up to you. So if you could convince him to take me away . . ."

"When were you thinking of going?"

"Two weeks from this weekend."

"That's quick. I need time to get it ready." Len cut the bread into squares.

Tina upped her game. "You could have an extra pair of tiny feet running around soon. Joyce would love that."

"What if you can't have any? The boy said you've been trying."

"I want nothing more than to give you a grandchild. We can only try." She tilted her head and let her lashes do the work. "What do you think?"

"You win! I'll have it ready in two weeks, as it's not hired out until June." He grimaced, transferring his weight to his other leg. "I'll mention it over tea. Now, let's get on."

"Thank you." She stood and kissed him on the cheek.

"I want no more of your outbursts. The boy has enough on his plate."

Tina smiled. "Promise. I'll be back in a minute. Just going to put my slippers on."

Len nodded his approval. She strolled down the hallway until she reached the bedroom. She closed the door and fist-pumped the air, wiggling her hips in the process. Phase one of her plan was complete.

*So easy! Now to convince Clive.*

The exertion made her legs wobble and strained her ribs. Feeling light-headed, she sprawled herself out on the bed like a starfish while the feeling passed.

"And you," she said, rubbing her stomach, "can stop making me feel like this. I can't keep you, you understand?"

A rap sounded upon the door. Tina sat up straight, swinging her feet to the floor. She then toed on her slippers as Len walked in.

"How long does it take to change your footwear?" he asked. "Come on. Tea is ready."

Tina looked him up and down, taking in his bowlegs covered by his brown trousers. She wasn't sure as to whether it was arthritis, or if he was born that way.

"Come on," he repeated. "What you waiting for? We can't wait for you, young lady."

His glasses slipped to the tip of his long nose. He pushed them up with his index finger and shook his head as he left.

"Coming." Bending over to straighten the bed made her feel woozy and the room began to spin. She could hear Len holler from the end of the hall.

"Come on!" he said, clapping his hands. "Chop, chop."

Tina sighed, giving herself a few minutes for the spell to fizzle out. *For goodness sake, give it a rest, you annoying little man.*

Using the walls on each side of the hall for balance as she walked along, she joined the others. Still gathered in the living room, Joyce rattled the walls with her snoring. Her double chin rested on her chest. The bottom row of her false teeth were about to ooze from her gummy mouth. Len stood behind Tina just inside the doorway.

"Wake your mum." He shot a look at Clive and returned to the kitchen.

Clive nudged Joyce's ankles with his foot. He laughed and signalled to Tina to watch. As her bottom plate fell onto her lap, saliva drooled from her mouth. Tina averted her gaze, watching would make her gag and she didn't want another episode like the one she had before.

He stroked her arm. "Wake up, Mum."

She lifted her head. "Oh, Ducky. I must have nodded off."

Clive lowered his voice and said, "Pop your teeth back in, Mum."

Joyce held the lower plate to her lips and sucked them into her mouth, wiping her fingers on her sleeve. Rolling forward and back several times like a pendulum gave Joyce the momentum to push herself from the chair. Tina saw her struggle and offered her an arm.

"It's okay, Duck. I manage when you're not here." She straightened slowly before she moved.

"Come on, Mum. Let me help." Clive wrapped an arm around her shoulders.

"Thanks, Ducky. You're a good boy."

Len sighed with exasperation. "Come on! Tea is ready. Boy, get in there, and you." He motioned at her with his thumb like a hitchhiker bumming a lift. "Come on, Nelly."

"I nodded off."

Joyce padded into the kitchen. Len clambered between the furniture and pressed the button on the telly.

"Not having that on, wasting electricity."

The square-cut sandwiches looked unappetising as they sat on an old chipped plate. A jug of squash sat next to it. Clive was the first to pile his side plate.

"Leave some for everyone else, greedy. There's two rounds each."

He dragged the plate away from his son and offered them to Joyce. Once everyone had taken their quota, Tina helped herself to two squares, opting for the tomato since she'd seen Len scrape the mould off the cheddar earlier.

Joyce spoke with her mouth full. "Is that all you're having?"

"I don't eat much at all. This will do me fine, thank you."

"You're so skinny. Isn't she, Len?" she asked, gripping Tina's forearm with her chubby fingers.

Tina slid her arm out of her grip.

"I keep telling her that, Mum. It's unattractive." Clive poured the drinks. "Tell me when. I wouldn't want to give you too much." He stood there, ready to pour the orange squash into her glass.

"Half a glass, please, darling. Thank you."

Tina nibbled on a corner of the sandwich. The spread was so thick it squeezed out of the bread's crusts and dripped onto the plate.

*I would like tomato with my grease sandwich.*

She smiled at the thought.

"I don't care what she eats. Cheap for me. I don't have to feed her, not like him," Len said, licking his fingers. "He's got bloody worms, he has."

"Worms at the tea table? You put me off," Joyce replied.

Tina doubted anything could put her off her food.

"He's a big strong boy." Joyce wrinkled her nose and shrugged.

"What are they doing about your thyroid?" Tina asked.

She raised the glass and took a big gulp, needing something to wash the foul taste from her mouth. The atmosphere in the room sank and they all grew quiet. Angry eyes were focused on Tina.

"That's not a nice thing to say." Len threw his crusts on the plate and locked his hands together, elbows on the table.

Joyce's mouth dropped open.

"What did you say that for?" Clive asked, mimicking his dad's actions.

"I was just concerned." Uncomfortable, Tina twisted in her seat.

"Nelly is very conscious about her weight," Len said.

"Yes, she is, Dad. You've upset her now." Clive stoked his mum on the shoulder.

Tina panicked. If Len changed his mind and told Clive about their conversation, it would ruin her plan. She took a deep breath to steady herself.

"I'm very sorry," she said, reaching out to stroke her arm.

"It's okay, Ducky. These two are overreacting. There is nothing they can do for me now." She reached for another square.

Tina left it at that, not wanting to elaborate and spoil her own intentions.

"These are yours." Len handed her the last two cheese squares on the plate.

"Thanks, but I'm full. Could you pass the squash, please?"

Clive filled her glass while Len cleared everything away and reached for the rubber key fob on the hook. He put it in his pocket and sat back down.

"Have you got any cake, Dad?"

"Patience, dear boy. Your mum cooked one special. Go and get it, lad. It's in the pantry."

Tina swallowed hard. *Oh, no! Not the cake!* The last one had upset her stomach for two days.

Clive returned and made fun of his mum. Holding the cake with both hands, he bent down so that it nearly touched the floor.

"What have you put in this? Concrete?"

They laughed. His mum slapped him on the arm. Tina wanted to join in, but she knew what was coming.

"It's a bit wonky."

"I would never have noticed. Thanks, Mum."

Clive kissed her on the cheek. She held his face and rubbed the side of his head.

"What flavour is it?" Tina asked.

"Victoria sponge," they said in unison and giggled.

"It caught around the edges a bit, but I scrapped the burnt bits off." Joyce wiped her eyes with her hankie.

"It will go down a treat," Len said, standing by with his knife at the ready. Cutting it into portions, he divided it up evenly and put a slice on each plate.

"Would anyone like a cup of tea with it?" Tina moved her chair back.

"No, we have squash. We will have tea later." Len picked up his piece and took a bite. "Not bad at all, Nelly."

Tina wanted to pinch her nose. She took a bite and swallowed as quickly as possible. Analysing it, she turned her plate. The cake was stodgy, but crisp around the outside, and undercooked in the middle. She guessed the oven was set too high and the flour beaten into the mixture and not folded. The easiest cake to make and she messed it up.

"Do you like it, Ducky?"

The 'Ducky' thing was starting to grate on Tina's nerves. She hated the way they spoke in this area, and had never been one for pet names.

"Filling, isn't it?" She persevered and devoured every crumb.

"It is," Joyce said, biting into the crispy edge of her portion.

Len put the key fob on the table and passed it to Clive, who was tucking into his slice of the brick.

"What are those for, Dad?"

"The keys to the *New Dawn.*"

"I know what they are. Why you giving them to me?" Clive leant back in his seat. "I can't help you, Dad. I know you have bookings, but I'm way too busy."

"No, idiot, it's so you can have a break with the missus. Just the two of you for a weekend."

"When?"

"Two weeks' time. Your mum and I thought it would be nice for you to . . . you know, have a romantic weekend together."

Joyce shot her husband a look. Len winked at her.

"I will never get the time off."

"You're going. Maybe you can use the relaxing time and try for a baby."

A look of delight spread across Joyce's face. "Oh, goodie!"

"What do you think?" Clive asked his wife.

"Why not? Sounds like fun." Tina smiled.

"What if you can't have children?"

Len tipped his head. A soft sigh escaped Tina's lips.

"We can try, can't we?" Tina asked. "I have no issues. It was attention seeking, and I'm over that now."

"If there is any reason you can't conceive, then I'm not sure I want my son married to someone who is infertile," Len said.

Joyce's head moved left then right between their conversations like a tennis match.

*Cheeky swine! We spoke about it earlier and he still brings it up.*

Tina bit her tongue and inhaled before she replied, "Of course not."

"It's bad enough him being married to a drama queen without this." Len looked at Clive, who nodded in agreement.

Tina's throat tightened. *Why don't you just say what's on your minds, you ungrateful pigs!?* She counted to ten and balled her fists under the table.

"I'm trying to change. It won't happen again."

"We know, Ducky." Joyce tapped Tina's elbow. "We know."

"That's settled, then. You go in two weeks. And look after those keys. They're the only spares I've got."

"Yes, Dad."

Tina uncurled her fists, drumming her fingers against her knees. All she had to do now was get through the next fortnight, and then it would be time.

# CHAPTER 14

**L**ATER that day, they watched *Colombo*. The volume was too loud and the room felt stuffy.

Tina shifted in her seat and said, "Would you mind if I went outside for a stroll in the garden?"

"It's too late now, Duck. Anyway, we are watching this," Joyce said without making eye contact.

"It's only seven."

"Just watch the telly," Clive said. He put his hand on her thigh and squeezed.

"It's bedtime drinks soon." Len picked at the end of his nose.

*Oh, yes, the bedtime ritual!* Tina had forgotten the ridiculous time they turned in.

"I'm just going to get my book." She tried to stand, but Clive's hold tightened.

"How rude! Reading? Don't you like this?" Joyce asked.

"Sit still and appreciate the family time." Len said, looking at Clive.

"Keep quiet. You're spoiling it." Clive nodded, satisfied with himself for putting his wife in her place in front of his dad.

The end credits rolled down the screen. An hour and a half of their moans about the detective irritated her. She didn't mind the program, but being confined in the same room made it hard to breathe.

Len looked at the clock. Tina watched him counting down the seconds. On the dot at eight o'clock, he rose from his seat and stood in the doorway.

"Drink time, Nelly. Now, what are we all having?"

"Tea, please, for me," Tina said.

"No, it's Horlicks or Ovaltine."

Tina predicted the response, but said it anyway. She knew it annoyed Len when she did so. Their last visit several months ago was only for the day. This was the third time she'd stayed overnight since their wedding, and it seemed their strict ways were getting worse.

To break the monotony, Tina thought back to the second visit and it brightened her spirits. Joyce hated cats, claiming she had an allergy. Clive had helped his dad clear the November leaves and a cat strolled through the garden. Joyce overreacted. It was the quickest Tina had seen her move.

Feeling a little mischievous, Tina had rubbed her hand over Joyce's calf, pretending to be the feline. She froze, the look on her fat face priceless. She grinned at the recollection.

"Well, I'm waiting." Len drummed his fingers on the doorframe.

Tina detested the malted drink. The thick milk with bits in it made her tongue feel heavy.

"I'm fine, thanks."

"I'm making four. Stop being fussy," Len said, his tone sharp.

"Make it, Dad. She'll drink it." Clive glared at her and nudged her ribs.

Tina winced. Although they were getting better, a direct hit still made the pain shoot across her chest. Joyce had nodded off again, spittle hanging from the corner of her mouth.

"Give Nelly a prod. I'll put the water on for your wash."

"It's alright, Duck. I'm awake. Just resting my eyes."

"Bedtime soon, Nelly." Len lifted his head and waited for Tina to reply.

"Err, no thanks. I can wait. Sorry to mess you about."

Len shook his head and left.

***

**T**HE in-laws turned in at nine o'clock after they locked up for the night. Clive had already changed and headed for the bedroom. Washing in cold water made Tina breathe sharply. She grabbed the towel and dabbed her face.

His and hers flannels were folded on the rail. Their toiletries rested on the wood table. Joyce's teeth fizzed in a glass, food embedded in the dentures. Unable to control the reflex, she put a hand to her mouth and suppressed the urge to retch on the way out. Her slippers slapped against her heels as she walked to the bedroom. Len called out to her as she passed their room.

"Night. You have ten minutes for lights out."

"Good night." Tina's eyes rolled.

Clive never slept this early, but there he was, in bed on his side with only his head showing above the floral covers. With her back against the headboard, she made herself comfortable and opened her book to chapter nine. Tina liked Lee Child's character about a handsome ex-military cop who took no shit and saved the day. Her eyes lifted at the sound of a tap on the door.

"Lights out," Len said as he peeked into the room.

Tina frowned. "I could have been indecent."

"Tough. I said ten minutes." He flicked the light switch and left.

In the darkness, she felt for her page mark and tossed the book to the floor. She then shuffled down the mattress.

"You should have turned the light off," Clive said.

*Smart arse,* she thought, and settled in for the night.

\*\*\*

**T**AKING her time to wash and dress, Tina was in no hurry for breakfast. Clive had awoken an hour ago and slipped out of the bed without disturbing her. She could hear their cheerful voices as she approached the kitchen.

"You're late, Duck," Joyce said.

"It's only eight."

Tina breathed through her mouth as the smell of stale cooking fat assailed her nostrils. Len stood at attention by the sink and waited for Joyce to pass the next clean dish for him to dry.

"Why didn't you wake me?" Tina asked as she stared at Clive.

"Don't blame me because you overslept," Clive said with his nose in the newspaper.

"I can do you a fried sandwich." Joyce put the pan on the ring as she turned and looked at Tina.

"Not sure I have ever had that. What is it?"

"Just fry them, Nelly. She'll like them." Len made fresh pot of tea, and then poured it into the cups. "What time are you leaving, boy?"

Joyce took the sandwiches out of the fridge and placed them near the cooker. Tina glanced over her shoulder. A thick layer of lard covered the bottom of the pan. The fat hissed and spat as it melted.

"I thought we ate all those yesterday?" Tina asked.

"These are stale, dear. They fry better if they're a day old."

She flipped the drowned bread over. Joyce's mouth salivated as the frying continued. With a delicate stomach, Tina stepped away and sat down before her legs gave way.

*How am I going to eat those?*

The burning fat started to smoke as the cheese melted.

"Bloody hell, Mum! Open a window. Mid-morning, Dad. It gives me a chance to sort a few things at home. I'm going out tonight with Ray."

Scooping the cremated offerings out of the pan, she placed it in front of Tina. "There you go, Ducky."

"Thanks." Tina's mouth turned down at the corners as she looked at the grease on the plate.

Len opened the window and used the tea towel to fan out the smoke.

"Dad, about the boat."

Tina straightened slightly, eager to hear what Clive had to say. Joyce mopped her brow and took a chair near the window.

"What about it?"

"Will it be ready?"

"Yes, but I won't be doing it. I'm too old for that now." He'd stopped fanning the smoke, drying his hands and hanging up the towel.

"There will be someone there to show us what to do?" Clive asked.

"Well, you're not having it if you don't know what you're doing."

Tina gulped, worried about her plan, and intervened. "You know how to do that."

"All I want to do is get on it and go. I don't want to be doing all these bloody safety checks." Folding the paper, he put it to the side and straightened. "Of course, I can sail the fucking thing." He glared at her.

"Language, please!" Joyce said.

"One of the lads at the yard will have it ready. All you have to think about is mating."

*What an awful expression!*

Tina grimaced. The thought of mating and the greasy smoke made her feel unpleasant.

"Excuse me, please."

No one spoke when she returned. At least not about her interlude or the wasted breakfast. They spent the next hour wandering around the garden, admiring the plants. Len had given Clive some useful items for the trip, which Tina lugged to the car, as well as their overnight bags. She looked at her watch, eager to make a move.

"I think we'll leave now, Dad."

Tina overheard and followed close behind. They said their goodbyes. Len winked at Clive and gave him a loose hug. He then turned to Tina and kissed her on the cheek.

"Don't forget that grandson," he joked.

"I will try my best." She returned the kiss.

"Bye, Mum."

They hugged.

"Bye, son. Don't leave it too long next time to visit." Joyce's eyes filled with tears as she clung to Clive and patted his back.

"Don't cry, Mum. Your cake wasn't that bad. You can visit us, you know," Clive offered.

"I don't like to travel these days, not with my thyroid." She wiped her eyes with a tissue.

"Nice to see you, Joyce."

Tina offered her a kiss on the cheek. She took it and leaned in for a hug.

"Good luck."

She wrinkled her nose and shrugged. Her hand moved to Tina's stomach and she stroked it gently. Tina flinched and pulled away.

"Thanks. You will be the first to know."

They strode to the car. Before Clive climbed in, he kissed his palm and blew it in his mum's direction. Clive caught one back and put it in his pocket. Sickened by the soppy gesture, Tina clicked her belt into place and gave him a fake smile.

*Get in the car, Mummy's boy,* she thought, and drummed her fingers on her shin.

\*\*\*

**LEN** and Joyce watched their precious boy reverse the car.

"She's pregnant."

"You don't know that, Nelly."

Joyce tapped the side of her head with a finger. "Oh, I do. Why else would she act like that and not eat her food?"

"We shall see what their weekend brings."

Len placed his arm around her shoulder. As the car pulled away, they waved goodbye.

# CHAPTER 15

**PRETENDING** to sleep, the glass felt cold against Tina's temple. Her legs were sprawled across the foot well. As Clive braked the car, her body jolted forward then back. Readjusting her position, she opened her eyes and glared at Clive.

"You fucking idiot! Get off the road, you wrinkly old bat!"

He turned his head to stare at the Corsa that got in his way. Ignoring his profanity and not wanting to engage in conversation, she looked in the other direction.

"Did you see that?" Clive glanced at her. "They should not be on the road at that age." He tapped her thigh with back of his hand. "Hey, I'm talking to you."

She ignored his irritation and rested her head against the window. Tina stared at the dashboard. Clive buzzed the window open. Cold air blasted her face, making her eyes water.

"Close it, please," she said, and sat up. "What did you say?"

"You should have paid attention. It doesn't matter."

The traffic on the A17 was busy. A few spots of drizzle splattered the windscreen. The wipers screeched on intermittent.

"For fuck's sake, is it bloody pensioner day on these roads today?" He punched the horn.

"Your dad's that age and he still drives," she replied. "What's the rush anyway?"

Clive glared at her and then contemplated the road ahead. "I want to get home. My dad is a male, therefore a better driver."

"Women are good drivers, too."

"No, they're not. They shouldn't be allowed on the roads at all."

The red lights from the car in front made Tina react. She pressed her feet to the floor.

"Don't start backchatting." He looked at her and then back at the road before slamming on the brakes. "Shit! You made me do that."

They bolted forward. She grabbed the door handle to steady herself and said, "It's not backchat. It's an opinion."

"We won't be going on any boat trip if you don't behave," Clive said, giving the driver behind them the finger.

"It was nice of him to offer, wasn't it?"

"Nice of whom?"

"Your dad."

"Yes, it was." He indicated right.

"You didn't seem too keen about going."

He sniggered. "Well, I don't want to sound too enthusiastic. I don't want him charging me for fuel."

"He wouldn't do that. You're his son."

"Don't you believe it! We have a free weekend and he does all the hard work. Suits me just fine."

Clive turned into their drive. Tina unclipped her belt, ready to make a quick exit. He let the engine idle and turned in his seat.

"Get the stuff out of the boot, and leave the bits for the boat."

"Aren't you going to turn off the engine?" Tina asked, and swung the door open.

"No, I'm going out."

"What? Now? I thought it was later on tonight."

"No, now."

Leaning into the passenger's side, she rested her forearms on the frame. "Oh, I see. When will you be back?"

"Not late. Hurry up. I haven't got all day."

With the bags at her feet, she stood at the front door and waved. Clive didn't look back at her once he'd pulled away. She smiled as the car disappeared.

*Perfect! Time to myself.*

"Hello, dear. How are you now?"

Mrs. Conerly's face appeared over the edge of her fence. Tina liked the sparky old woman who lived next door, and was saddened by the news of the loss of her husband a few months ago. She wandered over for a chat.

"How are you, Edith?"

"Not so bad, dear. Your husband was very rude to me. Such an angry man."

"Was he? When was this?"

"The day they took you in an ambulance. I only inquired how you were." Her hands gripped the fence for balance.

"Ignore him. He was probably just worried about me."

"Understandable, under the circumstances. Although, I did hear shouting." Edith took a bad step. She wobbled and held on tighter. "Are you sure everything is alright?"

"I slipped and fell down the stairs, but I'm okay now."

"The noise scared my cat. Look." She showed Tina her wrist.

"It was probably the TV. I must go now. It was nice talking to you." Tina rubbed her thumb over the back of Edith's hand. "You be careful on those legs of yours. I wouldn't want you to trip."

"I will, my dear." Edith began to turn. "You should come around for coffee. I get so lonely now that he's gone."

"Maybe another day. It must be very hard for you." Tina headed for the front door. "You take care now."

Once inside, she put the bags near the stairs. She could still smell Clive's lingering odour. Opening windows was her first priority. Tina then flung the keys on the kitchen table.

She couldn't help but to think of Edith. Clive disliked her, but she felt sorry for the woman. She'd lost her life partner to colon cancer and deteriorated herself since his passing. Somehow, killing her husband didn't seem fair or right. Neither did aborting the baby, but she couldn't think of any other way to make things right.

Hunting through the cupboards, she found what she was looking for. Why they owned a pestle and mortar was beyond Tina's knowledge. She supposed that it was another useless wedding present. Today, it had a use. She ground the handle into the bowl until the sleeping pills resembled a fine powder and threw the empty strip back behind the fridge. By the time they cleaned behind it, he would be floating on top of the river with his lungs full of water.

Alarmed by the sound of the key in the lock, she scanned the kitchen for a place to put the bowl. Her hands shook, spilling some of its contents onto the work surface. Hearing footsteps pound through the hall, her heart raced.

*Think! Oh, hell, think!*

Tina shoved the bowl under the sink behind the soap powder. She dusted the spilt residue from the worktop as Clive walked in.

"You're back early," she said, putting her hands on her hips, attempting to look casual as a burst of adrenaline pumped through her veins.

"Yeah, and you've done nothing. The bags are still sitting there." Clive gestured toward the foot of the stairs. "What have you been doing?"

"It's only been . . . what . . . ?" She looked at the clock "Two hours. I thought you were out with the lads."

"So you thought you could put off the jobs because I was out?"

"No, I was about to start. I—"

"What have you done since you got back?"

"I had a chat with Edith."

"You should have ignored her."

"I tried. It's hard to get away from her." Tina gulped, not liking the look in his eye or the change in his posture.

"What did you talk about?" Clive moved forward, standing inches from her face.

"The usual waffle about her husband." She took a step back, the corner of the work surface digging into her lower back.

"Why were you looking in that cupboard? Hiding something?"

He reached for the handle.

She shifted her position and gave him her best stare. "Of course not. I was thinking of taking everything out and giving it a clean. Something to do while you're out."

"Good, you're making yourself useful."

"Can I get you anything? I can rustle something up for tea if you like."

"No, thanks. By the way, I've invited Maggie and Ray on our boat trip."

Feeling stunned and deflated, she pulled out a chair. He'd scuppered her plan. How could she go through with it now? It had to be that weekend, otherwise it was all for nothing. This would be her only chance. In a couple of weeks, she would start to show, trapped in his clutch forever.

"Why did you invite them?" she asked, putting her head in her hands and massaging her temples.

"It'll be fun, don't you think? The four of us on the boat together." He smirked.

"No, it won't. It'll be cramped."

"Hardly. It's a four berth.

"Just the two of us to mate, your dad said."

"He said no such thing, and anyway, we don't need a boat trip to try for a kid."

She knew darn well what Len had said. "I don't want them there." Tina slammed her fists on the table.

"Watch your temper, or I will shut that gob of yours."

"Maggie, on a boat trip, in high heels." She rested her chin in a cupped hand. "It's a narrow boat, not a bloody yacht."

"Very accommodating, is our Maggie. Very adaptable, shall we say?" He rubbed at his crotch and gave a sharp thrust of his pelvis.

Repulsed, she focused on the dead flowers on the sill, and then made eye contact with him. "Listen to me, please." She stood and moved toward him. "I only wanted the two of us on the boat, you know." Tina hugged his waist. "So we could have some time together."

"We have the time now. All that talk of Maggie has made me horny as fuck." He rubbed his hips against her.

"No." Tina slid out of his embrace and took a step back. "Not now. I've got a headache and my ribs hurt."

"Pathetic excuse! Are you refusing me?" he asked.

He reached for her and pulled her close. Tina deftly disengaged herself from his hold once more.

"Please, not now." She moved to the other side of the room.

"How dare you deny me what is mine! I will fuck you when I want to, bitch. Now get over here."

"No, you disgust me, you vile pig."

Her hand shot to her mouth as she realised her blunder. Her eyes darted around the kitchen. With the knife block in sight, she headed toward it. Clive predicted her next move and blocked her advance.

"What? You going to try and stab me now?"

"Sorry, it slipped out. I didn't mean to say it." Frozen to the spot, her legs grew heavy and her arms limp.

"Too late, bitch."

Tina stiffened as his hand gripped the nape of her neck and forced her down. It was no use. She could already feel the cold worktop pressed against her right cheek. Every ounce of her being wanted to fight back, but it would be stupid to do so. She couldn't risk going to the hospital again. Nor could she risk her plans for the future.

"I'll do it, but please, let go of me."

The tension around her neck eased as his grip loosened. She faced him and then dropped to her knees, her eyes level with his zip.

*I don't want to do this, but it's got to be better than being raped from behind.*

"Hurry up." He unbuttoned his jeans and slid them to the floor, rubbing the end of his penis. "Now, this is what a good wife should be doing. Suck it."

"I can't! Please."

"Yes, you can. I may be a bit big for you."

"I can't. I feel a bit sick."

"Get your fucking mouth around it!"

Opening wide, the tip of his erection rubbed against her gums and pushed against her clenched teeth. His hand at the back of her head aided the invasion. Tina rebelled, but he pushed harder.

*Get it over with. You can do this. Two weeks, and it will all be over,* she repeated in her mind.

"Suck it, unless you want another beating."

Relenting, she relaxed her jaw and a mass of curly pubes scratched her lips as his shaft hit the back of her throat. The movement triggered a gag reflex.

"Mind your teeth."

An idea struck her. She could bite his cock, causing him excruciating pain, but after he recovered, she'd be punished. The idea, in itself, was a bad one. Her head rocked back and forth, the grinding from his hips penetrating deeper into her throat.

"Do it properly, and use your tongue as well."

The doorbell shrilled, cutting into the moment. Clive pulled away. Tina wiped her mouth, picking the pubic hairs off her tongue and jumping to her feet.

Clive tucked in his shirt and said, "Who the fuck is that?"

"I don't know." She watched him shake his penis back to a comfortable position.

"Well, fucking answer it, then. We can finish this later."

Tina scurried to the door and eyed the ceiling on the way. Once out of sight, she pressed her hands together and mouthed a *thank you* to the heavens above.

# CHAPTER 16

**W**HOEVER was at the front door had done Tina a big favour. For now, she was safe. In the background, Clive griped in his usual manner. She paid him no attention and answered. Edith stood in front of her, looking a tad sheepish.

"Hi."

"Sorry to bother you, dear. I thought you might like to see this." She held up a photo album and handed it over.

"Oh, thank you, Edith." She accepted it out of politeness. "I would invite you in, but now is not a good time. I'm in the middle of ironing."

"I wanted to go through the pictures with you." Edith gripped the edge of the door and had one foot on the top step.

Clive shouted in distance. "Get rid of her!"

Tina let out a sharp breath. If Edith heard his words, it never showed on her face.

"Maybe I can come around sometime." She passed the album back into her neighbour's hands. "I must go now."

Sensing his stride down the hall, she glanced over her left shoulder.

"I'll see you later. Move," he said, and barged his way past.

Tina fiddled with the brass latch as her husband nonchalantly passed by Edith without a word. He purposely brushed against her.

Unsteadied, Edith's grip tightened on the frame. "How rude!"

"I better go. Shall I walk you back to your house?" She could

126

have invited her in for coffee, but she wasn't sure when Clive would return and soon thought better of it.

"No, no, dear. I'll manage." Edith turned, gingerly moving her foot from the concrete step.

She visually escorted Edith to her home then headed back inside. Wandering through to the kitchen, she recalled the events from earlier. The taste of his flesh clung to her tongue. She gargled, whisking mouthwash around her mouth before spitting it out. Tina then dampened and smoothed down her hair.

He may want to continue when he arrived home. She could not refuse him. It was too risky. Ray and Maggie's invitation didn't help matters either. Clenching both fists, she thumped the work surface and then grabbed the vase from the sill, tipping stale water and flowers into the sink. She twisted the stems until her knuckles turned white and green slime covered her fingers. A growl escaped her lips.

Her frustration soon dissipated. She pulled the ground up medication out from its hiding place. Tina shook the mortar, powder forming in a mound at the bottom.

*I hope there is enough,* she thought, before tapping it carefully into a piece of foil. She folded it into quarters and hid it behind the fridge.

She spent the rest of the day being a piny woman. Tina did her chores so that Clive wouldn't go off on a tangent when he came home. Heaven forbid that the cups were an inch out of place!

Once early evening arrived, Tina took a long hot shower and went through her plan one more time. When they reached their mooring spot for the night, she would offer Clive a glass of wine laced with powdered pills. Upon taking hold, she would push him over the side of the boat.

*That sounds easy,* she thought whilst shampooing her hair.

If they did a post-mortem, they would find drugs in his system. His medical records would show he hadn't been prescribed any. Tina would say he took hers, that he had trouble sleeping as there was too much pressure at work. The dosage might be a problem, since no sensible person would take six at once. That would be suicide. No one would believe that anyway. She would have to give him a quarter of the powder, enough to make him drowsy.

*What if he refused the wine?* She stepped out and towelled dry. *In his coffee, maybe, but not potent enough.*

The wine and pills would add to the sedation. If need be, she'd provoke him, although that option wouldn't work with her plan.

"Food!" she said aloud.

If he refused the drink, she could sprinkle it on his meals. He had to eat at some point. She also added Maggie and Ray into the equation. Somehow, she'd find out their plans in the next few days. She could always drug Clive before they arrived. That wouldn't work, however, as they would be witnesses. The timing would all depend on their arrangements. Tina would not be deterred. She'd improvise if she had to.

Her favourite pyjamas were in the top drawer of the dresser. The material felt pliable against her fingers. Pulling on the bottoms, her hand traced her stomach. Another problem to sort, but how could she get rid of this life growing in her womb? She sat down on the edge of the bed. The tightness in her throat made it hard to swallow. Her hands began to shake and she started to cry.

*One thing at a time,* she thought.

She wiped her eyes and blew her nose, using a tissue she'd pulled from the box. How many weeks had gone by? She worked it out on her fingers and did the math in her head.

*Still plenty of time.*

Tina slipped on the fleecy top and glanced at her reflection in the mirror. Was that a slight bump now forming? It couldn't be. It was too soon, surely? Pulling the fabric over her hips in denial, she slid on a pair of socks and rubbed her palms over her face before she went to make herself a drink.

Her heart raced as she heard the key in the lock. The phone table scraped against the wall as Clive made his way inside. A second set of footsteps sounded followed by a swear word. Her husband had brought someone home. She could now breathe easy.

Tina popped her head around the door. Clive and his guest sat in the lounge. They were tipsy, but not that drunk.

"Get us a beer," Clive ordered.

"Did you have a good time?" Tina asked, and then looked at their guest. "How are you, Ray?"

"Fine, once you get that beer."

The men turned to face each other and laughed. Tina returned with two cold bottles. She passed one to each of them and sat close by.

"We're going to watch some sports. You should go to bed," Clive said, taking a swig of his beer.

Tina didn't want to leave. Not yet. She wanted to know a little more about the trip. It was the perfect timing. Inhaling deeply, she approached the subject.

"Have you asked Ray about the boat trip?"

Clive nodded.

"Yes, he has, and I accept."

"Will Maggie be coming?"

"No, it's way too . . . shall we say, unluxurious. She likes her mod cons."

Even better, she surmised, surprised that he could use such a long word.

"Are you meeting us at the mooring Saturday morning?"

"No, he's not." Clive butted in and turned to look at Ray. "You're coming early evening."

Ray nodded. "I know where your spot is for the night, so I will make my way there."

"It will be nice to have you with us," Tina said.

Clive shot her a look and shook his head. "Yeah, like you wanted him there."

"Tough. I'm coming. Bring your apron." Ray looked at Clive, who nudged him in the ribs.

"Oi, that's my wife. Pack it in."

Typical Ray, always so threatened by Clive, he had to mimic his actions. *What a sad man you are!*

Tina smiled through clenched teeth. "I shall go to bed, then." She leaned in to kiss her husband, surprised that Clive returned the peck and bid them both good night.

The TV echoed and laughter came through the walls. Tina knew he would turn it up to annoy her and disrupt her sleep. She didn't care. Instead, she jiggled her hips from side to side and punched the air with excitement.

# CHAPTER 17

*Two weeks later . . .*

**T**HE boathouse stood to the left of the Waterways Club car park and housed many pleasure crafts. A mud path ran along the river. Trees and shrubs banked the opposite side. Willow branches arched and licked the water's surface. Three hundred yards down, and nestled between two others, stood their narrow boat.

Not yet onboard, and there was friction between them. Tina stood to the side and looked on. The boat guard, dressed in his sailing club t-shirt and jog pants, advised Clive that he would need a practise run to familiarise himself with the basics before setting off. Clive had waved his arms in the air and shouted profanity at the poor man. He'd stormed off, shaking his head.

"Come on, then." Clive beckoned. "Get on."

The hull tapped the riverbank and the boat jostled in its tethers.

"Coming."

On first inspection of the vessel earlier to load luggage and food, she was not impressed, and wanted the trip over and done with.

"Untie the ropes."

Doing as she was told, she stepped over the small gap with the second rope in hand. Snatching it from her, he rolled it around his fist and then tucked it out of the way.

"Looks cloudy. I think I'll zip my coat up. It gets chilly on the water," she said, pulling the collar close to her ears. "Do you want yours?

"No, I don't."

They stood at the stern of the long boat. It was painted black with gold trim around its small windows. Snazzy coloured diamond shapes gleamed across the bow. *New Dawn* was written in green letters on the front starboard side.

"Give me some room."

She sidestepped to the left. Being in such close proximities with him got under her skin. The scent of his aftershave was the worst and would line her nostrils forever. As the diesel engine strained and the propeller churned, it caused a small wave to splash up the sides of the bank, unbalancing them both.

"You need to turn the tiller in the other direction." She took delight in his ignorance. "The bow should come out like this." She gestured the angle.

He glared at her. "What, you're an expert now?"

"Just trying to help." Tina stroked his arm. "Shall I get you a coat? You feel cold."

"Let me do this. Stop fussing."

He moved the metal rod to the right. The boat eased away from the bank, smooth and slow, at a ninety degree angle. Smiling inwardly, she choked back a laugh while the idiot figured out how to pull away. She glared into the water that smelt fresh and clean. Tall reeds grew deep within. Roaches and other small fish scurried about in circles and pond skaters danced nearby. She dangled her arm over the side and let the water run through her fingers.

*It looks shallow. It'll be deeper in the middle,* Tina contemplated.

"How deep is it here?" she asked, shaking the droplets from her hand and standing back up.

"How should I know?"

Watching him, she bit the side of her cheek. He shrugged and then put a hand on his hip, posing in his flip-flops, shorts, and t-shirt like it was a hot summer's day.

It was a beautiful part of the river. Wroxham was one of her favourite places. The wildlife was a spectacle. Birds sung, claiming their territory. Ducks laughed, some of their feathered tails bobbing and twitching. She let the gentle breeze caress her face. A strand of hair flopped across her brow and stuck to her top lip like a moustache as she looked back at their wake tumbling to the margins.

"It is lovely here. Look." She pointed. "A Kingfisher."

"It's the insects that piss me off."

"They're not that bad this time of the year." Tina held onto the side and scoured the area. "There's another cruiser. Shouldn't you be over to the left a bit more? They will never pass."

"I'm not moving. They have plenty of room."

She grabbed the tiller and Clive slapped her hand away. "Let's get them to move," he said, and veered farther to the right.

"We're going hit them. Please move over." She sucked in her belly and clamped her arms to her sides, attempting to make herself smaller, hoping it would make a difference and that the boat would pass without a scrape.

"Stop your whinging. There's loads of room."

"Err, mate, what you playing at? Don't you know the rules of the water?" a tall man shouted as they ran alongside with only four feet to spare.

Clive put two fingers up and mouthed a 'fuck off.' Tina looked away in shame.

"Idiots think they own the water. Make me a coffee."

Shaking her head, she lifted the wooden lid that closed onto two small doors known as the counter and climbed down three creaky steps. Stale musty air drifted through the belly of the *New Dawn*. She'd seen some smashing interiors in these narrow boats. Some had TV and WiFi, like floating hotels, but this wasn't one of them.

The small kitchen was equipped with the basic essentials, and the electricity was battery-powered. She filled the kettle, thankful for the bottled water, and spooned the coffee into two chipped mugs. Tina added a splash of milk from the mini fridge that sat under a tiny round sink.

*Should I do it now?* she asked herself as she poured the liquid into the mugs.

Clive wouldn't sail long before he would want to stop. This could be her only chance. As soon as the letch came aboard, the opportunity was gone. Getting him drunk tonight wouldn't work either now, since Ray would be joining them soon. It had to be done before they reached their destination. Tina drummed her fingers on the worktop and decided the time was right.

All day, the silver pouch tucked down the front of her trousers scratched against her skin. Looking around, she retrieved the package and sneakily opened one end, letting half of the powder slide into his mug. Out the corner of her eye, Clive's figure startled her, the foil slipped through her fingers and floated to the floor.

"Damn it." Stepping on it with her trainer, her hands began to shake, so she stirred his drink with more vigour than she'd intended.

He'd peered through one of the windows, balancing on the four-inch rim that ran parallel down each side from bow to stern. With her right foot planted, she twisted around to see him knock on the glass. A bead of sweat formed on her brow and ran down her temple.

"Is that coffee ready yet?"

"What are you doing?" Tina sighed and shifted her weight.

"What's it look like?"

"Shouldn't you be steering?"

"It's fine. We're on autopilot." Clive laughed. "Do you get it? Autopilot!"

In her courting days, that might have been funny. Now, he sounded like a prat.

"It's coming."

Once he'd disappeared, she picked up the drug packet and pocketed it once more. Bending made her feel queasy. Not again! She placed three fingers over her lips and strode the length of the hull. Walking across a beige threadbare carpet, she passed the built-in matching two-seater that made up the four berths when pulled out.

The chemicals emanating from the toilet made the nausea worse and she dry heaved.

Her feet stuck out of the shower room as she was unable to close the door. Swilling from a tiny sink, she dabbed at her lips and went back to the kitchenette. Nearing the bottom step, she made sure that Clive stood at the tiller and wasn't doing any acrobatics and climbing about.

*Okay, Mr. Comedian, see if you find this funny.*

She tentatively climbed the steps, not wanting to spill any liquid from the cup. Once on deck, she passed it to him.

"There you go."

Tina's eyes widened as she witnessed her husband take the first sip. He coughed and spat out the mouthful.

"It's instant," he said.

"You know it's instant. It's hot and wet." Tina blew across her cup and then took a sip of hers.

"Too much fucking milk!" He tipped it over the side and handed her the mug.

Tina hoped the disappointment didn't show on her face. "Should I make you another?"

"Don't bother. I'm having a beer soon anyway."

Leaving him to it, she made her way below. She cursed under her breath, hating every minute of his company and the trip. How far had they come and how long did she have left before Ray arrived? She downed the last mouthful of her drink and placed the cups on the side. She thumped the top of her thigh with her fist until it hurt, punishing herself for failing.

"Fetch me a beer!" Clive shouted, moments later.

Irked by his tone, she opened the fridge with force and then calmly closed it. Looking over her shoulder, and feeling for the foil pouch, she flipped the lid from the bottle, adding the last of the powder. It glided down the bottleneck and looked like her granddad's snow globe as it reached the bottom. It made the beer fizz and froth over the top. She looked for something to stir it with and found a metal meat skewer in the drawer. The creak of the steps made her heart pound.

"How long does it take to get a beer? I could have got it quicker myself."

Feeling the need to explain herself, she said, "Got it. I had to go to the loo."

She climbed the steps again and handed him the alcohol. "So, if Ray's coming, how are we supposed to try for a baby?" she asked, and swallowed.

"He's only here tonight, so stop whinging." Clive put the bottle between his feet.

"How far have we got to go?"

"How the fuck do I know?" He paused. "It's just after the next bridge, I think."

*Why couldn't he just say that instead of being an obnoxious git?*

"It's five o'clock. Do you want some food? I can do you a sandwich." She eyed his beer, willing him to drink.

"I'm eating at the pub tonight." He glanced at her and smirked. "You have one because you're not invited. You can sulk on the boat."

His foot bumped the bottle. It wobbled, but remained upright.

"Careful. You nearly knocked it over."

"No, I didn't." He turned to glare at her. The bottle fell on its side and rolled about, liquid oozing from its neck and spreading across the deck. "Bollocks! Now look what you made me do."

Her mouth fell open and her heart sank. The plan had failed. There was no way she could go through with it now. Fighting back the tears and gripping the fabric of her jacket pockets, she gazed at the sky. Everything looked dark and dull.

"It looks like we're in for a storm."

Clive smirked, picked up the bottle, and threw it over the side. "Better get me another beer."

Another commotion down the river left Tina feeling hacked off. Clive disturbed an angler and hit his rod, which poked out from the grasses. The old man shook his head and threw a ball of groundbait full of maggots at Clive, but it missed and hit the side instead. Disgusted with her husband, she looked skyward at the forming thunderclouds and bit her lip.

A large drop splattered her forehead. Then, a double flash lit up the murky sky, followed by a crack and a rumble. Tina pulled on her hood. The torrential downpour bounced off the water's surface, the droplets bouncing in unison as the rain grew harder.

"Get my waterproof, will you?" he ordered. "Fucking weather."

She scurried through the hull, leaving wet footsteps behind her as she padded through to fetch it. Tina returned with his grey jacket, purposely forgetting his beer.

"Here." She shoved it at him.

"Take hold of this."

With the tiller in her hand, she steered while he put on his coat and climbed on the rim that ran down each side.

"Why don't you go through? It's a lot easier."

Clive's eyes narrowed as he glanced back at her. "When I want your advice, I'll ask. I don't want to get the floor wet in there, you dozy mare. Pull alongside. We can use that space over there until the storm has passed."

"It's easier to get the canvas from the other end."

"I want to get the end covered. Concentrate on what you're doing. Fucking rain!"

Steering toward the bank, she kept watch while he shuffled down the side. The rain pounded on the roof and windows. He inched along and reached for the canvas cover that lay folded in a box on the roof.

Tina's jaw dropped open. She was unable to comprehend what happened next. Holding a hand over her mouth, she suppressed a laugh.

Clive lost his footing and fell overboard. His arms flailed about, causing a large splash. His body submerged, bobbing across the water. The trapped air in his coat made it look like he wore a life jacket, his arms splayed out beside him.

Tina reduced speed and leant over the side. "Clive, Clive."

Blood gushed from his temple. The rain washed it away, but more leaked from the gash. Tina's eyes widened with horror as his flip-flops rose to the water's surface.

# CHAPTER 18

**THUNDER** rumbled overhead. A silver streak flashed, lighting up the dark clouds. The torrential downpour blurred Tina's vision, raindrops pouring down the hood of her jacket. She stared at Clive's body floating nearby.

"Clive!" she cried, easing down on the throttle.

She looked up and down the river. Apart from a bridge up ahead, she saw no one. Given the predicament, she acted with a clear head. This could be the only chance to get rid of her husband forever. It was wrong, but the opportunity was too good to miss.

Battling with her conscience, her hands shook from the rising adrenaline. She wiped the moisture from her cheeks and face, and leant over the side once more. The blow to the head had knocked him out. His listless arms hung on the surface of the water and his eyes were closed. She wasn't sure she could cope with her inner torment if they were open.

The weather continued with its usual force, pounding harder against her and the boat. Her hood had fallen to her shoulders, and her soggy hair now clung to her face. Rainwater dripped from her nose.

If she could get him closer to the bank, it would make helping him die so much easier. She looked around the deck for something she could use as an aid. On the floor, to the left of where she stood, was a six-foot long metal pole found on most narrow boats.

Tina tried to yank it free, though it proved awkward to do so. She managed, nonetheless. Steering with one hand, she ran the boat alongside the bank. It was a couple of yards away and closing.

She stretched over the side and prodded her husband with the rod. In doing so, his body sunk before bobbing back up. She knew she needed to push him over to the side, but her arms ached and made it more difficult. An idea soon came to her. Tina hooked the end of the pole under his inflated jacket and rested the rod on the side. Doing so allowed her to push him over and guide the boat at the same time.

Tina nudged him further toward the water's edge until his head and shoulders hit the corrugated iron that supported the bank. The *New Dawn* came to a bumping stop. The mooring space was overgrown. Tall, flowing reeds and Yellow Flag Irises filled the perimeter.

She jumped the gap. With the rope in her hand, she tied both ends to the old fence posts, and then climbed back onboard, watching her footing on the slippery deck. She concentrated on Clive's inert form as it lay wedged between the back of the hull and the bank. Her breathing quickened and her heart pounded as she stared down at him.

"Please, let this work," she mumbled, wiping her eyes and drying her hands on her jeans.

A hint of blue broke out across the sky. The rain eased to a gentle pitter-patter.

She peered over the edge at her husband. Tina reached over the side, her hand trembling as it hovered over his mouth. She feared Clive's opening his eyes and his jaw snapping at her fingers.

It was no use. She couldn't tell if he was breathing. The wound on his head had closed to a thin line, and water had washed the blood away. His skin looked pale and slightly puffed.

*It's my only chance,* she thought. *Please forgive me.*

Making sure no one was about, she retrieved the pole. With all her strength, she forced his frame under the water, making sure to dunk his head. She held that position for a few minutes until realisation hit and her grip loosened. The pole slipped through her fingers and slid into the water. It half sunk, the other end lying across Clive's chest.

Now on land, she sat on the soaked ground and waited for the shaking to subside. The rain had diminished, leaving everything damp and soggy. A smile crossed her face and then her eyes started to well. She wiped her tears and stretched out her legs.

Tina dug into her jean pocket and found her phone. One bar showed up on the screen of her Nokia. She rose to her feet and waved it in the air. The signal dropped completely. Walking a little way down the path, she tried again. Three bars soon flashed on the device's interface, allowing her to dial the emergency services.

*** 

**H**UDDLED under the bridge, Ray crept out of the shadows and walked onto the path. His intention had been to show up early and pop up out of the reeds as a surprise to his mate when they passed. However, the commotion up ahead had caught his interest, and he'd quickened his pace, slowing to a stop before squatting behind the tall grass.

*Why have they stopped there?* he wondered.

Ray laughed at the sight of Clive's body floating in the water. He reached for his phone and swiped at the screen to open the camera.

*He definitely won't live this one down!*

Tina struggled with a pole to help Clive, while the boat headed to the bank. The sight made him chuckle. He resisted the urge to assist her. Watching her was much more fun. It would allow him to bust Clive's ribs for the rest of his life about it.

Crouching, he moved along the path, hiding behind the grasses until he was close enough to get some decent shots. The smile soon dropped from his face. Swapping to video, he let it roll, feeling flabbergasted by what he saw.

From his vantage point, he could see Tina clearly. She was using both hands and purposely holding Clive under the water.

*Should I race to help?* He thought better of it as an idea came to him instead.

Ray shook his head at Tina as she waved her phone in the air. He shifted position and headed back to the car park.

\*\*\*

**THE** dampness on the ground seeped through Tina's trousers, making her skin cold. Her legs buckled once she'd finished the call. She now sat there, staring at nothing in particular, until she heard a masculine voice coming from behind.

"Madam, are you okay? I'm Sergeant Mark Deegan from the Norfolk Constabulary." He knelt down beside her. "We are here to help you."

He placed a hand on her shoulder. The gesture felt reassuring.

"Can we get her a blanket, please?" He issued the order to the female officer that accompanied him.

Tina shivered and looked up, wiping her sleeve across her face. Her mind felt foggy and dazed.

"What's your name?" Deegan asked, whilst getting his bearings of the situation.

"Tina." She gulped hard. "Blythe." She wrapped her arms across her chest to keep warm.

"I think it may be best if you try to stand. The cold ground and your wet clothes aren't helping."

She stood on shaky legs and stumbled. The man held onto her elbow.

"Thanks." Her bottom lip quivered and her teeth chattered.

"I need to ask you some questions. Are you okay to do that?" Deegan looked about for the other constable.

"Yes."

His partner, PC Mary Adams, trotted back to the scene. She handed Deegan a sealed polythene bag. He nodded at her in thanks. She sped off to conduct an initial report on the incident. He took out a foil blanket and wrapped it around her shoulders.

"This will help you to keep warm. You're in shock."

Tina felt comforted by the tin shroud that offered her protection from the elements. Nervousness engulfed her as she saw the sergeant and the PC exchange glances between them.

*They'll treat me like a suspect. I will never get away with it.*

Tina knew she could do this. She had to. It could be the chance of freedom she'd dreamed about. It looked like an accident, after all.

*Oh, God! What did I do with the foil pouch!?*

She wracked her brains, trying to remember where she'd put it. The drug wasn't in his system, but it still didn't look good. Her heart started to pound. No, she was just being paranoid. She needed to stick to her story. Everything would be fine.

"Can I ask you some questions now?" Deegan tilted his head at Tina.

"Yes, of course. I feel a bit lost at the moment. I—" Tina noticed the sympathetic look on his face.

"You're in shock. You've been through quite an ordeal. Take your time."

He stood, poised with his notebook and pen at the ready. "What's the gentleman's name, and what is the relationship between you?"

# CHAPTER 19

**S**UNLIGHT broke through the clouds once again. Its rays bounced off the water. The wet vegetation smelt clean and fresh, as if the rain had washed the grime away and cleansed the canal.

Tina squinted at Deegan. "He's my husband. His name is Clive . . . Blythe. He slipped," she said through chattering teeth, holding the blanket up to her chin.

"It's okay. Take your time."

Deegan looked down the path at the other PC, who was now crouched by the body.

"Didn't you think about going in after him?" he asked, nodding at the PC before turning his attention back to Tina.

"I can't swim. I'm terrified of water. It all happened so quickly." She swallowed hard.

"From the beginning, please. When did you pick up the boat, and where did you start your journey?"

"Wroxham boat yard. We boarded at about 1:30 pm, I think."

"Did you hire it from them?"

"No. It's his dad's boat. He hires it out in the summer."

"Strange choice of holiday, considering you hate water."

Tina responded with a thin smile. She stared at the water and started to cry.

Deegan reached into his pocket and pulled out a cotton handkerchief. "There you go."

"Thanks," she said as she accepted it. She blew hard into the piece of fabric and then pushed it up her sleeve.

"We were having a weekend break, courtesy of Len. We were due to come home tomorrow." Tina sniffed, concentrating on holding in the contents of her delicate stomach.

"Len?"

"His dad."

"Ah, okay. I'll need his contact information."

Tina rattled off the address, and Deegan wrote it down. "All the numbers you need are on here." She handed him her phone.

"Thanks, but it's not necessary." He flipped a page. "Take me through the accident."

Tina lowered her head. "He climbed onto the rim." She pointed to the boat. "He nearly made it to the other end."

"The bow, you mean."

"Yes, the front. He wanted the canvas off the top. As he reached up, he slipped."

The sergeant cleared his throat. "Then what happened?"

"I took the pole and held it out to him." She paused for a second. "The storm got worse." Tina stared down at her feet. "He didn't move when I called, and that's when I saw the blood."

"Carry on. You're doing really well."

"I panicked. He was drifting away from me, so I slowed the engine. I just wanted to get to the bank to help him." Tina paused again. This time, she looked Deegan in the eye and thumbed a tear.

"Did you know how to steer the boat?"

"Not at all. That was Clive's forte. He was the expert."

"Would you say that Clive was competent then?" Deegan glanced over Tina's shoulder to see the coroner's officers walk down the path.

She glanced in the same direction. "Who are they?"

"It's okay. They're from the coroner's office. They attend all accidental and sudden death scenarios. They'll be responsible for removing your husband's body after they've looked at the scene." Deegan nodded at the team as they got to work.

The sight of the two-man team dressed in clinical uniforms and holding bags while walking toward the water's edge made her feel nervous. Goosebumps erupted across her flesh and her body began to shudder. For a moment, it felt like someone had just walked over her grave, though she knew it was just an old wives' tale.

"Could you answer the question, please?"

"Yes, very competent."

"Had he been drinking at all?"

She thought back to the powder in the beer and the remnants on the wooden deck.

*The rain would have washed it away.*

"He knocked his bottle over before he had a chance to drink it."

"What happened after that?" His hand rubbed his chin.

"I held the rudder and headed for the side, but it pushed him up the bank. I didn't know what else to do."

"You mean the tiller?"

"Yes."

"Could you excuse me just for a minute?"

Deegan ran down the path toward the other officer. They talked in hushed voices, making Tina feel nervous. A cocktail of emotions rippled through her body, leaving her feeling fatigued. The consequences of her actions were incomprehensible if they found out. Deep inside, she prayed they never would.

*Stay calm. You can do this!*

She dried her eyes with her sleeve. Several moments later, he was back by her side. She gave him a sad look.

"What happens now?" Tina asked.

Deegan inspected her face. "What happened to your nose? You have a fading bruise."

Tina gulped and said, "I walked into a door. Had too much to drink. I want to go home. I feel very weak. I need to make some calls."

"One of my officers will take you home after you have given a statement at the station."

"I . . . just . . . gave you one!"

"It's procedure, I'm afraid."

"What about Clive's . . . body? What will happen . . . ?"

Shifting her feet made her wobble and sway. Deegan steadied her.

"You need a hot drink. We can get a doctor to check you over if you want us to."

"No, thank you. I'll be alright. What happens now? I mean, after the statement."

"Your husband will be taken to the mortuary at the hospital, eventually."

"Eventually?"

"After we have checked things out. The coroner will need to do a post-mortem and—"

"He may still be alive!"

Deegan shook his head from side to side and said, "He's dead. The team just confirmed it."

*He's dead. I did it! Oh, God, what have I done? Act dumb.*

"Why a post-mortem?"

"I'm sorry, but that's what needs to be done. He needs an official cause of death."

Tina knew about the procedure, but had hoped things would be straightforward. Now there would be an investigation, which meant they might find something. It also meant they might get closer to the truth.

"I need to get home. I've phone calls to make and a funeral to arrange."

"Take some time. You're in shock. It will be awhile before the body is released. You'll have plenty of time."

*What do I tell people?*

Tina thought about what they might find that could incriminate her. There was nothing onboard to show that anything untoward had been committed. Wouldn't they only investigate if the circumstances were suspicious?

Feeling the lining of her pocket, she double-checked that the foil was there. It was, stuck in the corner like a ball bearing. She pushed it deeper into her pocket.

"What about the boat? I can't leave it here."

"We can sort that out and get it back to the yard."

"The car?

"Like I said, it will all be taken care of."

"Can I get our belongings from the boat?"

"No, sorry. They need to stay there, for the moment." He beckoned to the other PC, who briskly walked over.

"Hello, I'm PC Mary Adams. Let's get you to the car. If you would like to follow me . . ."

Tina followed her down the sandy path in silence. Two hundred yards and to the right, the wooden stairs climbed the side of the incline. She counted the steps as she made her way up. At the top was a small car park with about ten cars that were scattered in different spaces. The police vehicle and a van with a logo on the side sat near the entrance.

The PC opened the door of the vehicle. Tina felt a hand on the top of her head as she ducked into the back. She'd seen it done in crime dramas, and now felt like a criminal herself. In a sense, she was. She pushed it from her mind and buried it deep down. She kept quiet for the rest of the journey, not wanting to engage in conversation. Instead, she closed her eyes, thinking about the baby and the decisions she'd make soon enough.

\*\*\*

**H**IDDEN in his car in a corner of the car park, Ray replayed the video he'd taken while sipping a Coke. The images he saw were burned deep into his mind.

"You definitely held him under!"

He tapped his fingers on the can's side. The panda car passing by disturbed him and he shrunk in his seat. Ray caught a glimpse of

Tina looking down at something he couldn't see.

"Phew!"

He adjusted his position and crunched the can, throwing it into the foot well. He could follow the car and take the evidence to the police station to have the snobby bitch done for murder.

*Or . . .*

Ray drummed his fingers on the dash. He could earn something out of this, he decided. Clive was a flash git with plenty of money. By demanding a part of it from Tina, he'd be able to live comfortably. She wouldn't want anyone to know about what she'd done. Grinning, he started the vehicle's engine and drove away.

# CHAPTER 20

**D**EEGAN spoke into his radio and requested two more officers to assist with the situation at hand. One would be sent from the Boston Constabulary and would pay a visit to Len Blythe, who would be told about his son's death. This was the downside of their job, but someone had to do it. The other would arrive soon. He would have him look into things with the boat yard and car. In the meantime, he would do a sweep of the boat.

Jan McCloud and Nathen Jones were processing the scene. Both were in their late forties and had been on the job for over ten years.

Deegan squatted down and watched Nathen examine the body. "Hi, Nathen. What we got?"

Nathen grinned. "How are you today? The baby still keeping you awake?"

"Every night. I can't remember when I had a full night's sleep," he said, popping a mint into his mouth.

"It gets no easier when they get older."

"Thanks, I have that to look forward to. So what we got?"

"Well, he's not been dead long, but I would say within the last hour or so. He has a nasty gash on his temple about two inches long. The water washed the blood away, but you can see the cut. Look."

Pondweed clung to the victim's hair and twigs stuck to his colourless face. The temple wound had closed and was barely visible to an untrained eye. The cuttings from the cleared weeds floated near the water's edge. Clive's fingers had raked the debris from the surface, causing clumps to form around his hands. His flesh was tinged blue and he felt ice cold.

"What a waste. Poor fella," Deegan said, shaking his head with dismay.

"Always is."

"Did that kill him? The wife did say the boat pushed him along. Could he have been unconscious, but then drowned?"

"I wouldn't want to commit myself, but he could have haemorrhaged inside his skull. We'll know more when he's on the slab, but it does look like a tragic accident."

Deegan tipped his head to the side and looked at the body. "He looks asleep."

"That's because the critters haven't had a nibble yet. He is fresh and rigor hasn't set in either."

"You do have a way with words. May I have a look onboard? There are a few things I want to check out."

"Of course. Jan is on there now."

"Thanks." He rose and walked to the edge of the boat. It moved beneath his foot as he stepped onto the deck. "Hi, Jan. How are things with you?"

"We have to stop meeting like this," Jan quipped. "It's always at a grim scene. How are you, Mark?"

"Not so bad, thanks. Find anything?"

"Very clean, by all accounts. Had he been drinking? There is a faint smell of beer and a bottle top in the bin, but no bottle."

Deegan looked around. "Yes, the wife said he had a beer, but knocked it over."

"That accounts for that. Apart from the dirty coffee cups, there's not much else. Unless anything looks suspicious, then we can gut the boat, but I think we're done here." Jan snapped off the latex gloves.

Deegan sighed. "Poor woman just lost her husband."

"Tragic, isn't it? There was one thing, but it's probably nothing."

"Go on." Deegan rubbed a hand over his lower back and then stretched.

"He's barefoot. No sign of any footwear, only a pair of trainers in his holdall."

"Interesting."

"That's what I thought. No wonder he slipped and fell. No damp footmarks on the carpet either, but they could have dried, though."

He glanced at his surroundings once more. "Thanks, Jan. How are the wedding preparations coming along?" he asked, more out of politeness than genuine interest.

"The honeymoon is sorted."

"Anywhere nice?"

"Norfolk Broads, on a narrow boat." Jan raised an eyebrow and grinned.

"I didn't know you were into boats. Very nice. Don't forget our invite."

Deegan then cut her short. As nice as she was, she could talk forever about her wedding. He had a job to do. The time for pleasantries was now over.

"Was the husband a competent boatman?"

Deegan smiled at Jan's ability to jump from one conversation to the other, confusing everyone but herself. "According to his wife, he was. His dad owns the boat."

"Maybe he got complacent. You see it all the time on the roads with motorists."

"I think so, too. Can we get him bagged up and sent to the mortuary now?"

Jan nodded. Deegan turned, ready to leave the crime scene.

"Thanks, Jan."

"You're welcome."

Deegan cupped a hand over his brow to shield his eyes from the sudden glare. The breeze dried the moisture on his neck. A scuffle behind him made him look over his shoulder. Jan had tripped over her own feet. She recovered and now skipped to catch up.

"We can move him now, Nathen," Jan shouted.

Nathen nodded and waved a hand at her in acknowledgment.

"No problem. I'll fetch the stretcher."

Several minutes later, Deegan watched them manoeuvre the body out of the water and onto the PVC bag. They rolled him left, then right, pulling the bag over Clive's floppy limbs, tucking in his arms and zipping it up.

"Can I help you lift him?"

"It's okay. We got it, thanks," Nathen said.

On the count of three, they lifted each end and placed the morbid cargo onto the trolley. The wheels became hard to push on the dirt path's uneven surface.

"How are we going to manage the steps?" Jan asked, briskly walking alongside.

"We may have to carry him to the top. One on each end and one in the middle. There's not that many steps."

Deegan trailed behind them, speaking into his radio. In the car park, they slid the body bag into the back of their van. All three were out of breath with the effort of lugging him to the top. A police officer pulled up just as they closed the vehicle's back doors. Jan and Nathen said their goodbyes and drove away.

"Afternoon, Smith. Great timing," Deegan said. "What took you so long?"

"Sorry, I had another call. What would you like me to do?"

Deegan brought him up-to-date on everything and then said, "I want you to go to the boat yard. Find out if they can get someone to move the boat into its moorings. We may need to examine it, but we can't leave it here." Deegan popped another mint into his mouth and sucked on it. "Then, we'll take the couple's car back to King's Lynn. They should know which car it is at the Waterways Club. They're familiar with the couple and the owner."

Speaking in hushed tones, they walked back down to the canal.

# CHAPTER 21

**T**EATIME arrived at six o'clock. Len and Joyce eased themselves into their kitchen chairs, slurping their teas and eating Pilchard sandwiches, their usual fare on a Saturday. Len was about to raise the fishy snack to his lips when the doorbell rang.

"Who the hell is that this time of day?"

"I don't know, Ducky," Joyce said, halfway through her third triangle.

"Bloody inconvenient." He plonked his sandwich on the plate and stood. "Won't be a moment, Nelly."

He squeezed her shoulders as he walked past. His weight shifted from side to side as he walked on bandy legs to the door.

"Good afternoon. I'm PC Benet from the Lincolnshire Constabulary." He flashed his identification wallet. "May I come in, sir?"

Len's eyes narrowed as he glanced at the officer's ID. "What's this about? We're in the middle of our tea."

"It may be best if I come in." Len moved aside and let him enter. "Down the hall to the end room." He gestured and then followed behind the officer, shaking his head.

"Who is it?

"It's the boys in blue, Nelly."

Joyce's head peeked around the edge of the kitchen door as they neared the living room. "Hello. You look very smart. Doesn't he look smart?" she asked.

"Thank you. Madam, if you'd like to come through, that would be very helpful." Benet purposely hung back to let them lead the way.

"Yes, he does. Now get yourself in there." Len clapped his hands behind her back for motivation.

"Slow coach, I am. It's my thyroid, you see."

Panting, she waddled into the room. Joyce leaned on anything that could take her weight until she reached her chair. She flopped down onto it with no thought to the poor upholstery. Benet remained standing and cleared his throat. In these situations, it was best to offer the bad news with the family members sitting.

"What can we do for you?" Len asked. "It better be worth it. My tea is getting cold. It was a fresh pot, you know."

"Your son . . . His name is Clive Blythe, and he lives at . . ." He rattled off the address and swallowed hard, pausing before he carried on.

"Yes. What's he done?" Len sat on the edge of his seat.

Joyce looked up at Benet with puffy eyes and tongued bits of food from her teeth. "Is he alright?"

"I'm afraid he's had a tragic accident."

"It's that bloody car. How many times I have told him it's too powerful!?"

"Is my son okay? He's not hurt, is he?" Joyce's eye's darted between the two. "Tragic . . . He said tragic."

"Of course, he is, Nelly. He's had a prang, that's all."

"It happened on your boat, sir. I'm afraid your son is dead."

*** 

**TINA** avoided any attempt Adams made to make conversation. She caught the PC glancing in the rear-view mirror a couple of times. Averting her gaze, she pretended that she was asleep in the back of the car. She wanted to get things over with so she could go home and hide behind closed doors.

Adams assured her they only had ten minutes before they arrived at the station. Tina didn't need the reassurance, however, as the familiar sights already loomed in the distance. She thanked her, nonetheless, and closed her eyes once more.

Doing so gave her time to think. It wouldn't be easy from now on. Once his parents found out, they'd make things even more difficult for her. She never expected things to be easy, though. Clive's unfortunate death was the best thing that could have happened to the vile pig. She'd handle the in-laws when the time came. She had no choice.

Feeling lost and alone, she picked at the blanket sprawled across her legs. Her hair had started to dry, the long strands tucked behind her ears. Her body heat and the blower in the car had also helped to dry her clothes.

Tears filled her eyes. She let them fall. Tina wanted everyone to know how he'd bullied, raped, and mentally abused her during their two years of marriage. Yet, she knew she couldn't tell a soul.

She wrapped her arms around her shoulders, imagining her mother's hug, offering her the support she needed to carry on. In her mind, this was the closest she'd get to someone telling her everything would be all right. The hardest decision was one she still had to make, one that would scar her for the rest of her life.

Could she selfishly abort the baby, all to have a better life and a fresh start? Adoption was out of the question. How could she cope knowing someone else had her child, never being able to nurture him or her as she should have from the beginning?

Thinking about the negatives made her decision easier. The child was a part of Clive and could turn out to be just like him. Even with a good upbringing, she'd be reminded of her husband each and every day if it looked like him.

The in-laws would also take over. It meant she could never sever the ties needed to be absent from them for good. James would miss having a nephew. He'd always been playful with his friend's kids. Then, there was her mother. She couldn't go there at the moment. The endless fighting with her left her feeling too distraught and exhausted.

"Miss, we're here," Adams said, pulling into the station's car park.

Tina opened her eyes and climbed out of the vehicle, leaving the blanket on the backseat. She watched Adams swipe the security card across the panel near the double doors and the inner doors opened. Halfway down the corridor, Adams stopped at a door and pushed its long silver handle down, leading Tina into a small room.

"Take a seat. I'll be with you shortly. Can I get you a cup of tea?"

Tina nodded and pulled out a chair from under the table.

"Sugar?"

Tina looked up and gave her a wan smile. "No, thank you. Just white, please."

The room was dull in decor, all browns and beiges. She glanced about for a window, yearning for a bit of fresh air. It was small and too high up the wall. Fiddling with her fingers, she plucked at her nails.

*How long does it take to make a cup of tea?*

Growing impatient, she checked her wristwatch. Fifteen minutes had gone by. *Is that all?* It felt like an hour. Tina looked up as she heard the door's handle turn.

"Sorry to keep you." Adams placed a white cup and saucer beside Tina. "I brought you a couple of biscuits." Two Rich tea biscuits lay nearby.

"Thanks."

Parched, Tina took a hefty gulp. The strong hot liquid soothed her scratchy throat.

"Okay, I need a written statement from you today." Adams sat down opposite her and put the paperwork on the table with her biro poised at the ready. "Tell me how it happened from the beginning. Then I need you to sign it." Tina's look of bewilderment caught Adams' attention. "It's okay. Take your time. No rush."

Taking a deep breath, Tina recalled the events. She rigidly stuck to her story while Adams scribbled it down.

"Okay, I just need to get this typed up. It shouldn't be long."

Alone again within the depressing room, Tina sighed. The chill in the air sent a shiver down her spine. She got up to stretch her legs and placed a hand over the heater. It was cool to her touch. Tina returned to her seat and finished off the tea and biscuits before resting her head on her forearms. Her mind soon went blank.

Forty-five minutes later, Adams returned. "Sorry to keep you waiting."

"I expected it to take longer," Tina said, and sat up.

"I rushed it through. You've been through an ordeal and sitting around here can't be helping." Adams took her seat once more. "Now, if you could sign it and read the declaration at the bottom." She slid the report across to Tina, a pen lying on the top of it.

Tears welled in her eyes as she stared at the table. Tina bit down on her lower lip as a droplet escaped. It ran down her cheek and dripped onto the form. The moisture smudged the signature.

Adams nodded with approval. "Okay, that's great."

"Can I go home now?" Tina asked, her cheeks stained with tears.

"Soon."

Tina sniffled and nodded. "When can I bury my husband?"

"After the post-mortem, if all goes well. They usually release the body to the family as quickly as possible." Adams tilted her head and looked at Tina, sympathy shining in the depths of her eyes.

A soft sob broke through Tina's lips. "My life will never be the same."

Adams reached out to clasp her hand, patting it with understanding. "I know it must be very hard for you. The coroner needs to establish the cause of death."

"He drowned." Tina slid her hand free and fiddled with the corner of her sleeve.

"I'm sure he did, but it's procedure."

"That's what the other officer told me," Tina said, trying to stifle the sudden rise of hysteria. "Will they . . . Will they ring? I . . . I don't know how these things work. Help me figure it out, please. I don't know what to do!"

Heavy sobs rose from the pit of her stomach as she thought about what was to come. Tina prayed that things would turn out okay somehow. She wasn't sure if she could cope with more disappointments. Taking a moment to compose herself, she wiped her eyes with the edge of her cuff.

"I'm sorry. As soon as the coroner . . ." Adams paused to choose the right words. "After they release the body, the family can view . . . They can pay their final respects before the funeral."

Tina swallowed past the lump in her throat. "I . . . I want to go home now." She blew her nose on the hankie she'd tucked within her sleeve.

"It won't be long now. Come with me. You can sit in the waiting area."

She followed Adams out of the small room. The waiting room was a lot brighter, and even had a plant sitting on a windowsill. Tina sat down to wait and stared at the floor. Ten minutes later, she found herself sitting in the back of the car on her way home.

Adams manoeuvred the vehicle into Tina's driveway. She then accompanied Tina to the front door.

"We will be in touch. Is there someone I can call for you?" she asked.

"No, thank you. I'll be fine."

"You shouldn't be alone at a time like this."

"I can call my mum," she said. It was the first name to pop into her head.

Tina watched Adams walk back to the car and drive away. She leant back against the closed door and inhaled, deep and slow. Clive would never cross the home's threshold ever again. Exhaling, she headed inside, eager to take a much needed shower.

\*\*\*

"**DEAD?** How can he be dead? He's young and fit!" Len said, now standing. "This can't be right. There must be some mistake."

"There's no mistake, sir," Benet said. "He slipped and fell from your narrow boat this afternoon."

Joyce covered her mouth, rocking back and forth in her chair. "My boy, my poor boy! It can't be true, can it?"

"How did it happen?" Len asked as he moved to Joyce's side and wrapped his arms around her, hugging her tight.

"I only know the basics, at the moment, until we get a full report. We'll keep you informed." Benet swallowed hard. To see the poor mother who'd lost her son filled him with sadness. "I'm very sorry for your loss."

"It was her, that dizzy wife of his. She's wound him up again," Joyce said, pulling a hankie from her sleeve and blotting her eyes. "It's her again, up to her old tricks." A high-pitched wail left her throat.

"How long before we find out what's going on?" Len mimicked his wife and dabbed his eyes.

"Why would it be his wife's fault?" Benet asked, scrawling several notes into the pad he'd been holding.

"Because she's always having a go at him. Her and her stupid tantrums!"

"Now, come on, Nelly. We don't know all the facts," Len said.

"Is there anyone I can call for you both?"

Benet shuffled from foot to foot. The radio crackled. Ignoring it, he carried on.

"No, thank you. Can we see him?" Len asked.

"Not at the moment. I'm afraid there will be a post-mortem done on the body."

"They only do that for murder, don't they? I'm not having my son cut up." Len tensed. "I won't allow it."

Joyce's hysterical screech echoed the room. "Cut up, cut up, my boy cut up!"

"I'm sorry, sir. That's the procedure. You will be kept up-to-date, however."

"Where did this happen, and how? My boat! It will need collecting." Len reached for his wife's hand.

"That will be taken care of. As soon as we have the report, another policeman will come and see you." He slid a card out of his pocket and passed it to Len. "This has some numbers on it. You can contact us anytime."

"Thank you."

"I will see myself out." Benet turned and headed for the door.

He put his arm around her shoulder again. "Sorry, my love."

"We've lost another one. My precious boy has gone! Do you think it was her?" Joyce sighed.

A determined look spread across his face. "I don't know, but I'm going to find out."

# CHAPTER 22

**A**BOVE the sound of the shower, Tina heard the phone ring. Whoever it was could wait. All she wanted to do was rest and prepare herself for another emotional day tomorrow. Satisfied that the grime had washed away, she changed into her nightwear and looked at the double bed. There was no way she could sleep in that tonight. It would need fresh sheets to rid them of his smell. Instead, she pulled a blanket and pillow from the airing cupboard, took them downstairs, and spread them across the sofa.

The phone rang again. She wondered if it could be the police. Perhaps she should answer it. After all, people would want to know what had happened. Yet Tina couldn't be bothered to engage in chitchat about the how's and why's, and wanted to be left alone. She would ring them back in the morning.

Climbing in, she shuffled down and then curled her legs up to her chest before covering her head with the blanket. Every muscle in her body ached. She was hungry, but couldn't eat. The smell of food repulsed her and brought on the nausea. Even a drink turned her stomach.

The tick of the wall clock broke the silence. She tried to drift off to sleep. The phone, however, began to ring again. The persistent ringing drove her mad. She covered her ears, trying to drown out the sound.

"Go away!" she shouted aloud.

Clive had never set the answer phone on their modern landline, preferring to get any calls diverted to his mobile. She wished he had.

*It will stop in a minute,* she thought. And it did, only to ring again a few minutes later.

It was no good. The call needed answering, so she flung back the blanket and made her way to the hall. She glanced at the caller ID and hesitated for a moment before lifting the receiver.

*Damn, I forgot about him.*

"Where the hell are you both? I've been waiting here for hours. Both mobiles keep going to the answer machine. I only rung you at home on the off chance."

Tina bristled. "Hello, Ray."

"What are you doing at home? Clive should be at the pub. Where is he?"

"There's been an accident. I can't talk to you at the moment." Tina hoped the subtle hint would be enough to get the dick off the phone.

"What accident?"

"He slipped and fell from the boat this afternoon." She kept her answerers blunt and to the point.

"Is he alright? Shall I wait or come back? It's a two hours drive from here."

Tina rubbed the bridge of her nose between a thumb and forefinger. "He's dead."

"Dead? You're kidding me! How did that happen?"

"I can't talk right now. I need to be alone."

Tina put the phone down. No doubt, he would ring again. She left it off the hook, unwilling to put up with anymore phone calls.

\*\*\*

**R**AY hung up and smiled to himself. His phone call had unsettled her. Tina was in for a surprise. He couldn't wait to see the look on her face once things were said and done.

*This is going to be fun,* he thought.

He ordered another Fosters, and took the pint outside. Lighting a cigarette, he thought about what had yet to come.

\*\*\*

**B**ACK on the sofa, Tina's mind raced. She despised Ray and never knew much about him. He was a troublemaker, however, and was indirectly responsible for her shoulder wound. He'd seen her in town leaving a private house on her day off when she should have been at home.

Ray had tittle-tattled the news to Clive, saying he'd seen his wife exiting an unfamiliar door and that perhaps she was having an affair. Tina couldn't tell him where she'd been. He would never know, anyway. Clive was at work, and when he'd arrived home, he was pleasant and in an amicable mood.

The next day, however, was different. She couldn't believe he'd let the matter percolate a whole day before confronting her. She arrived home from work to find Clive putting up shelves in the living room. As she walked through the lounge to say hello, he'd held her up against the wall by the throat and forced the information out of her.

For four months, she went to her counsellor for an hour on her day off. Not once, did he ever suspect where she was. Tina always covered her tracks and made up the time when she got home.

Mrs. Armitage had helped her overcome some deep-rooted issues from her childhood. She made her realise it wasn't her fault that she had abandonment issues or insecurities. She'd called it primary attachment disorder, and it's something you learn when you're a child. After all, you look up to your parents and learn from them.

Tina could now make sense of that part of her life, and blamed her past for subconsciously marrying a man like Clive who had similar traits to her father. After all, she learned it was a normal part of growing up being beaten and abused. She'd even come to terms with the bullying, though she'd hated going to school and coming home. The youths would wait outside of the school gates, a whole gang of them, most days. They never stopped beating her until she cried, even capturing her in the toilets and repeating the whole process again, day after day.

*Sticks and stones may break my bones, and the horrible names did hurt me.*

She couldn't concentrate on exams or learning. When she got home, her mother would dismiss the black eye and bloodied lip. Her dad, depending on what mood he was in, would either sympathise, or add to the beating. Mrs. Armitage had encouraged her to get an education and filled her with hope and promise, a genuine person close to her heart she would never forget.

He'd laughed when she told him. It was then that it happened. She'd turned her back on Clive and stuck up for herself, calling him a vile pig. He lunged at her while holding a screwdriver, plunging it into her shoulder. She'd never seen so much blood. It had hit the bone and made her shriek out in pain.

The wound was deep. All Clive said afterwards was, "Clean yourself up and stop dripping on the carpet."

With that, she'd cleaned the wound over the bathroom sink, and remembered waiting ages for the blood to stop. She'd put on gauze and used surgical tape to keep it in place. The next day, she'd bought Steri-Strips from Boots and applied them to the area.

It had throbbed for over a week. Even now, the tissue damage was so substantial that she could no longer feel anything around the outside of the wound. Her shoulder and the scar were still sore, and it ached most nights. This happened eight weeks ago, and it still tortured her mind.

Tina pushed herself to her feet and headed into the kitchen. Her throat felt dry. She filled a glass with water and took a sip. She needed someone to talk to, a comforting cuddle, a few words of encouragement, but she felt alone and sorry for herself.

For the next few hours, she tossed and turned, unable to get a restful sleep. Maybe a hot drink would help. She padded back into the kitchen. The clock above the cooker said 9:00 pm. As she waited for the kettle, she pulled the milk from the fridge and smelt it. Clive had always bought full fat, and the creamy texture clung to the top of the bottle's rim. It made her stomach flip. She put it back and made herself a black tea instead.

Reaching into the cupboard for the Typhoo, the mint tea bags tumbled onto the work surface. She shoved them toward the back out of sight. Coffee was out of the question, and she no longer fancied a tea. She settled for another glass of water, and took it to the table, sitting down with her head propped on her hand. Twisting the bottom of the glass with the other, she stared at the wood.

Oblivious to her surroundings, Tina didn't hear her mobile phone ring. She felt dazed and so out of it. She could hear a shrill sound in the background, but her selective hearing chose to ignore it. The ringing grew louder. Startled, she picked it up and answered.

"Hello."

"Hi there. This is Sergeant Deegan. Are you okay, Mrs. Blythe?"

"I'm fine."

"I tried to ring your home number, but I couldn't get through."

"It's off the hook. I wanted some rest."

"Your husband's body is now at the Queen Elizabeth Hospital's mortuary."

"Thanks." Tina swallowed. "It was such a tragic accident. I'm not sure what to do now."

"You've had a terrible shock. We're sorry for your loss. We have informed your father-in-law."

Tina tensed. She now had the wrath of Len to contend with.

"Thank you again for all your help."

"If there is anything you need help with, or any questions at all, please don't hesitate to contact us. Bye now."

Tina replaced the handset onto its cradle. She then turned off her mobile and returned to the sofa, hoping to get some much needed sleep.

# CHAPTER 23

**T**HE sound of someone hammering on the front door brought Tina out of a comfortable sleep. She rubbed her eyes and put on her slippers and gown. The time was now 8:30 am.

*Who could it be at this time on a Sunday morning?* she wondered.

The shadow through the glass in the top part of the front door gave her a clue. Not ready for this conversation, she paused for a moment before taking a deep breath and opening the door. Len barged inside and stormed down the hall toward the living room.

"Why didn't you tell us what happened? You could have rang yesterday!" Len shouted. "I tried to ring. I had to leave a distraught Nelly to come here."

"Come in," Tina said under her breath.

She pushed the door closed and then dawdled behind Len. The scent of sweaty armpits invaded her nostrils. She pinched her nose to keep the smell at bay.

"I want to know everything. My son is dead and I need to know why." He sat down on the nearest chair.

"I lost my husband, too, but I am bearing up. Thanks for asking."

"This isn't about you. We've just lost our son. Nelly is hysterical at home. She won't eat."

*It will do her good then, the guzzling heifer.*

She stared at Len. "It was an accident," she said, her voice barely a whisper.

"How did it happen? Tell me, now!" He slapped the arm of the chair.

"It was raining. He walked down the side of the boat to get the canvas, and he slipped and banged his head."

"How the hell could he slip?"

"It all happened so fast. Please, do we have to talk about it now?" She wrapped her gown tighter around her waist.

"Yes, we do. We have things we need to discuss and arrangements to make."

"Let me get dressed first. I didn't sleep well."

Len snorted with disdain and rolled his eyes at her. "Hurry up, then. Do you have coffee?"

"Yes, top cupboard."

"'I'll make it while you get changed. Then, I want answers."

She watched him head for the kitchen from her perch at the bottom of the stairs. Tina hurriedly dressed, realising that he was being a little domineering again. Clive was dead now and she no longer had to follow rules or take orders from anyone. She decided to annoy him by taking a shower and dressing in her own time.

"How long are you going to be?" he roared. "Faffing about up there?"

Tina peered down at him from the top of the stairs. Len stood with one hand on his hip, the other resting on the banister.

"There, you are! In the kitchen, now!"

Len could make a good pot of coffee. The rich ground beans left a sweet smell around the house. She sipped the murky sludge, the first proper drink she'd drunk since coming home from the police station. Even the clotty cream that was on the neck of the milk bottle didn't bother her.

Len took a chair next to her, scratching his ear and then drumming his fingers across the table. "Now, tell me what you did to my son."

"I did nothing. Why would you say that?"

He stared at her. "You were always winding him up and getting him stressed."

"That's not fair. I've lost my husband and friend." She took a long gulp of her coffee and put the cup on the table. "I know you're shocked, Len." Tina reached out and rubbed his arm. "And you want answers, but so do I."

"He was competent and knew what he was doing." Len simmered down and took the offer of comfort.

"Maybe, he wasn't as good as you thought he was."

"What do you mean?" His voice rose several octaves.

"When we got to the yard, he refused to be shown anything by the boatman. In fact, he swore at him." Tina wasn't sure she should have told him that, but it was the truth and not incriminating at all. "At one point, he crossed over to the wrong side and nearly collided with another cruiser."

"You're lying." Len smacked the table with his fist.

She flinched. Len's eyes bored into hers, reminding her so much of Clive.

"Ask the man. When he fell, he was wearing flip-flops, not deck shoes." Lifting the cup to her mouth, she said, "So you see, it was an accident."

How long could she keep up this façade, when all she wanted was someone to care about her for a change? How many more faces would she need to use before all this was over?

"We're going to see his body tomorrow afternoon and you're coming with us," Len said, pouring himself a third cup from the cafetière.

"We can't see him. Not until the body is released."

"He is my boy, and I will see him when I want."

"You can't. You have to wait. Didn't the police tell you that when they came to tell you the bad news?"

"Yes, he did, but I shall do what I want."

"Please, calm down. Let them do their job. Then, you can see him." She sympathised with him, wanting to keep him calm, afraid of another outburst.

"Well, when we can, you're coming."

"I can't come. Sorry, it's too soon." She swallowed hard.

"Oh, yes, you are. Nelly needs the support, and it's best you're with her."

The nausea returned. This time, it wasn't morning sickness. As if she needed, reminding what he looked like, the imprint would always be there. She scrunched her toes inside her slippers.

A light of suspicion danced in his eyes. "I get the impression you don't want to go. "Why?"

"It's been such an ordeal for me. I need time to grieve and come to terms with what has happened."

"You're coming. Now, about the funeral arrangements."

"Do we have to go through this now? He only died yesterday."

"Yes, we do. Lots of things to organise, and I want the best for my boy." He gulped, his eyes filling with tears.

Tina looked away. She felt no remorse for this sad little man, and that fact shocked her.

"He's . . . going in with Nellie's . . . grandparents. We talked it about it last night."

*Why can't he call her Joyce? Stupid pet name!*

"Buried?"

"Yes, that's what he would have wanted. We want to plan it all. After all, he's our only son."

*Put him in a wicker basket and burn the rotten flesh from his carcass. I could scatter the evil ashy remains over stinging nettles.*

"Pardon?" Tina looked up, now back in the world of Len.

"We want to plan his funeral. He's our only son."

"Everything? I can't have a say about anything?"

"No, he is our boy, and we want to do it."

Under normal circumstances, this would be unacceptable. Who gave the right for the parents to take over? She was Clive's wife, after all. However, this was the best outcome she could have wished for. Besides, how do you plan a funeral for a man you hate? All she had to do on the day of the burial was to act like a distraught wife overcome with grief.

"Wouldn't cremation be better for the environment?"

"No son of mine is going leave the world that way." Len stood. "Sod the environment. He will be buried, and that's my final word."

"Whatever you think is best. Thank you for taking that stress away from me. I really couldn't face it."

"I will be in touch. Must go now and get back to Nelly."

Tina saw him to the door. "Please, send my love to Joyce. I really am sorry for her loss."

"It's a double whammy for us. We will never have the chance to hold a grandchild in our arms. We lost our first child, too." Len wiped his eyes.

"I know, and I'm sorry. My only wish would have been to have a child sooner," she said.

"Maybe, if you hadn't been so self-centred, you could have. No chance now, is there?"

"No, none at all."

Len walked down the path and gave her a backward half-wave, unable to turn to face her.

*That didn't go as bad as I first thought.*

Back inside, she dropped onto the armchair and glanced around the room. She would sell the house in due course. For now, she could grow to like it. The contents she loathed, and the bane of her life was gone, but apart from that, it had loads of potential.

Fantasizing about the possibility of the decor, she moved into each room with excitement. She would use vibrant colours. The bedroom furniture would be bright and airy. The spare room would make a lovely nursery.

*Where did that come from?* She pushed the thought from her mind.

Her paintings would hang nicely in her lounge. She could fill the surfaces with tasteful knick-knacks and make it homely. A bookshelf would spread across one wall, filled with her favourite books and signed first editions. She would have an office, too.

In the meantime, the first thing she would do was buy new

bedding and towels. The old ones would go to a charity shop along with his things. She'd shop this afternoon and pick up something for dinner.

A knock at the door brought her back from her mental bliss. Her mood dropped and reality struck. She opened the door to find an officer standing in front of her.

"Hello," she said, and peeked over his shoulder.

"Hi there, Mrs. Blythe."

"You've brought the car back!"

The hairs on her neck stood on end. It sat in the driveway with a police car parked behind it. Deegan sat at the wheel.

"We have, along with your personal belongings." He passed her the bags and the keys. "The boat is now back at the yard. We will be in touch if we need anything."

"Thank you. That was quick. I didn't expect them until after his release. You have all been so wonderful."

"You're welcome, and please accept my condolences."

She nodded. He turned and headed for the car. Deegan gave her a 'sorry for your loss' expression. The vehicle reversed, and they soon drove away.

There was no way she was going to sort through the luggage now. She tossed it against the wall in the hall, ready to dump it later. Everything could wait, for the time being.

Right now, she needed a little retail therapy. More importantly, another night on the sofa and her back would ache. Gathering her purse and keys, she headed out into the fresh air. Walking past the Audi, she decided to sell that, too, and replace it with a small town car. She'd always liked the idea of a Mini, just like the ones in the film, *The Italian Job*.

# CHAPTER 24

**T**HE stroll back from town was pleasant. As Tina turned onto her street, Mrs. Conerly's curtain twitched and Edith waved. With her hands full, she nodded in acknowledgment, wondering if the rumours had circulated and reached her neighbours' ears.

She halted at the mouth of her drive. *What's he doing here?*

Maybe she could double back and enter her property through the back entrance. That way, he'd get bored and leave. Sadly, it was too late. Ray had caught sight of her. All she needed this afternoon was this idiot turning up at her door.

"Hi! I thought I'd come and see how you are doing. Very sad business, you know."

She was halfway down the path when he thrust a bunch of blooms into her lapel.

"Sorry, can I help you with those bags?"

"What are you doing here?"

Pushing her way past him, she made it to the front door. She slid both bags into her left hand and then pushed the key into the lock. He'd squeezed in front of her and held the door open, waving his blooms about as if he'd invented the concept of giving.

"Let me help you."

"No, thanks. I can manage. What are you doing here, Ray?"

"I wanted to see how you were coping. Is there anything I can do to help?"

Without invitation, he waltzed down the hall. She followed in his

173

wake, bristling with annoyance.

"Err, do come in. Don't mind me."

"Where shall I put these?"

The way he waved them about like a flag unsettled her. She pointed to the side.

"I don't need your help. I want to be left alone, please."

He gestured to the kettle. "I'll make a drink. We can sit and talk."

"None for me, thanks. Talk about what?" She plonked the bags down on the worktop and then folded her arms about her chest.

"He was my best friend and work colleague. I would have come last night, but by the time I got back from Wroxham, it was too late."

"I know, Ray. I'm upset about everything, too. The only way for me to deal with it right now is to not talk about it."

"The boss needed to be told. I rang him this morning."

"You shouldn't have told him. It was down to me to tell him. How dare you go behind my back!"

"I thought it would help. Stop griping."

"Why didn't he ring me after you told him?"

"He did, and got no answer." Ray smirked.

Dubious of his reply, she bit her lip. All morning, she'd been in and wasn't out shopping long.

"You rang him on a Sunday?"

"Yep, he was at home. Like that, we are." He crossed his fingers in front of her face.

"I need to sit down. It's all too much for me."

"Go through to the lounge, and I will make a cuppa."

Tina did as she was told, more out of necessity than anything else. Playing along would aid his departure. She rehearsed what she would say to him within her mind, keeping the important details to herself, not that it was a secret. She just didn't want to give him the satisfaction of knowing everything. He and Clive might have been best friends, but it was one-sided, with Ray always standing in the background. She doubted whether Clive even cared for his mate.

A pang of guilt stabbed at her heart. She needed to contact Sam. Tina needed her now more than any other time in her life.

"Here we are. Get that down you."

"I didn't want one," she said, taking the drink from him.

The outside of the mug burnt her fingertips, so she went to place it on a coaster. Steam infused with mint escaped and drifted upward, the smell so intense it brought back bad memories. The mug slipped through her fingers. Some of the contents sloshed onto the coffee table and floor before she caught it. The liquid scalded the back of her hand and she wiped it on her trousers.

"Alright."

"Why did you make me this?"

"It was the first teabag that came to hand. It's your favourite, isn't it?"

Doubt crossed her mind. *They were at the back of the cupboard. I should know. I put them there.*

"How did you know that?" She twisted in her seat.

"Clive told me. Anyway, tell me what happened."

There were four other chairs in the room, yet he made himself comfortable beside her. She shuffled further up the settee. Ray followed suit.

"Sorry, but you need to give me some space."

"It's okay. I'm here for you."

Relaying events from the previous day brought tears to her eyes. She forced them back down.

"It was an accident. He slipped and fell."

"How did he slip and fall?"

"What difference does it make? He's dead."

"Well, he fell into water and could swim, so something must have killed him."

"He banged his head, okay?"

"Didn't you try to help?"

She tried to keep the uneasiness from her voice and said, "Of course, I did."

"How did you help him?"

Confused by the barrage of questions and the lack of mental preparation, it made her feel uncomfortable.

"Can we not talk about this now?" she asked, and tugged at the collar of her jumper to let the cold air dry her neck.

"Are you hot? You look flustered."

"So would you be, if you had been through this ordeal." She leant forward, resting her elbows on her knees.

"I find it strange that he could fall, knock his head, and die."

"Well, he did. We were in the middle of a storm, and Clive slipped from the side because he wore the wrong shoes."

"Did you jump in and help him?"

"Yes."

*Damn, why did I say that?*

"What happened to the boat, then? It must have drifted."

"I moored first and jumped into the water. He was too heavy to pull out, so I rang the emergency services." Her body shuddered. She hoped Ray hadn't noticed. "Please, can we stop talking about this now? It's too upsetting."

"It helps to get it off your chest. I'm here as a friend to help."

She doubted that. He wanted something to tell the lads at work in the morning. His cologne was the same as Clive's, and invaded her nostrils as he edged closer and stroked her back. She took his offer of comfort.

"It must be very upsetting for you. If you need me, I'm here." His thumb traced the outline of her bra.

Looking him in the eye, she said, "Everything will be taken care of," and shrugged his arm away.

"Anything I can do, just ask," he replied, replacing his palm and rubbing his leg against hers.

"Get off me!"

Unnerved by his persistence, she felt scared. Part of her wanted to push him away and smack him in the mouth. Experience and instinct had taught her to take what was coming. As she battled with her conscience, his right hand crept up her thigh.

"How is Maggie?" she asked, brushing it away.

"She's fine, but I'm more interested in you."

His left hand moved up to her chest and groped her breasts. He whispered several words into her ear.

"What are you doing? Stop it!"

"Come on! You know you want me. You make me so horny."

Repulsed by his inappropriate behaviour, she jumped from the seat and stood near the door. The thought of being molested by him made her cringe.

"Clive is dead, and you're trying to get it on with me. He was your best mate!"

"Yes, he was. Doesn't mean I can't have a go with you."

"How can you come here and be like this? I've just lost my husband. Have you no compassion?"

She raised her voice and then lowered it, in case Ray got forceful. As much as she knew Ray, to her knowledge, he'd never been a violent man. After Clive, she found it hard to trust again.

"Grief is a funny thing," Ray said, and stood, facing her.

Tina took a step back. "Get out of my house!"

"It's Clive house, not yours."

"Just leave and get out!"

"Not yet. I haven't finished."

His eyes looked wild as he headed toward her. Pinned against the wall, she felt weak and hopeless. She could make a run for it or fight back, but her limbs refused to move. Her hips stung as he gripped her hard, grinding his arousal against the top of her thighs and stomach.

"Stop it!" With every ounce of strength she could gather from her unwilling body, she pushed him away.

"Clive said you were a frigid cow. He could never understand it. After all, you were a prick tease when you were younger," Ray blurted out.

"I beg your pardon?" She choked out the words. "You know

177

nothing about me."

"Oh, yes, I do. Clive told me everything. You were quite the harlot, going off with strange men. He never liked that."

Refusing to cry, she said, "He had no right to tell you those things about me."

Now someone else knew the intermittent details of her damaged past, the very horrors she strived to leave behind.

*I am no longer ashamed of my life. I am strong, and I can do this.*

Silence filled the room before she spoke once more. "I'm . . . not ready for anything. Please, let me get over my husband's death in peace."

"I have to go, anyway. I will see you at the funeral."

"We don't have a date yet. Len's sorting it out." She swallowed hard.

"I know. Len told me," he said, leaning in for a kiss.

Tina clamped her lips tight.

"Oh, come on! One little kiss won't hurt."

Tina relented, eager to get rid of him. His rough hands scratched her cheeks as he cupped her face. His slimy tongue felt like a slug had invaded her mouth and penetrated deep in her throat. He tasted of sour bread dough. She pulled away, holding onto the contents of her stomach.

He left in a hurry and without a goodbye. After hearing the door click, she ran into the downstairs loo and dry heaved over the toilet. Once done, she rinsed her mouth, getting rid of any trace of saliva the letch may have left behind.

***

**C**URLED up on the sofa, she sobbed and played the recent events back in her head. Would she always be a victim? Her counsellor once said a sexual predator senses when a person has been abused. That was true. How dare he think that just because of past events, it allowed him to try it on? Damaged goods, so they must be desperate for attention, which was also true. After all, as a victim, you learned it must be normal, thus making you an easy target for other sexual predators.

*Always the victim. Never the survivor.*

Hopelessness swept through her, no longer able to take part in what was left of her life. She could jump from the tallest building and no one would care. In fact, it would do the world a favour.

Drying her eyes, she took a deep breath. She wouldn't succumb to the depression that clouded her judgment. Nor would she let the bastards win. Tina could do this.

The mantra worked and her inner strength began to flow. It started at her feet and threaded its way up to her brain. Her survival instinct, a seed she planted there herself after teenage boys cornered her behind some garages in her northeast home and did despicable things to her. She'd been six years old during a time when your parents let you play outside all day to give them some space.

Self-pity turned to anger. She stormed through to the kitchen, and threw both mugs into the sink. They broke into pieces. Tina never liked the pattern on them anyway.

Ray's flowers sat on the side. The fragrance reminded her of the blooms Clive had bought. Reaching for them, she slammed them into the sink and snapped the bunch in half, tossing them into the bin. Tina felt so much better.

After putting away the few bits of shopping, she stretched under the sink for a bin liner. She grabbed the scissors from the utensil drawer and made her way upstairs, taking the new bedding with her.

In the bedroom, she cut up the middle of the old duvet. As anger bubbled over, she ripped it to shreds, letting out a growl at the same time. The pillowcases were next to take her wrath followed by the bottom sheet. All in tatters, she filled the bag and tied a knot at the top before throwing the bag to the bottom of the stairs. It landed next to their belongings, which would remain unpacked. She then simmered down and remade the bed with crisp, clean bedding. It was deep purple, her favourite colour, which made her feel even better.

With a lot to contend with, she didn't know where to start. The first thing would be to refuel, as she hadn't eaten for a while. Tina hurried downstairs and walked into the kitchen, eager for a bit of sustenance.

Piercing the film and removing the packaging, she popped a tuna and pasta bake into the microwave. She turned the dial and then poured herself a juice. The bake started to fill the kitchen with fishy aromas. The scent made her salivate. She took the plastic container out and didn't bother to scoop it onto a plate. Delicately teasing it away from the sides with her fork, she played with the pasta. The phone rang as she was about to take the first mouthful.

"Now what!?"

She put her fork down, pushed the dish away, and headed toward the annoying shrill.

"Hello."

"Selfish, you are. When were you going to tell me? I had to hear it from Joyce. All day, you've had to ring. How dare you keep the news from me?"

# CHAPTER 25

**FOUR** inches away from her ear, and Tina could still hear the whiny voice offending her inner drum. When a pause came, she placed the receiver to her ear.

"Mother!"

"Don't take that tone with me, young lady."

She felt like a child at primary school after having backchatted the teacher for the first time. Sensing there was more to come, she remained quiet.

"Well, what supposedly happened? What did you do this time? It's disgraceful. You should have told me. Are you listening to me?"

"Oh, Mum!" She broke down and wept.

"I'm mum, now, am I? Now you want something. That poor man! What did you do to him?"

"I don't want anything. I just need some . . . support. I feel lost and empty." She was ready to open her heart. A small cry for help aimed at her mother, who was always too blind to see it. "I need you. Mum."

"You brought it on yourself, as usual, and will get no sympathy from me. It's him I feel for and his parents."

"I lost my husband. How is it my fault he had an accident? I'm so churned up inside." She sniffed and wiped her nose on her sleeve.

"Knowing you, you probably killed him like you killed your father."

"Don't be ridiculous! What an awful thing to say." She heard her mother sniffle and veered the conversation in another direction.

181

Incapable of taking any more emotional conflicts today, she asked, "Are you coming to the viewing when it's time?"

"With my arthritis, I doubt it. I would rather remember him as the kind man he was. Always had time for me, he did. Anyway, it's miles away."

Taking a deep breath, Tina counted to ten. If her mother knew what Clive really thought about her, it would wipe away her condescending and delusional manner.

"It's an hour away, not miles."

"I shall be at the funeral when the time comes. James will be there. Joyce will let me know the dates."

"Are you taking your medication for your arthritis?"

She softened. Where the caring side of her nature came from, she had no idea. Despite their fragile relationship, she hated seeing her mother in pain and discomfort.

"No, no, don't you dare start to care now. You want something, and it's not coming from me."

"All I ever wanted was a loving mum. Anything else means nothing to me." Tears coursed down her face and her bottom lip trembled.

"You should have thought about that before you started with the accusations about your father."

"Do we have to talk about that? I need you, Mum."

"I will never forgive you. Ever."

The line went dead. Deflated and alone, she sat at the kitchen table and stared at the cold pasta dish before binning it. Was it her fault that her father liked little girls and did things he shouldn't?

Thinking back to when she was younger and her dad sent a cold shiver up her spine. She rubbed the top of her arms to generate heat. When she misbehaved, he'd smash what personal things she had into smithereens as punishment. Whilst her other friends were having fun, she would be carrying heavy shopping back from town. He would slap her around the face and head because she forgot to clean the bathroom, while James and her mother sat back and did nothing. Not once, did her brother come forward and defend his baby sister.

Driving the thoughts to the back of her mind, she unplugged her mobile phone and sat in a comfortable chair in the living room. The screen lit up and it jangled to life. Waiting a few seconds, she tapped a number and waited.

"Hey, you! How are you, honey? Did you organise that surprise break? How did that go?" Sam asked.

Music played in the background. Sam's husband, Lee, sung along, though his voice sounded faint.

"Have I caught you at a bad time? Should I ring back later?" Tina asked.

"You're fine. You sound down. Are you okay?

"No, not really."

The sound of her cheerful voice brought more tears to her eyes. Sam was the best part of her life. They went to school together and were more like sisters than friends.

"I'm not sure how to say this, but Clive is dead."

There was silence on the other end. She heard Sam telling Lee to turn the music down.

"Sorry, I blurted it out. I had to let you know."

"Oh, no! How did it happen?" A long pause came before Tina heard her talk again. "I'm so sorry. I don't know what to say."

Tina tried to speak, but nothing came out.

"Are you still there?"

"Yeah."

"Do you want me to come round?"

"I think I'll just go to bed and get some rest."

"What about tomorrow?"

"Late afternoon would be best for me. I shall tell you then," Tina said in a raspy voice, rubbing her temples with the thumb and finger of her free hand.

"I'm here for you, always. Are you going to be okay on your own?"

"I'll be fine. Thank you."

"I have to go. Daddy's just arrived. See you tomorrow. Hugs."

Tina hung up. She put her phone on her lap and sobbed, not because she lost her husband, but because she'd deceived her best friend.

She loved Sam because she had a great perception of people, and would never ask how or why until offered. It was a gift she'd been given, amongst other things. The thought of her visit gave Tina the strength to get through another harrowing day. She could never tell Sam about the planned murder, or about the opportunity that presented itself.

There was also no point in mentioning her pregnancy. How could she tell her best friend about the abortion? Although given the full details of its conception she'd understand, but it was selfish and unfair because Sam miscarried two years ago and had never tried again since. What type of person would mention that? She'd keep it to herself and suffer the guilt alone. She rubbed her hands over her face in an attempt to freshen her mind. Her appetite had faded and all she wanted was a glass of water.

With the front and back doors bolted, and all curtains drawn, she felt safe and secure. It was now dusk and the table lamps dimly lit each room. It reflected her mood.

Opening the web browser whilst sitting comfortably in front of the screen, a blue hue filled the living room and gave off a pacifying shimmer. She never used the computer much, always afraid Clive would look at her history, or tell her off for pressing the wrong button or something pathetic like that. Even in incognito mode, she wasn't convinced that people couldn't access your history.

Everything she'd been through, and this was the worst task. Typing in abortion clinics into Google, a pang of guilt etched up her stomach. She fancied the Norfolk clinic she found a while back, but had forgotten the number. There was no harm in looking at the others first. It gave her a better insight as to what to expect.

NHS abortion clinics and procedures now filled the screen. Scrolling down the text, she read the information given. Referral by a

GP and one other doctor was essential in the first instance. She scrolled a little further and didn't like the sound of, 'waiting lists for the procedure after an initial consultation,' or the risk of bumping into anyone who treated her. She didn't want to travel too far either. She couldn't risk it.

Changing her search, she typed, Private Abortion Clinics Norfolk, into the search bar and hit enter. She found the one she'd liked earlier. She retrieved a pad from the kitchen, took a large swig of water and wiped her mouth, and returned to the screen, ready to take notes.

Private clinics were faster, unbiased, and very confidential. Tina wrote the number down first. She needed to book an initial consultation, and at that point, they offered a counsellor. She scribbled without looking at the paper. The next thing would be a time frame and pricing. Hovering the mouse over the relevant link, she saw that it could be done a week after the first appointment.

*That's quick.*

For the first consultation, the cost would be £60-£80. Tina scratched her head. If she wanted it done over a weekend, it was an extra £80. However, that wouldn't be necessary. Depending on what procedure she decided upon and how far into the pregnancy, it would cost £400-£600. Payment was given up front, or they did a payment plan.

She wouldn't need a payment plan. Paying up front worked best for her. The best part was that unless she agreed, they wouldn't divulge the information to family members or GP. No one would ever know. Nevertheless, she still had to live with the decision on top of everything else. She would ring first thing in the morning along with her boss. There was no way she could go into work tomorrow.

A little weight lifted from her shoulders made all the difference. She felt stronger and a little hungry. Her stomach grumbled, so she made herself a snack. Hot buttered white toast and jam and a builders' brew was more like it.

Wiping her mouth with a sheet of kitchen towel, she put the

plate and mug on the side. After a somewhat emotional day, she showered and had an early night, needing any energy reserves to get through the next couple of weeks.

***

**P**ARKED three doors down, Ray sat in his car. Ever since his visit earlier, he'd watched for Tina's comings and goings, but there were none.

"You've closed all of your curtains. Time for me to go." He spoke aloud, whilst starting the engine. "I'm keeping an eye you, Tina Blythe!"

# CHAPTER 26

**W**ASHED and dressed, Tina was ready for a new week. She was due to start work at 10:00 am today, so she needed to ring her boss soon. First, she would eat breakfast and ease into the morning. It gave her more time to think before she rang the clinic. As to whether it was the right thing to do, she had no idea, and it left her feeling perplexed. After three cups of coffee, the caffeine sharpened her thinking and she could compartmentalise the emotion from reality.

*Okay. Let's do this.*

Fifteen minutes passed before she got off the phone. Her heart fluttered and her hands shook the whole way through. The nice person on the other end made her relax and only asked the basic questions. All other details, they'd ask at her appointment, the receptionist had added. She was booked in for Wednesday at 11:00 am, and was surprised at how quickly she'd be seen.

*The quicker, the better. It can only be a good thing.*

She wrote the phone number down in her diary. The rest of the information remained locked away in her memory.

The earpiece on her handset was still warm. No way was she going to use her mobile when she had free calls on her landline. Dialling the office number, Linda answered. The staff had nicknamed her, Philly, after Philadelphia cheese, and she looked like the blonde-haired person with a squeaky voice in the advert.

"Could you put me through to Mr. Manning's office, please?"

"Who shall I say is calling today?"

"It's Tina Blythe."

"One moment, just connecting you."

She waited while Philly put her through. Any longer, and she would engage in idle chitchat.

"Hello, Tina. It's Mr. Manning here."

"Hi. I won't be in to work today."

"You could have told Linda on reception. There was no need to come through to me. Is everything okay?"

There was no easy way to say this, so she blurted it out. "I wanted to speak to you. I won't be coming back. I'm leaving."

"May I ask why? What's brought this on?"

"My husband died two days ago in a boating accident, and I . . . feel like I need to take some time off."

"Take as long as you need, but don't resign. You're a conscientious member of our team. I'm sorry to hear about your husband. If there is anything I can do to help, please ask."

Tina knew his offer was genuine, and he meant every word. He was one of the best bosses she'd worked for. Firm, but fair.

"Thank you, but I can't work at the moment. I should hand in my notice, but—"

"Please don't think of that, at the moment. Concentrate on yourself. You must feel awful. I know how close you were."

"Thank you for your concern." All she wanted to do was to get off the phone and forget the place ever existed. "I just need to be alone."

"Well, your job is always open here if you want to come back."

"Goodbye, Mr. Manning."

She cut him off, before he asked too many questions. It would be halfway round the office by lunchtime as it is.

A twinge of excitement made her smile. She was now unemployed and had made the decision for herself. Money had never been an issue in their relationship. Although Clive gave her a pitons for housekeeping and controlled their finances, she'd put a small amount away each month.

It didn't matter anymore. The healthy life insurance policy, the car, and the house would all be hers. Not even the family could influence that. She was his wife and it would go to her, unless he hadn't made a will. Tina knew he had. He'd always said he was far too young to make one, but Len being Len insisted. It would make starting her new life easier. It was never about the money, but a small compensation for putting up with him.

Nobody else rang all day. She assumed there was no news, as Len, nor the police, had made contact. Mind you, things were still in their early days.

***

**I**T was nearing 6:00 pm when the tap on the door came. Tina jumped up and looked out the window. Excitement rippled through her as she welcomed Sam inside. She held an armful of flowers and her burgundy bag had slipped down her shoulder.

"These are for you."

Tina relieved her of the blooms and said, "Thank you." She sniffed the red roses wrapped in red floral paper with a ribbon tied into a bow. "Beautiful." She arranged the ten thorny stems into another vase. "They're my favourite."

"I thought you would like them. Got you these, too."

Sam placed the dry white wine and the Thornton's soft centres on the worktop. Tina burst into tears, her shoulders shaking as she tried to hold in the sorrow.

"Sorry." She yanked a tissue from the box on the side.

"It's understandable. Come here." She gestured with her hands.

"Oh, Sam! I'm so pleased you're here."

Tina flung her arms around her neck and kissed her on the cheek. She felt Sam's warm hands stroke her back. The perfume Tina had bought her lingered on the collar of her work suit. As Sam pulled away, her hair clung to Tina's moist nose. Sam cupped her face and rubbed her cheeks with her thumbs, then smoothed her hair.

"I'm so sorry." She looked Tina in the eye. "Is there anything I can do?"

Tina shook her head. "On top of everything else, my mother was a bitch to me." She began to cry again. "Clive's parents treat me like dirt, and Ray came on to me." Sniffing once more, she wiped her nose. "I don't know how much more I can take."

"Oh, sweetheart, you go in the living room, and I'll bring you a drink. What would you like?

"Something stronger than caffeine."

Tina eyed the wine as she pulled out another tissue and walked into the lounge. She heard a clink coming from the kitchen. Two seconds later, Sam entered with the bottle, two glasses, and the chocolates in hand. Sam poured the wine and handed her a glass.

"Thanks."

"I'm here for you, if you want to talk about it."

Sam sat down next to her. Holding the glass by its stem, Tina downed it, the contents sliding down her throat and warming her tonsils.

"Refill?"

She nodded, squinting at the same time.

"It doesn't taste that bad, does it?"

"Not at all. It's a nice drop."

"You must have needed that."

"I did. Sorry about that little outburst."

"It's awful for you. I feel so guilty not seeing you for a while."

"It was my choice. I just couldn't—" Tina grew quiet. Not eating much and drinking the wine too quickly had absorbed into her stomach lining and hit her system fast. "I just wanted tonight to be how they used to be."

"We had some laughs, didn't we?" Sam placed an arm around her shoulder. "Was it an accident, or health issues that made him pass away?"

"It was on the surprise trip. He slipped and fell from Len's narrow boat. Can we not discuss it? I've been over the same things with so many people. I'm exhausted mentally."

Tina nestled her head in the crook of Sam's armpit.

"I'm here whenever you feel you want to talk about it." Sam rubbed her shoulder and said, "You could do without those negative people in your life. I don't know Ray that well. Do you want me to go and box his ears for you?"

Tina sat up and smiled.

"Thought that would cheer you up. Where does he live?"

Sam grinned and made a boxing motion with her fists. That's what Tina loved about Sam. There was never any pressure from her. Not like her brother, James, who always came across as dictatorial and nagged her to the point of rebellion. Or inconsiderate family members that barked at her, and nosy work colleges who liked the latest gossip.

Smart and funny, Sam had a wonderful way about her. Granted, she had the best of upbringings, and her parents were supportive and encouraging. She could have worked part-time for a large pay packet at her dad's gallery in London, but chose not to. Instead, she strived for her independence. Tina found it refreshing. She had seen it so many times in families where the children grew up expecting and wanting in their own world of self-obsession. Sam was level-headed and down-to-earth, putting others before herself. Tina admired that.

"One day, I'll tell you, I promise, when everything is sorted."

Sam reached for the bottle and offered her more wine.

"No, thank you. I feel a little woozy." She placed her glass on the table. "You have been so good to me over the years. I couldn't ask for a better friend."

"Now I know you've had too much to drink. You're getting sloppy on me." Sam laughed. "I could say the same about you. You were a rock for me a few years ago."

Tina smiled. "Let's make a start on those chocolates."

"I thought you'd never ask. They're yours, so you open them and have first pick." Sam passed her the box. "I bet I know which one you'll choose."

Tina waved them under Sam's nose, teasing her senses with the sweet smell before putting the box down on the table. She made her choice and popped it into her mouth. It tasted divine as the liquid centre coated her teeth.

"Let me guess, hazelnut caramel." Sam tittered and chose an orange crème.

"Enough about me. How are things with you? How's the family?" Tina asked, taking another chocolate.

"Mummy and Daddy are fine. They're off to Spain in a week."

Tina cringed as the words grated. Another pang of resentment came from out of nowhere. She squashed it down, using the technique her counsellor had taught her. It didn't always work, but this time, it locked itself away.

"This will cheer you up," Sam said. She fingered through the compartments of her bag and found what she was looking for. "This is for you."

Careful with her sticky fingers, Tina wiped her hands on her trousers before taking the square photograph and laid it on her right palm. It was black and white. The variation of the grey colours mingled together. Darker around the outside, brighter in the middle, she could almost make out what she was looking at.

"You're not . . ." Tina's eyes filled with tears.

"I am, or should I say, we are."

"I never thought you and Lee would try again. Ever." Genuinely pleased, Tina hugged and kissed Sam, holding back her own pang of guilt.

"You're the only person who knows, apart from Lee and the doctor, who is keeping a close eye on me."

"My lips are sealed shut." Tina gestured by zipping her mouth. "How far gone are you?"

"Ten weeks. I can't risk telling anyone, not until I've passed the critical stage. I'm scared, though. What if it happens again?"

"I hope not. You deserve this after all you've been through." She held Sam's hand across her lap, and bounced it up and down. "It's going to go full-term this time, you'll see. Do you know the sex yet?"

"No, although Lee thinks it's a boy. I keep telling him it's an arm." She pointed to the grainy picture."

"Oh, yes, I see it. I see what he means." Tina laughed.

"Not you as well!" Sam soon joined in the laughter. "I don't mind what it is, as long it goes well." She crossed her fingers in front of her face.

"We would love for you to be the godmother at the christening. I know I'm thinking too far ahead, but I need to keep positive."

Tina thumbed a tear. "I would be honoured." She passed the photo back to Sam.

"Thank you. You can keep it. I had two done."

Tina gave her watery smile and put it on the table.

"Could I ask when the funeral is? Sorry to blurt it out, but it's just I need to arrange the time off."

"Not sure. We're waiting for the release of the . . . body." Tina's lip quivered.

"I'm so sorry. I never meant to upset you. Come here."

Tina took a breath and sat up straight, holding both of Sam's hands on her lap. "I need to discuss something with you."

"Of course, I'm listening."

"I have my reasons, so please don't think this strange." Tina paused for a moment while she worked out how best to approach the subject. "I would rather you didn't come to the funeral."

"What? I was going to offer support, as I know you won't get much from the family."

Tina saw the frown spreading across her face. "I would prefer to go through it by myself." She stroked Sam's hands with her thumbs. "You see, all of those people that are going to be there are the ones I want out of my life. After the funeral, I never want to see them again." She paused once more. "I want you to be a big part of my new life without being contaminated by them."

Tina wasn't sure if she explained herself properly. What she meant was so hard to describe.

"I understand and I will abide by your decision. I've known you a long time. There is something I need to make you aware of."

Tina pulled her hands out of Sam's soft hold, dreading what was coming next.

"I'm not stupid. I've seen a change in you. I know the horrid things you went through as a child. I thought when you met Clive that it would be a turning point in your life." Sam took a deep breath and then said, "That day you texted me and asked me to cover for you . . . That was a lame excuse." Sam smiled. "He never liked you seeing me, did he? I'm betting he hit you, too."

"How could you tell?"

"Little things, like the bruises on your arms. The one you have on your nose that's now fading. The way he spoke to me on the only two occasions I met him."

"I see." Tina was shocked by the way her dearest friend knew all of this.

"When you used to come around to see me, you were always anxious and watching the clock. No sooner would you arrive, would you make excuses to leave."

"That obvious?"

"Only to me. His accident wasn't your fault. He was an arrogant, selfish man, and whatever happened, he brought it on himself. I wish you'd told me."

"I couldn't. You do understand that, right?"

"Yes, I do. And the way your family has treated you is diabolical."

"What I told you about them is all true. Every word. Please swear you won't tell a soul."

"Promise, but you know I won't say a word. You've done nothing wrong at all, my love." Sam stroked her face again.

"There is something else I need to ask you." Tina took a moment to compose herself.

"All ears!"

"I won't be able to see you for a while. I need to get everything out of the way and sorted in my new life before we meet up again," Tina said. "I know it sounds a bit strange."

"Not at all. I couldn't talk about my . . . well, you know, for months. I just wanted to be on my own, and I avoided coming into contact with people who meant well but didn't understand."

"Thank you for being so understanding. It won't be long, I promise."

"I better go. Lee gets home in an hour. We're meeting up for dinner at his mum's."

Tina showed her to the door. "Thanks again. You made my day."

"It's okay. Remember, I'm only a call away. Don't leave it too long."

They embraced, taking comfort in the moment they shared between them.

"Do you remember that friendship thing we used to do as kids?" Sam asked.

"Yes, I do. Shall we?"

"Is it silly? We're grown up now."

"No, it's not. Shall we?"

They raised their right hand and locked their pinkie fingers together. In unison, they repeated the phrase they made up during their teen years.

"Friends, always and forever."

Tears filled both their eyes as they kissed each others cheeks.

"Take care," Sam said.

"You too."

Tina waved at her as she made her way to the car. Upon driving off, Sam pecked her palm and blew in her direction. Tina reciprocated the gesture and then made her way inside.

Any positive energy she'd felt followed Sam out the door, and the house returned to its cold, depressive state. Tina needed a drink. The buzz from the wine faded, bringing her back to sobriety. Heading into the living room, the bottle was half-full and inviting, so she filled her glass with another.

The chocolates beckoned. She shoved two in her mouth at a time until she scoffed the lot, guzzling more wine to wash them down. Not since childhood had Tina eaten for comfort. Now, it seemed like a good idea. She wouldn't go to bed until the chocolates and wine were all gone, knowing the alcohol would aid her sleep.

Picking up the photo, tears formed as she held it to her heart. She had the whole day tomorrow to prepare herself for her appointment on Wednesday, yet she was so pleased with Sam's news. Feeling guilty, she poured the last drops of wine into her glass, finishing the bottle.

On unsteady legs, she made her way up the stairs, slowly taking each one. She set the photo down on the bedside table, unable to work out which way up it went. Tina climbed into her bed and was soon dead to the world.

# CHAPTER 27

THIRTY minutes before her appointment at the clinic filled Tina with dread. She paused on the doorstep and sighed. The Audi was the next challenge. She could have taken a taxi or bus, but she had to drive it sometime. Squeezing the key fob, orange lights blinked twice. As she climbed into the car, the scent Clive had left behind filled her nostrils. She'd come prepared with a body spray, squirting it liberally around herself.

Tina adjusted the seat and mirrors and made herself comfortable. Although the car was immaculate inside, she checked all of the compartments. His pile of CDs and a few odds and sods lay in the glove box. Gathering them up, she left the car and dumped them in the large black bin tucked at the side of the house before returning to the vehicle.

She could picture him, tapping along to the music as his hand bounced up and down on his knee. Tina dug through her bag for her cleansing wipes and cleaned the dashboard and the steering wheel, and any other place he may have touched. She then started the engine and drove away.

Stuck behind a lorry on the last part of the journey, and seconds away from the right turn, she felt apprehensive and guilt ripped at her heart. Thinking of Sam made her chin quiver. The pain her poor friend had gone through made her feel a little ill about the fact that she was aborting the child she carried. Some people were desperate to have children, yet she knew she couldn't keep the baby. She'd be frowned upon and judged because of her decision, but it was for the best.

Making the turn, she looked for a parking space in the small, but well-laid out, car park. Since it was mid-morning, there were plenty of spaces to choose from. She turned the bulky Audi into one with cars on either side close to the entrance. Tina locked the car and took a moment to compose herself, captivated by the building she was about to enter.

Pale lavish stonework stood out against the red brick. Ornate lion heads sat on pillars at the bottom of the steps. Baskets filled with green foliage hung on black metal brackets. The architecture was beautiful. Tina wondered about the building's history as she climbed the two sets of concrete steps. Anything to distract her from the oncoming consultation was welcome.

At the top, she hitched up her shoulder bag and folded her arms. The two doors hummed as they opened automatically. Never had she seen glass look so shiny that it was almost invisible.

The foyer looked like a posh hotel. A vase of lilies rested at the end of the highly polished reception desk. To her left were several unmarked double doors, and to the right, a waiting area. They had leather seats with a small coffee table in the middle with more flowers on top of it and the addition of magazines that looked new. This was unlike the NHS, who had odd-sized chairs, some of them plastic, with wheeled chairs that could only be pulled backwards, and well-thumbed ancient magazines. Even the coffee smelled expensive and there was no smell of overcooked cabbage that was commonplace in NHS kitchens. Under different circumstances, she'd be impressed by the plush surroundings, considering that it was a hospital.

*Unnecessary expenses. You certainly got what you paid for.*

A woman, not much older than herself, popped her head up from behind the desk. "Good morning. Can I help you?"

"Yes. I have an appointment with—"

"It's okay I can find it on here. What's your name, please?"

"Tina . . . Blythe."

"Take a seat in the waiting area. The nurse will call you shortly."

"Thank you."

Tina sat on the edge of the leather chair, resting her elbows on her knees and staring at the floor. The seating area was carpeted, and the remainder of the floor sleek and highly buffed. She waited for only a few minutes before they called her name and a slender middle-aged nurse led the way.

"Please, come in and take a seat."

The nurse held the door open, and Tina walked inside the room.

"Okay." She shuffled through some paperwork. "I just want to run through some details with you to make sure everything is correct. Then, I shall go through what will happen today."

Tina nodded and answered the mundane questions—date of birth, address, current age—waiting anxiously for what was to come.

"Now, this is what will happen today. We need to check how far along you are. We will also do a scan, a pregnancy test, and then you will see the consultant."

Tina's way of dealing with this situation was to see the baby as a thing rather than a forming life. The word pregnancy was far too real for her to handle. She stiffened, annoyed by the woman's patronising tone, which made her feel inadequate as she read the information like a well-rehearsed script.

"I'm going to take some bloods. This may scratch, but it will be over in a jiff."

The tourniquet tightened around the top of her arm and she wiggled her fingers. The needle slid into her vein. She flinched, watching the blood drain into the vials.

"There, all done. Press hard for me."

She held the cotton ball in place, while the nurse stuck labels on the relevant bag before sealing it and placing it in a plastic tray.

"Are you okay with plasters?"

Tina nodded and let the nurse put a brown patch on her arm. She pulled her sleeve back down and waited.

"I won't be a minute. I'll get this processed, and then we'll do your scan."

She left with the tray in hand. Tina took the time to glance around the large room. On the far side sat a metal framed bed, its mattress covered in white paper with a pillow on one end. Next to it were a few gadgets and machines. On the desk, she saw a computer and printer. The air smelt floral with a hint of disinfectant. A red bottle of alcohol rub sat near the tap of the small sink.

The door opened several minutes later.

"Okay, that's done," the nurse said. "Now, could you lie on the bed for me and pull your trousers down just below your tummy?"

She did as instructed while the nurse set up the scan and got everything ready.

"This will be cold."

Tina saw the nurse look at the fading yellow bruises on her stomach as she squirted the clear jelly, though she made no comment.

"This won't take long. You can look the other way if you don't want to see the screen."

The scanning implement glided over her skin. She faced the wall, not wanting to see the images. Curiosity and guilt got the better of her, however, and she tilted her head to look at the monitor. The image was grainy and grey. Her eyes filled with tears and she put a hand over her mouth.

The nurse gave her a compassionate smile and said, "It's okay. All done now." She wiped the excess fluid from her stomach with a tissue and tinkered with the equipment. "Pop your trousers back up and take a seat for me."

Tina nodded, her face full of pain, and wiped her eyes.

"You may want to consider going to our counsellor. We recommend that for any patients going through similar procedures."

"I don't need one," Tina said, her voice barely a whisper.

"It's a very traumatic event in your life. It can affect—"

"I have one already."

"Please, bear in mind that ours are specially trained in these areas."

Tina tilted her head in acknowledgment, cuddling her bag on her lap.

"If you would like to return to the waiting area, the consultant will call you through."

She needed air. The picture she'd seen on the screen tormented her. Her left calf shook, making her bag jump on her knee. Tina clasped it firmly as she stared at the scuff mark on the tip of one of her flat shoes. Not long after she'd sat down, a male voice called her name. He gestured her through a set of double doors and into his room.

"Please, take a seat."

He was tall and lanky, and wore a suit underneath his sterile coat. Taking a chair near his desk, she put her bag on the floor.

"I'm Mr. Cane. I shall be going through some things with you. Is that okay?" He looked at her over the top of the spectacles balanced on his nose.

She nodded.

"I shall ask a few questions, and then go through the procedures with you. What to expect, the recovery time, how long it takes, that kind of thing."

Tina slid her hand in her pocket and pulled out a tissue.

"What do you like to be called?"

"Tina."

"Now then, Tina, have you been to see your GP?" His hand was poised at the ready over his patient's notes.

"No. Your website said I could keep it confidential." She shifted in her seat.

"That's right, but only in exceptional circumstances. That's what I need to determine."

"Is rape exceptional enough for you?" she asked, feeling on the defensive.

"I know how hard this must be for you, but we do need to do this." He patted the open file on his desk.

"Does your husband know? Have you discussed it with him?"

"He is dead. I was raped and now I need to rid my body of this evil inside me." She wiped a tear. "No one is to know."

"Here, have a clean one." He passed her a box of tissues. "That's perfectly understandable. You're six weeks pregnant. So you're under the recommended fifteen weeks, which is good. It should be a straightforward procedure."

Blowing her nose, she looked at him. "Do you think I want to do this? It's the hardest decision I've ever had to make."

"Of course not. We're here to help. I assure you it will all be done in the strictest of confidence."

"Thank you."

"We have a procedure called, vacuum aspiration. We give the patient a local injection near the entrance of the womb, and—"

"Please, I don't want to know." It sounded awful, but she could take no more. "I just need to know how long it takes, when can I go home, and aftercare." Dabbing her eyes, she said, "Just do what you have to do."

"It takes ten to fifteen minutes. As soon as the local anaesthetic has worn off, and your pain is managed, you can go home in a couple of hours," Cane replied. "There are risks with any procedure, however."

Tina listened while he went through the risks and aftercare. He informed her that she would need a follow-up appointment in a few weeks. Unless there were any complications, she had no intention of turning up. He offered the following Wednesday at mid-morning for the procedure. She agreed to it.

Cane then requested that she go to reception and fill in the necessary financial forms. It was all so matter-of-fact and clinical, and she liked it that way. Handing over her payment details, Tina eyed the main doors, desperate to finally exit the building.

"Okay, that's all done for you."

"Thanks." Tina put the card and papers back into her purse.

"Bye, bye now. See you soon," the receptionist said.

She nodded at her and headed for the door. Outside, she inhaled and let the air cleanse her lungs. Going through this again in a week's time filled her with despair. Once it was over, it was another piece of the jigsaw filled in. When complete, her new life would emerge.

Trotting down the steps, she hurried to the car. Another had parked next to the Audi. Of all the spaces in the parking area that were free, the occupant had chosen this spot. It reminded her of the summer when holidaymakers clustered together near the amenities, most not wanting to venture further along the beach.

A light breeze blew against the corner of a white envelope placed under the windscreen wiper. She removed it and examined both sides. It was plain with nothing written on the front and sealed. Tina scanned the other cars' windscreens. None of them had envelopes left behind on them.

*Odd*, she thought, and shrugged off the sudden uncertainty.

It was probably advertising. She'd seen it before with pizza menus and double-glazing firms. She climbed in and threw the envelope on the passenger seat before starting the engine. Before pulling away, she paused for a second, curious as to what the envelope might contain. She should just dump it into the bin, but the fact that no other car had an envelope on them niggled at the back of her mind.

*I may as well open it.*

Thumbing the corner, she tore the envelope and slid out a sheet of A5 paper. Her heart thumped as she read the first few lines. Putting her palms over her mouth, it slipped through her fingers and floated down onto her lap. Her body trembled and her throat grew dry. Tina sped out of the car park and drove home as fast as she could.

***

**R**AY watched Tina make the turn out of the clinic and onto the main road.

*Oh, good, you read my little gift.*

He let three cars pass before he pulled away from the kerb. Keeping himself out of sight, he followed her home. Once she was in her drive, he parked at the end of the street and stalked his prey until she entered her house. He then left and headed home.

*Not long now, Tina Blythe.*

# CHAPTER 28

**B**EHIND closed doors, Tina sat in the kitchen, feeling compelled to read the note again. Her hand shook as she glanced down at the paper. It was typed in bold black letters.

*Well, well, well, does the family know you're pregnant? I think they would have something to say about that, don't you? Maybe, I should tell them.*

*I think I'll leave it for now. You have more pressing matters do deal with, like how you're going to lie your way through the service with false tears.*

*Oh, didn't I tell you? I know about your little stunt down by the canal. Sorry, that should be, I saw your little stunt. In fact, I have some pictures to show you. Maybe another time, though. I will be in touch.*

There was no way anyone could have seen her down at the canal. She'd checked the area and hadn't seen a soul. Another thought occurred to her, however. They could only know about the clinic by following her.

*Could it be a sick prankster? How do they know me?*

What if they told the family about the baby, or more importantly, about the other incident? She could go to prison. Her brain was so bogged down, she couldn't think straight.

She wanted to rip the note to shreds, but thought better of it. It could be evidence. Evidence of what? she wondered. That she'd aided her husband's death and was aborting her baby? That would incriminate her even more. No, she would keep it for her own record. A rap on the door made her jump.

"For heaven's sake, what now!?" she said under her breath.

Fighting with the zipper on her bag, she hid the letter in her secret compartment. Another rap sounded at the door, this time a little louder, harder, and almost impatient. She hurried to answer it. Two police officers stood in the doorway. She tried to remember what the PC's name was. It was on the tip of her tongue, but it was no good. Her mind refused to recall it.

"Hello, Mrs. Blythe. I'm PC Adams. This is my colleague, PC Smith."

"Yes, I remember."

"May we come in?"

"Yes, of course."

She stepped aside and gestured them through to the lounge. Tina sat on the edge of the sofa, clasping her hands around her bouncing knee. They took a seat opposite her.

"We have some news about your husband."

Her heart thumped inside her chest and a lump formed in her throat. Good news or bad, she was ready.

After the count of three, she said, "You have? Can I bury my husband now?"

Adams cleared her throat, shifting uncomfortably in her seat. "Mr. Blythe's body has been released, and a death certificate issued. This means you now have a burial or cremation order."

"That was very quick. I expected it to take longer."

"It was a simple case. The coroners work quickly on cases like these."

"What was the cause of death?"

"Accidental drowning, and he did have a bleed in the brain. You can request a full report from the coroner's office if you want to."

"Could I have saved him if I was able to get him out the water?" She didn't want a report, but rather clarification on the matter to satisfy her curiosity.

"It's hard to say, but like I said, it will all be in the report."

"Thank you," Tina said, and began to cry.

"We have also informed Mr. Len Blythe."

"Thanks."

"Your husband will reside at the hospital mortuary and can be viewed in their chapel, if you wish."

Tina sniffled and wiped her eyes as she nodded.

"We shall see ourselves out."

She watched them through the window until their car pulled away. A sense of happiness and relief swept up and down her body, and left her feeling giddy. She'd done it! Clive was gone and she was free, but the feeling of elation was short-lived. There were still plenty of obstacles in her way. The letter was foremost on her mind.

What should she do? Wait and see if anything happens and ignore the letter? She knew she couldn't act upon it. Having no choice but to suppress that thought, she made herself a hot drink and deliberated over the black and white image on the screen at the clinic. This time next week, it would be over.

*Is that what I really want?*

No sooner had she digested the information, her mobile vibrated across the kitchen table. Glancing at the screen, she wondered how long it would be before he called. It was unusual for him to ring her on anything other than the landline. She could do without him today.

"Where have you been? I tried to ring earlier," Len snapped. "Gadding about, I suppose. The boy's been released. The coroner rang me."

"I know. The police have just informed me."

"Accidental drowning! How could he drown? The water is not that deep," Len said.

The sobs in the background pulled on her heartstrings. She never meant to cause the family so much pain, but Clive should have thought of that before he'd used his fists against her. Len was just as bad with his put-downs. She buried any thoughts of pity for them. They didn't deserve her sympathy.

"How is Joyce bearing up?"

"How'd you think?"

"There is no need to snap, Len. We're all upset."

"I'm arranging to view the body on Friday. Nelly wants to see his face one last time."

"I think that's a good idea. It will help you both."

"And you."

"Pardon?"

"It will help you in seeing him one last time before the funeral."

"Err, I'm not going. I can't face it."

Tina didn't need to see his face or body again. She already had that image burned into her head.

"You're coming because Nelly needs you."

"I am not!" she cried, raising her voice. Why should she do something she didn't want to do?

"I shall pick you up midday. You better be bloody ready. Don't you dare let the family down!"

"I—"

The line went dead. Tina sighed and shook her head. Something else to add to her emotional pile. She'd hoped to worm her way out of the viewing. Still, that was two days away. She'd worry about that when the time came. In the meantime, she'd get some rest.

# CHAPTER 29

**I**T was precisely midday Friday, and Tina ignored the knock at the door. Len was as punctual as ever. He must have returned to his car as the horn beeped from the drive. In no rush to head out to the viewing, she let him grow impatient. Gathering her thoughts and inhaling deeply, she released a pent-up breath through pursed lips.

*Okay, let's do this!*

She stepped outside and proceeded to his car. It took them four miles to reach the hospital. No one spoke along the way. Joyce sat in the front and spent the whole time dabbing her eyes with a grey hankie she'd pulled from her sleeve.

She watched each traffic light, hoping they would stay red, anything to delay this misery. Len turned into the car park, moaning about the lack of space and crappy drivers. He found a spot, several seconds later. It was then that reality struck and Tina felt uneasy. Soon, she would face her worst nightmare.

A cool breeze welcomed her upon exiting the stuffy car. The vehicle's suspension expressed relief as Joyce hauled herself out and Len waddled off to find a ticket machine. Tina leant against the back door with her arms folded as she waited for Len, hoping they would all enter together. Joyce had other ideas and made a tremendous effort to walk inside on her own.

She followed and said, "Don't you want to wait for Len?"

"Leave me alone, Duck."

The entrance to the Queen Elizabeth hospital was spacious, but busy. The smell of coffee and baguettes drifted from Costa's up ahead. To the left, The League of Friends shop stocked essentials for a stay on the ward. To the right, stood a reception desk manned by volunteers doing good deeds, and the double doors nearby said, Outpatients.

Joyce aimed for the nearest chair just inside the entrance next to a cash machine and multiple vendors. She sat next to her wheezing mother-in-law, willing Len to come through the automatic door to ease the uncomfortable silence. An elderly woman smiled as she searched for a spare chair. Tina gave up her seat. Upon doing so, she spotted Len and waved at him. He marched through the double doors, shaking his head.

"Bloody parking! They charge the earth. It's ridiculous. You should have waited, Nelly, my love."

Joyce shook her head and dabbed her eyes for the umpteenth time.

Len scoured the area. "We need to get you a wheelchair. From what I understand, the chapel is on the other side of the hospital."

Tina pointed to a row of entwined black chairs all lined up like shopping trolleys. "Over there."

"This is new." He fished a pound coin from his pocket and slipped the plastic coated chain through the loop, pulling one free.

Tina offered him her assistance, but he snapped at her, so she backed off.

"Get in, Nelly. I'll take you to see the boy."

Len held the chair steady as Joyce slid across. It rolled sideways because the brakes were off, then she couldn't get her feet on the rests. Tina had never seen such a palaver getting from one chair to the other. Once Joyce got comfortable, and Len regained control of the wobbly wheels, they made their way to the chapel. Following signs, but getting lost in the process, they eventually found the right place. Tina walked alongside the couple, and let them get on with it.

"We're a bit early," Len said.

He took a seat and pulled his wife up close and at an angle. She took the seat the left of Len. All they could do now was wait.

From past experience, Tina found that the Chapel of Rest had a distinctive odour. Once smelt, it embedded itself in the lining of your nose. Even now, every time she entered a florist's shop, the fragrance of chrysanthemums rekindled the memories. It was unbearable and evoked fears she'd hoped never to recall again.

She was sixteen when her father died. They'd brought him here to this chapel. In her younger days, she was fond of her dad and looked up to him. Any attention from him was welcome. The only memories left were riddled with hurt and disappointment. When his moods swung for the better, he could be affectionate and loving, but that didn't happen often.

A part of her still loved him. After all, a girl needed a dad. Months of counselling and maturity taught her different. He was wrong because of all he'd done. Even in death, she would never forgive what a treacherous human being he truly was.

"Mr. and Mrs. Blythe?" A rotund man standing in the doorway beckoned to the relevant room. "Would you like to come through?"

They looked up together and then at each other. Len shifted his position before he stood.

Tina touched his arm. "Please, Len, may I go in alone?"

"I think it's best that way." He pointed Joyce in the right direction and entered.

After they disappeared behind the door, she rested her head back and tried to relax. Tina thought about happy things, distracting her mind from what was to come. A loud shriek soon made her jump. She knew it was Joyce. Loud painful sobs sounded in the distance followed by breathy pauses as they came back out. Tina stroked Joyce's shoulder, offering her a bit of comfort. Joyce looked away and blanked her.

"He looks so peaceful, like he's asleep." Len blew his nose. "Poor Nelly! She can't take it anymore."

Tina stroked his arm, but Len pulled away.

"You can go in now."

"I . . . I don't think I can."

"Get in there and say goodbye properly. You will thank me in the end."

He used the exact words her mother had all those years ago. He was right. You never get that chance again, and it does help the grieving process. Tina didn't want to grieve. She just wanted to be free of this messed up family.

"We will see you at the car. Don't be long. Think of her." He glanced at his wife.

"Okay."

She tilted her head and looked at her feet. Len waited for her to enter. She knew he would. Tina took a deep breath and counted to three before she entered.

Preservatives and the scent of decay whipped together with a hint of flowers filled her nose. It was the only way Tina could describe the smell that triggered her past. Clive's body lay in the middle of the room. He rested on a silver trolley bed decorated with a crisp white sheet pulled to his shoulders. The faint residue of his Hugo Boss cologne snuck its way past the heavy smells of the embalming fluid.

Skirting the room with her arms folded across her chest, she circled the body twice. She could have pretended to see him and turned her back on him, leaving the room within a few minutes. No one would have known. Yet her curiosity was tinged with guilt, and duty pressured her to look his way. Tina took a step toward him, her eyes fixed on his face. An unbidden memory surfaced as she stared at her husband.

*Her father's stubbled grey beard used to tickle her young cheeks when she kissed him goodnight. She held his hand, though it seemed like forever. A dead body was the most unnatural thing to touch. Your eyes tell you the skin should be warm, but its ice cold instead.*

*A fly disappeared up his nose and crawled out from the corner of his mouth. It was a gruesome sight to see for someone so young. She kissed his pale blue lips*

*and stroked his black quiff back.*
    *Goodbye, Dad.*


Closing her eyes, Tina forced the apparition of her father away. She leant over and slowly opened her eyes. With her face inches away from Clive's, she whispered close to his ear.

"Rot in hell!"

Satisfied, she rapidly left the room. She was afraid that if she stayed any longer, his body would rise from the slab and slap her one more time.

She pushed on through the busy foyer and hurried out into the fresh air. The in-laws sat in the car nearby. Len flashed the headlights as if she had somehow forgotten where they'd parked. Tina waved and headed in their direction. The heat of the vehicle was stifling and scorched her cheeks as she buckled up. Len pulled away and hit the queue of traffic waiting at the roundabout.

"You'd think they would sort this out. Bloody stupid! They should widen it." Len grumbled with impatience.

Tina shook her head. She'd only been in the car for two minutes and already he was griping.

"He looked peaceful. I'm pleased I came."

"Told you, it was for the best." He indicated right and made his turn.

"Are you okay, Joyce?" She patted her arm through the gap in the seats.

Joyce moved away and said nothing. Len spoke for her.

"She's drained. I need to get her home."

Tina waited until he took the turn and then asked the question. "Do we know when the funeral is?"

"Yes, we do."

"Do you need my help with anything?"

"No. I told you, I would do it all. But you can say something at the service, if you like. I want to see it first, though."

"I don't think I could. I don't want to have one of my moments again. Could you say something?"

Joyce spoke up. "It's your episodes that caused this with your attention seeking. I don't want her to say anything. Please, Ducky, don't let her say anything. He was my boy!"

Out came the hankie, and she dabbed her eyes again.

*It speaks!*

She wanted to tell them everything about their precious boy. That he was a wife-beating, rapist pig. Instead, she bit her lip and balled her fists across her lap.

"I think it's best if you don't. My poor Nelly is very distressed."

"So, when is the funeral?"

"Next Thursday at two. We're having the wake in the back room of The Walnut Tree. It was his favourite haunt."

*Great, the day after my abortion.*

Clive had only been there a couple of times. It wasn't his regular haunt. They were as delusional as ever, she surmised.

"Are you going to let me know the final details?"

"I will ring you. There is still some things to do. Don't you worry about that. All you need to do is turn up." Len turned down the next street.

"I'll order some flowers for his coffin."

"No, you won't. We're not having them. Monetary donations only, for the children's ward. He would have liked that."

"There are always some flowers on the coffin."

"Yes, but only ours."

A bunch of stinging nettles was too good for that imbecile. The heat raged through the car. Tina pulled her cardigan away from her perspiring neck. One more turn and she could get away from the claustrophobia that began to creep up on her.

He moved up to the kerb. "I'll drop you here. Saves me going around the one way system."

"Thanks. I could do with a walk." She opened the door and slid out of the car. Holding onto the doorframe, she leant inside. "Bye."

"I'll call. Shut the door. You're letting the heat out."

He thumbed his glasses up his nose. She tapped on the window to attract Joyce's attention, but she had nodded off. He drove away without a wave. Pleased that the ordeal was over, she stretched her cramped limbs, inhaling the sweet fresh air and strolling down the street to her front door.

Stepping over the threshold, something felt odd underfoot. She bent down and picked up a large brown unstamped envelope with her name written across the front. Tina gave it a squeeze. It felt thick with a lump in the bottom right corner. Tearing it open, she peeked inside. The contents slipped through her shaky hands and scattered across the floor.

# CHAPTER 30

**TINA** stared at four enlarged photographs, a letter, and a plastic memory stick. Shots of her at the canal with the pole in hand stared up at her. She saw the look on her face as she'd held Clive under the water. Her heart thumped as anger and helplessness flowed through her veins. She was reluctant to read the note, but curiosity won.

Anxious to get this issue resolved, she sat on the stairs and sighed, tearing the envelope open and sliding out a small sheet of paper. It was typed in the same font as the previous one.

*I sent you a gift. Do take the time to view the stick. It's so much better than the pics.*

*Did you enjoy your visit to the hospital? Hypocrite! Tell me, how did he look? How did he smell?*

*MURDERER! I will be in touch.*

Letting out a frustrated squeal, she gathered the items from the floor and stormed into the kitchen. Tina slammed the USB stick on the table, and dumped the note and the photos into the sink. She then hunted through Clive's drawer and found his lighter, left over from when he used to smoke, half full with gas.

Tina lit the corner of one of the photos. It curled at the end as the flames took hold. She let it float into the sink so that the others caught. After the contents had dissolved into grey ash, Tina ran both taps and washed the debris away, the evidence now destroyed.

Grabbing the USB stick, she headed to the tool shed. She had an inkling of what it contained and had no intention of taking a look.

Squatting on the patio, she raised the hammer and bashed the navy plastic into smithereens, concentrating on the circuit board that held the information. She picked up the pieces and put them in her pocket, ready to dispose of them down a drain.

Once inside the house, she put the items she'd brought with her from the shed under the sink. They'd be more accessible that way should an occasion arise to use them again. Next, she snatched her keys from the side and headed outside. Strolling down the street, she scanned her surroundings, in case the stalker followed in her wake.

*Maybe it's a neighbour.*

Wanting confirmation, she checked windows, doors, and gardens as she passed. Nothing seemed suspicious, apart from the people she knew. Down the next street, she did the same, even looking over her shoulder a few times. Ten minutes away from home, she pretended to tie a shoelace and discreetly threw the bits into the metal slats of the sewer drain.

"It's gone forever now."

A male voice speaking over her shoulder startled her. She stood and turned around to face him.

"Looks like it."

"I lost my keys down a drain once, never to be seen again." The stranger laughed.

"I was tying up my shoe and money fell out of my pocket."

"Gone forever. Bye now."

Tina smiled and said goodbye, making her way home. She could hear the blessed phone ring outside her front door. No way was she rushing to answer it. If it rang off, they would call again if it was important. In the mood she was in, ripping the wires from the wall would give her great satisfaction. It was still ringing as she entered.

*Leave me alone!*

Tina snatched the receiver out of its cradle. "Hello."

"How are you?"

Ray sounded breathless on the other end and tunes jingled in the background.

*What does he want?*

Before she had a chance to respond, he said, "Would you like me to accompany you to the funeral next week?"

With the handset to her ear, she made her way into the kitchen. "No, I need to do this on my own. How do you know when it is anyway?"

"Len filled me in. It's going to be quite a send-off."

"Thanks for your concern, but this is something I need to do alone."

"I could put a comforting arm around your shoulder."

"That won't be necessary. I need to go now. Bye."

Irritated, she threw the phone on the table, and then looked at her mobile. He'd tried to call three times. She let out a moan and turned it off. Ray being pals with the in-laws bugged her. After it was all over, would he continue his quest to hit on her? She never wanted to see the fool ever again.

No sooner had she put the phone back in its cradle, it shrilled. Tina let out a growl before answering.

"Yes."

"You're snappy! It's Len."

Tina rolled her eyes. Like she needed reminding of his name!

"I'm stressed. Sorry."

"Aren't we all? Think about poor Nelly."

Tina cringed, rolling her eyes toward the ceiling once more. She cleared her throat ready to speak, but he cut her off.

"We've done everything for our boy. You wouldn't know what stress is." He paused. "Imagine how hard it is for us, our boy dying before his parents. It's not right. It's just not right!"

"You offered, remember? You wanted me to keep out of it."

"We had no choice. You're unstable and selfish. You'd never have coped with it. Life is always about you. Think of others for a change."

"Why have you rung me?"

"At the funeral procession, you're sharing the car with Nelly and I. Oh, and Joan. We will pick you up at 1:30 pm. Be ready, and none of your usual faffing."

"Have you booked them? I wanted to make my own way there."

"Not yet, and you will be sharing the car with us. Making your own way there? What nonsense!"

Tina's heart sank. It was bad enough sharing the car with the in-laws. Now, she had to face her mother.

"Couldn't you have told me this earlier? We had ample time to talk things through at the hospital."

"I was far too distressed. Call yourself a wife to my boy? Nuts, that's what you are. Nelly will never forgive you. Ever."

Len wanted to control everything as usual. *No wonder Clive was like his dad. Like father, like son,* she thought, while Len gabbed on.

"Forgive me for what? It was an accident."

"Those outbursts of yours, and denying us any grandchildren."

She couldn't be bothered to reiterate over trodden ground. Tina felt too exhausted after another day of misery and anguish.

"Please, Len, calm down."

*Now, who can't deal with the stress?*

"Just make sure you're ready."

Len's nasal whistling stretched Tina's nerves.

"I'll speak to you before—"

The line went dead. She stared at the phone, feeling a little narked.

Back in the kitchen, Tina put her head in her hands and focused on the table's grainy pattern. She felt scared and unsure of what to do. Someone somewhere was blackmailing her and she didn't know why.

Tina worried about how she'd physically feel after the abortion and the funeral the next day. What if there was pain or bleeding because of complications? What would happen if she needed an overnight stay in hospital? How would she explain that to Len without him knowing the ins and outs?

On top of everything else, she had to sit in a confined space with her mother. Why did her relatives make her feel like an outcast in this family? Things would be different if she announced that a baby was on the way. There would be lots of fuss and attention instead. Yet, she couldn't do it.

*I will take pleasure in denying them that.*

She never meant it, though. Her emotions were beginning to fray. Confusion took hold. Not knowing what to do, or what to deal with first, she felt lost in a world of despair. Not even a shower or the promise of freedom could wash away the filth from her soul. Nor would it stop her from falling into the dark bottomless pit she'd climbed from so many times.

Giving herself a pep talk usually worked. It was another survival tool she'd taught herself.

*You can do this. One thing at a time. Prioritise!* Her body rocked back and forth as she repeated the words. *All you've been through from childhood until now . . . You are strong, and you can do this.*

As if at a séance, she sat with her palms splayed on the table, her back straight. With her eyes closed, she drew a deep breath. When she exhaled, it took the blackness from her heart.

Tina felt better and decided that she needed fresh air. A break from the walls that now cocooned her would do her good. She'd take a stroll through the park into town. Perhaps she'd sit on the grass and contemplate things whilst listening to the birds.

# CHAPTER 31

**D**URING the past week, Len had called Tina twice to keep her updated on how things were going and what costs he'd incurred in regards to the funeral. She hadn't heard anything from the owner of the photographs or letters either. Perhaps they'd given up on trying to intimidate her. Either way, no news was good. Ray hadn't pestered her with surprise visits or called, and work colleagues had sent a card attached to a bouquet of flowers offering their condolences from all the staff.

Another sympathy card had fallen through the letterbox on her way downstairs for her first morning cuppa. She picked it up and placed it with the other unopened ones on the side as she passed through the hall and into the kitchen.

From this point on, there would be no more anger, only strength and positivity. Whatever happened because of the consequences of her actions, she would learn to live with everything. The most important thing today was the abortion, and that would take every ounce of her emotional energy.

Leaving in thirty minutes would ensure that she was on time for her appointment. With one last check that she had everything, she closed the door on the way out. She climbed into the Audi and drove to the clinic, thinking of the good things to come on the way, trying

221

to keep her emotions in check.

No sooner had she booked into the reception, a nurse called her name. As they walked the corridor toward her room, the nurse asked if someone would be picking her up afterwards. Theoretically, someone should have accompanied Tina, or at least taken her home. After all, she would be in pain and still groggy, unable to drive. She'd lied and said a friend would be waiting for her later, when, in fact, she would take herself home.

*This is what it's like to go private,* she thought.

The room had an en-suite bathroom with a shower over the bath, a flat screen television, and a private sitting area. A table and a comfortable chair filled one corner. A mini wardrobe filled the other, unlike the battered locker at the NHS.

With all the pre-checks and admin done, she sat near the window in her surgical gown and waited. At least this one covered the whole body, whereas the NHS ones had the ties that never tied properly, causing you to parade your backside around the ward.

Contemplating her decision, Tina watched the clouds dawdle across the sky. Her body felt tired because of the emotional strain. She blanked her mind and tried to get into the zone. She'd done the same the last time when she had surgery to fix her back after a riding accident. Years of taking narcotics for pain at such a young age was a regret she felt on occasion, another demon from a past she couldn't outrun.

After numerous tests and scans, they decided to fuse the two vertebrae together after she'd crushed the bones in her spine. Her nervous system became dependant on Tramadol, an effective, but quite addictive, pain reliever. The withdrawal she'd suffered coming off them was horrendous, and she never took strong pain relief again.

Today, she hoped to be sedated, and would take Paracetamol afterwards, if need be. Tina was alone that day, too. At nineteen and in need of support, her mother let her go through it alone.

*It's your own fault. Horses are dangerous. Why did you take the medication in the first place?*

She always despised her daughter's love for horses.

*What type of mother lets you go through that alone?* Taking deep breaths, she tried to steady herself. *Am I doing the right thing? This is the only way.*

A knock sounded at the door. Tina turned her head toward a young woman wearing scrubs as she walked into the room.

"Is it time?"

"Yes, it is. Mr. Cane is ready for you now."

She nodded. Tears welled in her eyes. Holding them back, she approached the nurse.

"We're going to walk to the theatre from here. It's not far. Can you manage that?"

"Yes."

The grip she felt on her elbow gave her reassurance as the nurse guided her through a set of double doors where the surgical team clustered together around the waiting table. Tina swallowed past the lump in her throat as the doors closed behind them.

***

SEVERAL hours later, Tina felt the rush of cold air on her cheeks as she stood outside the clinic. A weight had been lifted from her heavy shoulders. For the first time in ages, she felt content. Tilting her head skyward, she exhaled through her nose. A murmuration of Starlings made patterns in the sky, and an aeroplane left long vanilla tendrils in its wake. Deep down in her heart, she knew she'd done the right thing.

She walked along with trembling legs, feeling exhausted by the time she made it to the car. Moving along was difficult, but she took her time in getting there.

*Oh, no, not again!*

A wave of queasiness overcame her. Bile rose up her throat at the sight of another envelope stuck under the vehicle's wiper. She tamped down the uneasy feeling and put it on top of the dashboard as she climbed in. There was no rush to read it.

Resting her head back, she slid a hand inside her trousers, circling the flat of her hand over the warm soft skin of her abdomen. Tina felt the dint in her bellybutton, and then started the Audi and drove home.

Inside, Tina took her time and made herself some brown toast and tea. This small bit of sustenance maintained her energy levels over the past few weeks, and it was all she could stomach. Popping the last crispy corner into her mouth and wiping her fingers down her thighs, she read the note.

*You went through with it, then. Shame, that poor little life gone. You cruel bitch! Now, we need to meet. I will be in touch.*

*That's what you think!*

She would do whatever she could to protect her new family. Tomorrow, it would be good riddance to her husband. For now, she'd spend the rest of the day relaxing and taking some time to rest.

# CHAPTER 32

**T**HOUGHTS of the funeral kept Tina awake for most of the night. Twice, she'd gone down to the kitchen to make herself a drink, only to go back to bed and toss and turn some more.

Rubbing the sleep from her eyes, she squinted at the clock radio. She'd overslept by several hours, and only had two hours before her lift arrived. Climbing out of bed, the carpet tickled her bare feet on her way to the shower.

Her clothes hung on the front of the wardrobe, black trousers and a frumpy black knit that she'd only worn once. It was another one of Clive's purchases. Today, she did not want to disappoint. She dressed, adding a squirt of his favourite perfume, and wearing her hair in a bun. This would be the last time anything he'd given her would touch her skin.

Downstairs, she gathered her bag and keys, and made sure her phone was on vibrate. Clive would turn in his coffin if he saw the mess that was building around the house. She took great delight in leaving everything wonky and unfolded. It felt good not to be controlled.

Glancing at the time, she said, "Twenty-five minutes."

The roses Sam had given her sat on the windowsill and looked spent. They'd lasted well, however. While she waited, she pulled his farewell gift from the vase. In the living room, she slid the curtain aside to watch out for the car.

*You can do this.*

It pulled up to the kerb five minutes early. Her heart raced and her palms felt clammy as she walked down the path. The limousine stretched down the side of the cul-de-sac and took up three spaces. Jet black and highly polished, there wasn't a dent, scratch, or nick on the humongous beast from what she could see. Its engine was surprisingly quiet as it idled, waiting for Tina to board.

*Len should have gone for a bigger car. Although a dustbin lorry would have been just as good.*

A solemn faced driver in a black suit and cap nodded as Tina neared. She knew the family were inside, sitting behind the blackened windows, ready to pounce. Blocking the sun from her eyes, she chanted her mantra to herself, giving herself a second before letting the chauffeur open the door.

Joyce sat facing the driver and took up two of the beige leather seats. Len sat next to her, their arms linked. Her mother sat opposite of them. Tina chose the option of looking out of the back window. She could have sat next to Joyce, but not only would it have been a tight squeeze, there was no way she wanted to see that overpriced coffin.

She made a mental note. A cardboard box would do upon her death. She didn't need a coffin just so someone could chuck a load of earth on it or burn it.

*What a waste! Scatter my ashes over a pile of horse dung.*

Tina said hello. No one spoke, at first, though three sets of eyes stared in her direction. Nausea returned at the most inconvenient time, triggered by the floral air freshener her mother called perfume and the stale sweat emanating from her in-laws' bodies. She glanced around the interior, hoping to hold on to her stomach's contents, not wanting to make a show of dashing from the car and retching down the nearest drain. Instead, she held the stem of the flower she'd brought with her to her nose and let its fragrance cleanse her nostrils.

"We said no flowers." Len's stern voice made Tina stiffen.

"It's one flower. I shall do what I want with it."

Her mother shot her a dirty glare. She then made a show of

taking out her hanky and blowing her nose. Tina stared back at her.

"You could have made an effort to dress better. You look like a scruff," her mother said, balling the tissue in her fist.

"Clive bought me this outfit. I thought it would be apt to wear it."

"No way," Len butt in. "He had better taste than that."

Tina bit her tongue as her mother nodded. Now, it was Joyce's turn to have a dig.

"Duck, you should have made a bit more of an effort."

Joyce put her arm up to her eyes and wiped them on her sleeve. She wore the same old knitted green suit that was probably unlaundered since their last visit.

*What a flaming cheek!*

"I lost my son . . . and . . . now I will never have any grandchildren."

*Not this crap again.*

Tina wasn't heartless, but Joyce's feeling sorry for herself was getting on her nerves.

Len put his arm around her and said, "There, there," like she was six-years-old and squeezed her knee.

The limo pulled away from the kerb so smoothly, Tina hardly noticed they'd made a turn.

"Don't worry, Joyce. She would never have made a good mum anyway. Selfish, she is."

Her mother's venomous words pushed Tina over the edge.

"How dare you all attack me like this! I've just lost my husband and not one of you gives two hoots about anyone but yourselves." Empowered by the burst of adrenaline racing through her system, she carried on. "None of you even care how I feel!"

Tears ran down her face, although none were for Clive. Shocked by her outburst, the three of them raised an eyebrow at each other. Her mother soon spoke freely.

"See, if anyone else gets the attention, she has an outburst. Just like that when she was a child, she was."

"Mother!" Tina shouted.

"Just speaking the truth, dear."

Tina needed to hold it together before she ended up giving her a slap. The car slowed and joined the rest of a black convoy.

Tina caught a glimpse of the pallbearer moving to the front of the procession through the window, ready to walk in front of the hearse. Doing so was better than looking at three sour faces.

It wouldn't be long before they made the turn into the church. Between Joyce's sniffles, Len's glares, and her mother's poisonous aura, she wanted to get out of this evil and contaminated space before her stomach lurched again.

# CHAPTER 33

**THE** peaty smell of freshly turned earth combined with the surrounding woodland drifted into Tina's nostrils and filled her lungs. A congregation had gathered around the oblong space at the graveside and waited patiently for the coffin to lower. Green Astroturf covered the ramps of soil to make it more presentable while the internment took place. Solemn faces and teary eyes looked on as the vicar voiced the final prayer.

She could recall most of the faces that turned up at the service. Clive's work colleagues sat at the back, and distant family and acquaintances, whom she never met, occupied the other pews. Close family sat at the front. She'd chosen her position wisely and stayed well away from her mother.

It was a wonderful send off. After hymns, prayers, and a few stuttered proses from Len in church, they were now ready to intern his body.

"Ashes to ashes, dust to dust."

The words sounded surreal in the background. She cried, not for her loss, but for the emptiness inside her soul.

Several men lowered the coffin with precision, letting the straps out an inch at a time, before its contents settled into its final resting place. Tina assumed that a few of the mourners were going to the wake, as they'd walked away, unable to see it through until the end.

Peeking over the edge, and down into the depths of the six foot hole, her heart skipped. He was gone and soon-to-be under a pile of freshly dug moist earth. The others stepped back. It was too much to bear for the likes of her mother and her in-laws. She didn't care to see the other people around the grave, only focusing on herself and her final message to her evil husband.

Her phone vibrated in her trouser pocket, but she ignored it. Tina twisted her marital band from her finger and looped it over the stem of the red rose. After taking a deep breath and giving the bloom a final sniff, she threw it into the grave. It landed on top of the classy lid, its petals scattering on impact and her ring pinging into the pit. Reluctant to move until she witnessed the first shovels of dirt sprinkled on the top of the coffin, Tina then turned and walked away.

A sandy path meandered around the graveyard. Wild and straggly grasses grew around the outskirts to attract wildlife. Different species of trees, decades old, made it look more like a woodland rather than a place of rest for the dead. Headstones, some at crooked angles, emerged from the undergrowth as if planted rather than placed.

It had been her favourite place until today. She would never come here again. How could she? It would be another constant reminder of the life Clive had forced upon her.

A tac, tac, tac came from the highest branches. Tina glanced upward at a Magpie chipping away.

*One for sorrow.*

She remembered a story her granddad once told her, about a complete armoured division saluting a solitary Magpie as they passed. Tina raised her hand to her brow, hoping it would rid her of bad luck.

Her phone buzzed, startling her. This time, she decided to answer it. When she looked, it was a text. Her hands started to shake as she read the five words displayed across the screen.

*Did you get my note?*

\*\*\*

**R**AY followed Tina, keeping low and out of sight. At the service, he'd sat at the back of the church with his work mates, but he didn't bother to see Clive lowered to his grave.

He had one thing on his mind. *Money.*

He'd gone as far as buying a cheap disposable phone to keep his identity hidden from Tina until it was time. His knees were starting to hurt as he crouched behind one of the larger over-the-top obelisks. The meeting would happen soon, as he needed the cash before the men he owed money to took away his kneecaps.

***

**T**INA scanned the area. Apart from Len, Joyce, and her mother, who were still at the graveside, and a few malingerers whom she knew, there was no one else in sight.

*Where did you get my number? Who are you, and what do you want?*

She tapped the screen and hit send. The phone buzzed in her hand.

*You'll find out soon enough.*

She sent out another message.

*Leave me alone.*

Another message came in.

*Watch your mouth. I'll be in touch. Looks like you have a visitor.*

A pat on the shoulder as she was about to turn made her take a step backwards. Her ankle gave away and made her wobble. The phone slipped from her fingers and landed on the dirt path. It all happened so fast. She panicked and a scream left her throat.

"Here you go." The stranger passed her the device.

"You startled me, James!" she said, snatching her phone back and putting it in her pocket. "I didn't see you at the church."

"I've only just arrived. The traffic was bad at Heathrow."

"Why are you here?" The words slipped out of her mouth before she realised she'd uttered the silly question.

"Er . . . the funeral!"

"Well, it's over now." She began to walk, hoping she could keep moving as they spoke. "You never even knew him. You only met him once at the wedding, and you were late for that, too."

"I can't help my job." He dawdled alongside her. "Anyway, I wanted to give Mum some support. It's been hard for her."

Tina bit down on the side of her lip. *Here we go again. Mum, Mum, Mum.*

With nothing to say, she upped her stride, putting distance between them.

"Tina, wait!" he shouted. "We need to talk."

She stopped and turned. "Really? Well, you could have picked a better day than today."

Tina assessed him from head to toe. From what she could remember, James had always worn his hair a little longer. Today was no different. In fact, looking at him evoked memories she would rather forget. The hair and looks she could deal with, but his eyes . . . His eyes brought back unwanted memories. It was like looking at her dad in his younger days.

"I do have a phone and a letterbox. Oh! And an e-mail account," she snapped.

"I've been so busy at work."

"For two years? Not too busy to ring Mum, though, and listen to her gripes."

"That's not fair. Mum is on her own now, and don't speak about her like that." James took a step back.

"Me! Speak to her like that? She treats me like dirt." She stared to walk again. "Why are we even having this conversation?"

Her attention was on the text and who it could be. In addition to that, a million other things fogged her brain. Now, James was here, raking up the past.

"You can hardly blame us. You brought shame on this family."

"What? How dare you! Where were you when I needed some help? You were supposed to be my big brother, instead you were so far up his arse—" Pausing, she inhaled and waited for her internal calm to come, but it was no use, her anger bubbled over.

"I was not!"

"Yes, you were. You knew what he was doing to me. You took his side, blaming it on attention seeking. I needed you. Why did you let it happen to your little sister?"

Tears welled in her eyes. It took a lot of strength to bite them back.

"Okay, you want to do this now? Fine."

"No, I don't want to do this now, but we have unresolved issues. It's not my fault if seeing you provokes them."

"I didn't come here for a slagging match. You need to learn to leave things in the past and move the fuck on," James said.

"Move on? When Mother brings it up every time we speak, pulling the guilt trip on me, how is that possible?"

Her heart raced. There were so many things Tina wanted to get off her chest, but what was the use when James was a part of her mother's clan?

"I need to have my say. Let's sit over there." He pointed.

Tina listened as they sat on a well-kept bench near the path. His voice calmed after the outburst.

"Mum is older now, alone, frustrated, and scared." His elbows rested on his knees.

"That doesn't excuse—"

"Let me finish."

Irritated, she folded her arms and looked around.

"She hangs on to things from the past. I'm worried about her,

Sis. She needs help."

"Can I speak now?"

"Please do."

"You know, you never even offered your condolences to me today. In fact, you haven't even mentioned it." She turned to face him. "I lost my husband and all your concerned with is Mum." After today, Tina wanted nothing more to do with her brother, the decision already made. She would have her say with nothing else to lose. "Not once in my life did you help me. Do you know how that felt when I was a little girl? No, you don't, because like the others, you chose to ignore it." Her hands trembled.

"I knew it was happening, and I did nothing. That's something I have to live with. At the time, I got everything if I played along. He was proud of me, as was Mum. They both brushed it under the carpet. Then the London thing happened." He twisted in his seat.

"You can say it, you know. I'm not ashamed. Not anymore," she said.

"I look back now and I know I was rotten to you. I thought you wanted attention and made it up."

"Made it up? How can you make sexual abuse up? Especially from a family member." She shook her head with disbelief.

"You hear it on the news all the time. Girls prick teasing and getting the men in trouble because they can't have what they want."

"At seven? Grow up, James. Why did you bother to come today?"

"For Mum. She needs looking after, and I'm away a lot. I thought maybe you could . . . help."

She knew it. He had an ulterior motive. He wasn't bothered about her. James just fed her what she wanted to hear. He'd been brainwashed since childhood. What did she expect? Compassion and understanding from a family who lived their lives in denial? It was better to go without them, she surmised.

"No, I have my own things to deal with."

"That's a bit selfish. She's your mum, too."

"Why don't you just fuck off and get out of my life?" Shocked by the profanity, she put her hand to her mouth.

"There's no talking to you. Mum was right. You're a waste of fucking space."

He stood and stormed down the path, kicking up dust as he went. A moment of pleasure crossed her pained face, pleased with herself that she'd finally had the guts to tell her big brother to go away. It didn't last long, however, as other pressing matters clouded her mind.

To the right of the bench was the back entrance to the cemetery. She'd used it all the time on her solitary walks while wildlife spotting. It led out on to a street. Further on, lay a narrow lane covered in brambles and fruit bushes. In the autumn, she shared the berries with the many birds, and picked the bitter, but sweet, fruit to make a blackberry pie.

Eyeing the entrance, she was tempted to sneak out and make the ten minute walk to her home. Instead, she took a slow dawdle back toward the church, taking in the wording on the slabs as she went.

*Matilder Cruckshank, 1868—1929.*

Her grave was neatly tendered, the flowers in the metal vase fresh. Tina wondered what life was like back then and what type of person she was. By contrast, the next one looked tired, the letters faded on the stone, the surrounding concrete green and washed out.

*Augustus Feodore Simpson, 1890—1929.*

*So young!*

She wondered if he'd died from the Spanish flu, and whether he was alone or loved. Maybe he died in battle, though her brain was too tired to work it out.

Tina shook the maudlin thoughts away and made her way up the path. Up ahead, James had his arm around his mother, helping her walk to the car. Still standing at the graveside, Len had gotten Joyce one of those camping chairs that pushed into the ground. All she needed was a picnic hamper and she could have made an afternoon of it. Tina approached in silence and stood next to Len.

"We've been waiting for you. What the hell have you been doing?" Len asked.

"I needed some time to think."

*Why do I need to explain myself?*

"I see you've upset James and your mother. Today, of all days!" He helped Joyce from the chair. Finding it difficult to remove the plastic stake from the earth, he said, "Nelly, you've pushed it right in. Look!"

A flush of colour painted her cheeks red. "Sorry, Duck."

"What's that got to do with you, Len? What I discuss with my family is my business."

"You're still our daughter-in-law. Now, let's get to the wake and give the boy a good send off."

"I'm not going." Tina stood her ground.

"Oh, yes, you are. Now, move!"

Tina shook her head. "No more. I'm doing what I want. You can't tell me what to do anymore."

Len glared at her and had one hand on his hip. The other steadied Joyce.

"Leave her, Ducky," Joyce said. "She would spoil it. It's her fault anyway."

Out came the hankie, and she dabbed at her puffy eyes once more. Tina could not be bothered for another heated discussion.

"We do need to sort out a few things. Maybe we can do that together."

"His money, you mean."

"No, I didn't mean that. I meant his personal effects. I'm sure there are a few things Joyce would like."

"Well, we'll get around to that. Come on, Nelly. Let's go."

Tina watched as they moved up the path. Now alone, she could hear life shuffling in the trees. She turned around and made her way home using the shortcut. Approaching the busy main road, she waited for a gap in the traffic before jogging to the pavement on the other side.

Not speaking to Ray was the only good thing to come from today. He'd sat in the back row with his egotistical work mates. The distance she put between them worked. He hadn't bothered her at all, and she managed the whole funeral without having a conversation with her mother. However, someone out there knew her business and phone number, and something had to be done about it.

Tina couldn't think straight. Her anger grew as she thought about her brother. She wiped her face with her sleeve. The phone buzzed again. She stopped at a side street to fish it from the pocket of her trousers and looked at the screen. Goosebumps covered her forearms as she read the message.

*Not going to the wake, then? We need to meet. Oh, and by the way, don't for one second think I won't show someone the pictures. Run along now, Tina Blythe.*

She looked up and down the street. Apart from an old man walking his terrier, she saw nothing else. Although he gave a nod in her direction, she pushed past him and jogged all the way home.

# CHAPTER 34

**B**EHIND the heavy laced curtains of his cousin's house, Ray watched as Tina scuttled past. An amused smile spread across his lips.

*You're in a hurry, Tina.*

He could have gone to the wake, but keeping tabs on her was much more fun. Making sure he'd put enough distance between them, he left through the front gate and shadowed her all the way home. On the corner of the street, he'd crouched beside a wall and stalked his prey.

*In, you go. That's it.*

He gave her a minute, and then took out his phone. Before he made the call, he placed a hankie over the mouthpiece. Ray prepared his best Scottish accent and then hit dial.

\*\*\*

**O**UT of breath and safely home, Tina wanted to barricade the house. She was scared of everything and her nerves were on edge. Her mobile buzzed in her pocket again, a call this time, but the screen said, caller unknown. She set the phone on the side.

With her foot on the first rung of the stairs, and her bag on her shoulder, the phone vibrated and danced along the teak table. She caught it before it fell and answered the call. Tina could hear background noise, a rustle, and an ambulance siren in the distance.

"Next time, answer the fucking phone!"

The sudden burst from the earpiece made Tina jolt. "Who are you, and what do you want? Leave me alone!"

"Shut up and listen."

Tina bit her lip. The voice on the other end carried a northern accent and some twangs of Scottish came through. Whom did she know that came from there?

"I'm listening," she said.

"Good." The line went quiet before the voice spoke again. "We need to meet."

"Why? How do I know you're not going to hurt me?"

Tina talked and walked at the same time, looking out of every window in the house, including those upstairs before she was satisfied nobody was there. She then sat on the edge of her seat in the lounge and massaged her temple with her free hand.

"You're worth more alive." He sniggered. "Now, do as I say, and we can both come out of this better off."

"Where?"

His accent wavered on the last few words. The caller now sounded local. She made a mental note of that fact.

"At the top of the bridge over the abandoned railway line in an hour."

The line went dead once more. There was no point in being insecure and scared anymore. The only person she could rely on was herself. She dug deep for inner strength, and repeated James' words aloud.

"Move the fuck on!"

She changed clothes, slipped on her trainers, and left the house with only her keys in hand. There had been a couple of muggings lately, even for as little as pocket change.

Thirty minutes later, she made her way to the meeting place. It didn't take half an hour, but she needed the walk. Exiting the park from the railway entrance, the King's Lynn to Kings Cross train whistled past. The barriers rose and a stream of cars pulled away. To the left, she saw the school, and to the right, were a line of trees and brambles. The path's prong in the middle segregated the walkway. Tina took the right fork.

Lined on each side were crooked trees and overgrown weeds. Moving aside to let a cyclist pass, she found herself on a patch of scorched dry earth. Empty bottles and takeaway containers showed signs of a recent party. Kindling lay at her feet. Snapped branches and twisted roots made easy seats for youths that gathered at night to exchange drugs.

She rested against a stump and let the sun's rays coming through treetops warm her face. Around the next bend, and she would be there ten minutes early.

A Whippet trotted past, his muzzle snuffling for a place to cock his leg. The owner trailed behind and gave her a curt 'afternoon' as he passed. Alone and frightened, she inhaled the sweet smell of wood and wild flowers, and then continued the journey.

Chipped green metal grew from concrete pillars that formed the bridge. Wild bushes entangled some of the handrail as she made her ascent toward the incline. Her thighs ached and her calves pulled. She reached the top of the ugly structure that stretched over wasted ground. With no one in sight, she took a breather, resting her hands on the cold, rough safety rail, peering over the edge.

*Could you kill yourself from this height?*

Rusted railway tracks with stones down the centre had clumps of grass and shrubs growing up the middle. Empty beer cans and discarded waste blighted the perimeter. The view in the distance was pretty in a bland landscape sort of way. Hearing footsteps and a click, Tina glanced over her shoulder.

*Could this be him?*

The old boy walked on by, pushing his bike. The time was now six, and there was no sign of the man who could ruin her life. Ten more minutes, and then she'd head back.

Coming from the industrial estate side of the bridge, another man approached wearing a black hoodie. Judging by the noise as he neared, he had his iPod on full blast. He limped past, though nothing seemed to be wrong with his legs. He was young and pretended to walk like a gangster.

Fifteen more minutes passed, and her agitation mounted. Contemplating as to whether to give it an extra five, someone tapped her shoulder, making her lurch forward. Instinctively, she slapped her hand against her chest as her heart skipped.

"You scared me, Ray! It's not nice creeping up on people."

"Are you alright? You look pale."

"What are you doing here?" she asked, looking around and feeling worried in case the unknown intruder saw them standing there chatting.

"What are *you* doing here, more like? Strange place to be after today."

"You have to go. You can't be here." Tina turned, feeling anxious.

"I can be wherever I like. Who you waiting for?" he asked, putting his hands in his pocket.

"Who said I'm waiting for anyone?"

"You waiting for your secret lover?" he teased.

"No, don't be stupid. I like it here, that's all."

Tina wanted to be rid of him. Her skin began to crawl as he moved closer to her.

"I think I will stay awhile and see who this mystery man you've arranged to meet is."

She stared at him with bewilderment. "No, you can't. You have to leave. H—How did you know it was a man?" Tina swallowed and looked him in the eye.

He smirked and said, "Let me show you something." Ray rummaged in his pocket and shoved his phone in her direction. "Take a look."

Speechless, Tina soon realised why he was there. *Oh, God! It can't be!*

"I have a video, too. Wanna see?"

"You bastard!" She slapped the phone out of his palm, but he caught it before it plunged to the ground.

"Now, now, don't throw a tantrum. One button on my computer is all I have to press to upload this to YouTube."

"You're supposed to be his frie—"

He pressed his finger to her lips. "Shush."

Tina swiped his hand aside and said, "Don't touch me!"

*How could he do this to me after all I've been through?*

It must have been factory changeover, as several people filed across the bridge after a busy day. He'd put an arm around her waist, and as Tina tried to pull away, Ray squeezed tighter, giving the passers-by the impression that they were lovers.

After the people dispersed, she said, "Get off me," and shrugged him off.

"Stop your fucking whinging. All I have to do is show this to the police and you're nicked." He shoved the phone back into his pocket. "Poor Len and Joyce. Depriving them of their first grandchild, huh? Now, that is harsh."

Refusing to approach such a tricky subject with him, she calmed down, wanting it to be over with.

"Please, just tell me what you want."

"Now, we're on the same wavelength!" he said, and gestured with his hands as if fanning himself. "We can both come out on top."

*How, when he's the only gainer from this?* she wondered. She nodded and gave him a thin rehearsed smile.

"I want money," he said.

"You don't need money. From what I can see, you're very well off," Tina replied, sounding puzzled.

"Never mind that. I want £10,000. In cash, obviously."

"I can't get that kind of money."

"Don't lie. You know you can." He adjusted his position. "Let's see." Ray counted on his fingers. "The sale of the house and the car . . . Oh, any life insurance, and what's left from Clive's bank account."

"Those things take time. Weeks, even months, to sort out."

"I want it by Monday afternoon. That gives you four days."

"Not a chance. It's unrealistic. Besides, it's the weekend soon, and I need at least a few days' notice for that amount." She tucked her hair over an ear and rubbed her hands across her face.

"Now, what have I told you about lying?"

"I'm not."

Inches from her face, his angry eyes bored into hers. The smell of garlic on his breath repulsed her, and tiny specks of spittle hit her face.

"You have a joint account. I know the fucking money is there." He eased himself backwards.

"It's joint, but I can't touch that now since he's dead. It has to be sorted out properly." She sucked her bottom lip into her mouth.

"Well, I'll take this to the police, then." He turned to leave.

"Wait, please! Let me see what I can do." She fiddled with a tissue in her pocket, poking holes in it with her thumb.

"See, that wasn't too hard, was it? I'll be in touch. You'll know it's me. I'm the caller unknown." Pulling on his hood, he turned to leave and then glanced over his shoulder for one final dig. "Oh, and don't call the police. Oops! I forgot, you can't, can you?" He smirked once more. "See you."

Shocked, she held onto the rail and watched as he disappeared down the ramp. How could Ray be so callous and stoop so low? He was supposed to be Clive's best friend.

She sighed and made her way home. Under normal circumstances, she would never walk through the woodland alone at night. Tina preferred the safer route under the streetlights, but this way was much quicker in getting home.

Pausing at the entrance, she took a breath and shook her hands at her sides. Eerie light made the woods come alive. Clusters of grey branches reached out like arms beckoning her to come through. That didn't make her nervous. What lurked in the shadows sent prickles down her spine. She glanced about and upped her pace, almost power-walking along the way. Now halfway through, a round bright moon lit the path with its gentle blue rays.

A whiff of bonfire floated through the night air, and a snap rippled and echoed through the trees. She heard voices up ahead, amber flames flickering from the small patch of ground she'd seen earlier. Four men sat on the tree stumps opposite each other, the fire glowing in the middle as they puffed on long cigarettes.

"Fancy joining the party, lovely lady?" one called out to her.

"Evening. It looks fun, but I think I'll pass, if that's okay," she said. Her heart thumped so hard, it pounded in her ears.

"We have good shit," another man said, holding out his spliff before passing it to the next bloke who already looked out of it.

Tina nodded and carried on.

"Where you going? We need a bit of female action. Come join us."

One of the docile men stood. That was enough to make her jog until she reached the park's entrance. Tina thought better of it and walked along the pavements to her house.

Glad that ordeal was over, she chained and bolted the door, doing the same with the back entrance. Although she still felt scared, adrenaline pumped once again, making everything feel a little dreamlike.

Making herself a drink to warm up, she positioned herself at the kitchen table, fed up with feeling like a jittery mess. She would take positive steps. If she could go through all of this, she could handle that . . . that moron. He'd walked away, thinking he had the upper hand, but now that Tina thought about it, she might have an advantage over him.

The thing that still hurt the most was his betrayal of friendship. Even though she despised him, he was supposed to be . . . It made no difference now. The only thing that mattered was what she was going to do about it.

Knowing where he lived and worked, even his favourite drinking place, would play in her favour. After all, if she gave him the money, it wouldn't stop there. He would want more, always having that threat to bargain with. Ray would throw it in her face at every opportunity, and she couldn't have that, not in her condition. When this was all over, she never wanted to see any of her family or acquaintances again. The thought stung, though she pushed it from her mind.

There was one way, but it was risky. Tina had nothing to lose, however. He would suffer the same fate as Clive.

# CHAPTER 35

**T**INA thought about how to outwit Ray. She wasn't going to let the sleaze get away with blackmail. The first thing on her itinerary would be to make him believe she'd arranged the money at the bank, just in case he monitored her every move.

After breakfast, she headed for town, keeping an eye out for him, but he was nowhere in sight. The clear blue sky and a few dotted clouds made the day feel summery and calm. There was no mid-morning traffic to contend with, nor loads of people loitering about.

The bank had several customers and that was good for this time on a Friday. Joining the queue, she tapped her foot with impatience and observed the counter. The next light flashed and another person approached. Four more to go, and then it was her turn.

Recognising the girl from the restaurant, she tried to hide behind the tall man in front of her. He shuffled forward. That didn't work, so she re-tied her shoelace instead until she saw the girl skip out the door. Tina stood and wiped her brow, pulling her collar away from her neck as a bead of sweat ran down her centre spine.

Once it was her turn, she requested a checkbook, using the 'I spilt tea on my last one excuse' to get it. Whilst the teller did her job, Tina swapped pleasantries and waved her arms back and forth for effect. Upon completing the transaction, she said, "thank you," and promptly walked out of the bank.

The brightness stung her eyes, making her squint. She took a few minutes to cool off, as it was incredibly stuffy. Why they insisted on having the hot air blowers on in this weather was beyond her.

The "(Don't Fear) The Reaper" ringtone came from her handbag. She'd set it specifically for the caller unknown. Balancing on one leg with her bag on her other knee, she rummaged about until she found her phone and viewed the text. Her body tensed.

*What took you so long? Bit of a queue, was there? Did you get it sorted?*

Browsing the area, she couldn't see him. He wasn't in the bank either. Where was he hiding? Tina hit send.

*What do I do now?*

She waited a few minutes for his reply, though he didn't answer, and it made her feel paranoid. Sliding her phone back into her bag, she pushed through crowds of shoppers that were mooching about. She checked faces and doorways, keeping an eye out for Ray. Was he keeping an eye out for her, too?

Rounding the corner to her street, Mrs. Conerly waved a white hankie. It looked like she was surrendering. Tina waved back and joined her at her gate.

"Hello."

"Hello, dear. I'm sorry I couldn't make it to the funeral. Are you okay? Too many memories, you see. It brings it all back."

"It's alright. I'm doing . . . well . . . pretty crappy. How are you?"

"Not so bad. This blessed knee keeps playing up and my hip. Bits drop off at this age, dear."

Tina tittered at the quirky old woman. She was very sweet and smelt of roses.

"You do very well, Mrs. Conerly."

"Thank you, dear. Fancy a coffee? I would love some company. I have some Swiss rolls I can cut up to go with it."

"Now, I'm tempted. Lead the way."

"Oh, how nice! Follow me, dear."

Mrs. Conerly was a chatterbox the entire time. Two hours later, Tina managed to pry herself away. She'd enjoyed their conversation about the war. Everybody stuck together and helped each other in a time of crisis. The rations they lived on and the bombs that fell, tearing families apart, she doubted society could cope in this day and age with such stringent rules.

She was pleased by the fact that Edith didn't ask her about the ins and outs of Clive's death. Tina offered the frail old lady some company instead, and listened to what she had to say. It made her forget her troubles for a few hours.

Feeling mentally refreshed, she skipped to her front door. The moment she stepped inside, her phone jangled. Two lines from the song played before another text came through.

*Did you have a nice time with the old bat next door?*
*Now, Monday, same time, same place for hand over. I will be in touch.*

\*\*\*

**£** *10,000 . . .*
Ray number crunched and punched the air. Enough to fund his secret venture and pay off the person who wanted his kneecaps. When his balance said zero, he would blackmail her again.

He'd done all he needed to do today. It was time to sit back and wait.

He drummed his palms on his legs with excitement. Fancying a drink, he headed out to his favourite pub for a pint or three of their finest best bitters.

\*\*\*

**M**ONDAY, *same time, same place.*
Tina thought it over one more time. There was no way she wanted to meet on the bridge. Stalling him until she

figured things out properly was the best action to take. She could try to tease the information out of him, but she would need to be clever. The other option was to follow him and see where he went each day. It could prove awkward, however, as he was also spying on her.

If she could collar him at the pub, maybe, just maybe, her idea could work, but only if he left his car behind. Of course, he may insist on meeting at the bridge, nonetheless. She would have to think about that and come up with a reasonable scenario. Only having until Monday piled on the pressure.

"It's here somewhere," she said to herself, thumbing through Clive's telephone book for Ray's real mobile number. She swiped her finger down the page of his work list.

"Found it!" Tina dialled and waited for him to answer.

"Why are you ringing this number, and what the fuck do you want?"

"Secret Smile," by Semisonic, played in the background. Tina remembered it from 1999. Knowing what the song was about sent shivers down her spine. Struggling to hear, she guessed he was at his local haunt.

"We can't meet on the bridge."

She yelled the words into the mouthpiece and hoped he could hear above the racket in the background. A click sounded followed by a dialling tone.

"Bastard!"

*Calm down. Breathe. He's toying with you. He isn't in charge. You are,* she thought, whilst pacing the kitchen.

Within thirty minutes, he rang back. The noise on his end of the line sounded quieter.

"Couldn't speak earlier. Too busy having fun. What the fuck do you want?"

"To meet."

"Well, I say where and when. I will call when I'm ready."

Tina reckoned he was a little tipsy, as he slurred a little at the end of his words. This meant his barriers were down.

"Please don't put the phone down. It can't hurt to chat, can it? It's about the money."

"You better fucking have it."

She moved the mobile away from her ear a fraction until he stopped barking. "Of course, I'll have it."

"What then?"

Tina thought back to a movie she once saw and used the same line. "How do you want the cash?"

"Twenties."

"About the meeting place. Could we change it?"

"No, why?"

"I'm not comfortable carrying that amount of money through the park to the bridge."

"Drive and pull up at the bottom of the ramp."

This wasn't going to work. He was right. You could pull over. He already knew she drove to the clinic. Tina changed her tactics.

"You hung up on me earlier. Were you at The Angel?"

"Why?"

"It was Clive's favourite haunt."

"Yeah, I know. The lads will miss him on Sunday. It's the pool final."

She kept herself calm as she asked another question. "Are you playing?"

"What has it got to do with you? Just get the money."

"I . . . I will." She fiddled with the corner of the table.

"How you feeling? You've pissed me off. I'm telling Len and Joyce everything."

The phone went dead.

"Damn it!" she bellowed down the hallway.

If he uttered one word, then she would not hand over the money. Bile rose at the back of her throat. She hated him with every ounce of her being. In a quandary, she drummed her fingers.

*Ring him back.*

She hit redial and the engaged tone filled the line. Panicking, she scrolled through the contacts list and tapped the screen. An intermittent beeping came from Len's line.

*Oh, no! The bastard has told them!*

It could be a coincidence. Did it make any difference if they found out? Tina knew the answer to that. Trying again, but to no avail, she slammed the phone onto the chair. It bounced off the upholstery and slid down the side of the cushion.

In the kitchen, she splashed her face with water before drinking a glass. Tina dabbed at her chin with the tea cloth, instinctively folding it and making sure the cloths were level on the rail.

*What am I doing?*

She messed them up, leaving one on the side. Taking a deep breath, she retrieved her mobile from within the folds of the sofa and hit redial continually until she got through.

Len's Bostonian accent sounded gruff when he answered. "Hullo."

"Hi, Len. It's me. I—"

"What do you want?"

Tina twisted a length of her hair around her finger while she spoke. "I'm just ringing up to see how you both are. How did the wake go?"

"How do you think?"

"I do hope Joyce is a little better." She injected compassion into her voice, though she really didn't care about what happened to her mother-in-law.

"Not good, not good. It's knocked her for six. I'm a man, and therefore a lot stronger mentally."

Tina half smiled. *What a dick!*

"Is there anything I can do?" She already knew the answer, but asked the question anyway.

"You've done enough damage to this family as it is. Nelly will never forgive you now."

*Like I'm bothered!*

Her smile broadened. Ignoring his flip comment, she

approached the next subject on her mind.

"I know it's not a good time, Len, but I have to ask." She gulped, feeling apprehensive. "There are some things we need to sort out, both financially, as well as his . . . belongings."

"The wheels are in motion."

She hated it when Len spoke in clichés.

"Good."

"It will take awhile, but don't worry, you will get what you're owed."

Tina seethed. "I didn't mean that. Things have to be finalized. I want to get his personal effects sorted."

"All in good time. I must go. Things to do."

Relieved by the knowledge that Len knew nothing, she sighed. Ray was only playing games with her.

She remembered the last night Clive played pool. Having downed several chasers and turning up plastered, he'd finally arrived home during the late hours, swaying through the door.

Sunday night would be her aim. Chances are all the blokes would end up sloshed after a thrilling night of pool, including her target. At least this way, she stood a chance to be free completely. Of course, she wasn't callous. The guilt would make itself known when the time came, but it would remain locked in her heart forever.

*** 

SUNDAY evening came, and she found herself parked fifty yards from The Angel Public House. Tina pulled into the lay-by and twisted in her seat to look around.

The needle on the dashboard's clock said 9:30 pm. Any earlier, and her presence in the car might arouse suspicion, that's if boredom didn't take over first.

She climbed out and closed the door quietly behind her. Not wanting the orange indicators to penetrate the darkness, she left it unlocked. Dressed all in black for the occasion, she hoped to blend into the pub's tall hedges to glance inside the window.

The night was calm and refreshing, the sky clear. Country smells hovered in the air, a mixture of spring onions and cow excrement. An owl twitted on a tree branch. Another hooted a little further down the path, answering each others call. What sounded like a screech from a toddler came from the farmer's field. A fox, Tina imagined.

She took in her surroundings. The only house she saw was twenty yards back from where she'd parked. Tina wondered if its occupants could see her. It was the only place to pull over. The big blue P told her it was okay to do so.

Sneaking about at this time of night made Tina feel a little on edge. She briskly walked along, keeping an ear out for the odd car passing by. Acres of land had been cordoned off, some with mesh and others with wood. The landscape was flat, not like her hometown. In the north, the houses slanted on steep inclines, just like the Hovis advert filmed in Gold Hill in Shaftesbury.

Up ahead, the lamps outside the pub shone. Hanging baskets hung above the doorways. Picnic benches sat neatly on mown grass. A play area for the kids stood nearby with swings and climbing frames, the metalwork tarnishing the beer garden.

Eyeing the car park, she tiptoed amongst a few cars, crouching if she heard movement. Two lads were sitting in the newly assigned smoking area positioned at the side. With no sign of Ray's car, she crept over to the window and glanced inside, bobbing her head up and down over the windowsill as if playing peek-a-boo with a child.

Ray's leg dangled from the pool table as he went to take the shot, his upper body flat on the green cover. Six other lads surrounded him and looked like they were cheering him on. She'd gotten her confirmation, but a thought soon struck her, something she'd missed. Won't they leave together, or offer him a lift?

She huffed into her coat and made her way back to the big P. How would she know when he left? She questioned herself as she sat in the plush leather seat. Hitting the steering wheel with her palms, she cursed under her breath.

*Why didn't I think things through?*

It was now 10:30 pm. The pub would close in half an hour. Unless they had a lock-in, which is against the law, but some pubs still did it.

*Think! It's your only chance!*

# CHAPTER 36

**TRAIPSING** back to the pub, Tina hunkered down in the shadows behind a bush. The spring evenings were chilly, so she hitched the collar of her jacket over her ears and waited. Three of the original six men were ushered out the door by a tired-looking proprietor. The car park was almost empty with two cars remaining. She deduced that the others had left and hoped Ray wasn't one of them.

Raucous voices echoed in the stillness, the men in high spirits presumably after their pool and copious amounts of alcohol. The bolts on The Angel's door clunked and the exterior lights went off, leaving only the inside lamps to show them the way.

Tina exhaled and stepped back to keep herself well hidden. Ray was amongst them. She recognised his stance.

*Please don't take a lift.*

The taller one headed for his car, not quite as drunk as the other two, and drove away. One down, two to go.

Overhearing their slurred voices, she tried to make sense of what they were saying. The words, "I'll wolk, snot far, sne you mater," made Tina titter.

Ray's friend had tried to get into his car. He fumbled for the handle to the door, only it was the boot. Tina put a hand over her lips to squash a laugh. After managing to get into the driver's seat, he gingerly pulled onto the road without the vehicle's headlights on and weaved in the direction of Tina's Audi and the lone house.

His actions were funny, but in reality, she would have reported him for drunk driving. Other people were at risk because of his selfishness. She kicked the ground with her heel, annoyed by the fact that she hadn't been able to nab him and get him banned for life.

***

**R**AY stood alone and shuffled along on wobbly legs. His untucked shirt rode up his back, flashing a bit of hairy flesh. He took three steps to the right and one left.

He tugged his phone from his pocket and put the screen close to his eyes as if he needed reading glasses. Ray then waved it about for a signal.

The motion of the fresh air and the movement affected his equilibrium. He lost his balance and bent over his knees, throwing up and tumbling to the ground, his phone skidding across the tarmac.

***

**T**WIGGY spikes poked at Tina's head as she looked on. Placing a hand to her mouth, she held back a gag. Stepping back, dead wood cracked under the soles of her shoes. She suppressed a laugh and peeked around the bushes.

After a few attempts, he managed to get to his feet and staggered down to the exit. She gave him a few minutes until he reached the main road. At this rate, it would take him a while to get home.

Tina took one last look around to make sure the coast was clear and stepped out of her hiding place. The landlord cleared glassed from the tables, and it looked like he gazed out the window. She darted back into the shadows and watched his movements. Once it was clear, she crept out using the shrubs and bins as cover.

The smell of acid stomach contents penetrated the surrounding air and bits of carrot speckled the pool of vomit. She crouched and held her breath. Bunching her cuff around her hand, she picked up his phone and put it in her pocket. Her heart raced. Luck was on her side. What were the chances that he would drop his phone? She would deal with its disposal later. With another glance over her shoulder, she jogged to the car.

*Ray shouldn't have gotten far.*

The engine purred. With the heater on full blast, she blew on her hands. Two cars passed by, causing her to duck down in her seat. The house across the road had its curtains closed and showed no signs of activity. A lump formed at the back of her throat, and her stomach knotted at what she was about to do. Adrenalin mixed with guilt and sadness made her feel a peculiar high. Inhaling for ten seconds, she let out a long breath.

*No choice, no choice!*

"Okay, let's do this!" she said under her breath and pulled away.

Focusing on the road ahead, she kept her speed down. Two sets of headlights flashed in her rear-view mirror. Tina slowed down even more, forcing the cars behind her to overtake her vehicle. Once they passed, she speeded up once more. Too fast, and she would damage the car. Too slow, and she would wind him.

Minimal damage and maximum impact was the aim. The first place the police would look would be at car repair centres. Therefore, it had to look like an accident. Slowing her speed to a little less than 30 mph, she saw him zigzagging along the road, stepping over the white line in the middle like a solid object that needed negotiation. Ray hadn't gotten very far, and if he wasn't so inebriated, he could have walked on the pavement.

Grasping the steering wheel tight, her knuckles whitened. Tina flexed her fingers and adjusted her grip, checking for other vehicles before turning off the headlights. She aimed the car toward him and braced for impact. It all happened so fast. She swerved, changing her mind at the last minute, but the car didn't respond.

Before she knew it, his body hit the bonnet and crashed into the wing. A loud thud shattered her nerves. Slamming the brakes, her body catapulted forward and the engine stalled. Tina jumped out of the car and looked around. There were no cars or people in the vicinity.

The damage to the car was the first thing she checked. There were scratches on the paintwork and a dint, but it was nothing major. The passenger side window was streaked with blood and saliva. She'd hoped it had been enough to kill him.

Another burst of adrenaline made her hands shake. For a moment, she felt invincible. His body lay contorted on the pavement. Blood dribbled from the corner of his mouth. His arm stuck out at an obscure angle. Broke or dislocated, she wasn't sure. It was almost as if he'd bounced, the booze making his body look relaxed and bendable.

She resisted the temptation to touch or go near his body without protection. Having the phone was the important thing. Anger and guilt rose within her, however, and sobered her thoughts.

"You despicable bastard!"

Tina wanted to roll him closer to the side, so he wasn't found too soon. She wondered if there was anything in the boot she could use to push him aside. Flipping the lid, she rummaged through the items and found two carrier bags. She tipped out the contents and placed one over each hand, closing the boot.

Squatting near him, she leaned over and put one hand to his shoulder and the other to his hip, rolling him onto the verge. Pleased that he was out of sight of oncoming motorists, she put the bags in her pockets and hurried to get in the car before anyone came by. Turning the key, the engine clicked, but nothing happened. She tried again.

"Oh, shit. Oh, shit!"

Tina remembered that it had an onboard computer. You needed to give it a few seconds before starting up. She let it sit for a bit. It seemed like the longest twenty seconds of her life.

"Come on!" she said as she tried again.

Pumping the pedal like an old Vauxhall Viva with the choke pulled out, it soon started. Tina slapped the wheel and drove away. On her way back home, an odd pair of lights loomed in her rear-view mirror. She tensed as the vehicles manoeuvred past.

Turning into the drive at midnight unnerved her. It was a free county. She could go anywhere she wanted, but her nerves remained on edge. Tomorrow, she would wash the car and leave the repairs.

Tina took a couple of wipes from the glove box and rubbed away the snot and blood from the window, running it along the wing mirror. There were several excuses she'd make for the damage. Some people drove around all the time with dints in the bodywork and it wasn't that bad. Who would see it anyway if it sat in the driveway unused?

Taking the stairs two at a time to her bedroom, Tina collapsed on top of the bed. The events of the evening finally caught up with her and she began to sob. The guilt wrenched at her heart. He had family, too.

*What have I done!?*

# CHAPTER 37

**D**EEGAN pulled over to the side of the road. Two of his team members were already at the scene. Yellow tape cordoned off the road, putting a halt to any traffic wanting to come by. A van from the coroner's office parked further up.

"What we got?" he asked, popping a mint into his mouth.

"A body at the side of the road. This lady," Adams pointed to a woman standing nearby, "spotted it on her way to work."

"What time was this?"

"Seven-thirty this morning. The poor woman is in shock."

"Thank you."

Strolling toward the area, he circled the crumpled figure. Adams tagged along behind him. A man lay on his side, his clothing dishevelled. The side of his face was purple and mottled. Deegan's knees clicked as he crouched to take a closer look.

"He'd been drinking. You can smell it from here." Deegan rubbed his chin and stood. "Looks like he's been sick. It's encrusted around his mouth and dried on his shirt. Best check the pub. Chances are he came from The Angel."

"Could he have had too much to drink, stumbled, passed out, and died of hypothermia?" Adams inquired.

"It doesn't account for the way his limbs are twisted like that, or the dried blood on his face."

"Would he have rolled this far if a car hit him?"

Deegan liked Adams' attitude. She had a keen eye and was

260

always inquisitive. The woman would go far in this profession.

"What you saying? It's a hit and run?"

Adams' eyes brightened.

"I won't commit myself. We'll let the team do their job and see what they come up with." Deegan scratched his head and scoured the area. "In the meantime, check out the pub. Then, we shall go from there."

"Okay." Adams spoke into her radio.

"I'll speak to the witness," Deegan added.

Adams nodded. Heading in the middle-aged woman's direction, he found her resting her bike on her thighs. The basket at the front of it carried her handbag.

"Hello. I'm Sergeant Deegan. Thanks for your patience today."

He held out his hand. She shook it, her own hand trembling slightly.

"That's alright. Terrible business, just terrible," she said.

She had a weathered face and short black hair covered by a headscarf. Old-fashioned for this century, but expected in that age bracket.

"What's your name, please?"

"Mrs. Judith Palmer. I already told your pals that." She glared in their direction.

"I know, and it must seem strange, but I have to ask again," he said, removing a pad from his pocket. "You cycled past at about 7:30 am, is that right?"

"Well, yes."

"Could I ask you where you going at that time of the morning?"

"I was on my way to work at the old people's home at the end of Willow Street." Judith shuffled her feet, rebalancing the bike. "I shan't go into work now. It's too much of a shock, and will be on my mind for the rest of the day."

"I understand, Mrs. Palmer."

"Judith. Please, call me Judith."

Deegan smiled. "Okay, Judith, did you see anything or anyone around at the time you noticed the body?" He pressed on, not wanting to veer off point.

"Nothing. The road was clear. I only spotted it because it looked like a black bin bag. I hate fly tippers, you see. It annoys me. Of course, when I looked, it was a body." She looked Deegan in the eye "Awful, it was. How another human being could do that to one another is beyond me."

He cut her ramblings short. "We don't know what happened yet. It's too early to speculate. There are all kinds of scenarios to this situation." He didn't want her blabbing before he even knew himself, and he got the impression that she was a bit of a gossip.

"Did you touch the body at all?"

"Why would I touch it? Full of disease, no thank you."

"You would be surprised. Some people like to help, especially if they think the victim is still alive. It's perfectly understandable for them to do so."

Rotating his shoulder blades, he carried on. The cool morning air made him feel a little stiff.

"It also helps us to eliminate you from our enquiry if we were to find any evidence that belongs to you."

"Very technical, I must say. You sound like one those shows on the telly. I didn't touch him. I just looked from about here." She gestured the distance. "It was obvious he was dead."

"I can assure you. Mrs. Palmer—"

"Please, call me Judith," she said once more, and smiled at him.

"I can assure you, it's not like it is on the television."

*A man, presumed dead in a ditch, and this woman revelled in it. Some people!*

"I just need your contact details and you can go home." Deegan wrote it down as she rattled off the information. "If you make your way up there," he pointed, "the gentleman will let you through the tape."

"Oh, thank you, yes. I may hear from you. Bye then."

"Goodbye. Thank you for your assistance today."

Deegan shook his head, turned, and walked away. He watched the team at work, bagging evidence and trawling around the outskirts of the scene. Jan approached, wearing a white all-in-one and gloves on her hands.

"We meet again. What we got?" he asked.

"How are you? Nice to see you again."

Standing parallel with each other, he could smell the scent of fresh soap emanating from her skin. "Not bad. Could do with a massage. I'm all tense."

"That's a job for the Eve. How is she?"

"Not bad. The baby likes to keep us both awake."

"I bet."

"Anyway, you know me and idle chitchat. So, can you tell me anything?"

"We will be able to tell you more after the examination. Judging by the injuries, something hit him for sure."

"Thought so. Any idea, what?

"A car. Van, maybe? He has a broken arm."

"Would that have killed him?"

"You know I can't tell you that until the PM." Jan smiled, raised her brows, and squinted with one eye.

Deegan frowned, accepting the naughty glare, knowing she could not divulge the information.

"Any ID on the victim?"

"Well, no ID, but just a wallet in his pocket." She held up the clear plastic bag she'd taken from the case on the ground. "Ten pound note, no credit cards."

"Any phone, keys?

"No mobile. Keys, he may have dropped. There's a pool of vomit just inside the entrance to the pub. We took some samples. My guess, he was very drunk. But as you know—"

"I have to wait for the PM."

"I wasn't going to say that." Jan smiled. "He was dressed in black and drunk. It would have been hard for any motorist to see him until it was too late."

"True, but the driver should have stopped."

"He could have been mistaken for an animal. Most people don't stop if they hit a deer or a fox on a country lane at night."

"Okay, let's see what the PM tells us."

"He will be priority. I hope to get to it later today." She put the bag into the case. "We will be moving the body shortly."

"Thanks, Jan. A positive ID would be a great help."

"You're welcome. As soon as possible, I promise." She stepped away.

Deegan turned in time to see Adams canter down the road toward him. Out of breath, the female PC approached his side.

"You need the gym."

"Tell me about it. Here's me thinking I was fit," she said through a lungful of air. "I managed . . . to . . . speak . . ."

"Get your breath back first and then tell me."

Her breathing slowed, and she spoke. "The pub was closed, but the landlord lives above. I had a chat with him."

"Do go on."

"They had a pool night. Six of them, all in high spirits. Other than that, the pub was quieter than usual for a Sunday night."

"And our victim?" He grew impatient. "Spit it out."

"Only one walked home."

"Does the landlord know who it is?"

"Sorry. I briefly explained what had happened. Apparently, the rest drove or got lifts."

"Of course, it could be random and he never came from the pub at all," Deegan surmised.

"Bit circumstantial being paraletic so near a pub, don't you think?"

"I bet those others were over the limit."

"Probably, although the landlord—" She looked at her pad. "Ian Jones says not. Oh, and he wasn't happy to be disturbed at this time of the morning."

"Tough, and he would say that in trying to protect his customers."

"Anyway, just in case, I got some information about the guys. They all worked in the same place and were regulars. I also got the lone walker's name. You never know, we may get lucky."

"Good work, Adams. What's his name?"

"It's . . ." she began, and rattled off what he wanted to know.

# CHAPTER 38

**A**FTER another restless night, Tina's bones ached. She'd felt bilious all morning and had a raging headache. Regret and the memory of the night before tumbled through her mind. She wouldn't get away with it. How could she? The police were hot on DNA and ferreting things out.

"Why did I do it?" she asked herself. "What choice did I have?"

It was now late morning. The only thing she could think of was cleaning the car and ditching the evidence. Resisting the temptation to take it to the jet wash, she grabbed a bucket from under the sink, filled it with soap, and got to work.

Mrs. Conerly appeared at her gate. "You cleaning the car, dear?"

"Morning. I thought it could do with a spruce."

Tina wiped her brow, thankful for Mrs. Conerly's fence being in the way. She could only see the tail end of the Audi.

"Nice weather for it."

"It is a lovely day."

Tina began scrubbing the wheels and cracking on with the bodywork.

Edith took the hint and said, "Cheerio."

She finished with a polish of the interior. The less people who saw the damage, the better. Tina re-positioned the car and parked closer to the hedge-covered fence to obscure the passenger wing. Once out of the car, she looked at the gap. Unless you were super skinny, no one could get in.

Back in the kitchen, she rested her hand on the counter to ease herself up after putting the bucket and cloth away. For a moment, she felt a little queasy. She sat down until the feeling passed. Stroking her stomach with the palm of her hand, she looked at her tiny bump at the same time, thinking about the consequences of her actions.

It would be a massive impact on both their lives if she got found out, having decided to keep the gift forming inside her womb. She didn't have the heart to dispose of it so clinically, no matter what the circumstances of its conception were. What type of mother would she be if she went to prison? The child would be orphaned. She'd do all she could to not be caught.

Suppressing her thoughts, she moved on to more pressing matters, the discarding of the evidence. Tina reached for her coat and dug into its pockets for the bags she'd used last night and Ray's phone. She wasn't interested in scrolling through the photos, and started to dismantle the mobile. Her fingers fumbled in doing so, but she persevered. Retrieving the hammer, she smashed the screen and got to work on the rest of it before bagging everything.

Another thought crossed her mind. He'd threatened to put the video on YouTube, but nothing could be done about that. If it was on his computer, she could hardly break into his house and erase it. She hoped it was just an idle threat.

Tina collected her keys from the side and made her way outside. On the way to the park, she dropped the pieces down several drains and in bins. She then sat in her favourite spot opposite the pond full of ducks. Their tails twitched as they waddled toward her in the hopes of getting a tasty morsel. On her right sat a bin full of empty bread bags. She added hers and shoved them down as hard as she could. She circled the park twice to watch the squirrels before reaching the main road and going home.

At the end of the street, her chest tightened and she couldn't breathe. Tina leant on the neighbour's brick wall, trying to comprehend what she saw. She willed her legs to move, but they refused.

*Breathe. You can do this.*

Tina's heart was still pounding in her ears when she approached the drive.

*Stay calm and breathe.*

Two figures stood at the front door. She greeted them with a smile.

"Hello again, Mrs. Blythe. May we come in?" Sergeant Deegan asked.

It took every ounce of willpower she had within herself to stop her hand from shaking as she slid the key in the lock. She was sure they could see it tremble. They had come to arrest her. The life she wanted was now nothing more than a dream.

"Yes, of course," she said, and cleared her throat. "Please, come through. What's this about?"

"May we sit down?" Deegan asked.

"Yes, what's this about?" she repeated once more, sitting on the edge of the seat, her knees bouncing up and down.

"We have reason to believe that you know a man named Ray Johnson."

The female officer who took her statement, whose name she could never remember, sat next to him.

"Yes, well, not me, but my late husband."

*You can do this. Pretend. Pretend!*

"He was found dead this morning, and we are appealing for witnesses. We also want an insight into his friends and family." Deegan leaned forward. "We know he was a friend of yourself and your husband."

"He was more Clive's friend than mine. They worked together."

"Would you know anything about this incident?"

"No."

"We have to ask, so don't look so worried. Did he have any enemies or grievances with anyone that you know of?"

"I only met him once or twice. Maggie and his family are the best ones to ask."

*Ask the question. It's odd if you don't.*

"How did he die?"

"We can't say until after the post-mortem. Maggie, you said? She's his wife?

"No, girlfriend. Don't know his parents at all. Where did he die?"

In full flow, Tina relaxed and took things in her stride.

"Do you have her address and phone number?" Deegan asked.

Adams spoke up and answered Tina's question. "Morris Lane, down by The Angel Public House."

"That was his local haunt. All I know is, he did like a drink and often went out with Clive."

"Could I have Maggie's details, please? Oh, and sorry that I have to ask this, but where were you last night?"

"I shall get my book." She went off to fetch it and returned to give Deegan the relevant information.

"Thanks. Where did you say you were last night?"

"Here, in my bed in this house. Ever since my husband's death, I can't face going out." She scratched her calf.

"I know, it's still very fresh in your mind, but I have to ask." He frowned at Tina. "Did anyone know you were here?

"Of course, my friend, Sam. She has been a massive help to me."

"Could I have her number, too, please?"

"Why do you want her number? She doesn't know Ray."

"Elimination purposes. We're just doing our job."

Tina gave him Sam's number. "There we are. I do hope you get to the bottom of whatever happened to Ray. Nice chap, he was."

"So do we. We'll be in touch if we need to talk to you again."

"Anytime." Tina saw them to the door.

"Goodbye now," Deegan said.

Adams nodded at her as she passed. She waited at the door and watched as they strolled past the Audi, glancing at its bodywork before climbing into their car and driving off. Tina scurried into the kitchen and picked up her mobile. With shaky hands, she dialled Sam's number.

# CHAPTER 39

**THE** incident room buzzed. Deegan stood by a white board at the front of the room as the other officers went about their business. Some tapped on computers with phones attached to their ears, others stood by fax machines and printers. Telephones shrilled in the distance.

The room was large and square with walls painted in sterile colours. Desks were piled with mountains of paperwork, ready to topple at the slightest vibration. Coffee cups filled with black diesel adorned their workspaces, keeping them alert and ready for action. The scent of bacon drifted through the vents from the canteen, enticing his taste buds. His stomach grumbled as he blu-tacked the last bit of information to the board.

"Okay, listen up, everyone."

Many heads turned in his direction. They stopped what they were doing, their ears at attention.

"Right, this is Ray Johnson." He pointed at a photograph with a biro. "He was found in the early hours this morning at the side of the road near The Angel Public House."

Nods and low groans came from the team.

"He was inebriated and passed out on the verge. Now, Jan rushed the post-mortem through for me this afternoon. It turns out he was hit by a vehicle or a van and left for dead. The victim's cause of death was hypothermia, as his injuries didn't kill him. He had several broken bones, but no internal bleeding. He'd been drinking and vomited. As you can see," he pointed again, "he was dressed in black, a motorist's nightmare. It could be that the driver panicked and thought he hit an animal." Deegan circled his shoulders to loosen the crick in his neck. "We have appealed for witnesses, but so far, we have nothing."

Another officer coming in to the room and grabbing something from the desk distracted everyone's attention. She mouthed an apology and left.

Deegan nodded and carried on. "I know some of you are familiar with the case, so what did we find?"

Mary Adams said, "As you know, I paid the landlord a visit. We were able to find the victim's name and work place. However, he was reluctant to cooperate."

"Yes, that's right, Adams. We also paid Tina Blythe a visit. Turns out that her late husband, who died in an accident not long ago, was the victim's best friend."

"Has the body been officially identified?" a fresh-faced black man asked from the back of the room.

"Yes, and the family has been informed." He tapped his pen on the photo and turned around to face the classroom.

"Anything on his girlfriend, Maggie? Barnes, you were investigating that. What did you find?" He popped a Polo mint into his mouth.

"It's strange, if I'm to be honest." She riffled through her notes.

"Go on."

"Their relationship was, shall we say, more of a sexual one. She didn't seem shocked about his death at all. Apparently, they socialised with Mr. and Mrs. Blythe often," she said, fidgeting in her seat. "Maggie was more interested in slating Mr. Blythe's wife than she was in the victim."

"Maybe, they were having an affair," another voice chipped in.

"This Maggie sounds like a sort," a rookie also sitting at the back of the room replied.

"Quiet down! We're getting carried away. Barnes, look a bit more into that, please. Find out where they socialized together.

Maggie can't be ruled out." Glancing around the room, he asked, "Where is PC Smith today?"

"Day off," someone said.

"Not now, he isn't. Get him in. We need the help."

Adams cleared her throat. "The victim's parents are friends with Mr. and Mrs. Blythe. I know it's going off point, but again, like Barnes said earlier, none of them seem to have a good word to say about the wife."

"Interesting." Deegan rubbed his chin. "Let's see what the trace evidence shows up. In the meantime, Adams, I want you to go to the house near the pub and see if they heard or saw anything."

"Yes, sir." She swigged the last dregs of her coffee.

"Let's step up the pace, people. I want eyewitnesses. Find me some. I don't believe that no one saw anything."

Some of the PCs scurried out the door to run the errands requested by their boss. Deegan went back to his desk and started to read the file. He'd turned one page when his phone rang.

"Deegan. Yep, one sec."

Putting the earpiece in the nook of his shoulder, he reached for the relevant information. "Yep, great news." He licked his lips and listened. His heart rate increased with the news. "Excellent." He put the phone back in its cradle once he was done with the phone call.

"Any news on Smith?" he yelled into the noisy room.

"He's on his way."

"Thank you, Adams. Come here a minute."

"Sir."

"After you've been to the house, I want you to check out body repair shops. We are looking for a dark car with possible wing damage. See if anyone took a car in for repairs. Take Barnes with you."

"Barnes. Barnes!" he shouted. "You're going with Adams."

Liz Barnes nodded and grabbed her coat. She bumped into Smith on her way out of the room.

"Hello . . ."

"Can't stop. We still on for tonight?" she asked.

"I hope so. See you later."

Adams followed close behind and smiled at the new budding relationship. She was happy for them.

Smith walked up to Deegan's desk. "Afternoon, sir."

Deegan looked him in the eye and tilted his head. "Ah, there you are! Sorry to call you in."

"That's okay. I just need bringing up to speed." Smith shuffled his feet.

He raised a brow at him. "I want you to have a look at the victim's house. See what you can find." He handed him a slip of paper containing the address. "Look for any clues to a grievance he might have had. Anything suspicious, you know the drill."

Smith glanced at the information and slid the paper into his pocket. "Do we have a warrant?"

"Yes, we do. A couple of officers will meet you there."

"Sir."

"It could be that the person who knocked him over was on their way back from work and panicked. Maybe it was pre-meditated. It can't hurt to check."

Smith turned on the balls of his feet and left. Swivelling in his chair, Deegan scratched his head. Something didn't add up and it niggled at him. Why did he keep hearing the name Tina Blythe from so many unexpected sources?

# CHAPTER 40

**T**INA slammed the phone down before it connected. What was she thinking? Not only could the police trace the call, but was it fair to expect Sam to cover her back? It would be selfish to bring her into it. After all, Sam was having a baby after a horrid two years. Now, she was going to ask her for the unthinkable.

She pondered her predicament. Sam being her alibi meant the difference between prison and a fresh start. She would speak to her, though Sam didn't have to comply. Deep inside, she knew she had to try.

Driving to Sam's house to speak in person was out of the question. One, she wanted to leave the car in place, and two, she may be at work. Talking to her from a phone box was the only way.

*Where's the nearest one?* she wondered. With mobile phones and modern devices, they seemed outdated.

*How much do they take?*

Searching through her purse, she found three one-pound coins.

*Would that be enough?*

Deciding that it was, she headed into town. A few years back, the bus station had a line of phone boxes situated near the supermarket. She wasn't sure if that was still the case, but she would try there first.

Tina's self-esteem felt beaten and deflated. With CCTV and Big Brother these days, how could she possibly expect to get away with another crime? Shaking off the negative vibes, she carried on.

The station was packed, and as usual, people formed wobbly

lines, queuing for their buses. The smell of exhaust fumes and food outlets churned her stomach. To the left, stood the museum, and further on, the public conveniences. A waft of urine and disinfectant drifted from the toilet as she hurried past. Pinching her nose, she weaved through the pedestrians to the other side of the station.

The windows from Sainsbury's loomed in the distance, advertising their bargains and offers. Tina was pleased to see that the bike sheds were still attached to the side. They hadn't been demolished like so many other buildings in the area, making it a part of history. This was where the telephones used to be. Glancing through the hordes, one box remained. She made her way in its direction as an old woman entered the cubicle. Tina stood outside and tapped her foot with impatience.

"Won't be long. Need a taxi."

Tina gave her a thin smile. *Why don't you use one from the rank? It's just over there.*

A few moments later, the old dear held the door open so that she could slip inside. Tina nodded and thanked her.

The glass walls of the *TARDIS* surrounded her like a shroud. Tina had never seen such a modern booth. They were more soundproof than the old red ones. It took a short while for her to figure out the newfangled features. Once she did, she dialled Sam's home number first. If there was no answer, she would ring her mobile. She shuffled her weight from one foot to the other and waited.

"Hello."

"Hi, Sam! It's me."

"What number are you calling from? I thought you were trying to sell me something."

"A phone box. I'm pleased you're not at work."

"I have a few days off. You sound stressed. Is everything okay?"

"Not really. I have a problem I need your help with."

"What's happened? Just tell me, Babe."

"This is going to sound strange, so please forgive me for asking.

275

Could you cover for me and say you were with me last night?"

"What's wrong? You're scaring me now, Babe."

"I'm frightened I may lose everything." Tina held back the tears, her voice low as her hand shook, making the receiver tap against the side of her head.

"Hey, come on now. Is it the funeral? Did something happen?"

"No, that went as well as it could under the circumstances. Would you . . . cover for me? Say I was with you? Please."

"From who?"

"The police."

A long pause crackled through the line. The sun shone into the booth and the temperature rose. Sweat beaded her forehead. Swallowing, her throat craved moisture.

"What have you done?" Sam asked. "Please, tell me, is everything alright?"

"Nothing, I swear." She felt bad fibbing to her best friend. "I'm paranoid, I guess."

"I can help, if you tell me."

Not sure how to phrase the next line, she blurted, "Ray is dead. He was found near the pub."

"What's that got to do with you?"

"He was Clive's best friend." Tina shielded her eyes from the sun, and then pulled her top away from her neck with her free hand, letting the air dry her skin.

"I know he was, and it's a shame he's dead. How awful, but I still don't see what it has to do with you."

The pips alerted Tina that she was getting low on credit. She slid another pound in the slot.

"Don't you see? First, Clive has an accident, and now Ray. It all points to me."

"I can see why you think that. They have no reason to involve you. How did he die?"

"I don't know. They just found his body. The police paid me a visit and told me."

"What do you want me to say? That I came over?"

"Yes, thank you. One more thing, the police may pay you a visit."

"I sort of expected that, as you want me to cover for you."

"Sorry, my head is all over the place."

"It's okay."

"Thank you."

"I will have to tell the hubby, though."

"Why?"

"If they asked, it would be odd, don't you think, him not knowing where I was?"

"Yes, I see. Could you say you walked to mine from work?"

"Of course. Now, please stop worrying."

"Time . . . What time did you leave?" Tina asked.

"What time would you like me to say?"

"You stayed over and left in the morning." Her heart raced.

"Okay, I know you and your nerves must be shattered, but I'm not stupid. You're hiding something. You have your reasons, and I understand."

"Promise, I will tell you everything, but not yet."

"I have to go. Someone's at the door. Speak soon. I'm here, always and forever."

"Always and fore—" she began, but the line had already gone dead.

The temperature felt comfortable as she left the booth. Air dried her forehead and sent a chill down her spine. Without Sam in her life, she would feel empty. She wanted to see her baby grow up and become a step-aunt. More guilt coursed through every inch of her body like an incurable disease. Not wanting to go home, she decided to have a wander down by the riverside after she bought some rolls.

The Customs House and the statue of Captain Vancouver were on the left as she strolled by. Cobbled streets paved the way in the old part of town, steeped in history with wonderful old buildings. Strolling over the bridge, she reached the dockside and looked over the side. The tide was out on the river Ouse.

Webbed feet made patterns over the exposed mud flats. Tearing bread into tiny bits, she flung it over the side. From nowhere, a selection of sea birds squawked, talking to her as if thanking her as they eyed the tasty pieces. The light made their wings look silver and precious, their plumage clean. Those with black heads were ready for the mating season. A Heron crossed the sky, coming in to land.

Inhaling the salty air and taking in her surroundings calmed her nerves and eased her aching heart. These moments from nature lifted her soul.

With the rolls devoured, she put the bag in the bin and walked the front. Taking a seat near the newly built moorings, she began to people watch. She kicked at the ground, unsure of what to do next, feeling lost and alone.

There would come a time when Sam needed to know the truth. Maybe Sam would never forgive her for what she had done to Ray.

*I will take it all to the grave.*

Scared to go home, in case the police came back, thoughts of the car tumbled through her mind. What could she do about the damage? She needed to stop acting as if she was guilty and start acting like someone who had no clue about what happened.

*Stay in character and convince yourself you didn't do it.* Standing, Tina stretched and took a deep breath before heading home. *I can do this!*

# CHAPTER 41

**D**EEGAN thumbed through the paperwork on his desk. He'd sent out a memo the day before and wanted everyone involved on the hit and run back in the incident room by 10:00 am the next morning. It was now 9:45 am, and he waited for his officers to arrive.

Sipping at a cup of coffee, he'd succumbed to the canteen aromas and took a careful bite from a bacon roll, just in case ketchup dripped onto his white shirt. He wiped the grease from his chin with a napkin and brushed the crumbs from his lap.

Adams and Barnes were the first to arrive. They took their places at their designated workstations.

"Morning," he said, throwing the remnants of his breakfast into the bin.

"Morning," they replied in unison.

"We caught you having a crafty snack!" Adams jested.

"You did. I recommend the canteen for its fine bacon rolls."

They snickered.

"I might try one," Barnes said.

Shuffles, door bangs, and chairs scraping attracted Deegan's attention to the back of the room. Everyone involved had started to congregate at their desks, and waited for updates and a debrief.

"Okay. Morning all."

Mumbled mornings came from his team.

"Any developments?"

For a second, all was silent. No one wanted to talk over each other or appear rude.

"Barnes, shoot," he said, and moved to his position in front of the board, pen ready to point.

"The last time they socialized together was a few weeks ago. They only went out as a foursome on occasion." She took a deep breath. "Clive and Ray went to pool night every Sunday with the lads from work." Barnes flipped through some pages. "I did go to the restaurant where they ate. A really posh place in town, very formal."

"It's nice there. Expensive, though. Great steak," Adams said.

"You should try the Roulade. It's to die for," Barnes replied.

Deegan coughed. "I'm sure it is, but can we leave the chitchat until later, please?"

They looked at one another like naughty school girls being ticked off by the teacher.

"Barnes! Carry on."

"Anyway, I paid them a visit and spoke to the owner, who then passed me on to Helen Watt, their waitress." Barnes found the relevant information. "Helen Watt reported that Ray was a normal guy. Pleasant, polite, nothing untoward. In her words, he was a bit of a charmer. However, she did say that one of the women looked uncomfortable, and Mr. Blythe ordered for his wife."

"Ordering for your wife is not out of the ordinary," Deegan said.

"It turns out later in the evening, Tina Blythe stormed into their bathroom and was gone for about fifteen minutes. When she came back, her eyes were red. Oh, and the waitress got the impression that Mrs. Blythe had an eating disorder."

Deegan digested the information. Being pernickety and thinking outside the box is what got him the position as sergeant. He knew he needed to stew.

"Adams, how did you get on at the house near the pub?"

"They arrived home after the incident. They'd been on holiday and left the lights on timer to give the impression they were home. So, nothing there, sir."

"Damn, no eyewitnesses as of yet, either. Repair shops and

garages?"

"Not looking good there either, sir. I left our number with the local ones and asked them to ring if anyone shows up wanting repairs that fit our description. The thing is, we need more officers. There are so many to check out, and so few of us to go around." Adams crossed her ankles under her desk and leant forward. "A thought did occur to me, though."

"Share it with us, Adams."

"If this is a hit and run, and nothing to do with friends or family, then the car or van who hit the victim could be halfway up the country by now. This makes it almost impossible to find them."

"Good point, but not impossible. We will find the culprit. It may take a while, but we will find them. Barnes, I want you to talk to the other lads that were with him that night. They all work in the same place, so that should make it easier."

"Okay, sir."

"Smith! Have you fallen asleep back there? You're very quiet."

"No, sir, just listening."

"How did you get on at the victim's house?" Deegan scratched his head and then folded his arms about his chest.

"A normal bachelor pad. Lots of porn, some illegally obtained. I seized his computer. The techs are looking at it now. This man was sick in the head. Some of the DVDs . . . Well, I've never seen filth as bad as that."

Smith presented a bag filled with paraphernalia and placed it on Deegan's desk.

"How do you know?" Deegan skimmed through the titles, stacking them neatly on the evidence table.

"The victim had one in the player, sir. I watched a few minutes before I removed it. Maybe this has something to do with his death. Here is another thing. This Maggie . . . his girlfriend appeared in it. He had a room with filming equipment, too. We seized it all, sir."

"You could be right. It is certainly another avenue to follow."

"His house showed no foul play, only what I've just told you.

Did you find a mobile phone? Was it found on the victim? I noticed a charger."

"No. We think in his drunken state he may have dropped it. We combed the surrounding area, but found nothing," Barnes added.

"Right. Smith, keep me informed on what they find on his computer. Try to find out where he got those films from."

"Adams, you're coming with me."

"Where are we going, sir?" Adams gathered up her things, ready to move.

"To pay a visit to Mrs. Tina Blythe."

"Why."

"You'll see."

***

**D**EEGAN stopped his car at a red light, drumming his fingers on the steering wheel. Adams pulled the visor down to protect her eyes from the sudden glare.

"So, tell me, why we are paying her a visit?"

"We had the trace evidence results back. They found fragments of dark paint in his wounds. I want to check her car."

"Do you really think she could be a part of it? After all she's been through?" She shifted in her seat.

"We have to look at everything, and go where the evidence takes us. Of course, this is just my gut instinct."

"Your guts again? You should see a doctor about that," she joked.

He made his last turn. Not long after they left the station, he said, "Here we are," and pulled into Tina's drive.

"She might be out," Adams said.

"Then we can still take a look, can't we?" He eased the car to a stop. "Oh, look! A shiny car!"

"It's been cleaned."

"Yes, it has. Let's have a look first. Then, we can have a chat with her." Stretching as he got out of the police car, he rubbed his hands together.

Adams crossed the short drive to inspect the Audi. "It's parked really tight up against the fence."

"I wonder why."

\*\*\*

**THE** sound of crunching gravel came from the drive, as well as the low murmur of voices. She peeked out from behind the bedroom window's curtain.

*Oh, no!*

The sight of two uniformed officer's checking out the Audi made her heart rate drop. Feeling light-headed, she flopped onto the bed and brought her knees to her chest. The lampshade in the centre of the ceiling circled and the bedroom swirled before her very eyes. Panic spread through her body, but the rush of adrenaline raised her pulse and the dizziness faded.

Any moment now, there would be a knock at the door. She was doomed! Steadying herself and making her way down the stairs, she stopped. Should she go out and greet them? Would that look too obvious?

Tina sat on the bottom of the stairs and waited. Soon enough, the tap came. She inhaled, counted to ten, and exhaled before she answered the door.

"Hello again. May we come in?"

"Hello, of course. Please, do come through. What can I help you with today?"

"We'd like to ask you a few questions regarding Ray Johnson." Deegan's eyes met Adams' inquisitive stare.

"Would you like some tea? I have no milk, though." Tina's eyes darted from one to the other.

"No, we're good. Thank you. Sit down, please."

She sat down on the sofa. "How can I be of help? What's this about?"

Deegan got straight to the point. "How did you damage your car?"

"It's not mine. It's my late . . . husband's. The car is too powerful for me. I knocked it into a bollard. I dare not drive it now. It scares me. Why?"

"The car involved in the hit and run involving Mr. Johnson—"

"A hit and run? Oh, dear! Have you found anyone yet? I don't know how I can help." Tina kept her tone soft and fragile.

"As I was saying, the car or van we're looking for is consistent with the damage to your car."

Tina knew he was trying to utilise scare tactics to get her to say what they wanted her to say. They would need to have a paint sample taken as proof, and she knew SOCO would take the car.

"You can't think it was me, surely?"

*Did I say the right thing? Did that sound incriminating? Breathe. Stay nice and calm. You can do this.*

"Why would you say that, Mrs. Blythe?"

"Well, if you think it's Clive's car, and it's not been stolen, what else am I to think?"

"Would you mind if PC Adams took a look round? I don't want to get a warrant."

"Why would I mind? I've nothing to hide. Please excuse the mess. I haven't cleaned up since his . . . death." Tina ran her finger along the nearest piece of furniture. "Look?"

"You had time to clean the car, though," Deegan said, nodding at Adams, giving her permission to look around.

"It was Clive's pride and joy. He would have hated to see it dirty. I needed to keep it clean."

"You don't get on with many family members, do you?"

"How do you know that, and what's that got to do with anything?" Tina's armour cracked. Tears flooded her cheeks. "I . . ." Sobs wracked her entire body. "I've been to hell and back, and just lost my husband. His funeral was only last week. Now you come here and treat me like this." She rubbed her eyes with her sleeve. "I've always had a fractured relationship with my . . . family. Please, leave me alone to grieve."

In his urgency to solve the case, Deegan felt a pang of remorse. He'd pushed her too hard. She wasn't even a suspect. He'd taken a lucky guess at her relationship with her family based on his instincts and what'd he'd learned, thus far, about her.

"I'm just doing my job."

Adams came back into the room, shook her head, and said, "Everything is fine, Sarge."

"Okay, Mrs. Blythe. The accident happened on Sunday evening. I have to ask you this, so please do understand that it's procedure. Where were you from around 9:00 pm?"

"My friend stayed the night." She sniffed. "She left in the morning."

"Friend's name?" Deegan gestured to Adams to write it down.

"I have already given you the details from your previous visit."

"I just need to make sure the information is correct."

"Samanther Williams."

"Address."

Adams wrote everything down as Tina rattled off the information once more.

"What time did she arrive?"

"About six-ish, and she left early the next morning."

"We will check out your alibi. Sorry to have bothered you today. We may be in touch."

He headed for the door. Adams hung back and rubbed Tina's arm, passing her the tissue box from the side. Tina blew her nose and mouthed a, "thank you."

After they both left, she curled into a ball on the sofa. All of the pent-up stress and anger had bubbled over. What strength she had left fizzled out. Her limbs felt too heavy to move, so she stared at the walls and gave in to the hysteria roiling within her.

# CHAPTER 42

**D**EEGAN made a call from Tina's driveway. "Barnes," he said, shifting in his seat as he slid his hand into his pocket and retrieved the information Adams had given him. "I have an address here. Could you find out and check phone records for me? Mobile and landline." He relayed the information. "As soon as you can. Yep, bye."

"What do you think?" Adams queried, clicking the seat belt into its holder.

"Not sure." He put the car in gear and reversed.

"She's either an incredible actress or very genuine. Maybe we are barking up the wrong tree."

"I put a lot of pressure on her in there, unjustifiably so. I wanted to get her reaction."

"Well, you did that, sir. What about the car damage?"

"Let's speak to her alibi first, and see what the phone records show." He indicated right. "It's about a fifteen minute drive to Mrs. Samanther Williams' place."

"That name rings a bell. That's not the Williams family that owns and runs the electronics factory out of town, is it?"

"That's the one. He owns an art gallery in Cork Street, London, too. Paintings sell for thousands. Very respectable man in the community," he said, changing gear. "Samanther is his only daughter, apparently." Looking over his shoulder and to his right, he tutted. "Why is it when motorists see a police car, they slow down to a ridiculous speed? As if we don't know!"

Adams chortled. "Well, it reduces speed. That's got to be a good thing."

"Not to below 30 mph, it isn't."

The soft tones of his satellite navigation system repeated they had reached their destination. He turned into the cul-de-sac. Blossoms had fallen from the weeping cherry tree and covered the neatly cut lawn in a pink blanket. Spent Daffodils filled the borders. As they approached, the lemon scent from the potted fir trees on each side of the white front door irritated their nostrils.

Adams wiped her nose as Deegan rang the bell. Its shrill sounded sophisticated. A beaming smile from a fresh-faced woman in sloggey trousers and a t-shirt opened the door.

"Hello, Madam. I'm Sergeant Deegan from the Norfolk Constabulary." He flashed his credentials from a black wallet. "And this is PC Adams. May we come in, please?"

"Okay, what have I done?" she asked, holding both wrists out in front of her. "You better slap the cuffs on me now."

Deegan held in a smile. Adams looked away and bit her lip.

"Mrs. Samanther Williams?" he inquired.

"Please, call me Sam."

"We need to speak with you."

"Please, come in and go on through."

She directed them through to the lounge. Deegan entered first. Adams shuffled on behind him, both sets of shoes clicking across the laminated floor.

"Please, take a seat."

The cream leather sofa whooshed as they sat down. The black glass coffee table in the middle was a good contrast to the other décor in the room.

"Can I offer you both a tea, coffee, or fruit juice?"

"No thank you."

Adams raised her palm to decline. Sam took a seat and thoughtfully gazed at the pair.

"So, how can I help today? Sorry about out there." She tipped her head to indicate the front entrance. "We've had some wonderful news, so we're both a bit excited."

"We?"

"Me and my husband, Lee. What's this about?"

"Do you know a man by the name of Ray Johnson?" Straight to the point, he nudged Adams, who took out her pad.

"Vaguely, why?"

"He was found in the early hours of Sunday morning by the side of the road near The Angel Public House."

Sam's hands flew to her mouth. She then cupped her face before putting them on her knees.

"Oh, my God! How awful? What happened?"

"He was involved in a hit and run, and we are appealing for witnesses."

"I don't know how I can help. I hardly knew him. Ray was a friend of a friend."

He cleared his throat. "You do know a Mrs. Tina Blythe?"

"Of course, she's my best friend. I've known her since childhood, although I can't see what this has to do with her."

"Where were you on Sunday evening?" he asked.

"I was with Tina." Sam locked her fingers across her knees, and rocked back and forth.

"You have proof of that?"

"Yes, ask my husband. He's in the shower right now, though."

"What time were you there, and when did you leave?"

"Please. I don't like your sternness," Sam said as she looked at Deegan. "I was at Tina's from about six and I left in the morning. She has just lost her husband. I was comforting her, as she has no family to rely upon. Before you ask, it's none of your business."

"Apologies, Mrs. Williams. I'm just doing my job, and this is an urgent case."

"Is he always like this?" Sam asked Adams.

"Just doing his job," she said with a serious face.

"Could you tell me what you chatted about? And what you did, please?"

"You mean in between tears and the comfort? We had wine and chocolates. I took some flowers, too. I didn't want to leave her in that devastated state, so I stayed over and walked to work the next morning."

Footsteps thudded from the ceiling above Deegan's head. "Is that your husband?"

"No, it's the milkman."

"May I remind you, I'm conducting an investigation into a death."

"Lighten up, I was only teasing. We've just found out we're having a baby, so please forgive the high spirits. It cheered Tina up, too. I gave her copy of the scan. Thought it would take her mind off things."

"Can I speak with your husband?"

"Yes, I'll go and get him."

Sam left the room and yelled up the stairs. Deegan and Adams looked at each other, and then back at Sam as she came into the room.

"Two minutes."

He twiddled his thumbs while he waited. Adams looked about. The smell of body wash and hair gel drifted into the room as Lee walked into the lounge.

"We have guests," he said, and plonked himself down beside his wife. "Hello, how can I help?"

"I shall keep this brief. Your wife can fill you in after we've gone. Where was your wife on Sunday evening?"

"She was at Tina's. Poor lass has just lost her husband." He swivelled in his seat and eyed Sam, who was making circular motions across her stomach.

"Are you both off work?" Adams asked.

"Holiday, to buy things for the baby, and what's that got to do with anything?" Lee prodded in a gruff voice.

"Just curious."

Her words went in one ear and out the other, however. Lee was now stroking his wife's stomach as they playfully smiled at each other. Deegan saw their gestures and smiled.

*Time to go,* he thought, nodding at Adams.

"Congratulations to you both. We may be in touch."

They rose and made their way to the door.

Sam saw them out and said, "I do hope you find whoever did it. Sorry I couldn't be more help."

Deegan heard Lee shout to his wife in the background.

"Mrs. Mummy, come here so I can cuddle you!"

Feeling a little uncomfortable by the soppy behaviour, he groaned inwardly. *Still, better to be like that, than beating the crap out of each other.*

His phone rang as he was about to open the car door. Pressing his back against the hard metal, he folded an arm across his chest and spoke.

"Deegan."

"Sir, I checked the records for the phone. I mentioned it was urgent and they rushed them through."

"Thank you, Barnes. Anything?"

"No, not for the time frames you were looking for. In fact, nothing in the last week. Not from the numbers you gave me. Did you want me to check all the calls out?"

"No, that won't be necessary. See you back at the station."

Sliding his phone back into his pocket, he got into the car. Adams was already belted up. Adjusting his position, he turned toward her.

"Nothing on the phone records."

"Sir . . ." Adams rubbed her nose and then stared at him. "Earlier, when I browsed through Mrs. Blythe's house, there was a scan on the dressing table by her bed. I did wonder, at the time, who it was from." She picked a hair from her uniform and dropped it in the foot well. "It seems to me her alibi checks out. There were also some dead flowers on the windowsill, along with an empty box of chocolates and a wine bottle in the kitchen. I don't think she did it, sir."

Deegan rubbed his chin and scratched his head. "She has no motive either, but there is damage to the car," he said, more for himself than to inform Adams.

"Are you going to impound the car?"

"To be honest, there wasn't that much damage on it. It could quite easily have hit a bollard. I can't justify spending the money on forensics just to get it checked out. Doesn't seem worth it for something so simple. We shall see what the other evidence shows up."

"You really bullied Mrs. Blythe, poor woman."

"I know. Sometimes, you have to up the pressure. Quite often, people crack when doing so. You're a newbie, so I know this is still new to you, but when you've done the job as long as me, you'll see what I mean."

"I suppose."

"Watch and learn, Kid." He clicked his tongue against the top of his mouth and winked.

***

**B**ACK at the station, the scent of coffee drifted through the corridors. Deegan's throat felt parched. Helping himself to a cup, he took it with him as he made his way back to his desk. He gulped down a large mouthful before Barnes approached, sounding out of breath.

"Hello, sir."

"I didn't ask you to run a marathon."

"Trying to get fit. Every time I go anywhere, I try to do it briskly. Sometimes, I even jog."

"You wear me out just thinking about it. What you got?"

"The lads from the pub, I spoke to them all this morning at their workplace. They were very saddened to hear of Ray's death."

"Ah, Smith, just the man!" Deegan called as he entered the room. Smith nodded and pointed to the coffee pot. "When you're ready. Sorry, Barnes, do carry on."

"Nothing untoward. I got the impression they didn't want to speak to me. The last couple of men to leave said Ray was about to walk home when they drove away. I think they clammed up, knowing they were inebriated and didn't want to get nicked for driving under the influence."

"More than likely. I think from now on we will station traffic down the lane to see if we can nab them in the future."

"One did say, a Mr. . . . ." She rifled through her notes. "Jacobs, he got the impression his friend was having a bit of money trouble. But apart from that, he was just a normal guy."

"Thank you, Barnes."

"Smith," he hollered across the busy room. "Have a minute?"

"Sir?"

"Anything on the computer that came from the deceased's home?"

"Can of worms, sir. They found porn on his hard drive, as you know. It looks like he was distributing. Maggie, his girlfriend, starred in several. It's hardcore, sir. There's sex videos and sick crap like this." He pointed to the table.

Barnes scrunched her face in disgust. "Tell me it's not kiddie porn." She transferred her weight from one foot to the other.

"No, thankfully."

Deacon breathed a sigh of relief. "I want to see these movies. Maybe this has something to do with it, and someone was after him."

"There is some information the technical guys are still looking for. I should get that information soon," Smith said.

"Okay, Barnes. Smith, I want his financial records looked into. I want to know who he was selling to and his girlfriend's role in it all."

"Yes, sir." Smith turned to walk away with Barnes on his heels.

# CHAPTER 43

**A**FTER such a busy previous day, everyone gathered in the incident room. Some rested their elbows on their desks and yawned. Others chatted amongst themselves.

Deegan stood at the front of the room in his usual manner. Smith tapped his foot with impatience, ready to spill the information that had taken him most of yesterday to compile. Barnes, on the other hand, had been assigned to another case that had just come in. He projected his voice to the far end of the room as if it were a theatre.

"Anything on the financial front, Smith? You and Barnes were dealing with that."

"Yes, we were. Barnes got called away this morning to take care of another case, however."

Deegan rolled his eyes. "I know that. I sent her on another job. Stop stating the bleeding obvious and tell us what you found, if anything."

"Quite a bit, Sarge, in fact." Smith fingered the edge of his notes and looked up. "I think Ray Johnson may have been a target, and his death is no accident."

He raised a brow at him. "What makes you say that?"

"His bank account showed irregular transfers. Some large, some small."

"How much are we talking about?"

"Anything from £100 to over £5000. On his death, his balance showed a few pounds in credit. The men he was dealing with are part of a dangerous gang. They kidnap young girls for the sex trade. They're groomed for their looks and virginity. These girls are runaways, homeless, that kind of thing. He's sold his porn to the sickos. Maggie was taking a cut, too. Her salon is just a cover. Not only did she appear in these videos, she befriended the girls and passed them on."

"Interesting. He was into something deep. Where did you source your information?"

"Our snout. He couldn't say where the operation was taking place, only what he'd heard on the grapevine. However, he does know the pub they use sometimes, so that's another starting point."

"Right. I want missing persons checked out, and the bank account this money was transferred into. This could be a money hit. Also, bring Maggie in for questioning. Tell you what, let us talk to the informant again. This is a lot bigger than we first thought."

"I'm on it."

"Take some extra officers to help you with the legwork. In the meantime, I shall pay a visit to Mrs. Blythe."

"Yes, sir."

Deegan raised his voice once more. "Adams!" He looked around the room. "With me, please."

She trotted up to his desk, ready to go. They made their way out to the car.

"Mrs. Blythe didn't do it, did she?" Adams asked, whilst buckling up.

"No, she didn't. The thing is, and you will learn this over time, sometimes the crime committed is so close to home that you have to suspect friends and family."

Adams sighed and shook her head. "That poor woman! What she's been through, and how she holds it together, I will never know."

Deegan offered her a sad smile. "That's why we're paying her a visit. My gut instinct was wrong this time."

"It was probably that bacon roll you ate from the staff canteen."

"More than likely. I was wrong. She deserves the truth. It's the least I can do to ease her mind about this matter at hand."

Turning right at the next junction and then a left, he turned the car into Tina's drive. The Audi was still parked close to the fence.

\*\*\*

**S**INCE it was just the middle of the afternoon, Tina was still dressed in her pyjamas and dressing gown. After a restless night's sleep and then severe morning sickness, she decided to slob out. With nothing to do and nowhere to go, she could relax and enjoy reading her book and drinking hot chocolate, if she could keep it down. She was about to read the first line of a new chapter when a knock came from the front door.

*What now?*

She tightened the sash of her gown around her waist and pulled the collar up around her ears. Tina walked down the hall, heading toward the inconvenient annoyance.

*Whoever it is can take me as they find me.*

Deegan smiled as she opened the door. "Hello again, Mrs. Blythe."

The sight of him and the officer standing in front of her made her heart thump and her palms sweat. She wondered if they'd found any incriminating evidence and had come to arrest her. That would look good, as she was still in her dressing gown. All of a sudden, her legs felt weak. She steadied herself against the doorframe.

"Hi. What can I do for you?" Her throat felt dry and needed moisture.

"May we come in again?" Deegan asked.

"Please excuse the way I'm dressed. I wasn't up to it today."

He nodded. "Don't worry about that. We just want to have a quick chat."

After she let them in, she looked up and down the street, expecting several police cars and the media to be overtaking her drive, but only their car was parked nearby. Tina closed the door and shut her eyes, repeating her mantra for a second or so. She opened them and made her way to the lounge.

"I would offer a drink, but I . . ."

"That's okay. We'll decline," Deegan said, taking a seat next to the window.

Adams sat next to him like his lap dog. Tina sat back on the couch and covered her knees with the flaps of her gown.

"What can I do for you this time? Did you check out my alibi?"

Deegan smirked at her, amused by her sudden gumption. "Yes, we did. You've nothing to worry about. We thought we'd update you on the hit and run, as your husband was friends with the victim."

Tina wasn't bothered, but smiled sweetly and pretended to show an interest in what they had to say. "Have you found the person that did it?"

Her legs had stopped shaking, and her voice returned to normal. In addition to that, she felt relaxed.

"Not exactly, but we do think we know who we're looking for. Was your husband into pornographic movies and making them?"

"No. At least, not that I know of. Why?"

Deegan filled her in on a few of the grisly details about Ray and his extracurricular activities. It now made sense to her as to why he wanted to extort the money from her. Maggie's involvement in the matter surprised her, however.

*No wonder she needed implants and Botox!*

"I also wanted to send you our deepest sympathies regarding your husband and the interrogation we put you through."

"You were only doing your job," she said.

"I know, but it doesn't help that we made things worse. I honestly assumed you must have been a part of this new occurrence. We now know that's not the case."

She shifted in her seat and sighed dramatically. "It's all right."

Adams glanced at Deegan and said, "Madam, we just want to say we're sorry. You've nothing to worry about now."

Tina nodded. "I appreciate your coming here to tell me."

Deegan stood and offered her his hand. Tina took it and allowed him to shake it. Adams offered her condolences once more before making her way to the door. They took their leave, moments later.

Half an hour later, Tina's body unwound and she felt even more relaxed. She would never take it for granted that she'd gotten away with murder. Not once, but twice.

Granted, she would always carry the guilt for what she'd done, but she would keep it locked down deep inside. Tina was now free. Free to be happy with all aspects of her life. She would never have to worry about having someone breathe down her neck ever again.

She flopped back down into the chair as a broad smile spread across her face. Tina turned on the TV and watched re-runs of *Only Fools and Horses*, the classic episode to *Hull and Back*. Contentment rippled through every part of her body as she made herself comfortable.

# CHAPTER 44

**TINA** put the final touches to the canapés she'd made for Sam's visit. This lunch was way overdue. The last time she'd spoken to her best friend was from the bus station. Tina had taken some time to herself, hoping to clear her mind, once and for all.

She owed Sam an explanation, and knew that it had to be today. Sam, being the person she was, had waited for Tina to make contact, and gave her the time and the space she needed to sort herself out. Now two months on, she was stronger and ready for a fresh start.

The absence of the police around the area filled her with hope. The last time she had any contact with them was six weeks ago. They'd informed her that the investigation was still ongoing, and had wondered if she knew anything about the seedy sideline Ray was involved in.

She'd gotten away with Ray's and Clive's murders, knowing that both of their deaths had been a necessity. They would have made her life hell should they have continued to live. Tina hadn't relished the thought of always having to look over her shoulder at any given moment.

Tilting her head to the side, she eyed the plate of smoked salmon and cream cheese blinis. She added a sprinkle of cress for garnish before admiring the other scrumptious dishes and placing it on the table next to them.

A quick glance at her watch told that she had time to change. Tina pulled on a sleeveless loose frock, cream-coloured with bold red flowers printed on the fabric. She'd loved it from the moment she'd laid eyes on it. She twirled, admiring herself in the mirror, and then toed the matching red sandals before heading downstairs.

Sam would arrive in about half an hour. The thought of seeing her best friend filled her with excitement.

Midday arrived. The doorbell chimed. Tina had added the accessory to the once dreary home. Rushing to answer the door, her heart fluttered. A broad smile crossed her face as she twisted the latch.

"Hey you!"

Tina's eyes widened. A bump protruded through the baggy top pulled over Sam's hips. "It's so good to see you." She flung her arms around Sam's neck and squeezed tight.

Sam grinned. "Missed you."

"Missed you, too."

Sam hugged her and then stepped back, holding onto Tina's fingertips. "You look amazing. Nice dress. Have you put on some weight?"

"Monsoon. Got it on sale. And yes, I have." She twirled again, hanging onto Sam's fingers as she went under her arm. "Look!" Tina stopped and nipped the skin below her ribs. "I can pinch more than an inch."

"Little pudding, you!" Sam teased.

"I know. It's great, isn't it? My clothes fit better and feel great. You look well, too. The pregnancy suits you. Come through. I've made some lunch."

The corner of the lace tablecloth lifted with the breeze coming in through the open window. It ruffled the leaves of the potted plants sitting on the windowsill.

"Tada!" She held out her arm and gestured to the delicious food on the table.

"Wow, are they blinis? My favourite! You're doing really well. I'm proud of you." Sam tucked her hair behind her ear and leaned in for a sniff before she sat down. "Nice Mini you got there in your driveway. It suits you." She put her bag on the floor. "Got rid of the Audi, then?"

"It was too big, and a reminder."

"I don't blame you."

"Before we eat, I want to show you something upstairs."

She reached for her hand and led Sam into the hallway. Like two school kids up to mischief, they bounded up the stairs.

"Close your eyes." Tina led her into the small bedroom. "It's okay. You won't trip." Once in position, she said, "Now, open them."

Sam's eyes fluttered and her mouth dropped open with surprise as she stared at the room's splendour.

"Oh, wow! Are you . . . ? I . . . I'm speechless!"

Tina offered her a tentative smile. "Yes, I am."

Sam's mouth curled into a perfect O. "Is it . . . Clive's?"

"Yes, it is." Tina swallowed, anxiously taking in her reaction.

"Well, that's wonderful news!"

Sam gazed about at the half decorated baby's room. Animal stencils were etched halfway up the wall, burgundy on a delicate pink background. Tins of paint sat on the bare floorboards. A stepladder was propped up against the adjacent wall. A crib and a pram, still in its packaging, rested in the corner.

"Are you pleased for me?" she asked, her voice barely a whisper.

Sam turned to face her. "Of course, I am. Why didn't you tell me?"

Tina's mouth trembled as she stared at her best friend. "L— Let's go downstairs. We need to talk."

"I see you've changed some things in here, too," Sam said as she glanced into the living room.

"It's temporary. I'm not staying here for long. Anyway, please, take the seat," Tina replied, and smiled.

"I noticed. Where's the rest of the furniture gone?"

"Len and Joyce. They wanted everything that Clive had bought. It's a bit sparse."

"They had no right. Why would they do that?" Sam shuffled up the two-seater and made room for Tina.

"Glad to get rid of it. They said, as I had the house, which is now mortgage free, and a couple of other life policies, they should have Clive's furniture and belongings."

Sam stroked her arm with reassurance. "You can start fresh now."

Tina nodded. "The funny thing is, Clive left them nothing in his will."

Sam's eyed widened. "Really? I bet they were miffed."

"Yes, they were. Haven't spoken to them since. Let me get us some drinks. Then, we can talk properly. What would you like?" Tina asked as she unfolded her legs to get up.

"Juice would be great."

"Two ticks." From the kitchen, she raised her voice and said, "Orange, okay?"

"Yes, it's fine."

Tina popped her head around the door. "Shall we go into the kitchen instead? We can eat and talk at the same time."

Sam grinned and stood up. "Sure."

Facing each other at the table, they helped themselves to nibbles.

"So, how do you feel about the baby?" Sam asked as she selected a blini and took a bite.

"I'm okay with it now. There is something I must tell you."

Sam nodded and let her have her say. She listened without commenting and sipped at her juice.

"I'd planned to have an abortion. I went to the clinic shortly after your visit, but I couldn't go through with it." Tina switched her position. "He raped me . . . repeatedly. At first, I couldn't bear the thought of having it."

Sam reached out and clasped her hand. "Darling, I'm so sorry. I could have helped and supported you. What made you keep it?"

"The baby," Tina said, circling a hand over her stomach. "I'm going to name her Martha, and when I change my last name, it will be my late grandmother's maiden name of Simpkin. And you did."

Sam angled her head to the right and looked Tina in the eye. "Did I?"

"The day you left me your scan. I thought, 'how could I get rid of the baby after all Sam's been through in trying for one?' It made me realise life is precious."

Taking a few minutes, and feeling stumped for words, Sam nodded.

"I know how you feel. I've passed the stage I was at last time. Lee is acting like a big kid. He won't let me do anything. He would have had a fit if he saw me bounding up those stairs earlier."

"How sweet! Top up." Tina motioned to the juice.

"Yes, please. These really are delicious." Sam shoved another blini into her mouth.

"You've demolished the whole plate." Laughing, Tina filled their glasses and sat back down. "Here you go."

"Does your family know?" Sam crossed her legs and reached for the next plate of goodies.

"No. I haven't spoken to Mother since the funeral, and James can piss off."

Sam laughed. "You used a swear word!"

Tina put a hand to her mouth in jest. "So I did," she said, and giggled.

"What about the in-laws? They have a right to know."

Tina's face dropped at the mention of them. "Maybe in the future I might tell them. For now, I'd like to keep it to myself."

"Won't they pay you a visit? You're bound to be seen by people in town, and you know what the gossips are like."

"I'm only staying here until the baby is born. Then, I'm moving away. I had to change the décor and everything. I got a firm in." She smiled. "I may tell them in the future, as it's not fair on Martha."

"I love the name, and . . ." Sam made a gesture across her mouth as if she were pulling a zip closed. "Sealed!"

Tina reached over the table and held Sam's hands, stroking the backs with her thumb. "I wanted to say thank you for giving me an alibi." Their eyes bored into each others.

"I must admit I was shocked when the police came round, even though I knew they were coming. I wanted to ring, but I thought it was best to give you time. Why were you implicated in that?"

The dreaded question brought spasms to Tina's gut. How could she lie to her best friend? She would tell her a half-truth instead, knowing it was better this way. It left her with a modicum of decency, at least.

She took a deep breath and said, "I think because Clive was Ray's best friend, and they died so soon after each other, it roused suspicion."

"Even so, what did that have to do with you?"

"The Audi had wing damage, and they were looking for a dark car or van." Her mouth had gone dry.

"I see. How did you prang the car?"

"Stupid thing was too powerful. I hit a bollard. That's why I needed your alibi."

"Where were you that night, then?" Sam asked.

"You sound like the police. I was here, Officer Sam Williams." Tina chuckled, and Sam joined in. "They would never have believed me being here on my own, now would they?"

"True. Did they ever find the person who ran him down?"

"I forgot to mention that. Did you know that Ray was into seedy sex videos and distributed them?"

"No way! Do tell."

"I got another visit from the police asking if I knew anything about it. Did you ever see Maggie?"

"Yes, once. Mrs. Barbie Doll, that's what I thought when I first saw her." They laughed as Sam rose from her chair and strutted across the floor doing an impression of Maggie. Tears of laughter ran down their faces. "Don't tell me she played lead role?"

"Yep. Would you have thought the man capable of making porn?"

"No way. What a thought! Mrs. Foster Tits with a knob in her mouth."

"Sam! Profanity. Well, rude, anyway."

Sam playfully stuck her tongue out at her. "My turn."

They both giggled and sat back down.

"I think they're looking at that angle now, as he owed money, apparently. Haven't heard anything else since."

Tina carried the plates to the sink. Sam's phone rang as it sat in her bag. She pulled it free and glanced at the message.

"Oh, shoot! I forgot I'm meeting Daddy later. He wants to buy me some bits and bobs for the baby. I have to go."

Tina waited for the resentment to rise, ready to squash it back down, but nothing came. She'd turned a corner and had moved on. For the first time in her life, she felt closure.

"We can see each other soon," she said, showing Sam to the door.

"Of course, we can. We can have regular visits from now on, and go to antenatal together and chat about babies. I never even asked how far a long you are."

Tina patted her hand and smiled. "Next time. Go on. You're keeping your daddy waiting."

Sam smiled. "See you soon. I love you so much, and thanks."

She hugged and kissed Sam on the cheek. Sam held out her little finger. Tina hooked hers around it, and in harmony, they shouted the words.

"Always and forever!"

Tina watched as she moved down the drive, waving goodbye from her perch by the door. She then made a start on the dishes. Later, she would spend the rest of the day finishing off the baby's room. Temporary or not, she wanted the best for Martha.

Once the washing up was done, she made her way up the stairs. Halfway up, the doorbell rang. She hurried back down to answer the door.

"What, have you forgotten something? Your head should be

screwed . . . on."

Two figures cast a shadow through the pane of glass. Tina bristled and opened the door. The sight nearly brought her to her knees. Her heart raced as the police officers she recognised spoke.

Deegan nodded at her. "Hello again. May we come in?"

She held an arm out before her. "Come through."

Tina's thoughts soon turned to dread. This was it. They'd found evidence, and she was going to jail. She followed them into the lounge.

"You may want to sit down," Deegan suggested.

"I'm okay standing, thanks. What can I do for you today?"

Deegan and Adams eyed each other before he spoke. Tina's heart beat fast. She expected another squad car to come flying around the corner like they do in the movies.

"I have some bad news, I'm afraid. As you're familiar with us, I thought it best it came from me. "

Tina gulped, ready to blurt out that she was the killer and that she never meant it.

"Do you know a Mrs. Joan Morris?"

Tina's face paled. "Yes, she's my mother."

Deegan took a deep breath and said, "I'm afraid she was found by the milkman on the kitchen floor."

Tina's voice shook. "I—Is she alright?"

"No. I'm sorry. She's dead."

Her cheeks blanched further. "How?

"A heart attack."

Tina's mouth grew dry. "I see."

Adams took a step forward and clasped her hands, hoping to offer her a bit of comfort. "You've my condolences. It's not easy having someone else you know die so soon after the loss of your husband."

She nodded and looked down. "Y—Yes. I . . . appreciate you're coming to tell me about my mum's death."

Deegan tapped Adams on her shoulder and tilted his head in the direction of the front door. "We should go. You've my condolences as well."

"T—Thank you," she said, her voice barely a whisper.

They walked past her and promptly headed out the door. Tina pushed it closed and leaned against it. She then burst into laughter.

*Things just keep getting better and better!* she thought.

She'd expected the worse, only to be told that her mother had died instead. Never once, had she thought about coming out on top of things. In her mind, she'd assumed that they'd find some evidence to implicate her in both Clive's and Ray's murders. She'd been waiting for that moment to come, day in and day out.

Now she knew that she'd no longer have to worry about a thing. She was free at last. Her new life lay on the horizon. It was never too late to make a fresh start, she realised. This was her chance to make the most of things, and she was more than ready to embrace the unknown.

# THE END

Connect with Susannah Hutchinson via the following social media outlets online:


**Website/Blog:** http://susannahhutchinson.wordpress.com
**Email Address:** author.shutchinson@yahoo.com
**LinkedIn:**
http://uk.linkedin.com/pub/susannah-hutchinson/8a/a19/515
**Twitter:** https://twitter.com/2English5Rose
**Facebook:** http://www.facebook.com/authorsusannahhutchinson
**Goodreads:**
https://www.goodreads.com/author/show/13486757.Susannah_Hu
tchinson
**Author Interview:**
https://authorsinterviews.wordpress.com/2014/03/27/here-is-my-
interview-with-susannah-hutchinson

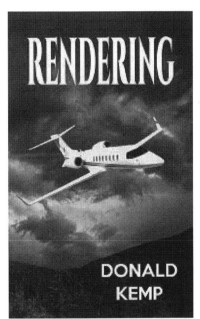

# ABOUT THE AUTHOR

Susannah Hutchinson was born and raised in Sunderland in the North East of England. She spent most of her childhood with either a book in her hand or riding horses. She moved to Norfolk in 1990, where she now lives with her long-term partner, artist Gerald Marsland.

Susannah turned to writing in the hopes that one day she would find a publisher and embark on a successful career as an author. She's written several short stories and has one printed in a local magazine. Another was accepted and read in a podcast in the USA. Her ambition is to become a novelist.

At the age of 46, she finished writing what will be her soon-to-be released debut novel titled, *Never Too Late*. Her genre of choice is Social Thriller. As well as entertaining the reader, she tries to send out a message within her work, while bringing social issues to the forefront of people's minds. She is also a conservationist and supports several animal charities. She enjoys traditional art, reading almost any genre of books, and is very interested in Forensics and Psychology.